Secrets of the
ITALIAN
ISLAND

BOOKS BY BARBARA JOSSELSOHN

BARBARA JOSSELSOHN

Secrets of the
ITALIAN
ISLAND

bookouture

Published by Bookouture in 2023

An imprint of Storyfire Ltd.
Carmelite House
50 Victoria Embankment
London EC4Y 0DZ

www.bookouture.com

ISBN: 978-1-80314-781-9
eBook ISBN: 978-1-80314-780-2

To Betty and Irving; Sarah and Jacob; Ida, Rose, and Bessie
My grandparents and my great-aunts
How I wish I'd known you better.

ONE

2018

Thursday

"I hate when it gets so dark so early," the woman in the seat behind her said. "Don't you hate this time of year? I mean, it's not even six thirty! And it's only... what, October eleventh? The clocks won't even change until next month!"

The woman's seatmate mumbled something in reply, but Mia didn't bother to catch the words. Instead, she put her elbow on the metal armrest and peered out her window, the noisy clatter of the rails changing to a gentle metallic purr as her train emerged into the outside air from the depths of Manhattan. The woman was right—the city landscape looked dramatically different from even fifteen minutes ago, when the lowering sun still lit the sky as she'd entered Penn Station.

But unlike the woman behind her, she didn't mind. Each year, she waited with growing impatience for fall to come and the days to grow shorter. She loved how streetlamps and traffic signals, headlamps on cars and flashlights on phones, became weak substitutes for daylight. They aimed to make the night appear tame and restrained, like a tiger tucked behind a glass enclosure at the zoo. But their power was an illusion. Nobody controlled the night. The best you could do was make it your friend.

Mia tucked her collarbone-length brown hair behind her ears and pressed her forehead against the window, cupping the sides of her eyes with her hands to block the glare from the train's overhead fixture. That was one of the lessons her grandmother had taught her when she was little—that the night could be a fine friend, but only if you understood all it offered. Growing up, she'd had many friends who were scared of the dark. Their parents were, too, it seemed. Many families in town kept their porch lights on all night; and when she'd go on sleepovers, she was amazed at the plethora of nightlights—in bathrooms, in hallways, even in the bedrooms where she and her friends slept. But her grandmother had always craved the dark. She'd claimed that lamps, chandeliers, and so on were unpleasant and unhelpful, with their harsh bulbs and the distracting shadows they threw.

The night sky is bright if you look closely, she'd say. *It tells you exactly where you need to go.*

Mia's phone rang, disturbing her memories, and she bit her lip as she looked at her bag on the seat next to her. She hoped it was her friend Erica confirming that she'd be at the station near the ticket machines at seven thirty, waiting to pick her up so they could head to dinner. But when she pulled out her phone, the number was Ryan's. She hesitated before putting the phone to her ear.

"Hey," she said, trying to sound pleased. "Where are you, at the airport?"

"About to board," he told her. "And you?"

"On the train."

"Will you go straight to the house?"

"No, Erica's picking me up. We're going to get dinner. Then she'll drop me off."

There was a pause, and then Ryan continued, "You sure you want to do this?"

Mia pressed her lips together, stifling her sigh so he wouldn't hear it. "I have to," she said. "I can't let the house keep sitting there."

"But I'll be back soon. Two weeks won't make a difference. I can be there *with* you. That's what boyfriends are for, you know." He chuckled and then went on, more serious now. "You don't have to do this alone. You don't need to prove anything—"

"I'm not trying to prove anything," she told him. They'd been over this a lot. Ryan liked being needed, and it bothered him that she didn't want him to come with her when she returned to the house for the first time since her grandmother died.

"I want to spend the night there by myself," she added. "Then tomorrow I'll meet up with Erica again, and Saturday we leave for the Adirondacks."

She waited, sure he was going to protest further. But thankfully, a voice in the background announced the last boarding call for Flight 1642 to Los Angeles.

"Is that yours?" she asked.

"Yeah," he answered, resignation in his voice. "Okay, but look, make sure to get the exact measurements for the two upstairs bedrooms and the hall. I can't make out the handwriting on the old floor plans you picked up from town hall, and I want to be able to talk intelligently with the architect if we decide to break down that wall. And make sure the gardener cleared the leaves. You want the place to look nice, no matter what you decide to do with it. And set a timer on the hall light, for God's sake—"

"There's no need—"

"Mia, this is my business. I work in real estate, remember? I hear these stories all the time—a property looks vacated and it's as if the owner sent a personal invitation to any burglar in a twenty-five-mile radius—"

"Okay, I've got it all covered. Go ahead, don't miss your flight."

"And call if you get scared or creeped out. Call *anytime*, okay?"

"I won't feel creeped out. I grew up there."

"And that's *exactly* why you might feel weird, Mia..."

There was a rustling as his voice trailed off, and she pictured him getting up from the plastic airport chair, throwing his coat over his arm, and starting to wheel his carry-on toward the gate.

"I gotta go," he said into the phone. "I love you. I'll call you tomorrow, okay?"

"Okay," she said. "Have a good flight."

She waited for him to end the call, then studied the screen for a moment before returning her phone to her bag. It always surprised her, how effortlessly he tagged the words "I love you" onto the end of their conversations. He'd started doing it a few months ago, and she still didn't know if he meant it or it automatically came out without his thinking about it, simply because they'd been dating for almost a year now. She wondered if he'd noticed that she never responded with "I love you, too." But she didn't feel it, not yet anyway, and she wasn't the kind of person who said things without meaning them.

Still, she understood his frustration about tonight. She could have arranged this trip for a time when he could have joined her. But she'd scheduled it for today specifically because she knew he was flying out on a business trip. She hoped he bought her story, that she merely wanted to be alone. She didn't relish keeping secrets from him. But she couldn't bring him to the empty house.

Because there was something there he couldn't see. Something that she had to find and deal with before she could ever let him in.

She settled in for the seventy-minute ride and when the train slowed as it approached the Soundport train station, she pulled on her tan fall jacket and slung her bag over her shoulder. Standing, she gave a quick smile to the woman upset about the dark, then pulled her suitcase from the overhead rack and made her way to the exit doors. They slid open, and she stepped onto the station platform, feeling an almost imperceptible autumn coolness in the breeze that swept around the hem of her straight-leg pants and touched the skin above her brown ankle boots—a foreshadowing of the cold weather not too far in the future. The air held a familiar, faint scent of wood-burning fires, sweet and earthy, no doubt coming from the chimneys of nearby houses, and the leaves on the tall oak trees on either side of the station house glowed orange, reflecting the light from the half-moon and the sprinkling of stars above. These were the smells and sights and feels of home, and although she wasn't the crying type, she couldn't stop her breathing from becoming a little jagged. It was her first autumn here without her grandmother.

"Mia!" a voice called, and she looked down the short flight of concrete steps to see Erica waving out the window of her idling Civic. She took a deep, cleansing inhale, and went down to the car.

Tossing her suitcase into the back, she climbed into the passenger seat and gave her friend a hug. "I am so glad we're doing this," she said. "It's going to be great to get away."

"I know," Erica said. "A whole week of hiking. Are you hungry? I'm starved. Let's head straight to Caryn's."

They drove the short distance to Main Street, which ran through the center of the small town and was lined with bars, restaurants, and an array of food markets, home goods shops, and pretty clothing boutiques. Erica pulled into a parking spot in front of a single-story building with a bright-blue sign in the window that read "Caryn's Fine Eats." Mia loved that Erica knew Caryn's was exactly where she'd want to go. They'd been coming here since they were old enough to drive, hanging out with friends when they were in high school, meeting up during college breaks when they were both home, and more recently stopping in for a drink or a bite whenever Mia was in town visiting her grandmother.

They ordered their usual—cheeseburgers, sweet potato fries, extra sweet pickles, and some local beers that were impossible to find anywhere else. Erica slid her menu back into the rack and leaned forward on the table. "So. How are you doing?"

Mia took a sip of the beer the server placed before her. "I'm okay. Tonight's going to be hard. But she'd want me to be okay in the house without her."

Erica ran her fingers through her wavy, champagne-colored hair. "I can't believe Lucy's gone," she murmured. "I saw her in town all the time, right up until the end. She had so much energy, and you couldn't miss her, with that gray sweatshirt and short white hair, and that no-nonsense walk of hers. And the way she looked at people when they were talking—you know, with her eyes narrowed and intense, and her lips pursed so tightly. Like there were a million problems in the world and she wanted to make sure she didn't miss anything, because she needed to solve them one by one."

Mia nodded, picturing that very expression, the way Lucy's amber eyes would become narrow, her eyebrows would draw close, and her thin lips would press together when she was listening intently. Even when she was young, Mia always strived to be serious and insightful when she and Lucy were talking. Because there was little as wonderful as saying something that was worthy of her grandmother's complete attention.

Erica tilted her head. "You know, you have that expression too sometimes," she said gently.

"Me? Really?"

"For sure. I mean, mostly you don't look like her at all. The whole shape of your face is different—hers long and yours rounder. But your eyes are exactly the same, that clear goldish-brown. And when you're focusing in on something and you purse your lips—like just now when you were reading the list of beers to see what they'd added to the menu—I swear it was like I could see her in you."

Mia pressed her chin back in surprise. "No kidding? I guess I picked that up from her. Although it probably doesn't have the same impact as when she did it. She was so strong, right? It drove people crazy sometimes. Ryan could never get used to her. But I always thought she was easy to love, in a funny way. Don't you think?"

"Absolutely. And she loved *you* so much, Mia. I don't mind telling you that with three sisters, I was always kind of jealous of that. When I would run into her in town, you were all she wanted to talk about. She was so proud when you started your job at the hospital and moved into Manhattan. One of the premier research institutions in the world, she loved to say. And she couldn't wait for you to go back to school to earn your PhD so you could run your own lab. Her whole world was you."

Mia lowered her eyes, smiling modestly in agreement with Erica. Her grandmother didn't say it often; she was a person of few words, none of them sentimental. But Mia always knew that Lucy was proud of her.

The server returned with their meals, and she and Erica both dug in, the burgers as thick and juicy as Mia remembered.

"So, what are you going to do with the house?" Erica said, swirling a long trail of ketchup onto her fries.

Mia shook her head slowly. "I don't know. I need to sleep there and get used to her... being gone..." She nodded, rein-forcing that plan. "And then I'll be able to decide."

"Well, I know what *I* think you should do," Erica said. "I think you should move back and live here. It's a great little house, right on the water. There are lots of hospitals and pharmaceutical companies around here that conduct medical research. You can do exactly what you're doing in the city now."

Mia smirked. "You, too?" she said. Everyone had ideas for what she should do with the house.

Ryan, who always had his real estate developer hat on, wanted to help her renovate it and then sell it; he was convinced it would earn a mint if they put in a little work. Milt, her grandmother's longtime lawyer and the executor of her will, thought Mia should rent it out, so she could benefit from a steady income without having to make any huge decisions right away. And now it seemed that Erica, who was an elementary school teacher and lived nearby with her physical therapist boyfriend, was hoping she'd move back to town.

They were all good ideas. But Mia didn't know which one was best—or if there was a better alternative she hadn't thought of yet. She didn't see how she could know, when she hadn't set foot in the place since the funeral last month. She had to go into the house and through all of the rooms: hear her footsteps on the wooden floor in the kitchen, now unaccompanied by the shushing of her grandmother's slippers; sink her toes into the old, wool rugs her grandmother had never wanted to waste time replacing despite the worn spots; handle the arms of the kitchen and living room chairs that would no longer resonate with the warmth of her grandmother's long fingers and tiny body. That's how Lucy had taught her to make decisions: You got down and dirty, coming face to face with the evidence available to you. You explored through your senses. And then you moved ahead.

But even before she could get to that point, there was something else. Something her grandmother had left. And although Mia had no idea what it was, she knew it was something she couldn't talk about. Not to Ryan, not even to Erica.

Something for her to find alone.

TWO

2018

Thursday

After dinner, Erica drove Mia to Lucy's home, a small, split-level house on a tree-lined, unpaved street that backed on to the rocky shore of the Long Island Sound. Mia got out of the car and grabbed her suitcase.

"Are you sure you won't stay with me tonight?" Erica said. "It's going to be super sad inside. Dylan already left for Stamford for his brother's bachelor party this weekend, so it'll be just you and me. You're sleeping over tomorrow night anyway, so why not tonight, too?"

"No, I'm fine," Mia said. "I need to spend tonight on my own. I'll see you tomorrow after you finish work, okay? I'll be at your house at three thirty."

"And we're off for the mountains first thing Saturday morning!" Erica said with a cheery lilt in her voice.

Mia nodded and waved as Eric drove off. She reached into her bag for the ring that held the keys to her grandmother's house and car, and wheeled her suitcase to the door. The house was dark, and it was hard to find the keyhole with only the dim light of the streetlamp, but after living with her grandmother so long, she was used to that. And she was relieved that Erica had accepted her decision without a fight. She needed tonight to search every nook and cranny in the house—that had become clear when Milt called last week to ask about a storage unit renewal notice in her grandmother's mail.

"It's the oddest thing," he'd said. "I handled *everything* for her—taxes, utilities, bills, you name it. But she never mentioned renting space in a storage facility... I had no idea she kept anything in storage at all until I started going through her forwarded mail.

"I suspect the key to the unit is somewhere in the house," he continued. "I can go and try to find it. But as long as you're coming to town next week, Mia, maybe it's best if you take a stab at it. She always said that if anything was missing, you'd be the one to know where it was."

It was that conversation that had spurred Mia to decide to spend the night in the house alone. Her grandmother had been meticulous about her affairs, and she'd entrusted Milt with everything. If he didn't know about the storage unit, then she'd held that information back intentionally. And the last thing Milt had said, that Mia would know where everything was—she couldn't help but believe it was her grandmother's way of signaling that the contents of the storage unit were for her eyes only.

Inside the house, she switched on the lamp on the front hall table. Thanks to the cleaning service that had continued to come weekly, the place looked spotless and smelled faintly of eucalyptus, her grandmother's favorite scent. Looking away from the lamp, she found herself studying the four small family photos on the little table—the only decorations in the house. The most recent one was Mia's college graduation picture from a decade ago, which sat alongside her high school one—both images of Mia alone in cap and gown taken by the respective school's photographer, as Lucy liked neither snapping photos nor appearing in them.

The only exception was the third photo—her grandmother's black-and-white wedding picture from more than 60 years ago. She was wearing a plain white sheath dress, and her short, wispy hair, then dark brown, was pushed behind her ears. In her hand was one long-stemmed rose. Her gaze was sideways and her expression impatient, as though there were a dozen things she'd prefer doing than posing for the camera. Mia's grandfather, an older, dapper man with slicked-back hair and a mustache, looked at his bride with amusement—most likely, Mia thought, because he knew exactly what she was thinking.

The fourth photo was of Mia's mother, taken in the backyard when she was maybe seventeen or so. She was a beauty, with golden hair that draped down to her slim shoulders. She looked as though she'd been fun, like someone Mia would have been friends with had they met as teenagers. But Mia never knew her mother at all. Or her father either, for that matter. Her parents had died in a car crash when she was just an infant.

Mia picked up her grandmother's wedding photo and held it for a moment, running her fingers along the edges of the rectangular silver frame. She looked far from a joyous bride. It wasn't the first time Mia had observed that her grandmother never appeared truly happy. And yet as Mia had grown up, she'd come to recognize those quiet moments when her grandmother seemed... well, if not unabashedly happy, then untroubled and content. There was something in her bearing that showed that emotion—an alertness, an uplifted brightness, like a far-off star glittering in an otherwise dark sky.

Mia had always been on the lookout for that expression and would bask in it when it appeared: during her high school and college graduation ceremonies; when she'd received her first job offer as a research tech at a lab on Long Island; when she'd garnered her next job, as lab manager at Weill Cornell Medical in Manhattan; and whenever she'd come back for a visit after moving to an apartment in Manhattan near her job. Lucy's deepest contentment came when Mia was happy, and it filled Mia with guilt that her grandmother had never seemed truly happy herself.

She studied her grandmother's face in the photograph for another moment. Erica was right—she really didn't look much like her grandmother at all. Her face was round and her cheeks full, while Lucy's cheeks often appeared flat, even sunken. And Mia's hair was thick and straight, while Lucy's was fine. Mia remembered how hard her grandmother would work to comb the knots out of her freshly washed hair when she was young. "Goodness, Emilia, such hair!" she'd sometimes exclaim when the knots were particularly stubborn, as she'd press the trigger of the detangler spray and then went back to combing.

"Emilia?" Mia would demand, looking up at Lucy in the bathroom mirror. "I'm Mia!"

"Yes, yes, Mia," Lucy would say. "Keep your head straight so we can get this done."

With a sigh, Mia returned the frame to the table, then grasped the handle of her suitcase and climbed the first flight of stairs. Leaving her suitcase at the entranceway to the living room, she went into the kitchen and over to her grandmother's most prized possession—her telescope—perched on a stand. She gingerly touched the smooth metal. How many nights had she and her grandmother spent together out on the patio, staring at the sky and contemplating how far away the stars were?

How she wished her grandmother had lived long enough to see her save the money she needed so she could leave her job and go back to school for a PhD. It was Mia's dream to study at one of the top cardiovascular research programs in the country —Boston University, Columbia, or Duke—and then join a major academic research institute. They were alike in that way, she and her grandmother—both students of the natural world. But while her grandmother had been drawn to big things like the wide sky and the deep ocean, Mia gravitated toward tiny ones: cells and molecules, antibodies and enzymes. Still, Mia knew they'd both felt the same deep urge: to search the void for answers.

Opening the kitchen door, she stepped outside onto the raised stone patio and looked up, thinking that the sky appeared even darker now than when she was inside the train and the glare from the overhead light interfered with her view. She could hear the gentle lapping of the water just steps away. Her grandmother had loved living so close to the sound.

Back inside, she searched through a few kitchen drawers to see if the storage unit key was there. But, like everything in the house, the things in the drawers—gadgets, recipe books, a calendar, eyeglasses—were neatly arranged, and no stray keys were visible. Not that she'd expected to find it so easily. It must have been well hidden, if her grandmother wanted no one else to find it. But Mia knew her heart wasn't in the search tonight. She was tired and missing her grandmother, and wanted only to undress and go to sleep.

Retrieving her suitcase, she dragged it up the next flight of stairs. Before she reached her old bedroom, her gaze landed on the attic door ahead. The attic had been Mia's favorite place in the house, with its fascinating features—the steepled ceiling, the exposed beams, and the long casement windows that produced the most interesting shadows on the floor, their shapes changing by the hour as the sun crossed the sky. In middle school, she'd begged to be allowed to do her homework there, and so Lucy had set up a small desk for her.

Mia caught her breath. She suddenly knew that if her grandmother had wanted her and only her to find the storage unit key, she'd have stashed it in the attic.

Climbing into the attic, she switched on the light. The cleaning people never went up here so it was a little dusty, but everything was orderly, nonetheless. Her small wooden desk was still flush against the wall, the ladder-back chair pushed in. There were storage boxes around the room's perimeter, all neatly taped and labeled in her grandmother's angular hand-writing: Photos; Mia's School Records; Books; Linens; Miscel-laneous.

Still, something was off—and soon Mia noticed what it was. There was a small walk-in closet in the corner of the room, where her grandmother had kept their off-season clothes—heavy sweaters and wool scarves in the summertime, and sundresses and shorts in the winter. And the door was slightly ajar. In most homes, maybe this wouldn't seem strange—but Mia knew Lucy would never leave a door ajar unintentionally: drawers and closets were always closed after you'd gotten what you needed. There was no question in Mia's mind that her grandmother had known she'd come up here looking for the key, and she'd left the door open so Mia would look inside.

With even steps, she walked into the closet, feeling a chill run up her neck to the back of her scalp as she did. The space was almost entirely empty—so different from how it had looked for most of Mia's life, with clothes draped on hangers spaced evenly apart on the rods or neatly stacked on the grid of shelves. Now there were no off-season clothes at all. The only item inside was a gray fabric garment bag stuffed with something voluminous and hanging from the rod on the far wall. She walked in further and touched the bag with her fingertips. Then, slowly, she unzipped the bag—and gasped.

Inside was a wedding gown.

She slipped off the bag and let it settle on the floor, then studied the gown on its hanger, her hands gliding down the length of the garment. It was the most elaborate piece of clothing she'd ever seen. The bodice was covered in hundreds of tiny glittering beads, and the neckline and sleeves were constructed of lace, the skirt made of layers of fine tulle, the hemline scalloped. The zipper was hidden by delicate pebble-like buttons that shone with a faint, opalescent pink hue. The dress had clearly been made decades ago, as the silk was yellowed and the tulle felt aged to her fingertips, the section near the waistline missing some buttons. Still, it was the furthest thing in the world from the simple sheath dress her grand-mother was wearing in the wedding photo downstairs. Whose wedding dress was this, and why was it in her grandmother's attic? And why had she wanted Mia to discover it?

She ran her fingers again along the bodice, which looked as though every bead had been handsewn, and wondered who had designed this dress. It looked not just beautiful but amazingly engineered, the way the different fabrics and textures held together organically, as though each section of the dress was a natural extension of the sections next to it. She slipped her fingers inside the neckline, wondering how a dress this delicate could possibly support the weight of all the beads...

And that's when she felt it—a little tissue-paper packet basted inside the bodice. Sure that her grandmother had intended for her to find this, she ripped the thread and unfolded the paper. Inside was a metal key attached to a small silver medallion with the words "Hempstead Self-Storage."

Mia shuddered as she held the key. Rewrapping it in the tissue paper, she held the packet to her chest and headed back downstairs. There was a story behind the wedding gown, she was sure of it, and the information had to be in the storage unit; otherwise, her grandmother wouldn't have sewn the key into the bodice. Tomorrow she'd go to Hempstead Self-Storage and see what she could find.

In her bedroom, Mia put the packet with the key on the night table. Her grandmother hadn't changed the room at all since Mia had graduated high school. The shelves by the window still held all her old science trophies, and the bulletin board beside it displayed her awards and certificates for outstanding school achievements. She pulled her phone out of her bag, and that's when she noticed she'd missed a message from her grandmother's lawyer, Milt, while she was at dinner. It was unusual for him to reach out to her in the evening. And when she opened the text, the words were even more surprising:

> *I know you're getting ready to head out with your friend to the Adirondacks, but can you work in a few minutes to stop by in the morning? There was something in your grandmother's mail that I think you should see.*

THREE

2018

Thursday

In bed a little later, Mia tried to decipher the tone of Milt's message.

He'd never asked her to come in at the last minute like this. That was one of the things that she'd always liked about him—how calm he was. As the executor of her grandmother's estate—the word still sounded funny to her ears, since her grandmother owned nothing but the house and her old car—he'd periodically ask her to sign a document, or to review a bill or financial statement that had shown up. But she could sense something different in the tone of his text. He sounded... not alarmed, so much as puzzled. As if whatever had arrived had left him stumped.

But there was nothing she could do now, as it was too late to call him. She turned off the light and tried to fall asleep. Still, his text kept her awake for some time. As far as she knew, her grandmother received little mail other than circulars addressed to "Occupant," since Milt had been handling her routine bills for a while now. What could have shown up that she needed to see? An unpaid loan they hadn't known about before? An issue with the house or car? Nothing like that seemed plausible, as Milt had been involved in every aspect of Lucy's life for years.

On the other hand, maybe the mail didn't contain something bad. Maybe it was a condolence card from someone who didn't have her New York City address. But if that were the case, she knew that Milt wouldn't have been so cryptic. She stayed with this thought for a moment, then turned onto her side. If her grandmother were here, she would tell her it was useless to speculate. The explanation was right there in Milt's office, she'd have told her—*so get yourself down there and get the answers.*

The next morning she woke up early and dressed in jeans and a blue cotton sweater. She pulled her hair into a ponytail and then picked up the storage unit key from the nightstand so she could drive straight to the storage place after seeing Milt. That would leave her plenty of time to return here, put the car back in the garage, grab her suitcase, and take a taxi over to Erica's at three thirty as planned. Slipping on her flats, she started for the bedroom door—but then stopped and turned back to make the bed. Her grandmother would never tolerate tousled covers or unfluffed, unaligned pillows. And it wasn't just that she liked things neat. No, taking care of your home, her grandmother often said, was an act of courage, even defiance. It told the universe that no matter what arose during the day, you knew that you'd be coming home that night and you'd want things in good shape.

She yanked the sheets and tucked them under the mattress, then spread the comforter on top, running her palm over it to smooth the lumps. Satisfied it would have met Lucy's scrutiny, she grabbed her shoulder bag and went downstairs to the kitchen to make a quick cup of coffee. But she changed her mind the moment her fingers touched the coffeemaker. Her grandmother belonged here, she thought. Setting out the mugs and spoons; cranking open the windows to let in fresh autumn air; planning her day—maybe a walk on the beach or a bike ride through town. Mia couldn't bring herself to switch on the machine or fill the tank with water in all this silence and emptiness. She'd grab a cup somewhere in town instead.

Continuing further down the steps, she looked into the small den off the hallway. Though she'd been only five when her grandfather had died, she'd always known this was his room. She could picture him sitting on the brown leather armchair opposite the fireplace on rainy days or chilly evenings, reading some esoteric book about quantum physics or doing a jigsaw puzzle, his wire-rimmed glasses low on his nose and his pipe protruding from the side of his mouth. It was funny, how different her grandparents had been. Her grandmother had never wanted to be in this room. She always said she preferred to be outside exploring life, rather than inside studying some representation of it.

At the threshold, Mia took a deep breath, knowing where she had to go next. With deliberate steps, she walked through the room to the heavy door just past the sofa, then proceeded across the breezeway and to the garage. Inside, she headed for her grandmother's old red Camry—but no matter how hard she tried, she couldn't divert her eyes from the pair of pale-blue bicycles in the corner, each with a white biking helmet perched on one handlebar. She felt a heaviness in her chest that made her shoulders sink. The bikes looked like abandoned animals who once were lean and fearless, but now were merely shadows of themselves. From the time she was a teenager, she and Lucy would hitch the bikes to the car every summer and take the ferry to Shelter Island for a one-week holiday, visiting nautical museums and strolling nature preserves, and eating fresh seafood and pies made with local peaches and berries.

But what they'd both loved most on those trips was riding alongside the hilly terrain so close to the water. The evenings were warm, the sky staying light until eight thirty, the sunsets fiery over the sound. Her grandmother had been a strong cyclist and was enchanted by the natural world—the moon, the oceans, the clouds, the pebbly beaches. Mia remembered there'd been tears in her grandmother's eyes when they'd loaded the bikes back on the car to come home six years ago. It was the week before Mia was starting her job at Weill Cornell and moving into the city, subletting a tiny studio from a co-worker who was relocating to Los Angeles. Lucy had been having worsening heart trouble for years, and with the arthritis in her knees also intensifying, even gentle bike riding was painful and taxing. They'd both known—though they hadn't said it—that it was the last bike trip of her life.

Shaking off the memory, Mia reached into her bag and pulled out the key to her grandmother's car. The interior still had the familiar, somewhat minty smell of eucalyptus, which had lightly suffused all areas of their home when Mia was growing up. Lucy had even used silver-dollar eucalyptus leaves as a centerpiece every morning, always with a lily in the center —because, as she'd say, *A breakfast table should be fragrant and aesthetically pleasing.* Mia had never known how she'd managed to arrange the centerpiece even in the dead of winter, when the variety of fresh plants and flowers in local stores was limited. Lucy's lifestyle wasn't extravagant, but when she wanted something, she usually found a way to get it. She liked being in control, so Mia knew it must have been devastating to feel her health deteriorating. But she never said anything. She would never have burdened Mia with complaints.

Inside the car, Mia started the ignition and took off for the short drive to the corner of Main Street and First. It was one of the things she loved about Soundport—the simplicity of the street names. Front Street was at the front edge of town; First,

Second, and Third Roads were perpendicular to it; Bridge Street ran across the small inlet between First and Second; and North Road abutted the town's northern border. There was something reassuring about this. No strange words that few understood, and nothing silly—no streets named after random trees or flowers, and no neighborhoods where all the street names began with the same letter of the alphabet. Lucy had felt the same way. She liked that her street was named Shore Lane precisely because the houses backed on to the water. Mia could hear her now: *It's good to always know where you are, Mia. Keep your eyes focused and you'll never be lost.*

She parked and walked into the familiar brick building, the entranceway sandwiched between a bakery and a clothing boutique. Down the hall, she spotted the familiar office with "Milt Kander, Attorney at Law," engraved in white letters on the door. She used to love coming here with Lucy when she was little. Milt always had a colorful, swirly lollipop and a sharpened pencil and notepad to give her, which kept her occupied while he and her grandmother had talked.

She opened the door and Milt's assistant, Janet, a white-haired woman partial to bold-patterned scarves, looked up from the reception desk. Also a widow, Janet had been one of her grandmother's few close friends. Several years ago, she'd urged Lucy to go with her on a seniors' tour to Europe. But the answer had been no. Although she had been born in Italy, her grandmother had never desired to go back there.

"Oh, sweetie, how are you?" Janet said, coming over and taking Mia's hands in hers. "Milt said you were alone at the house last night. I'm sure that must have been so hard..."

Mia smiled, knowing her grandmother would expect her to be calm and unemotional. "Hi, Janet. I'm doing okay, thanks. Milt texted me last night and asked me to come in this morning. Do you have any idea what that's about?"

"No, only that he wants to see you right away. He said to

interrupt him when you arrived. I think he's on the phone—
have a seat and let me peek in and tell him you're here."

She went to an interior office, but soon emerged and waved
her over. Mia nodded and went into Milt's office—a modest but
sunny room, with a simple light-wood desk and some contempo-
rary artwork on the walls.

"Mia!" Milt said as he stood and opened his arms, and she
went around his desk to hug him.

Although she had known him forever, his age was a bit of a
mystery. He was completely bald, so there was no way to use
any gray or white hair as a clue. He had an athletic build, with a
firm stance and slim waist. His shirt and tie always looked crisp
and fashionable, the knot always perfect, and his eyes were a
clear, youthful blue. Still, he had a warm, paternal way of
speaking to her—something she'd always appreciated, having
grown up with neither a father nor a grandfather. He had to be
in his late fifties or even sixties now, judging from how long
she'd known him. But he definitely could have passed for
younger.

He stepped back, holding her by the shoulders. "How are
you, Mia? How was it last night?"

Unlike the way she'd been with Janet, she decided to be
more honest with Milt. She knew her grandmother would
understand. Since Lucy had no siblings, so no actual nephews,
Milt had taken on the role of surrogate nephew. He would stop
by her grandmother's house weekly for coffee, and when Mia
had gone to a two-week science conference in New Orleans last
year, he'd called her grandmother every day and even took her
out to dinner a few times. Last December, she and Lucy had
attended Milt's annual Christmas party. He and his husband,
Danny, were amazing cooks and, as always, they prepared a
festive multicultural buffet that was out of this world.

"It was hard," she told Milt as he went back behind his desk
and she sat down opposite him. "Seeing our bikes... And I

couldn't bring myself to make coffee this morning. I couldn't stomach the idea of taking a sip in that house without her there drinking it with me."

"Well, it's going to take time. Baby steps, right? And as for coffee—that's no problem. Hey, Janet?" he called toward the door. "A mug of coffee, please?"

"Thanks," she said, smiling. "I appreciate it. And I appreciate you, of course. Everything you did for her, as well as all you're doing now. So, what is it you need to show me?" she added. "Your text scared me a little. Is it bad?"

"No... no," Milt answered, but his tone wasn't all that convincing. Janet came back in and set Mia's coffee on the desk. Milt thanked her and, when he asked her to close the door, Mia's back stiffened. She didn't know what he had to show her, but it certainly was more serious than a condolence card if he didn't want Janet to overhear.

He folded his hands on his desk. "Mia, did your grandmother ever talk to you about going to Italy? A trip she wanted to make? Something she had to do?"

"No, she said she never wanted to go back to Europe. You know that. She wouldn't even go with Janet that one time."

"Yeah," he said and scratched his head. "Did she ever... talk about anyone from Italy? Or an island in the Mediterranean? I mean, you know she was born in Italy, right?"

"Of course," Mia said. "But she came here when she was young. She never talked about it. Why? Milt, what's all this about?"

He opened the folder on his desk and pulled out a business envelope. "This letter came addressed to your grandmother," he told her. "From a law firm claiming to be based in Rome. I'm sure it's some kind of mistake. But I didn't want to respond until you'd taken a look at it."

He pulled the letter out and handed it to her. It was printed on some kind of official letterhead.

Dear Mrs. Abrams:

The owner of Isola di Parissi has retained my law firm in connection with the recovery of a certain object of historic significance. He is in the process of renovating the historic castle on this island and has recently become aware that the object was stolen from the castle sometime in the early 1940s.

We have uncovered information that indicates you resided at the castle during that time period, going by the name of Annalisa or Pippa. Our information also links you to the stolen object. We would like to speak to you to discuss any knowledge you have that will enable us to swiftly return this object to its rightful owner.

Please reply promptly by post or email so we may resolve the investigation.

Regards,

Enzo Battista

"Oh my God," Mia gasped. She felt her chest tighten, as though she herself had been accused of a crime. "What is this? Who on earth are Annalisa and Pippa?"

Milt lifted his palms in a "beats me" gesture. "And it came with a picture of what this lawyer says was stolen." He reached back into the envelope and handed her a photocopied drawing of a large bowl on a black base, with alternating bands of gray and pink, complete with gold veins. There was a hinge attached to the rim and something that looked like a tiny mallet sticking inward toward the center of the bowl, with a silver shaft and a pink ball at the tip. At the bottom of the paper were two Italian words.

Mia struggled to pronounce them. "*Schianto... Grandioso?*"

"It's something like great crusher or grand crusher. That's

how it's translated online," Milt explained. "Looks like a mixing bowl to me. With a strange-looking spoon attached."

"This is crazy," Mia said, handing the drawing back. "What does this have to do with my grandmother? And she never went by any other names!"

"I know. But it's a real island, this Parissi place, and there is a castle on it, also called Parissi. And evidently there's some big Italian financier who's recently bought the whole thing, island and castle together."

Milt took another look at the letter, then shrugged. "It's got to be a mistake," he decided. "Maybe there's someone else with a similar name that they're trying to contact. Or it could even be a scam. There are lots of bad guys out there who get a whiff of something big and then prey on older people. Trick them into giving up their bank account information or credit cards, or whatever. Usually they do it on the internet, although sometimes they use the mail, especially when older people are involved. Maybe the letter wasn't even mailed from Italy. These guys can be pretty clever when they set these schemes up."

"So what do I do?" Mia said.

"You don't do anything," Milt said firmly. "I'll send a letter demanding they drop the matter immediately or face harassment charges. No matter if it's a mistake or a scam, that should get them to back down. I just wanted to check first, in case any of this rang a bell."

"Not at all," Mia emphasized. "This is so creepy. What if my grandmother had seen this? She would have been terrified."

"No, she would have brought it to me and I would have told her not to worry. Just as I'm doing with you. Unfortunately these things happen, but I'll take care of it. Now that I've upset you sufficiently, my work is done." He chuckled as he reinserted the papers into the envelope. "Really, don't worry about it. You've got bigger fish to fry. Have you given any thought to what you want to do with the house? Any more ideas about selling or renting?"

Mia shook her head. She knew Milt realized she was rattled and was trying to get her mind off the letter, and she appreciated his efforts. "No, not yet."

"Is Ryan still itching for you to sell it?"

She nodded. "Yeah, but he went to L.A. for meetings. So I probably have a breather before he brings it up again." She laughed, hoping she sounded good-natured and not annoyed. She had to force herself to remember that Ryan really did believe he had her best interests at heart.

"And what about that storage unit? Any luck finding the key yet?" Milt asked.

Mia inhaled sharply, surprised by the question. "Um... no, not... yet," she stammered. "Wow, look how late it is. I'd better get going. Lots to do, packing and things..." she added, hoping he wouldn't notice that she'd commented on the time before seeing it on her phone.

"So you're heading out with your friend Erica soon?" Milt asked.

"Tomorrow. Her school has a fall break next week." She rose from her chair, wanting to leave as quickly as possible so she wouldn't have to lie more about the key. She hated deceiving Milt; but she was certain her grandmother had wanted no one but her to see what was inside the storage unit, and she needed to leave quickly so she wouldn't have to keep up with the deception.

"Perfect," he said, rising to walk her out of the office. "Have a wonderful time then, and don't worry about a thing. I'll take care of this letter and I'll keep an eye on the house. We'll speak when you're back, okay?"

"Thanks, Milt," she said, and gave him a quick hug. With a wave to Janet, she was soon outside and back in her grandmother's car. Leaving the parking space, she exhaled slowly before starting to drive, her thoughts turning from the key to the frightening letter Milt had shown her. She knew Milt was right, that the letter was either a mistake or a scam. But it was still upsetting. She couldn't help but think how vulnerable her grandmother had been all these years, living by herself in that house. She supposed that her grandmother wouldn't have done anything without contacting Milt first. But as Milt had said, there were bad people in the world, and they could be clever. Although she'd always felt certain her grandmother was safe here in Soundport, she wondered now if she'd told herself that simply to set her own mind at ease.

She pressed her head back against the headrest as she headed down Main Street. Why was she allowing herself to feel so anxious? Milt said the letter was nothing to worry about, and she believed him. Maybe it was all too much, coming to the house alone. Maybe Ryan was right and she should have waited until he could come with her. Her grandmother had been her only family. And now she had nobody at all.

But she couldn't have come with Ryan, she reminded herself. Because her grandmother had wanted her and *only* her to see the wedding gown and the storage unit key.

She continued toward the highway in the direction of the storage facility, hoping that what she would find in the storage unit was no big deal. Maybe a note saying that the wedding gown belonged to a friend. Or a friend's daughter. Or maybe Lucy had bought it somewhere and was fixing it up so Mia could wear it someday. Maybe the storage unit had sewing or fabric restoration instructions. Or maybe just a letter from Lucy explaining why Mia should have it.

That's all she wanted from the storage unit, Mia thought. No news from overseas lawyers, no scammers, no mysteries. Just information. And closure.

Then she could call the last twenty-four hours a success.

FOUR

1943

August

The small fishing boat rocked in the darkness, the water below crashing rhythmically against its side, sending cool droplets into the air that landed on Annalisa's skirt, her hands, and occasionally her face.

If this continued, she mused, she might very well be drenched by the time they reached the island. But she didn't mind. The night was warm and the water was cool and pleasing, the anticipation of each new spray a welcome diversion. She loved the sea. She loved how it glistened and moved, how hypnotic and yet powerful it was. Each smack against the boat had more force than she expected. Each splash seemed as charged as electricity—a spark of energy and then a gentle withdrawal.

What she didn't like was the sound of her younger sisters quarreling on the bench behind her. She turned to see Emilia huddled close to Giulia, her fingers wrapped around Giulia's elbow. The plaid bow Emilia had fixed to the crown of her head was falling to one side, and the moist breeze was causing her thick curls to tighten and swell beside her jawbone, making her face appear even rounder than usual. With her dark eyes swimming in tears, she looked far younger than her fifteen years.

"I'm scared!" Emilia cried. "I don't want to do this anymore."

Giulia groaned as she yanked her arm away. "Emilia, enough! Get off me!" She pulled herself loose and tilted her head, first one way and then the other, to fluff her honey-colored hair. The ends curled under just below her collarbone in the style so popular in her fashion magazines. Annalisa watched her try to fix the portion that was supposed to curve along the top of her cheekbone, although the breeze was playing havoc with her hair as well as with Emilia's.

"There's no going back," Giulia added crossly, although Annalisa suspected she was more annoyed with her failing hairdo than with Emilia. "So you may as well stop complaining."

"But we can go back," Emilia insisted. "If we turn around right now—"

"And we'd ruin *everything*," Giulia said. "Is that what you want to do?"

"No, but—"

"We're past the point of no return." Giulia sliced her hand through the air. "If you didn't want to come, you should have stayed at home."

"I wasn't going to stay home while you both left—"

"You're *such* a baby—"

"And you're so *mean*—"

"Both of you, stop," Annalisa whispered harshly. "You're making too much noise."

Although the truth was, there was no need to be quiet. They were still a ways from the island, and there was almost nobody around who could hear them. Just Vincenzo, the son of one of the shopkeepers on the mainland, who regularly transported supplies to the island and had agreed to sneak the boat out tonight. But she wanted the quiet so she could think about where they were going and what they would do when they got there. It wouldn't be all that much longer now.

She had come down to the shoreline yesterday evening to explore the sand, the water, and the sky, keeping everything she'd seen and heard and felt at the forefront of her mind as she calculated the length of the trip to the very minute. She'd always had a scientific mind, and she approached problems and questions the way a scientist would: by coming face to face with the available evidence, exploring it through her senses, and settling on the one solution that all the data pointed to.

There was quiet in the boat for a few moments. Then Emilia whispered, "At least it's not too dark. Isn't that something? Why is the sky that color?"

Annalisa nodded, acknowledging Emilia's observation. The baby of the family, Emilia was spoiled and cried far too often. But she was attentive and curious, qualities Annalisa appreciated. Qualities that Giulia, who could be impulsive and quick to anger, lacked, despite being two years older than Emilia. And Emilia had noticed something fascinating, Annalisa thought as she faced front and looked out over the water. The night was, in fact, strangely bright, even though there were a few stars out and no moon in sight. It was the sky itself that seemed to be aglow, its color rich blue, not quite royal blue but almost. And the way that color lightened the sky was distinct but also very subtle, so you might not even notice the lighter hue unless you were out in the night, focused on your surroundings and guarding against any danger.

As they were.

She lifted her chin to look straight up at the sky. How she wished she could understand why a nearly starless night sky could still be so luminous. How could this distinctive blue color blanket them as far as the eye could see? Did it have something to do with the water, or the soil below the water, or the island they were approaching, their final stop? The islands in this part of the Mediterranean were well known for their steep rock formations—could the reflection of the formations cause the appearance of the sky? Or was there something about the weather, the climate, the water and its shifting salt and oxygen density with the changing of the seasons? Ever since she could remember, questions would keep her up at night, the ones that went unanswered. Because the answers to everything were somewhere. They *had* to be. How could she live on this planet otherwise?

"I'll figure it out," she whispered softly to herself. She'd figure everything out in time.

"Look!" Giulia called, and when Annalisa turned again, she saw Giulia pointing toward the right of the boat. The dim outline of a sprawling stone castle could be seen at the top of a mountain.

Annalisa shook her head in wonder. She'd been thinking of, reading about, and picturing this castle for so long, it was hard to believe it actually existed and they were coming closer with every stroke of Vincenzo's oars. Castello di Parissi was its formal name—but it was more commonly known as Castello del Poeta —the Castle of the Poet. The island and the castle showed up in countless books, newspapers, and magazines. The famous and extremely wealthy Parissi family had bought the island and built the castle hundreds of years ago, and had passed it down from generation to generation. And over the centuries, it had become a revered destination for the greatest inventors, scientists, philosophers, writers, and artists from all over the world, who all dreamed of receiving an invitation to stay there.

Annalisa gazed up at the castle, which was lit from within, golden light pouring out through the uppermost windows. It was rumored that two of Michelangelo's pupils, who had gone on to sculpt some of Florence's most beloved fountains, had sketched out their designs while visiting, and the French architectural team of Blanchet and Allaire, who helped carry out the nineteenth renovation of Paris, had drawn their early sketches here. Many of Europe's greatest painters of the seventeenth and eighteenth centuries were believed to have been castle guests at one time, and three Nobel Prize-winning scientists had done their early research up in the tower. The castle had also been home for a time to numerous composers who'd gone on to write world-famous symphonies, and some early scientific devices— including a telescope that preceded Galileo's—had been conceived within its storied walls.

It was the castle's singular history—all the scientific and artistic achievements inspired or completed in its vast halls and spacious rooms—that had first captured Annalisa's imagination. But it was the person who was here now, the person whose invention might save her father's life, that had made her decide to risk everything and set sail for this island.

Vincenzo cleared his throat. "Now's the time," he told her gently. "We're getting close."

She reached behind the bench for a cloth sack she'd stowed there. Loosening the drawstring, she removed a long white shirt, which she wriggled into, pulling it over her cotton blouse and pushing her arms through the sleeves. Then she pulled off her skirt, revealing the men's trousers she'd been wearing underneath. She took a pair of brown leather boots out of the sack and, kicking off her own shoes, inserted each of her feet into a boot. They were way too big for her, but she laced them up as tightly as she could and assured herself they'd be fine.

The last step was to gather her dark hair, which she routinely kept in a pageboy style pinned away from her face, and tuck it under the black cap she found at the bottom of the sack. She then adjusted the cap's bill, pushing a few wayward strands under the band. She turned to look at her sisters, and Emilia started to giggle. Giulia rolled her eyes.

"It'll be fine," Annalisa told them firmly.

Maybe it wasn't the best step in her plan. But it was a necessary one. She'd calculated from the few maps she'd found that given the darkness and the suitcases she and her sisters would be carrying, it could take them as much as an hour to walk up the path to the castle once Vincenzo dropped them off. She doubted they'd encounter anyone—it would be close to two a.m. by the time they started out, and the castle was the only structure on the island she'd been able to find in her research, aside from the boathouse on the shore. Most of the island's inhabitants and guests would likely be sleeping within the castle walls —but if they did happen to pass anyone on their long walk, she'd thought it would be safer if they appeared to be a man and two girls, rather than three young women alone.

She slipped her skirt and shoes into her nearby suitcase and rubbed her hands together. Her palms suddenly felt clammy, even on this warm summer night, and she gritted her teeth, willing herself to stay focused. She couldn't allow nerves to strip her of her concentration. At eighteen, she was the oldest, and she needed to keep a clear head. She was in charge of her younger sisters—and, while she'd rethought her decision to bring them at least a dozen times, she'd had no choice but to allow them to come. She'd confided in Giulia early on because she thought someone at home should know the truth—but then Giulia threatened to expose her plan if she left without her. And once she'd agreed to bring Giulia, it would have been cruel to leave Emilia behind. Cruel to Emilia, but even crueler to Papa, who would have had to deal with Emilia's simpering. Not that she wanted to be alone, but being the leader entailed responsibility. She was the one who had to make sure everything came together.

Her plan was a good one, she reminded herself. Sound and

comprehensive, and it had worked so far. And if all continued to go right, they would arrive at the castle with time to catch a little sleep among the trees before dawn. She assumed the kitchen staff roused early to begin fixing the day's meals, and after she gave them time to get their work underway, she'd lead her sisters inside and speak to the person in charge. She hoped that by the end of the morning, the three of them would be in the castle's employ.

Vincenzo eased the boat onto the shore, then hopped over the side and stood by as the three sisters stepped onto the wet sand. Annalisa went last, and she watched as Vincenzo helped Giulia out, then continued to hold her hand, even as Annalisa directed her to assist in pulling out their suitcases. Instead, Giulia ran the fingers of one hand along Vincenzo's bare forearm. They had met Vincenzo, a cousin of their neighbor, only three days ago when they'd reached the coastal town of Anzalea. There'd been little time for conversation, let alone romantic encounters. But Giulia was a romantic and liked to fall in love, and she had fallen for Vincenzo hard. They'd all spent two delightful evenings together—enjoying the food, the people, and the nightlife of the town—while they waited for a series of storms to pass and the sea to calm. Annalisa hoped that Giulia would forget about Vincenzo the same way she forgot about all the boys she fell in love with once they were out of sight. The last thing she needed was a lovesick sister on her hands.

Emilia came up close behind and put her head on her shoulder, and Annalisa stroked Emilia's cheek as she looked up at the castle. The lights inside were bright, and now that they were closer, she could make out people through the windows. They looked small from this distance, but she was sure she saw couples dancing and women in colorful gowns, red and deep purple and sunflower yellow. And if she tuned out the sound of the water lapping against the shore and Giulia and Vincenzo whispering, she could even hear the sound of beautiful music, a Viennese waltz.

"Do you think Papa will be okay?" Emilia asked.

Annalisa knew what Emilia was thinking. Papa was in a lot of danger, partly due to his health. But also due to what was happening in the world—the increasing threat to Jews like her father. It was no secret that Italy had come down on the wrong side of history, allying itself with Germany, and the battles it had launched in North Africa had been an unmitigated disaster. Food was getting scarcer. Not to mention all the laws restricting Jews from many types of employment and banning marriage between Jews and non-Jews—something that would have prevented her own parents from marrying. For now, the laws weren't being enforced in many small towns, including theirs, Caccipulia, not too far south of Rome. But with the world so unstable and Germany so unrelenting, who knew how long the status quo would remain? Many Jews were leaving Italy for America, and Annalisa thought her family should do so too. But her father, who'd worked hard all his adult life as a tailor, was unwell and couldn't make the trip. Not in his current state.

"I'm sure he's okay. For now," Annalisa answered. But she needed to act fast, before Papa got any worse. Her next goal, after obtaining kitchen jobs, was to meet Patricio Parissi, the head of the Parissi dynasty, whom she'd read lived alone in the castle's tower. One way or another, he was going to show her what she'd come to see.

Emilia's question about their father reminded her of the small white packet she'd basted to her blouse, and she reached inside her clothes and ripped the thread with her fingers so she could give the packet to Vincenzo. It was the letter she'd written to Papa. She had composed it in her mind the night they left home, and had repeated it so often to herself—adding a better word here or a more precise term there—that she knew the finished product by heart:

Dear Papa,

I know you must be surprised that Giulia, Emilia, and I have left. We didn't want to be so secretive, but we knew you'd try to stop us if we told you what we were going to do.

Please don't be angry that we left you alone with the shop, and don't be worried because the stress will only make you sicker. I have a plan to get you well enough so we can all go to America. Please take care of yourself and take your medicine. We miss you and will be thinking of you until we are all safely together again.

Your loving daughter,

Annalisa

She gently nudged Emilia's head off her shoulder and walked over to Vincenzo to hand him the packet. "You'll make sure this gets to him?" she asked.

"Of course," Vincenzo answered, then gave Giulia a tender kiss on the cheek. He took a few steps back and faced all three of them.

"Goodbye, my friends," he said. "And good luck." He climbed into the boat, and Annalisa felt the air change, felt something new—a quietness, a soberness—which intensified as Vincenzo grasped the oars. They watched Vincenzo start to row off, and then Annalisa picked up her suitcase and waited until her sisters followed suit. The hardest part of their journey was ahead. The sooner they arrived at the top of the steep hill, the more rest they'd be able to get.

She looked around until she noticed a small gap between

two bushes just beyond the beach that most likely signaled the start of the path to the castle. Tilting her head toward her sisters to indicate they should follow, she began to lead the way. But before she could take more than a couple of steps, a harsh voice called out from behind them.

"Stop! Where are you going? If you don't want to be arrested, you'd better get back on that boat!"

FIVE

2018

Friday

A half hour after leaving Milt's office, Mia entered the parking lot of Hempstead Self-Storage.

She expected to have to explain to the man at the desk who she was and why she was entitled to enter the room, having nothing but the key, but after glancing at her driver's license and tapping some keys on his computer, he told her she was listed as a co-owner of the contents in the room and free to take whatever she wanted. Mia looked at the man for a beat, unsure if she was annoyed or simply dumbfounded that her grand-mother had arranged this path of discovery without ever letting on. It was like a perverse treasure hunt, the kind Erica's mom would organize for birthday parties. But Mia wasn't ten years old and this was no party. Why hadn't her grandmother told her about this?

The man pointed to the elevator and she followed his direc-tions to the fourth floor. The hallway smelled like fresh paint, and the floor was covered in gray industrial carpet that looked brand new, the silver garage-type doors on either side sporting identical shiny latches. She supposed most people found this a good thing—who wouldn't want to store their possessions in a place that looked clean and well-tended? Lucy would have surely found such organization appealing. But, to Mia, the place felt overly sanitized, as though the simplicity and order were intended as a distraction, a diversion. It made her think not of security, but of whatever secrets were lurking behind these doors. She shuddered.

She inserted the key into the lock. Even though she'd known it had to be the right one, she was still a little surprised when it easily turned. Her hand trembling, she removed the lock and slid the bar to the left. Then she kneeled to pull up the handle of the garage-type door, and she walked inside.

The unit was about the size of a large closet with a motion-activated light fixture on the ceiling and a concrete floor beneath her feet. In the center of the room was a dusty wooden cabinet about shoulder height, with three deep drawers. As Mia stepped forward, the word *armadietto* suddenly came to mind, along with a memory of this exact cabinet in the attic. She must have been very young, maybe no older than five, and she remembered going to open the top drawer. "No, don't open!" her grandmother had said. "Don't ever touch the *armadietto*!"

"But why?" she'd asked. "What's an ama... amadee—"

"My, how late it is," her grandmother had said hurriedly. "We're going to miss the full moon if we don't have dinner right away."

She'd taken Mia's hand and they'd gone downstairs quickly to eat and then head outside. But there'd been no moon that night. And now that Mia thought about it, she couldn't remember ever seeing this cabinet again.

Until now.

She ran her hand along the top. Despite the dust, it was a pretty piece. Slowly she lowered her wrist and grasped the pull she'd reached for so many years ago. The metal runners slid smoothly along on their tracks. But the top drawer was empty. As was the second one. Kneeling, she pulled open the bottom one.

This drawer wasn't empty at all. It held a white cardboard cube, like a gift box before it's covered in wrapping paper. She picked it up and placed it on the floor. Settling onto her knees, she lifted the top and removed the sheet of white tissue paper inside.

The first thing she noticed was a slim silver rod with a rounded pink ball at the end. And then she saw the inside of a wide stone bowl, with alternating bands of rough gray granite and smooth pink marble with gold veins. Along the rim was a gold plate with Italian words inscribed: *Schianto Grandioso*.

"Oh my God," she murmured. It was identical to the drawing Milt had shown her in his office. The stolen crusher.

And now it looked like the Italian lawyer was right. Her grandmother had known exactly where it was.

Right here, in her storage unit.

"I can't even begin to think," Mia said to Erica later that day as the two friends sat next to each other on Erica's sofa, two glasses of wine on the coffee table in front of them. Across the room, the *schianto grandioso* sat alone on the center shelf of Erica's bookcase. "I have no idea what to do."

She shook her head, glad that Erica had understood why she needed to put all thoughts of their trip aside as she sorted this out. After leaving the storage unit, she'd driven back to Soundport and waited at a coffee shop on Front Street until three fifteen when school was over and Erica would be on her way home. She hadn't known what else to do with herself. Though she couldn't explain it, she didn't want to go back to her grandmother's house. Suddenly her grandmother seemed a stranger to her, and the house she'd grown up in no longer felt like home.

She'd arrived at Erica's house just as Erica was pulling into the driveway.

Erica got up from the sofa and went to the bookcase. She ran her fingers along the bowl's rough upper band. "This is stunning," she murmured. "Look at the color of the marble. And this delicate little hammer thing." She turned to Mia with a mystified look. "Where did you say the letter was from?"

"Milt said it was from a law firm in Rome. I guess the lawyer was able to track her down from when she lived there. He also mentioned these other names he said she went by, Annalisa and something that starts with a P. That's one of the reasons Milt and I were so sure he was looking for someone else."

"I didn't know your grandmother came from Italy," Erica said, returning to the sofa. "I thought she lived here all her life. Did you always know she was Italian?"

Mia nodded. "Yes, although she never talked about it. Maybe my grandfather told me. Or maybe Milt mentioned it once when I was little. I have no idea."

"I always thought she had a bit of an accent. I just couldn't place it. I knew she didn't sound like all the other moms—I mean all the other grown-ups—in town."

"I sometimes asked her about where she came from," Mia recalled. "But she'd always change the subject. Talking about the past was off limits. And back then I didn't mind. It was already strange to have no parents and be raised by your grandmother. I wasn't looking for other things that would make me different."

"So, where is this place where this thing supposedly came from? And who's looking for it?" Erica asked.

"I don't know. I wish I'd taken the letter from Milt's office. But I thought he was right, and that it had to be a mistake or a scam. And he needed to keep it so he knew where to send his reply." She pressed her forehead with her fingertips. "Let me think. Some island... Isola di Parriso, Parissio. I think Milt found it online. Let me look it up."

She went to Erica's desk and typed on the computer keyboard how she thought the place might be spelled. "That's it, Castello di Parissi, on the island of Parissi," she said and clicked on a link that led her to a website called ItalianIsland-Castles.com. The home screen had a stunning picture of a castle at the top of a rocky summit on a tiny island, surrounded by still, turquoise water and a vast blue sky.

"That's gorgeous..." Erica murmured, looking over her shoulder. "What does it say?"

Mia scrolled down and they both read the paragraph below the picture.

A sixteenth-century stone castle, Castello di Parissi sits on the hillside of Isola di Parissi, a small island off the western coast of Italy. Owned for centuries by the wealthy Parissi family, who invited celebrated guests to vacation there, the castle gained fame in the early twentieth century when it was inherited by Patricio Parissi, a scientist who made a practice of hosting the brightest minds of his day to set up residency there.

Similar to Paris in the early twentieth century, the island and castle, which was nicknamed Castello del Poeta or Castle of the Poet, became a magnet for promising writers, scientists, painters, and inventors, who appreciated the temperate climate, magnificent coastline, and glorious accommodations provided by their host and benefactor. An invitation to live at the castle was an invitation to balls, parties, lavish meals, and space to dream and create.

The island was stormed and overtaken by the Nazis in 1943, and the castle was used to house high-ranking military officials. Following the war, the island changed hands many times, most recently to a hotelier with plans to convert it into a five-star resort.

"Wow," said Erica. "Do you think your grandmother could have been there? Maybe she was the daughter of a guest there? Ooh, maybe you're the great-granddaughter of some famous writer or painter..."

"No, no way," Mia said firmly. "I don't know what her connection to the castle was, but it can't be that. She didn't come from wealth or fame or anything, I'm sure of it. It's not who she was."

"Hey, what's this?" Erica said, reading from a box at the bottom of the web page. "*Isola della Notte Brillante*? What could that be?"

Mia clicked on the link, which took them to another page with a view of Parissi Island at dusk, the sky a deep but shimmering blue. Below the image was another text box:

Isola della Notte Brillante—Island of the Brilliant Night—was the nickname given to Isola di Parissi, the private island off the coast of Italy where many of the most promising artists and writers of the early twentieth century lived for a time. According to legend, the tides and the topography of the island's rocky coast lent the night sky a bright intensity not seen elsewhere. Many of the island's guests relayed this feature in poetic terms, describing how the glowing sky helped them find their muse. Sadly, the sky's reported luminescence also made the island desirable to the Nazis, who believed it would enable them to ferry plans and documents back and forth from the mainland in the overnight hours.

"Wow, Island of the Brilliant Night," Erica said. "So romantic. And so awful, the Nazi part, that is."

Mia nodded. "*The night sky is bright if you look closely—it tells you where you need to go,"* she murmured. "My grand-mother always said that. She made it sound positive, although it sometimes frightened me, too, the idea that I might someday have to rely on the night to get somewhere. If she'd heard this name, Island of the Brilliant Night, she'd have been so intrigued. She would have wanted to know more." She paused. "Although... maybe she did know more. Maybe she knew all about it. If she really went there and just never told me."

Mia went back to the sofa, picking up a pillow and clasping it tightly to her chest.

"What is it?" Erica said.

"It feels wrong," Mia said slowly. "I mean, here we are, talking about this island, these people and the Nazis. And my grandmother—as if she's some character in history. The daughter of a painter, or—"

"I'm sorry, Mia. I didn't mean to talk about her like a character—"

"I know." Mia dropped her forehead into her palms. "I'm just saying she was *my* grandmother. She loved me so much, and all she ever wanted was to make me feel safe. And even with no parents, I always felt that way. Safe and loved." She raised her eyes to look at her friend. "And now there are people dragging her name through the mud, accusing her of having stolen property and wanting to pry into things that were so private that she didn't even tell me about them."

Erica came over and sat beside her. "Maybe you should talk to Milt about this bowl you've found?"

Mia considered this, then shook her head. "If I tell him about it, he'll want to return it. He'll feel it's the only right thing to do. But my grandmother never told him about any of this, even though she told him everything. I don't think she wanted him to know. She only wanted *me* to know. She wanted *me* to decide what to do with it. That's the way she arranged it."

She thought for a moment, then looked up at Erica. "And

there's something else that I didn't even tell you about yet. There's this beautiful, elaborate wedding gown that I found last night in the attic. And the key to the storage unit was sewn into it. They have to be related, Erica—the *schianto* and the wedding gown. She wanted me to find them both, one and then the other. She led me to them, I know she did. I just don't know why.

"But you know what? There's one thing I do know for sure," Mia added, hearing her voice grow stronger again. "My grandmother wouldn't have stolen anything and she wouldn't have kept something she knew was stolen. She had too much integrity to do anything like that. There has to be a good reason that she hid this thing from the world. And I need to find out what it is before I tell Milt, or anyone else, that I have it."

"So what are you going to do?" Erica asked.

"I think... no, I *know* that I'm going to this island," she said. "To get to the bottom of this story and clear my grandmother's name. He's not going to back down, this Italian lawyer. I read the letter he sent and he knows he's on to something.

"I'm sorry, Erica, but I can't go to the mountains with you," she said. "I only have one week off from work, and I need to take care of this right away."

"Screw the mountains!" Erica exclaimed. "Of course you have to go to Italy. And you won't need to go alone. I'm coming with you!"

SIX
2018

Friday

That evening, in between sips of white wine and mouthfuls of cold sesame noodles, steamed shrimp dumplings, and cashew chicken called in from the Thai place in town, Mia huddled with Erica at the kitchen table to plan their trip.

She was glad Erica had decided to come with her. She would have gone alone if that were her only choice, but she'd never been to Europe before, and the presence of her best friend made the prospect much less daunting. She was glad, too, that Erica was taking the lead with the planning, as she was familiar with the range of travel websites, having worked part-time at a local beach resort while she earned her teaching degree.

"So we can take an eight fifteen flight from JFK tomorrow night that arrives in Rome on Sunday morning," Erica said, turning from the computer to insert her chopsticks into the dumpling carton. Chewing, she looked back at the screen. "We probably should plan to stay in Rome for one night to get our bearings and deal with the jet lag. And hey, if things go smoothly, we'll have a whole day to explore Rome. How bad could that be? Then we catch the train southwest toward the Mediterranean coast on Monday morning—well, technically I guess it's the Tyrrhenian Sea, but it says here it's part of the Mediterranean—and take it to... um..." She clicked on the links to the various station stops along the train line. "Well, it looks like we need to get to this town, Anzalea. It seems to be a launching point for ferries to these tiny islands. See on the map? There's a whole slew of little islands in this area."

Erica typed in the search box and clicked. "Although... it looks like you can't get to Parissi Island at all. I guess it's still not open to visitors. We'll have to stay on one of the nearby islands and wing it from there."

Mia felt her jaw drop. "Really? Just go somewhere close and try to figure out what to do when we get there?"

"I don't see any other way. I know you like things all neat and tidy, but it'll be okay. Let's think of this as an adventure. And try to embrace the uncertainty of it all."

Mia exhaled loudly, thinking how lucky Erica was to be comfortable when things weren't nailed down. It was one of the things she said she liked about being a teacher—that with twenty-five rambunctious third graders in her classroom, her workdays always seemed to hover on the brink of chaos. She leaned in closer to read the web page Erica had pulled up on the screen: a list of all the islands reachable by ferry with brief accompanying descriptions of each one.

"Well, we shouldn't go anywhere too small or remote," Mia said. "We're going to need a hotel that's used to helping Americans. With people who speak English."

Erica nodded in half-agreement, and Mia chuckled, knowing that if Erica had her way, they'd aim for somewhere almost entirely off the grid.

"I mean it," she insisted. "Neither one of us speaks Italian."

"Okay, okay," Erica said and began scrolling down the list of islands, clicking on links and then returning to the home page. A few moments later, Erica pushed herself away from the laptop and folded her arms across her chest.

"I think Piccino Island is where we should stay," she said firmly, gesturing with her chin toward the screen. It showed a photo of a small, airy hotel lobby, with wide-open doors looking out on to a glistening aqua sea. "It looks tourist-friendly. There's a garden and a restaurant on the terrace, and it's close to a sweet-looking beachfront with cafés and shops. And see on this page..." she added, switching quickly to another screen. "Look, the hotel gets good reviews. People say the staff are very helpful. If any place around here has people who can help us get to Parissi Island, I think it's going to be this one."

Erica went on to pull up the reservation page and keyed in all the requested information, setting up their trip as though it were no different from ordering burgers and fries from Caryn's for take-out. But to Mia, the trip felt like something out of a fairy tale, a journey you contemplate only theoretically. It was hard to wrap her head around the idea that by this time tomorrow they'd be flying to Rome, and then making their way down the Italian coast, ferrying onto a tiny Mediterranean island barely visible on a map, and somehow exploring an even tinier island where no outsiders were allowed. Up until now her only trip abroad had been to Quebec City, when her high school biology club competed in a science fair and all the arrangements were made by the school. She could hardly imagine stepping onto a plane in New York, then finding herself on the other side of the ocean seven hours later.

Lucy had never explained why she refused to travel, and Mia had always known the subject wasn't open for discussion. As a child, she'd felt very protective of her grandmother when the subject of travel came up. "My grandmother likes New York too much to leave," she'd tell school friends who asked where she'd be spending Christmas break. "My grandmother thinks there's no better place than home." And it felt so good to say that, as though she knew something that the rest of the world didn't. Maybe because she'd never known her parents, it made her feel safe knowing that her grandmother wanted nothing more than their home and their life together. Just the two of them.

But it wasn't that simple, she reminded herself. No, there was something desperate, frantic even, in her grandmother's refusal to go further than Shelter Island for their annual summer vacation, and her reluctance to engage with anyone other than the people she knew in town. She'd always been uncomfortable speaking more than a few words with the parents of Mia's friends, and often canceled routine parent–teacher conferences, avoiding any phone calls with teachers to reschedule until they finally gave up. As a teenager, Mia had wondered what made her grandmother act this way. She'd always known there had to be a reason...

With the transportation booked, the hotel reservations made, and last-minute chores—such as adding international service to their phones and packing plug adaptors—done, Erica closed her laptop with a sigh. "Why don't you sleep here tonight?" she said. "I can drive you to your grandmother's house tomorrow to get your suitcase and then we can go to the airport together."

Mia shook her head. "All I brought was hiking stuff. And anyway, my passport's at my apartment in the city. I'll drive back to my grandmother's now to get my suitcase and drop off the car, and then I'll call a taxi to take me to the train station."

"Well, that's silly, I can at least drive you to the train station," Erica said. "You head over to the house now, and I'll leave in a few minutes to pick you up."

It was a good idea, so Mia carefully rewrapped the *schianto* in tissue paper, put it into its box, and took it with her back to her grandmother's house. Pulling into the driveway, she could see that it was dark inside, which reminded her that she hadn't gotten around to buying timers and attaching them to indoor lights, as Ryan had asked her to. Nor had she remembered to call the local hardware store to have someone come out and install motion detectors around the property. She supposed she could ask Milt to handle those tasks. He'd be happy to help, she knew. But even though she felt guilty for neglecting Ryan's requests, she wasn't sorry for the darkness. No; she enjoyed bathing in it as she parked the car in the garage, then walked up the slate path to the front door. Inside, she switched on the table lamp in the front hall, letting the glow of the moon, as it traveled in through the windows, cast patches of light on the stairs. It reminded her of the way the house would look when she'd arrive home from a party or dance when she was in high school, her grandmother already asleep upstairs.

She put the *schianto* on the hall table, intending to go right upstairs and grab her suitcase. But she found herself pausing as her gaze landed once again on her grandmother's wedding photo. Her dress looked even simpler than it had when Mia had examined it last night. Actually, it looked plain and sad by comparison with the beaded, flowing gown up in the attic. Had her grandmother had that gorgeous dress upstairs for a long time? Perhaps even as long as she'd been in this country? Mia knew deep in her heart that if her grandmother had had the choice between the two dresses to wear on her wedding day, she'd have chosen the plain one. "Oh, Nana," she whispered, staring at the photo. "Why didn't you think you deserved anything special?"

She went to her bedroom and was wheeling her suitcase back into the hallway when her phone rang. She knew even before she looked that it would be Ryan, and she took a breath as she sat down on a stair and tried to decide what to tell him. She wasn't sure she could possibly convey to him why she had to go to Italy, at least not in a way he'd understand. She'd have to tell him about the letter Milt had received and the *schianto* hidden in the storage unit—and he'd no doubt tell her to tell Milt the truth and have him contact the lawyer in Italy to return the object and be done with it. He wouldn't understand why she felt so strongly that she needed to prove her grandmother innocent.

On the other hand, she didn't want to lie to him. How could she let him think she was a few hours north of New York City, instead of on the other side of the Atlantic? Ryan was always making plans for the two of them for the future, as though there was no chance they'd ever part ways. He was planning to leave his company sometime in the next year to start up his own real estate development firm, and he hoped that at some point, Mia might consider leaving her career so she could help him get the business up and running. Surely by this point, Mia thought, there shouldn't be any secrets between them, other than maybe where she'd hidden a birthday or Christmas present.

"Hey," she said when she answered, trying for a casual tone. "How's L.A.?"

"I wouldn't know. I've only seen the inside of conference rooms and my hotel. Going into another meeting now, and then heading to a dinner right after. I'm exhausted. How about you? Are you and Erica set to leave tomorrow?"

"Yeah... well, there's been a change," she said. "I know this is going to sound crazy. But we're not going to the Adirondacks after all. We're going to Italy instead."

"You're *what*?" She heard the confusion in Ryan's voice. Her own resistance to uncertainty was barely perceptible compared to his. "What are you talking about? You're going where?"

"I know it's a shock," she said, trying to keep her voice casual. "I'm surprised, too. But something came up while I was here in town."

"What? What could have come up that made you need to go to Italy?"

"I came across an object that I don't understand. My grandmother evidently had it forever and never talked about it. So I have to decide what to do, and I... I have to check out the whole story before I make any decisions. And that's why I'm going to Italy, and then Erica offered to come, since we both have the week off and were planning to travel together anyway..." She paused, waiting for his response. "I know it sounds crazy—" she started.

"*Really* crazy," he said, jumping in, as though his thoughts had been blocked behind a dam, and her repetition of "crazy" had sent them pouring out. "What is this thing? What does Italy have to do with it?"

"It's not just 'a thing.' It's an object that meant a lot to her. And there's some indication that it originally came from Italy."

"So what is it? Is it valuable?"

"I don't know. I mean, it was clearly valuable to her. But I don't know what it is or what it means. Or where it should be now that she can't tell me herself. I have to learn more about it..."

She let her voice trail off, not wanting to admit her grandmother was under investigation concerning the *schianto*'s whereabouts. Ryan had always thought her grandmother was a little strange. "Off"—that's how he'd put it. He never tired of telling her he'd almost decided not to date her because he was scared that any granddaughter of Lucy's would probably be a little off as well. Her grandmother had never warmed to Ryan either, although she tended to stay aloof from most people. But she did say she believed he'd make a dependable husband.

"So you're going all the way to Italy to find out about this thing—this object? I don't get it. This has to be Erica's doing. She's always coming up with random ideas—"

"It's not random and it wasn't Erica's idea," Mia's said

sharply as her back stiffened. Ryan often thought she was being influenced by someone else. As though she didn't have much of a mind of her own. "*I* had the idea, not her," she added.

"So why can't it wait? I'll be home in two weeks. Why can't we talk about it when I get back?"

"Because it can't wait."

"Why not?"

"Because... because there are people in Italy who think it belongs there. And they want it back. And I only have a week off from work. I only have this coming week to take care of it."

"What? This is starting to sound a little dangerous," he said. "If there are people trying to claim your grandmother's property now that she's dead, this isn't something you should be handling. Let Milt take care of it."

"I can't let Milt take care of it. I have to take care of it."

"But why, Mia? *Why*?"

She looked up at the ceiling and pressed her tongue against her upper lip. How could she not tell him the complete truth? Even she would have trouble accepting all this evasion if the tables were reversed. "Okay, here's the story," she said. "There's a lawyer in Italy who sent Milt a letter claiming that this object is stolen. It's a kind of a bowl or something, and it seems to have some historical importance. But my grandmother would never have stolen it. She must have had a good reason for having it."

"Then let Milt tell them that," Ryan replied, his tone dismissive.

"But they believe it's stolen and they're not going to back down. And I can't let people go around saying my grandmother had something to do with the theft."

Ryan exhaled loudly, and she could picture him puffing out his cheeks, the way he always did when he thought someone was being illogical. "Look, Mia, your grandmother's gone. I know it's sad and that she meant a lot to you, but she is. What does it matter what someone in Italy thinks about her? If this person has a legitimate claim to this bowl thing, just give it back."

"But it does matter. It matters to me! And there's something else, too, a wedding dress I never saw before in the attic. She wouldn't have hidden these things all my life and then left them for me unless she wanted to tell me something. I can't just send the *schianto* off to Italy."

"The what?"

"The *schianto grandioso*. That's what it's called. It means great crusher or grand crusher, something like that."

"Grand crusher? Mia, this all sounds so ludicrous—"

"But that's how it is. She wanted me to find it after she died. There's a reason for it or she wouldn't have done it this way. I can't just let it go..."

She sighed. Why did she always end up having to explain herself to him? Of course, he had a point. There he was in California, having this news sprung on him. Maybe she'd be upset, too, if he suddenly ran off with a friend to Italy. But she wasn't suddenly running off. Her grandmother had died. She was going through her grandmother's house. There were feelings she had, things she felt she had to do to get some kind of resolution. Why couldn't he say, "Okay, then if this is what you need to do, go ahead. I'll be here if you need me"?

"Look, I have to get to this dinner," he said. "Think about what I said, okay?"

"There's nothing to think about, Ryan—"

"But I think we should talk some more. I don't know what kind of... of unsavory people you're going to run into, or what they're going to want from you. Milt should be handling this. I'll talk to you tomorrow, okay?"

He said goodbye and hung up, and the absence of his voice on the other end of the phone made her shiver. It was upsetting to be cut off like that, and it made her start to question her decision, even though she knew in her heart it was the right one to make. She hated doubting herself like this. And she hated that Ryan could make her so easily doubt everything that had made sense up until his call.

She stayed on the steps, wondering what to do, until she heard the crunch of Erica's tires on the gravel outside. For a moment, she turned her frustration toward her grandmother. Would there ever be a time she could take her grandmother's life at face value again? When she could hear Lucy's voice in her head without feeling that all her words were loaded and secretive? A time when the thought of her grandmother didn't call up questions and add so many complications to her life? She was like her grandmother—she liked life to be simple. Why had her grandmother saddled her with these discoveries?

Taking the *schianto* from the hall table, she switched off the lamp and left the house, the clang of the lock snapping into place reverberating in the warm night air. Crossing toward Erica's car, she left the darkened house behind. Strangely, the sight of the car's harsh headlights felt comforting.

Would she be able one day to again embrace darkness the way her grandmother had—and not wonder what it was hiding?

She hoped that in Italy, she'd find her way back. So she could again be the person who was satisfied with Ryan. The person who unequivocally loved her grandmother. The person who believed she knew her grandmother, backwards and forwards.

The person she was before last night.

SEVEN

1943

August

With the threat of arrest hanging in the air, Annalisa willed herself to stay calm so she could assess the situation.

The first order of business was to deal with her sisters, who were close to hysterics. She could hear Emilia breathing loudly and shakily, and when she glanced toward them, Giulia pointed to the water, her head jerkily nodding, as though asking if she should run along the shoreline to get Vincenzo's attention. She gave them both a hard look to convey that she would handle everything and that all they needed to do was stay put and not make a ruckus. They both evidently got the message, as Giulia lowered her arm and moved closer to Emilia, nudging her with her elbow. Emilia clasped her hands in front of her chest and looked down at them.

As her sisters thankfully fell in line, Annalisa watched the silhouetted figure heading toward her, annoyed with herself for not being more thorough in her preparations. Why hadn't she foreseen this complication? She'd read so much about the island

and the castle before she left; countless articles that she'd hunted down at the library after helping customers each day at her father's tailoring shop, countless chapters in books about the Parissi family. The island was a paradise and the castle a haven, a place where the guests' every desire was anticipated. For centuries nobody would have thought to come to the island without an invitation. But these days, everything was changing. War was spreading across Europe, and people from all walks of life were on the move. Of course Patricio Parissi would want to protect his Shangri-La, this one-of-a-kind artistic fortress he had worked so hard to create.

Certain that silence was better than a panicked response, she continued to watch the guard hurry toward them. And that's when she saw that he wasn't a guard at all—or at least not a particularly menacing one. Thanks to the glowing sky that Emilia had pointed out and the lantern he was holding, the man's features became visible as he approached. And, despite his authoritative tone, he was barely a man, certainly no more than her age, maybe nineteen or twenty at the most.

But a very beautiful one, she couldn't help thinking. His hair, wavy on top with a few thick curls that grazed his fore-head, was a rich dark brown, like the carob syrup her mother used to drizzle onto figs and fresh pears, the texture smooth and silky. His lips were pillowy, especially the lower one, and she could hardly pull her eyes away from them. They gave him an air of vulnerability, of tenderness, and she felt herself blush at this intimate observation.

When she finally looked away from his face, she saw that there was more to admire. His physique was strong and almost rugged—his chest solid, his waist trim, his legs long. She'd been determined from the moment she'd stepped into Vincenzo's boat that evening to stay single-minded and impassive, to not let her guard down for even one second during this long, pivotal night. So it unnerved her, how intensely her insides responded to this young man. He was wearing light-colored trousers—tan or light green, it was hard to tell—that were cuffed at the bottom, and a thin cotton shirt with buttons open halfway down the front. The top of his chest was exposed, and she couldn't help but imagine how his clavicle would feel—the skin soft, the bone hard and muscles firm—beneath her fingertips.

With one hand holding his lantern, he rubbed his eyes with the other, and Annalisa pressed her lips together firmly to remind herself where she was, and what was at stake. And equally important, she had to remember that he was her adversary. She analyzed his behavior a moment longer, taking stock of her best advantage—that she was alert while he had apparently just awoken. The evidence led her to conclude that to get what she wanted, she would have to go on the offensive before he could.

"Arrested?" she exclaimed. "Do you know who you're talking to? We're the newly hired kitchen staff."

He paused and she thought she saw him smile with skepticism. "Kitchen staff?" He asked the question with a disbelieving chuckle. "Showing up in the middle of the night?"

"We're arriving now because we start first thing in the morning," she told him. "Signor Parissi is expecting us for tomorrow's breakfast preparation. This was the only time we could arrange to come on such short notice. We need to be up at the castle before dawn."

"Let me see if I understand this," the young man said, his hands on his waist, the lantern dangling from his fingers down along his side. "You come here in that old boat, sneaking onto the island after midnight, because Signor Parissi is *expecting* you?" He laughed again. "Am I supposed to believe that? Just like I'm supposed to believe I'm talking to... a boy?"

She gasped and then looked down, feeling her heartbeat quicken. She'd forgotten how she was dressed and hadn't thought to lower her voice when she spoke. Suddenly the idea of dressing in boys' clothing seemed ridiculous. The truth was, she hadn't planned on there being someone at the shore who'd hear them arrive and ask her questions. She knew that he knew they weren't really hired cooks, that he'd caught her in a lie. Still, his taunting—and the possibility of failure at this point— made her angry. She had no intention of backing down.

"And are we supposed to believe that you have the authority to question us? Half asleep and *barefoot*? Are we really supposed to believe you're the person Signor Parissi has guarding his island?"

"That's exactly who I am," he said. "Okay, you're right, I fell asleep. But I'm awake now. And you need to leave. Signal your man back. He hasn't gotten very far. Call to him now."

Giulia cupped her hands around her mouth, but Annalisa hurried over and yanked her hand down. "No," she told him. "We're not bringing him back. We're going up to the castle. We're going to find work—"

"So you're not already hired, huh?" he said, smiling. "Well, that's not how it works. It's a private island, don't you know that?"

"I know that perfectly well. And we're here because we want to work here. My sisters—we're sisters, the three of us—my sisters and I are hard workers. And we're smart. Signor Parissi is going to like having us here once he meets us."

"Don't you understand? You're never going to get to meet him. And if you don't leave now, you're going to be in big trouble. Is that what you want?"

"And if we're discovered, then you're going to be in trouble for falling asleep and not stopping us from coming ashore when the boat was approaching. You'll be sent off the island right along with us. Is that what *you* want?"

He went to reply, then stopped with his mouth open. Letting out a breath, he shook his head and looked out toward the dark sea, rubbing his chin with one hand. She smiled at the thought that she'd outsmarted him. He was not nearly as tough or scary as he was pretending to be. And he clearly understood she had a point.

"It seems we're in this together now," she said, making her tone more conciliatory. "We can either protect each other, or we can all be losers."

She held out her hand. "I'm Annalisa, and this is Giulia and Emilia."

He looked at her, then at her sisters, and then back at her. He cupped his free hand around the nape of his neck for a moment and gazed at the sky before sauntering toward her.

"I don't know when you all ate last," he said. "But if your plan is to climb all the way up to the castle, you'll need your strength. It won't do any of us any good for you to pass out halfway up. I have some fruit and cheese in the boathouse."

He took her hand and gave it a quick shake. "I'm Aldo, by the way. Follow me."

A few minutes later, they were all sitting on the wooden steps outside the boathouse, eating grapes, bread, and chunks of hard cheese. Emilia, who was on the bottom step, rested her cheek on Annalisa's knee.

Just as Annalisa would have expected, her sisters had panicked when Aldo had confronted them: Emilia had been wide-eyed, like a caged animal, while Giulia was willing to call Vincenzo and hop back on the boat as soon as he could return. And yet, as annoyed as she was, her heart ached for them. They were with her because they loved her and trusted her, and they didn't want to be left at home without her. They felt safe with her, maybe even safer than they felt with Papa, who was frail and sick. And she was grateful for their love. Still, at moments like this, when she thought about how much was riding on her own shoulders, it was hard to always be the one in charge. She sometimes wished that she had someone she could rely on, someone who could step in and help. Someone that would allow her to relax and be carried along. Not for always; just once in a while.

But she didn't have that at home, at least not anymore. It had been awful when her mother died, but at least Papa had made her and her sisters feel safe and kept their family strong. He loved them so much. He'd changed, though, when his heart started to fail a few years ago. Suddenly he became scattered and impossible to rely on. She had to get Papa better, had to take him and her sisters to America, and every second counted. She had a month, maybe five weeks at the most, to accomplish what she needed to. She didn't think her father's health would hold out past then.

That's why she was drawn to the island. For transformation.

When they were finished eating, Aldo went inside and came back out with a second lantern, which he gave to her. They returned to where they'd left their suitcases and, guided by the glowing sky, began the long, steep climb up the stone stairway to the castle. Aldo took Emilia's suitcase, and while that irritated Annalisa at first—it wasn't a good idea for Emilia to get used to people making things easier for her—the gesture showed that he was feeling kindly toward them, and she knew that was a good sign. Despite their rocky first encounter, he was proving himself to be generous and kind, which somehow made him even more pleasing to gaze at. In a show of solidarity, she took Giulia's suitcase as well as her own. Aldo grinned and gave a quick nod, his eyes twinkling, and she felt her cheeks burn as she relished his attention.

The steps were narrow and uneven, and they moved slowly and in single file—with Aldo in the lead, Annalisa next, and Giulia and Emilia behind her. The route was winding, with separate staircases of about twenty steps that led to a square landing with each new change of direction. As they drew closer to the castle, the music grew louder, and occasionally when Annalisa lifted her eyes toward the windows, she caught glimpses of dancers, the women's jewel-toned ball gowns flowing and swaying.

"Is it like this every night?" Annalisa murmured to Aldo when they reached the next landing and stopped to catch their breath.

Aldo nodded. "Sometimes opera, sometimes lectures and readings. Often music and dancing. Nights are important here. That's when everyone comes together."

"And does it always continue this late?"

"Not always. But more so in the summer. Especially this summer."

"Why this summer?"

"Because the war is worsening. Everyone knows it. They just don't want to believe it. So they dance. They dance as though it will stop the future from showing up. They know it won't. But they act like it will."

He shrugged and gave her a kind of apologetic smile, as though he hated revealing this undeniable truth. She noticed his deep-brown eyes shaded by impossibly long eyelashes. Back at the shore, she'd thought his dark eyes made him look intense, quick to anger. But now, she believed his eyes and eyelashes signaled earnestness. That he was someone whose cards were all on the table.

He started toward the next staircase and she followed, looking again at the top-floor windows. The music had picked up in tempo and from this closer vantage point, the dancers looked as though they were floating on air. Although she could never let herself forget that she was here for a purpose, she gave herself a moment to bask in the wonder of it all. She loved learning, and she especially loved being so close to people whose capabilities and talents were on a whole other level to anything she'd ever known before. These were geniuses. Virtuosos and visionaries. How she wished she had no other task than to stay here and soak it all in.

They reached the top landing and Annalisa froze, with Giulia and Emilia on either side of her. The castle entranceway was spectacular. They were standing in a vast courtyard in between two thick groupings of shrubbery arranged in diamond patterns. Ahead of them was a stone walkway lined with tall black iron streetlamps, the gaslit flames in their faceted glass cases twinkling golden. At the end of the row of streetlamps was an arched stone doorway surrounded by a semicircle of white marble steps. The actual door, set deep inside the arch, was dark and barely visible.

"Come on! Don't stop!" Aldo hissed to them from the far end of the courtyard.

Annalisa shook herself to attention and nudged her sisters, pushing them in front of her toward Aldo. Of course, he was right, they couldn't just stand there or someone might see them. How ridiculous would that be, to get caught after she had made a pact with Aldo to protect each other. She'd never forgive herself if all was lost because she couldn't control her own foolish gawking.

Aldo proceeded to the side of the castle, then stepped onto a dirt path that led to a forest thick with leafy olive, beech and fragrant eucalyptus trees. They continued for a few more minutes, until he turned off the path and went deeper into the woods, the leaves above forming a dense canopy. He placed Emilia's suitcase down and sat upon it. Annalisa and Giulia settled onto their own suitcases, and Emilia kneeled on the ground.

"You should probably get a little sleep," Aldo said. "Just make sure not to sleep past dawn. Things get started early, and it won't do for anyone to catch you lying here. There's a..." He paused, looking like he didn't know the word to use.

"A... building for the groundskeepers and such a little ways past these trees, and I'm sure nobody's there now if you... well, you know. Parissi believes in cleanliness, which is why he had the thing built out here, with running water and everything."

She nodded, thinking it was cute that he was embarrassed to use the word toilet or anything like it.

"The kitchen is at the back of the castle," he continued. "It won't be hard to find in the daylight. When you get inside, ask to talk to Signora Russo. She runs the kitchen and she's busy in the mornings, so as long as you get there early, she won't ask too many questions. With any luck, she'll put you right to work." He stood and lifted his palm in a wave, then turned toward the path.

"Wait—you're leaving?" Annalisa blurted out.

As sorry as she had been to meet him back at the shore, now she didn't want him to go. Though she'd only just met him, in an hour he had proven himself essential as well as pleasant to be around. He had led them up here to this hidden spot—something she wasn't sure she'd have been able to do on her own. She felt safe with him, which was pretty remarkable, considering that she and her sisters were trespassers.

Nevertheless, she didn't like how desperate she'd sounded. "I mean... we haven't even had a chance to say thank you. Do you have to go right away?"

"I need to get back to the boathouse," he said. "And even though getting down the hill is quicker than coming up, it still takes time."

"Will we... see you again?" she asked quietly. She hated herself for hoping so strongly that the answer was yes.

"Sure," he said, his tone upbeat and reassuring. "It looks like a big place from the outside, but it's not as big once you're in. And I do a lot of different things, so I'm around often during the day. I'll keep my eye out for you." He looked at the three of them, one at a time. "Good luck, Emilia, Giulia, and... Annalisa," he said, pausing before he said her name and holding her glance with his eyes for an extra moment. "Good luck in the kitchen. Or wherever you end up. Something tells me you're here for more than just kitchen work. I hope you get whatever it is you came for."

He nodded, and Emilia and Giulia called out their thanks. "Bye, Aldo," Annalisa said softly, watching him disappear into the darkness. When she turned around, she saw that her sisters were staring at her, their wide eyes glowing by the light of the lantern she still held.

"What?" she asked.

"You think he's cute!" Emilia said.

Annalisa put her free hand on her waist. "No, I don't," she said scornfully.

"You do. You like him," Giulia teased. "Anyone could tell."

"I do not like him," she insisted, feeling her cheeks warm. "I was nice to him because we needed him to bring us up here. So stop being ridiculous, okay? Lie down and go to sleep!"

"But Pippa, I don't want to sleep outside," Emilia whimpered.

Annalisa gave her a look. "You know I hate when you call me that. That silly nickname Papa made up. Don't test my patience!"

"I'm sorry, Annalisa, okay? But I don't want to sleep on the ground."

"It's only for a little while," Annalisa said, her voice softer. She felt bad for speaking so harshly a moment ago. "By tomorrow we'll have a better place to sleep. I promise."

"But it's bumpy—"

"Then take some clothes out of your suitcase to use as a pillow," Annalisa said. "We've been up so long, I bet you won't have any trouble falling asleep."

"What if we oversleep and they come out and find us?"

Giulia asked. "Could they really arrest us, like Aldo said at the shore?"

"I'm so scared!" Emilia said. "I wish neither of you ever told me about this—"

"Emilia, you're *impossible!*" Giulia said. "You wouldn't have wanted to be left behind and you know it. So don't you dare start crying—"

"Okay, stop, both of you," Annalisa scolded, even though she knew they had a right to be upset. Planning to sleep outdoors had sounded a lot better back when she was home and in her soft bed, thinking things through. She was the head of this family—at least while they were here—and it was her responsibility to keep her sisters calm. "Actually, I don't even think I could sleep at all," she said. "How's this? I'll stay awake and watch for dawn, and I'll wake you both before anyone can notice us. You're both going to be sorry if you don't get a little sleep."

"Don't *you* fall asleep," Giulia said. "Don't even close your eyes, okay?"

"And don't go too far away," Emilia said. "Make sure you stay hidden."

"I will," she said, and waited until they'd gotten themselves settled. Then, walking out from under the canopy of leaves, she sat down with her back against a tree, watching the rear of the castle. Though she could no longer see the windows that revealed the couples dancing, she could hear the music playing again. This time it was a bit more upbeat, like a swing beat. She wondered how the party could still be going on. Wasn't everyone tired? Could they really work on their inventions and creations all day, and then party until dawn?

But then she thought about what Aldo said. How the war was worsening and the island wasn't immune, no matter how much the people dancing wanted to believe it was. If war was coming, that meant she'd have to work even faster, strategize even harder, to meet Patricio Parissi. He was the man she'd come here for. He was the person who could save her father. But only if she could get him to agree to do so. Which would probably be her hardest task of all.

Because Parissi hated her father.

There was no one on earth he hated more.

EIGHT

2018

Saturday

I'm really doing this, Mia said to herself the next evening, as she stepped out of the cab at JFK Airport.

She relinquished her suitcase at the check-in counter and continued through to security, startling every time the muted sounds of conversation and footsteps were interrupted by announcements about gate changes and final boarding calls. She didn't know why she felt so jumpy. It wasn't flying that unnerved her; no, she understood the physics of flight. It was more the thought of leaving what she knew to be fixed and reliable. Like the furniture in her small sublet apartment, her bed with its blue comforter and two plump pillows. And her building on the east side of Midtown, the guy down the hall who walked his Bernese Mountain Dog every morning and the super, whose permanent scowl made him look irritated even when simply saying hello. Her grandmother's house. Erica's laugh. Milt's office. Janet's scarves. Ryan, too—his firm voice and neatly combed hair, the way his shirts fit so well, the untucked hem resting in line with the center of his hips. All familiar.

But what was also familiar was her grandmother's determined voice, telling her that the only way to solve a problem was to face it outright. *You need to use your senses,* she'd say. *You need to examine things with your eyes, your ears, your hands.* It was why her grandmother hated puzzles—they were mere representations of things. And she thought picture-taking was a waste of time, too, as the expression on her face in her wedding photo reflected. *Don't memorialize things—investigate them,* she'd urge. *Know what you know and face what you don't.* It was good advice, Mia had always thought, but now it rang a little false, coming from a woman who had gone to great pains to keep the *schianto* and the wedding gown hidden, seemingly for decades. What could have made her go against her most cherished philosophies?

Pausing at a small snack shop on her way to the gate, Mia grabbed a bottle of water and an energy bar and took them to the counter. Ahead of her in line, a young father was buying a packaged ice cream cone. His little daughter looked up with wide, expectant eyes as he pulled off the wrapping and handed it to her. "Good?" he asked as she took her first lick.

She nodded. "Thanks, Daddy!" she said.

After paying for her snack, Mia watched the pair, the little girl grasping her father's arm with her free hand as she skipped alongside him. She didn't often think about it, but sometimes it hit her, that she'd never had a father to skip alongside. She couldn't even remember any conversations at home about her father.

But there had been a conversation about *Lucy's* father, she now remembered. On a warm, early-September evening when Mia was seven or eight. She'd been looking for Lucy so she could say goodnight, and had found her outside on one of the hard-backed patio chairs. Mia hadn't been surprised to see her there, since she often sat outside, even on the coldest nights. But on this night, she was holding a tissue and making small gasping sounds.

"What are you doing?" Mia had asked, anxious. She'd never seen her grandmother in such a state before. "What's wrong?"

"I'm fine," Lucy had croaked after clearing her throat and pressing the tissue for a moment against her lips.

"Then why were you crying?"

"I wasn't crying. I was thinking."

"About what?"

Lucy's answer sounded curt. "I was thinking about my father. I don't usually do that, but tonight I did. He died on this day. Many, many years ago."

Mia had moved closer, resting her belly against the arm of the chair. "I didn't even know my dad," she said, trying to offer comfort by showing that they shared the same absence. "Did you know yours?"

Lucy nodded.

"How did he die?"

"He was sick. It was his heart."

"How old were you?"

"Much older than you. Almost an adult." She shook her head. "I tried to save him. I thought I could. How foolish. I couldn't save anyone..." she murmured.

Mia dragged a chair over and sat down on her knees, reaching out to stroke her grandmother's hair. They were so alike, she remembered thinking: both daughters left behind. She didn't ask why Lucy thought she could save her father, or who else she wanted to save. Even so young, she knew her grandmother had probably already said more than she'd intended. So she continued to stroke Lucy's hair, feeling lucky to have her grandmother to take care of her.

And it was on that night that Mia decided she wanted to be

a scientist. So she could find a cure for sick hearts. A cure that would have made her grandmother's father better.

The next thing she knew, it was morning and she was waking up in her own bed. She and Lucy never spoke about that conversation, never spoke of their fathers again, and Mia didn't even remember going upstairs to her bedroom. But she'd promised herself that from then on, she'd never ask about her grandmother's father. She never wanted to see her grandmother cry again. It had been too hard to watch. Yes, she liked to ask questions and learn things. But some things, she'd thought that day, were maybe not worth learning.

Because who knew what she'd find out—and how it would cause things to change? If anyone had asked her about her life up until now, Mia would have insisted that she had the best childhood possible, with a grandmother who kept her safe and was utterly devoted to her. But sitting here at the airport, a place far from familiar, she suddenly remembered other feelings she had growing up. Uneasy feelings when she was nine, ten, eleven, and even older, maybe until she left home for college. There'd always been a layer, a smidge, of impending threat just beneath the surface of her life. Often it felt like walking on an asphalt driveway in winter, not knowing where the black ice lay. She clung to the regularity, the unchanging routine of her days, the sameness of the old furniture in the house, the cycle of the moon that her grandmother loved to gaze at, because those things kept her stable.

Reaching her gate, she sat down and sipped some water, and her hand instinctively touched the fabric of her carry-on. She had decided last night to bring the *schianto* with her on the trip because it felt more dangerous to leave it alone in her apartment. At first, she'd packed it in her carry-on, but then wondered if the hinge connecting the arm to the bowl could trigger the metal detector when she passed through security. So she'd rolled the bowl in a couple of thick sweaters and tucked it deep within the suitcase she was checking. She'd worried last night about what she'd do if her suitcase didn't make it onto the plane for some reason, and she thought about that possibility again now. But she reminded herself that despite all the horror stories, the vast majority of checked luggage arrived at the same airport at the same time as the owner. Probability was on her side. And anyway, her suitcase was gone; much as she hated uncertainty, the matter was literally out of her hands.

Placing her shoulder bag on the seat next to her to save it for Erica, she ripped the wrapping on the energy bar. It was Ryan's favorite flavor, chocolate peanut butter. He'd called that morning while she was packing and suggested again that she either let Milt handle the situation, or wait until he was back from California, and she'd repeated that she wanted to get to the bottom of things before the Italian lawyer took any more steps. She told him that she understood he was worried, and that she appreciated his efforts to protect her; but she'd said it mostly because she had a lot of packing left to do, and it seemed an expedient way to bring the call to a close.

And she wanted to end the conversation fast. She was still bothered by how he'd spoken about her grandmother last night: *Your grandmother's gone... What does it matter what someone in Italy thinks about her?* What an awful question to ask, she thought. How could he not understand that it mattered a great deal that her grandmother not be called a thief? Especially now, when Lucy wasn't around to explain or defend herself. And even if Ryan couldn't find a way to agree with her, even if he didn't have the capacity to put himself in her shoes, why had he continued hammering home how misguided he felt Mia was being? Why call again this morning to repeat himself, as though he hoped to eventually wear her down? Couldn't he have simply offered his opinion once and then accepted that this was a decision *she* needed to make?

She finished the bar and, as she went to throw out the wrapper, she noticed the digital clock high on the wall. Seven thirty —where on earth was Erica? She sat back down and tried her best to relax, but a few minutes later, the agent announced that the flight would start boarding in five minutes. She nervously gathered her hair away from her face and twisted it behind her neck, then scanned the crowds of people coming from the direction of the security checkpoint. Surely she'd see her friend's face at any moment. Erica could be a little reckless, but she'd never miss the flight. She'd never leave Mia alone at a moment like this.

When the agent announced the first group to board, Mia texted Erica but received no response. She finished her water and tried to slow her quickening breath. When the agent announced the next group of passengers to board, Mia tossed the empty bottle in a recycling can and texted Erica again. It was seven fifty now. Another group would soon head to the doorway. And then it would be time for the two of them to board.

Finally her phone rang, and the screen showed Erica's number. "Hey, what's going on?" Mia said when she answered, her voice high-pitched and shaky. "The plane is boarding."

"Oh Mia, you're not going to believe it," Erica cried out. "My passport expired. They won't let me through!"

Mia found it impossible to take a breath, as though her chest muscles were glued to her bones. "*What?*" she said, somehow pushing the words out. "What do you mean?"

"It expired two months ago. I never even looked."

"But this can't be. You travel all the time—"

"I haven't gone out of the country since I started at my new school. I never thought about it. I just forgot."

"So what happens now? What do you do?"

"I don't think there's anything I can do. The passport offices don't open until Monday, and I may not even be able to get an appointment then. And even if I do, it could take a couple of days to process."

"So what are you saying? You're not coming?"

"I don't see how I can. There's not enough time. We both only have a week off."

"But... but—" Mia stopped and held her breath, paralyzed by this news. Erica was the one who knew all about travel and who'd designed the whole trip. How could she manage by herself?

"Maybe I shouldn't go either," she said. "Maybe I should postpone—"

"No, you *have* to go," Erica told her. She lowered her voice. "They think your grandmother stole that thing, remember? You were going to do it even before I said I'd go."

"But you're the one who made it doable! I don't know if I would have done all this without you. Maybe Ryan was right and I should think it over. He thought it was a bad idea to go in the first place. He doesn't see what the big deal is. Maybe I should wait until he's back so we can talk about it—"

"No! Don't change your mind! It won't be that hard."

"But I don't speak the language—"

"Neither do I. Lots of people go to Italy who don't speak Italian. Everyone speaks English there."

"But—"

"I'll feel horrible if you cancel this trip because of me. And you will, too, I know it. You can call me anytime, day or night, if you need me. Don't let Ryan make you doubt yourself. And don't let my stupid mistake mess this up, or I'll never forgive myself..."

Mia looked over at the gate, where people were filing toward the open door. The truth was, she could walk away. She could leave the airport right now. Except, of course, her suitcase would be flying to Rome without her. She wondered how long they would hang onto it at the Rome airport. What would they do with it if she was unable to reach anyone in Italy and explain? Might she never see her suitcase—or the *schianto* —again?

She looked through the windows out onto the airfield. Night had arrived, the sky a deep bluish black. Her grand-mother had taught her to look to the night when she was feeling anxious. And sure enough, the view soothed her. Planes glided along the runways, lifting up like magic. It was orderly and beautiful, both at once.

That's when she felt her mind starting to filter out all the noise and the useless thoughts in her head. Sure, it would be easier if Erica came, but now that wasn't an option. And in the end, it didn't matter. Erica was a good friend, but this wasn't Erica's trip. Nor was it Ryan's decision to make, whether she went or not. It was her trip and her decision. And it was her story to uncover, the story her grandmother had left to her. Now was not the time to turn away.

Stepping toward the gate, she took one last glance out the terminal window. The night sky was vast and peaceful, dotted by shimmering, white-hot stars.

Her grandmother had always told her to embrace the night sky. Because it had all the answers.

She just hoped her grandmother was right.

On board, she ordered a vodka tonic. She wasn't much of a fan of mixed drinks, but she thought it would help her relax. Sure enough, she closed her eyes and the next time she opened them, the sun was streaming in through the small space between the window and her lowered shade, and the plane was starting its descent.

A short time later, she emerged from the jetway. It was a relief that Leonardo da Vinci Airport was very similar to JFK, with lots of English being spoken around her and all the directional signs in multiple languages. She found her way to baggage claim, glad when her suitcase came around the carousel as expected. Setting her carry-on on top of her suitcase, she made her way out of the terminal. Outside, the sun was shining and the air was pleasantly warm, the temperature in the mid-seventies. All was good so far, she thought.

She paused a moment to get her bearings. To her right was the taxi stand, the taxis white instead of the yellow she was used to in New York and a bit smaller but certainly recognizable. Positioning herself in line behind about a half-dozen travelers, she waited her turn but then saw through the window, to her dismay, that there were no credit card readers facing the back seat. It was a surprise, since that was how she always paid when she took cabs in New York. She pulled a card from her wallet and showed it to the driver through the front window, but he shook his head, then pointed back toward the arrivals building where, through the glass doors, she could see what appeared to be an ATM. With a nod to the driver, she went into the building to get some euros, then returned to the taxi line. A minor setback, she told herself. If this was the worst thing, she'd be in good shape.

A few minutes later she was in a taxi with enough euros to cover her ride to the hotel and more. Taking out her phone, she found the home page of the hotel Erica had chosen, and the thin, grandfatherly driver took a look and nodded as he pulled away from the curb. Sitting back in her seat, Mia studied her surroundings through the window. The road signs were different colors than she was used to, with information and symbols that she didn't completely understand. It was like looking in a fun house mirror, knowing you're seeing your own image even though it's all out of whack.

Before long she noticed a tall stone barricade alongside the highway. It was part of the Aurelian Walls, she realized—the ancient structures built to defend Rome from invasions, which she'd learned about in tenth grade history. Still, it was one thing to read about an ancient monument and another to see it right there next to her taxi—broken up in spots, solid in others. It wasn't so much the age of the construction that struck her; she'd grown up looking with her grandmother at stars and planets billions of years old. No, it was more the feeling that the wall evoked. She remembered traveling from Soundport into New York City on school field trips, the way the trains would descend into darkness as they sped toward the Midtown Tunnel and crossed the East River before emerging in Penn Station. She'd always hated that tunnel. She'd never quite understood how tunnels could exist underwater and why they didn't sink or float or flood, and trying to come to grips with the matter always made her queasy.

Before long, they'd reached Trastevere, the neighborhood where Erica had booked their stay. It was lovely, with winding cobblestone streets, old stone buildings in shades of tan, brown and burnt orange, and window boxes overflowing with ivy and floral vines. But what stood out the most was how empty the streets were. There were bicycles and motorized scooters parked against the buildings, and plenty of outdoor cafés, but no diners—only the occasional worker wiping down tables or pushing in chairs. She'd never seen such an absence of people when the sun was up and morning was well underway. Even Soundport, a small town by any measure, had plenty of people on the streets by eight a.m. or earlier—fetching coffee, stopping at the bank, shopping for groceries, or picking up breakfast before heading to the train station.

The quietness here was strange and unsettling. Not that she had anything to say to anybody right now, but in a place so foreign to her, she would have liked the sights and sounds of people starting their day. Being almost the sole person around in one of the few moving vehicles, she couldn't shake the feeling she was doing something wrong.

"Where is everyone?" she said to the driver, leaning forward in her seat. She saw him lift his shoulders and shake his head, and even without the benefit of seeing his face, she knew he had no idea what she was asking.

They arrived at the hotel, the Albergo Carina, a yellow building with a small patio surrounded by an iron fence and pretty pink flowers in stone planters at either side of the front door. Calculating the fare plus a tip, she paid the driver, took her change, and murmured *"Grazie"*—one of the few Italian words she knew. He smiled as he carried her bags from the trunk and set them down before her. She gave herself a moment to look around before going inside and navigating the check-in process.

Just then, on a high ledge surrounding the building next door, she noticed a tabby cat with dark swirls on its face and orange patches along its sides. It reminded her of the tabby she and her grandmother had encountered back when Mia was in middle school. They'd been sitting outside on the back porch one summer night when they'd heard a loud mewing, and a moment later saw the cat climb onto the deck. Although it had a collar and looked well cared for, the mewing made Lucy think it was hungry. Mia went inside to get a bowl of milk, but by the time she came back out, two kids from a few streets away had shown up to bring it back home.

The next day, Mia's English teacher assigned the class to write a series of linked tales, where the ending of one led right to the beginning of the next. With the tabby still on her mind, Mia decided to write her series about a cat that keeps getting lost. "The kids who own her get into a big adventure when they try to find her," she explained to her grandmother that evening as she set the table for dinner, excited to share her idea. "And each time they track her down, they see her striped tail as she runs off again, and that's where the next story starts."

"So when do they bring her home?" Lucy asked.

"They don't. That's the whole point."

"They never get the cat back?"

"That's the point," Mia repeated. "They keep going on new adventures—"

"With no end?"

"It's a series—"

"But doesn't the cat ever find a home? What if it's hungry?"

"I guess people give it food. Like you were going to do with the cat that came here. Nana, it's just a story—"

"The cat can't keep running," Lucy said, turning away from the chicken on the stove. "She'll get sick, she needs food. Medicine. Find another story. I don't like this assignment."

"But—" Mia protested, although by that time, Lucy had turned off the stove and left the kitchen.

Mia looked after her, baffled. She hadn't meant that anything bad would happen to the cat. It was just a series, and the cat was what kept the series going. There was nothing wrong with the assignment. There was nothing wrong with her idea, she was sure of it. In the end, she wrote the series the way she'd envisioned it, and her teacher gave her an "A." But she never showed the grade to her grandmother. Nor did she show her the teacher's comments: "Very inventive! Well done!"

And now, standing here on the empty street in Trastevere, she understood what had bothered her grandmother and sent her rushing out of the kitchen. It was the idea that the cat would never be found. That her story would never be completed. That her ultimate fate would remain unwritten. There was a lack of order to that, a lack of closure. And Lucy hated it.

Mia watched the cat scurry on along the ledge until it reached a curve and moved out of sight. Then she took her first steps toward the entrance to the hotel.

NINE

2018

Sunday

Luckily, the clerk at the front desk spoke English, and it wasn't long before Mia was checked in. The hotel was charming, as Erica had predicted, and Mia's second-floor room, though small, was well furnished with floral linens on the bed and plenty of towels in the bathroom. There was a tiny balcony on the far wall with green wooden shutters that opened out, revealing a romantic view of the cobblestone street and still-empty cafés below. Knowing it was smart to adjust to the time difference as quickly as possible, Mia resisted the temptation to take a nap, and instead showered and changed into a fresh pair of ankle pants and a light-blue cotton top. Before she left the room, she kneeled by her suitcase, feeling for the *schianto*. There it was, wrapped deeply in her sweaters, just as she'd packed it. Safe and sound.

Downstairs, she asked the clerk where to get an early lunch, and he directed her to a café across the street, where servers were starting to welcome diners on the outdoor patio. A few people were out and about now, which made her feel more comfortable. Pointing to the pictures on the menu, she was able to order a cappuccino and a tasty sandwich of tomatoes, cheese and spices on thick, toasted bread. As she waited for her food, she sent quick texts to Ryan and Erica saying that she'd safely arrived and was having her first meal. Neither responded right away, as it was still the middle of the night in L.A. and not even six a.m. yet in New York. But then she noticed that Erica had sent her a text last night with an itinerary. "These are some things you should see today. All walking distance from the hotel. Can't believe I'm missing it!" she added with a sad-face emoji.

Mia considered the long list—Trevi Fountain, Pantheon, Spanish Steps, the Colosseum, and lots of churches, squares, and monuments. Erica had been overambitious for sure—there was no way to squeeze in all these places in just one afternoon. But it made no sense to sit in her hotel room doing nothing but anticipating the train and ferry trips tomorrow, which would be far harder to navigate than her transfer from the airport. The *schianto* was secure in her suitcase, and tomorrow morning was a long way off. She'd never been to Europe before, let alone to Rome, so it made sense to take advantage of this beautiful day and her free time. Plus, the distraction would be good for her.

After reviewing the route on her phone, she set off on the half-hour walk toward Rome's historic center. Of course, this wasn't the way she'd have planned to explore Rome. If she and Ryan had been taking this trip, she'd have read up for weeks beforehand to have the complete historical context in mind, while Ryan would have created a spreadsheet with the most time-efficient itineraries. She liked to be prepared, and Erica's random list felt far too ad hoc. Although, she had to admit, there was something magical about crossing the wide pedestrian bridge and seeing the river below and more old bridges in the distance before consulting her phone to learn that she was on the Ponte Sisto, which dated back to the Renaissance. A trio of musicians was playing jazz halfway across, and she stopped to listen, then counted out some coins and tossed them into the open guitar case. In the distance, a huge white dome rose above the greenery. It felt refreshing to look at it for a moment before checking to confirm that it was St. Peter's Basilica.

She reached the other side of the bridge and quickly realized where all the people she'd expected in Trastevere were—right here, crammed into this popular area of Rome. The streets were so packed with bodies, it was almost as if the city were composed of sidewalks where cars and taxis could attempt to drive, rather than streets made for moving vehicles. So different, she thought, from the jammed yet relatively orderly grid of Midtown Manhattan, where pedestrians mostly waited at the curb for a "Walk" sign before descending en masse into the intersection. Rome was chaotic on a level she'd never seen before. And she didn't know how all these people seemed to take the whole scene in stride.

Her first stop on Erica's list was the Trevi Fountain, with its huge stone statues and frescoes, and clear water flowing into a large aqua pool. The area was bursting with tourists—romantic couples and groups of friends and what looked like big extended families, everyone laughing and embracing, snapping selfies and videos, as they tossed coins over their shoulders and into the water. Two men nearby were savoring huge cones filled with creamy pink and white gelato topped with biscotti, and they offered each other hurried tastes as the creamy scoops melted in the sun. Stopping to check her phone, Mia read that according to legend, if you threw one coin into the fountain, you were assured a return to Rome. There was another part of the legend regarding tossing multiple coins, but she was being jostled and shoved so much by people trying to get closer to the pool, it was impossible to read on.

Fishing a coin from her bag, she took a selfie as she threw it over her shoulder, thinking she'd send it to Ryan and Erica. But her smile looked awkward and artificial. There was something sad about being here all by herself, and she wondered again why her grandmother had never brought her here. Why hadn't she wanted to show Mia the country where she was born?

She spent the rest of the afternoon following the crowds, the centuries-old structures making her feel displaced and alone, even though she aimed to quell those thoughts by focusing on the wonders of the architecture and the historical significance of her surroundings. By late afternoon, she was ready to return to her hotel and Trastevere's less hectic setting. But to her surprise, the neighborhood was as busy as the historic area of Rome. The shops and businesses were all open, and the cobblestone streets were filled with people, the outdoor cafés overflowing. The density of the crowds, along with the sounds of a language she didn't understand, only reinforced her feeling that she was a stranger with no business being here, and she decided on room service for dinner. It was a revelation to think how rarely she'd been anywhere unfamiliar.

She wished that her grandmother were still alive and she could go back home. To have dinner on the patio, just the two of them. What she would give to see the stars come out as the sky grew comfortably dark!

And then it was morning and her adventure was continuing, taking her even further from home.

She'd thought the coastal travel Erica had booked would be complicated, but it turned out to be smooth sailing, getting a taxi from the hotel to the train station and then finding her way through the enormous terminal. With help from an English-speaking agent in the ticket office, she located the correct plat-form. Soon enough, she was boarding the train, proud that she'd made it with no drama. Relaxing into her seat, her suitcase visible on the luggage rack at the front of the train, she realized that she'd done it—the first leg of her journey was complete.

The train set off down the coast, passing alongside a few industrial areas but mostly revealing rocky cliffs, peaked mountains, deep-green vegetation along the hillsides, and the gorgeous blue water of the Mediterranean, sparkling as it reflected the brilliant sunshine. The separation from home wasn't bothering her today the way it had yesterday. Instead, she felt invigorated and curious. Even though she was still jet-lagged, she didn't want to close her eyes and miss this vista. For the first time since she'd left her apartment for the airport, she felt glad to be exactly where she was.

The two-hour trip passed quickly, and she easily transferred to the local train that would take her to Anzalea. It was then an easy walk from the station to the ferry pier, despite having to wheel her suitcase. As Erica had said, Anzalea was a big transfer location so lots of passengers were heading in the same direction, and she simply followed the crowd toward the water. Ferries were coming and going and the way to the one stopping at Piccino Island was well marked. She'd loaded her ticket onto her phone last night, so boarding was a breeze, and she found a seat on the deck. It was exhilarating to be sailing on the Mediterranean, watching the mainland recede and the spattering of tiny islands offshore come closer. The sun was out again in full force, and she was glad she'd decided to wear a short-sleeved top and casual cotton skirt for travel, as the soft breeze felt delicious on her arms and the back of her neck.

Twenty minutes after leaving the pier, the ferry arrived at her island, and she followed the other passengers and disembarked. On the dock, she looked around for an information kiosk to see how she could get to her hotel—and spotted a long white van with a driver standing beside it, holding up a sign with the words Piccino Hotel. Surprisingly, most of the people who'd left the ferry were heading to that van, so she joined them. Although maybe it wasn't so surprising, she thought. Likely there was only one hotel on the entire island.

Falling in with the others—about thirty or forty altogether— she noticed that everyone was speaking English. In fact, they all sounded American, conversing about the fall weather back home in the States, or their plans for Thanksgiving next month, or the similarities between this view and the view off of various coastal cities in Florida. They were wearing jeans or shorts and tee shirts with the names of U.S. sports teams, and many were slathering sunscreen on their faces and arms, pouring the white lotion out of containers with recognizable labels. She couldn't believe so many Americans were here. How had she and Erica not realized what a popular destination this was?

The driver greeted each of them with a friendly English "Welcome" tinged with an Italian accent. When it was her turn, he took her luggage, and she murmured "*Grazie*" as he put it with the others in the open-air trailer attached to the back of the van. Trusting that the driver had hauled luggage before without any problems, she stepped inside and found an empty row. Within a short time, the van was filled, and it left the shore and started a winding, uphill climb. The roadway overlooking the water felt a little too narrow for Mia's comfort, but nobody else on the van seemed concerned. The higher up they got, the more expansive the view of the sea, dotted by several small islands. When they were about halfway up the hill, the driver pointed to the left and spoke to the group through a microphone: "Castello del Poeta."

Mia looked where the driver had indicated—and sure enough, there it was, looking exactly as it had online. The gray stone castle was set atop the island's highest point, bordered by greenery alongside steep cliffs, with domes rising at either end and a tall, narrow tower set at the back. Behind it, the ocean and the cloudless sky melded in the distance, the horizon barely visible. There was something otherworldly about the whole picture, Mia thought, as the island and castle looked like something from an old, weathered storybook. Or a dream.

What must it have been like in its heyday, with all the great thinkers of the world coming to write their books and their music, make their discoveries and craft their inventions? She could only imagine the energy that must have suffused the place —a castle devoted to supporting and promoting the best thinking in the world. And how awful that all that energy and creativity, all that vision, was destroyed.

The van turned, and suddenly they were on a gravel road. It led to a narrow, circular building with arched windows and airy terraces. The van parked, and she stepped out with the other passengers as two men came to offload the suitcases onto wheeling carts. At the front entrance to the hotel, three servers in white shirts and vests and black bow ties appeared with trays of champagne in crystal flutes. Her companions from the van started helping themselves, not looking nearly as surprised by the five-star service as she was. From the way Erica had talked as she made their reservations, she'd thought the hotel would be modest. Its biggest assets, it had seemed, were a restaurant and a concierge who spoke English.

A moment later, a strikingly good-looking man jogged out from the hotel's raised entranceway. He looked to be in his late thirties and was wearing a white button-down shirt and khaki slacks. His tousled, chestnut-colored hair was cut in a jagged style that reached the top of his collar, and he had a short, well-groomed beard.

"Good afternoon! Please may I have your attention?" he said. With his deeply tanned skin and dark hair, she would have felt it a safe assumption that he was Italian. He also spoke like an Italian—at least, like the Italians she had encountered so far, with their languid cadence and sensual emphasis on vowels. But while this man's speech had that cadence, his English had an American tinge.

"*Buongiorno*," he said with a welcoming lilt when the group had gathered around him on the stone patio, Mia having been pulled along with the crowd. He held his fingers to his ear, his eyes wide and inviting, and the people around her responded in unison: "*Buongiorno.*"

He nodded approvingly, his smile assured and charming. "I'm Leo Bonetti, and I'll be guiding you this afternoon. You've picked a wonderful week to visit us—the forecast calls for sunshine and temperatures higher than we usually have in October. All the better to enjoy our beautiful Mediterranean paradise. We have a welcome lunch set up on the back terrace, where you'll also find your name tags and some extra itineraries. Our first excursion begins immediately afterward. So please enjoy your meal and return here to board the van in an hour. *Benvenuti*. Welcome."

Mia looked around as the people she'd arrived with started to walk along the stone path where this man, Leo, had indicated. Now she was starting to understand: this was some kind of tour group, and she had glommed onto it by accident. Weaving her way in the opposite direction from the crowd, she went inside to check in to her room.

The lobby was cool and furnished in dark wood, a subtle scent of citrus circulating through the air. To her right was a wood-trimmed sofa and two floral-upholstered armchairs surrounding a square coffee table on a red rug. Hoping the clerk behind the desk spoke English and feeling guilty that she knew no Italian, she walked over and smiled in greeting.

"Yes, Signorina?" the young woman said.

"Hello, I'm Mia Abrams. Checking in."

The woman tapped on her keyboard, waited several moments, and then tapped again. "*Si*, yes, here you are. I see you made your reservation independently rather than through the association website. But that's no problem. You'll find your name tag and luncheon setting outside with all the others. You're traveling with a companion, yes?"

"I was supposed to, but she couldn't make it at the last minute."

"Oh, I'm sorry. Well, they've put you in a room with two full beds. Would you like me to switch you to one queen?"

"Sure," Mia said. "Thank you."

"Not a problem. Now, Signorina, I suggest you go ahead and enjoy your lunch with the others. Your tour of the Castello del Poeta is leaving promptly."

"Well, that's the thing, I'm not—" She halted in mid-sentence. Had this woman just said that the group was heading to the castle on Parissi Island?

"But... but I thought the castle isn't open yet," Mia said.

"Well, yes, it's not open to the public. You're the only group that is allowed to visit before the resort opens next year."

"So... so nobody can get to the castle except this... our group? Not even other guests staying here?"

"That's correct. Only your group and only this afternoon. Did you not get a chance to look through the itinerary with all your outings?"

"Yes, of course," Mia said. "It's just... I'm so jet-lagged, I can't keep anything straight." She forced a laugh and pointed to her temple, rolling her eyes to emphasize the level of forgetfulness she was trying to convey.

The woman smiled impatiently. "There are extra copies out on the terrace, near the name tags," she said, evidently ready to get rid of Mia and move on to the next guest who needed help. "Enjoy your lunch and your afternoon, Signorina Abrams!"

"Thank you," Mia murmured as she moved away from the desk.

The lobby was small, and before she knew it, she'd wandered out through the open sliding doors and onto the stone terrace where lunch was served. To her right was a long table with lanyards attached to name tags and a stack of stapled papers held in place with a rock so they wouldn't fly away in the warm sea breeze. In front of her were about a dozen small, round tables set for four, with floral centerpieces and silverware enveloped in pale-green napkins, each of which had been folded into a narrow rectangle and tied with a slim green vine. Beside each napkin was a place card, the names handwritten in calligraphy. The hotel had gone all out for this group.

And that was true not only of the setting but of the food, too. At the end of the terrace, Mia spotted an exquisite spread, with plates of cheese, antipasti platters with sliced meats, olives and peppers, and baskets overflowing with long, crusty loaves of bread. There were bowls of green and purple grapes, and round, vibrant oranges. To one side, a bartender was standing behind a row of wine bottles with colorful labels, and adjacent to the food, four servers in white full-length aprons were poised to serve.

Not quite sure how to proceed, Mia walked to the waist-high stone wall and looked out across the shimmering water. There it was, the Isola di Parissi: the place where the most important and influential artists and scientists and writers had assembled for centuries; the place from where the *schianto*, whatever it was, had supposedly been stolen; the place that was somehow connected to her grandmother, maybe even to where her grandmother had been at some point in her life. The place that might possibly hold her grandmother's secrets.

And now, as far as she could tell, there was only one way she could get onto that island. By pretending she was a part of this group, whatever it was.

Suddenly she felt a tap on her elbow, and she jumped in surprise.

"*Scusi*, Signorina," said one of the servers. "Lunch is about to be served. May I help you find your name tag and your table?"

She looked at him, then at Parissi Island, and then back at him.

"Yes, *si*," she said. "My name is Mia Abrams. *Grazie*. It all looks delicious."

TEN

1943

August

At the edge of the woods, Annalisa allowed herself to doze for a few minutes at a time, lurching back to consciousness when she felt her mind floating off too far. She knew she wouldn't fall deeply asleep.

She had good control that way, unlike her sisters, who would happily sleep until noon or later back home if no one came in to wake them. Her father had always admired her both for being his most capable daughter and for knowing herself so well. Her mother had been like that, too, he'd often said. It was one of the reasons he'd been so in love with her, one of the main reasons he missed her so. "Your mother was my anchor," he once told her. "Without her, I'm adrift."

She hoped her note would make it to him at the shop. As lost as he'd been when her mother died, he probably felt even more so now, without his daughters as well. She hoped he'd have faith in what she'd written, and would understand how hopeful she was. She had come to this island for him, and she truly believed she could make him healthy again.

The fourth time Annalisa pulled herself awake, dawn had broken, the sun a golden-orange ball rising above the horizon, its glow so bright that it made the turquoise sea sparkle and turned the sky a blinding white. She stood and squinted into the light, feeling its warmth envelop her limbs. She wished she could stay to examine the sun's power here on the island, to see how it evolved with the passing hours, how the sky's color changed as the morning played out. But Aldo had given them both instructions and warnings. She needed to wake her sisters so they could make their way to the castle.

She went back to the shaded spot where they were sleeping, the sun sending pale-yellow rays down from the sky that darted between the branches of the trees and formed random spots of light on the grass. Kneeling, she gently shook Giulia's shoulder and then Emilia's, and put her finger to her lips to remind them to stay quiet. She scooted out of her boy's clothes, and the three of them put on fresh skirts and blouses. Then they each took a turn in the lavatory. Annalisa led the way, thankful that the building was equipped with a sink and even a few cracked mirrors on the walls, so they could rinse their faces and fix their hairpins, arranging their hair into presentable buns.

Back by the trees, she tucked their suitcases beneath some bushes. With any luck, they'd be able to retrieve them and bring them inside before any groundskeeper discovered them and came to ask questions. She motioned to her sisters to follow her as she continued on the path they'd taken last night, which wrapped around the back of the castle. Aldo was right, the kitchen was easy to find, the clatter of dishes unmistakable. Approaching the entryway, she took a deep breath.

"Stay quiet," she whispered to her sisters. "Let me do all the talking."

Inside, the kitchen was larger than any she'd ever seen before, and there were at least a dozen young people—about the same age as she and her sisters, some perhaps a little older—in white aprons that covered them from their shoulders to their knees. They scurried about, opening drawers and lighting ovens and setting food on china plates. It was chaotic, but also exciting and energizing. An unexpected and welcome change from the silence and isolation of last night.

A girl carrying a tray of teacups walked by them, and Annalisa lightly tapped her elbow. "Excuse me—Signora Russo?"

The girl gestured with her chin to a woman, probably in her mid-thirties, rolling dough on a marble slab atop a wooden table. The woman was very pretty, with a tiny waist and stylish hairdo with rolled sides. She looked as though she belonged on a fashionable street in Milan, rather than here in this busy kitchen. Annalisa would have expected that the head of the whole kitchen would be far older, and would look much more weathered.

With a nod to her sisters, Annalisa led the way toward the woman. She wasn't sure what to say, so she figured the less said, the better. "Signora Russo? We're here... to work—"

"Oh, finally! They sent us some new workers," the woman said, her matronly tone of voice in stark contrast to her younger appearance. Annalisa suspected she'd been at this job a long time. She'd have to be, to speak with such authority. "We've been so busy, and I've been waiting for *days*," she continued. "Now... wait, which one of you is the baker?"

"Um... my sister... this sister," Annalisa said, pointing to Giulia.

Evidently Signora Russo was expecting three new staff members, one of whom was a baker, and luckily Giulia knew how to bake. Now Annalisa could only hope that the actual new employees didn't show up, or at least not very soon. Or that Signora Russo was so overworked, she wouldn't even realize there were double the numbers of new staff that she needed.

"Oh, sisters? I didn't realize they were sending over a

family. Now what are your names? Just first names, I don't bother with family names here, I'll just mark you as siblings so you'll share the same room." She went to a small metal cabinet and pulled out a notebook, then opened it to a page that was half-filled with names. Some names were followed by a triangle and some additional words that Annalisa couldn't make out, but the triangle seemed some kind of code. The woman added their names to the list and then drew a bracket that grouped them together, which she guessed was how Signora Russo kept track of siblings.

"Now, you—baker girl," she said, pointing at Giulia. "You head on over to the ovens, they're preparing tonight's dessert. And you, the little one—you can go to the big sink and help scrub the pots. There'll be more coming soon, so best get a quick start. Got it?"

Emilia looked at Annalisa pleadingly, and Annalisa stared her down, keeping her eyes fixed until her sister dropped her chin and headed toward the sink.

The woman turned to Annalisa. "And you—the big sister. You'll be a tray runner, third and fourth floors, and Signor Parissi's suite in the tower, too, if you're the first one back. Don't get the trays mixed up, they all like their breakfasts a certain way. And keep the hot food covered! I understand things went late last night, so some may be taking it slow this morning. And for goodness' sake, remember to leave the tray on the table outside each door. Whatever you do, don't knock! It's essential that we don't interrupt the creative process. Got it?"

Annalisa nodded quickly.

"If you have any questions, you can ask one of the others. Everyone helps everyone here. After breakfast I'll show you and your sisters where you'll sleep and take your meals, and then you can unpack your things. But no time for that now—let's go, everyone!" she added, raising her voice. "The day has started. Breakfast is served!"

Relieved at how easy that had been, Annalisa went to where Signora Russo had instructed. There was a long metal table with trays arranged in long rows. Trying for an air of confidence, she picked up one of the lists on the corner of the table and then surveyed the name cards, handwritten in calligraphy, that were perched at the front of each tray. She tried not to gawk, but it was eye-popping to see the names of people she'd read about. Names like Gunter Wilde, the Dutch sculptor working on a scene from Dante's Inferno on a scale never attempted before. And Marietta Basi, the French soprano. Annalisa looked further along the table, recognizing two more names: a Nigerian poet whose work she'd read in school, and a famous scientist from India. It was remarkable that all these people were here, now, under the very same roof that she was.

She grabbed her first tray, and soon realized why Signora Russo had given it to her as opposed to her younger sisters. It was painstaking work. The only way to get the job done was to take one tray at a time, walk up the grand, carpeted staircases until she reached the intended floor, make her way down the long hallways lined with paintings and sculptures, and place the tray on the table adjacent to each doorway. Then she had to go back downstairs to get the next one. Some of the tray runners were able to stack two, three, or even four trays on top of each other to save themselves extra trips. But she didn't dare try that. Having had almost no sleep last night, she felt weak and jittery under the weight of just one tray; the last thing she needed was to fall on a staircase, sending cheeses and fruit bowls and baskets of croissants and cups of hot coffee flying in all directions.

On one of her trips, she passed the ballroom where she assumed the dancing had taken place last night, and she paused to drink in the sight. The marble floor was gleaming, and long architectural friezes decorated the walls. There were two grand

pianos on opposite walls, and three chandeliers lining the ceiling, each one about the width of her entire bedroom at home.

"It's really something, isn't it?" Another tray runner, a girl
about her own age, had come up beside her and was speaking in
just above a whisper. "I love the whole castle, but I love this
room the most. You can only imagine what the Nazis would do
to it. I pray every night that no soldiers ever discover this little
island paradise."

She continued down the hall and Annalisa watched her,
thinking about last night, how Aldo had mentioned the tension
simmering beneath the revelry. Back home, she'd been aware
that the war was intensifying, but Papa's ailing heart had been
her most pressing worry, and she'd assumed she had time to get
him cured and then bring him and her sisters out of Italy. The
girl's comment felt ominous, and for a moment her heart
sped up.

Back in the kitchen, she went to the metal table to fetch the
last tray, Signor Parissi's, to take up to the tower. She didn't
know if she'd see him as, aside from the staff, nobody in the
castle seemed to be awake yet. But that didn't matter. It would
be good to get a feeling for where his room was, what the tower
was like, what his living space contained. Information was
always helpful, and the more she could get, the better.

Which was why she was disappointed when she reached
the kitchen to find his breakfast tray gone. She groaned. One of
the other runners must have finished with their own trays first,
and had taken Parissi's up. Maybe it was the boy who'd been
carrying four trays—he'd probably finished his own list very fast.
She couldn't help but be angry at herself for missing this opportunity to set foot in Signor Parissi's private part of the castle.
She decided she'd start with Parissi's tray tomorrow, even
though Signora Russo had said to deliver to the lower floors first.
She couldn't afford to lose another chance to see his
surroundings.

And if war was indeed coming to the island, she had even less time than she'd thought.

"It was fun... kind of, because—*ouch!*" Emilia exclaimed later that evening as she sat on the bunk bed's bottom mattress, her pajama-clad legs crossed. She pulled back a section of her freshly washed hair away from Annalisa, who was sitting behind her, trying to comb out the knots.

"Can you please be a little more gentle?"

"I'll try—but Emilia, such hair!" Annalisa scowled as she took the section back and tried again, this time with less force, to nudge the comb downward.

With no mother, it was her job to comb Emilia's thick hair, which was beautiful when dry, its brown color glowing with natural highlights of caramel and sienna, but a headache when wet. Still, she was glad that the three of them were settled now and had been able to bathe this evening and change into their nightclothes.

Their room wasn't luxurious by any stretch, and it lacked the niceties of the bedroom they shared at home—the sunflower-gold quilts that Mama had made for them long ago; the soft sheets and plump feather pillows; the narrow bookshelf near the door filled with Annalisa's not-yet-due library books, Giulia's romance novels, and storybooks that Emilia intended to give to her own children one day. But the room was clean and functional. The staff quarters, which were connected to the kitchen by a short tunnel, were designed as doubles, but Signora Russo believed the sisters shouldn't be separated, so she'd had a bunk bed and extra dresser squeezed into this room to accommodate them.

"Okay, all smooth," Annalisa said, giving Emilia a quick kiss on the back of her head before dividing her hair into two sections for braiding. "So what were you saying? You had fun?"

"Well, it wasn't fun scrubbing black grease off the pans," Emilia clarified. "Signora Russo likes things *clean*. She sent three pans back to me twice to redo them. But the other girl is nice and the boy is very cute. Did you know, they let the kitchen workers use the library and even listen in on lectures and concerts? Some even get to be apprentices to the guests."

"They said that?" Annalisa asked.

Emilia nodded. "They told me that Signor Parissi believes in education and wants everyone, even the workers, to learn something every day. He even gives gifts like books or colored pencils to the ones who show interest in learning. That's what those triangles were in Signora Russo's notebook—she keeps track of all the gifts. Isn't that amazing? I hope *I* get a gift."

"I'm glad you liked it—but don't get too attached to this place," Annalisa warned. "We're not staying here to have fun." She rose from Emilia's mattress and went to her own bed, which was set against the opposite wall.

"I know, I know. It just feels good to be somewhere so..." Emilia sighed. "So special." She rolled onto her back and kicked the mattress above her. "How about you, Giulia? Did you like it?"

Giulia, who was reclining on the upper mattress, shrugged. "It was nice to work in such a fancy kitchen," she said. Then she sat up and faced Annalisa. "But you know what I found out? There's a painter who needs apprentices to sew dresses to model for a mural he's starting. When I told Signora Russo that our father is a tailor, she said maybe I can meet him."

She looked down at her lap. "But I miss Vincenzo. I miss Papa, too," she added softly.

Emilia looked at Annalisa. "I'm worried about him. Do you think he's okay?"

"I'm sure he's no different from when we left," Annalisa told them. "It hasn't been that long."

"So what's the plan now, Pippa?" Giulia said, sounding a little aggressive to Annalisa's ears, with her use of that awful childhood nickname. "Now that we're here—what's next?"

"I'm too tired of your whining and silliness to talk anymore," Annalisa said. "Missing Vincenzo—honestly, you hardly know him! I think we'd better get some sleep before we all say even sillier things. I'm turning out the light now. And I told you before, don't call me Pippa!"

She reached over to the small lamp on her dresser and pulled the chain. With the curtains drawn, the room was completely dark. Turning on her side, she hoped that the little gasps she heard from the other side of the room were just the sound of sleeping and not of Emilia crying. She hadn't meant to scold Emilia or snap at Giulia. But she was frustrated that she hadn't set foot in the tower and gotten a glimpse of Signor Parissi. She couldn't believe how foolish she'd been not to take his breakfast tray up first. There'd been no other time to see him since, as she'd learned later from other tray runners, he didn't come downstairs for lunch or dinner as all the other guests did. So despite the fact that she'd gotten the three of them jobs here at the castle, her misstep at breakfast made today a failure. And she couldn't afford failure.

But even more than frustrated, she was tired. Her arms were sore from carrying the trays and her legs ached from going up and down the stairs all morning. She turned on her side and closed her eyes, trying to ignore the slats she could feel through the thin mattress. She hoped a good night's rest would make things look better in the morning. She'd only been here a day, and yet she felt as though she'd aged ten years.

Suddenly she heard a light tapping on the bedroom door. She froze. Could someone have found out they hadn't actually been hired and now was here to take them away? She lay there for a few moments, stuck in the limbo of uncertainty about what to do. But then she heard a voice coming from the other side of the door.

"Annalisa? It's me!"

Aldo! She recognized his voice immediately. Relieved, she scrambled out of bed. Since she was in her nightdress, she opened the door just a crack. "What are you doing here?" she whispered.

"I wanted to see how you did today," he whispered back. "And to bring you a treat. I've got wine and some leftover sweets from tonight's dinner. You haven't tasted anything until you've tasted Signora Russo's specialties."

Annalisa looked over her shoulder at her sisters' bunk bed. "I can't let you in. My sisters are sleeping."

"Then come take a walk with me," he said. "The sky is amazing tonight. Trust me, you're not going to want to miss it."

"But it's so late..."

"Late?" he said, sounding surprised. "Not to me. No matter, we can find each other another time—"

"No, wait!" she whispered, still peering through the crack between the door and the frame. Aldo looked different than he had last night. Neater. His hair was combed and parted on the side, and he was wearing a white button-down shirt and brown wide-legged trousers. She assumed he had other responsibilities during the day that called for a neater appearance than his work down at the boathouse. He'd looked appealing last night in a cute kind of way, but now he was even more handsome than she'd realized. And she was curious about who he was and how he came to be on the island. How he was able to get his hands on Signora Russo's desserts when that hadn't been offered to her and her sisters.

She knew she should go back to sleep. She didn't need any wine or sweets. But she felt something deep inside her stomach as she looked at Aldo's dark eyes and open-hearted smile, and the tiny cleft in his chin that she only now noticed. If she let him leave, she'd never get to sleep, knowing that she could be outside with him, under the stars and the glowing sky.

"Let me get dressed," she said, thinking she could be making the biggest mistake of her life, letting her feelings, instead of her judgment, determine her actions.

But she couldn't help it.

ELEVEN

2018

Monday

Mia followed the server across the patio to search for her name tag. She wondered what would happen if it wasn't there. How far was she willing to go with this lie? But there it was—her name tag at the long table as well as her place card at one of the round tables. Clearly someone had made a careless error and included Erica's reservation with this group's booking. As far as the staff was concerned, she belonged right here and was entitled to the same hospitality as everyone else on the terrace for lunch.

The server held out her empty chair at the otherwise filled table for four, and she thanked him and sat down. To her left was an older woman with round sunglasses and a huge sun hat, and across from her was a man around the same age, with wispy gray hair and an impossibly long neck. On her right was a young man in his twenties whose features resembled those of the older man. She placed her napkin on her lap, pretending to concentrate on smoothing the napkin's wrinkles as she wondered who these people were and how she could possibly make them believe she was one of them.

"Hello, there," the woman said, lifting the name tag hanging across her chest. "I'm Missy Carruthers and this is my husband, Charlie, and our son, Pete. We're from Baltimore."

"Hi, I'm Mia Abrams," Mia said, smiling and nodding for what felt like a ridiculously long time. Another server appeared and she politely waved away his offer of wine. It was best to stick with water. "Oh, and I'm from Long Island," she added.

"Is this your first time in Italy? Or have you done this before?" Missy asked.

Oh no, Mia thought—done *what* before?

"First time," she answered. It seemed the safer choice.

"Ours, too. The Italian ones have always been so small. Of course we've been on others. France mostly, but Spain and Greece, too."

"So how's business up there on Long Island?" Charlie asked.

"O... *kay*," Mia said, as though she'd given the question her deepest analysis. She wished she had taken one of the itineraries the hotel clerk had mentioned, so she'd at least have a clue as to what was going on.

"Tough for us, not gonna lie," Charlie said, tearing off a chunk of bread from one of the slim loaves in a basket on the table. "Five years ago, I'd have sworn that by now we'd have closed shop for good. But thanks to our brilliant son here, we transitioned to a different business model. High-end, service-driven. We have a base of affluent clients who want exotic locations. Status vacations, you know? It's worked beautifully. And, of course, the richer our clientele, the better our options. As in..." He stretched his arms wide, proving his point.

"It really helped," Missy agreed. "We changed our name this year from Carruthers Travel to SEE Incomparable Adventures. Service, Exclusivity and Excellence is what that stands for. We can't wait to see the castle. We already have three clients waiting to book."

"No kidding," Mia said as she took a sip of water. Now it was starting to become clear: she was with a group of travel agents and tour company owners on a junket to promote the resort planned for Parissi Island. No wonder the castle was the premier visit on their tour.

The first waiter returned and poured circles of olive oil onto their bread plates, while the second set down square luncheon plates with an artfully arranged selection of meats, cheeses, fruits and bread from the display table. Charlie forked some prosciutto and dipped a hunk of bread in the oil, then took a hefty bite.

"So what's your secret to success?" he asked her, putting down the remaining bread and wiping his glistening lips with his napkin.

"I have a very small clientele, too," she said, studying her plate.

"Been around a while?"

"Not really. I kind of just fell into it. It was... my grand-mother's idea—"

"A family business, just like ours!" Missy said. "What made her decide to go into the business? Love of travel?"

"No, not that," Mia said. "But she was from Italy and had a very unusual past. So I'm specializing in Italian travel. I'm trying to recreate her life. Yes... yes, that's what I'm doing," she said, suddenly energized.

Because sitting here with this family of strangers and speaking off the cuff, she had finally zeroed in on what she was doing here. Mostly the trip was about the *schianto* and the Italian lawyer's accusations. But it was about more, too. So much more that she was able to travel seamlessly by herself, to interact casually with new people, to lie with impunity and take on a whole new persona. Sometimes lying was necessary. Like when your very identity was at stake.

Because above all, this trip was about understanding the woman who had raised her. About learning, for real, who her grandmother was.

After lunch, the group reboarded the van, and when they arrived at the shore, Mia was more delighted than she expected to see Leo standing alongside the ferry landing. He was now sporting a wide-brimmed sun hat and dark sunglasses which, coupled with his slim build and broad shoulders, gave him a movie star quality. He offered his hand to steady people as they stepped onto the boat, which was smaller than the one they'd been on before. It was rocking significantly, so she was grateful for the support. His skin felt smoother than she would have guessed, and his fingers were slender but strong as he clasped them around hers.

"*Ciao,*" he said, and she looked from his sunglass-covered eyes to his wide, even smile to his square chin, covered in that beguiling scruffy beard. She knew it was childish to study him so closely, as though she were a schoolgirl watching a TV show starring the newest teen idol, but his focus on her was magnetic. Forcing herself to turn away, she murmured "*Ciao*" in return and took back her hand. As she slid onto an empty bench, she realized she wasn't the only one who'd noticed his good looks.

"Jeez, is that guy dreamy or what?" a woman seated in front of her said, and the two beside her both nodded.

"A real Adonis..." one of the others murmured.

Leo exchanged a greeting with the ferry captain, who ran up the short set of steps to the wheelhouse. Then he removed his sunglasses, dropping them into the pocket on his shirt, and grabbed a microphone from the boat's front panel, its spiraled cord draping across his body.

"*Ciao*," he said and again put his fingers to his ear, and the crowd responded "*Ciao!*" in return.

He laughed. "Good, good! Nice to see you all speaking like native Italians! We are now heading to the Isola di Parissi, and as we make our way, I'd like to give you a little background."

He raised a knee and rested his foot on a bench, revealing a tanned, bare ankle above his boat shoe and beneath the hem of his pants. "The Parissi family acquired the island with its magnificent castle way back in the sixteenth century," he said. "And while they often hosted luminaries and aristocrats, it wasn't until the period leading up to the Second World War that the castle became the very heart of European art and invention. And ironically, it's this transformation that made the island a target for the Nazis," he added. "The invasion cut short the lives of the best young thinkers and scholars of the time and denied their descendants, and the whole of humankind, a treasury of inventions and creations perhaps more astonishing than we can even imagine."

Mia crossed her legs and sat back as she took in Leo's words. She'd attended many lectures in her life at college and even at her lab, as scientists routinely gave talks about their work that were open to all employees. She loved hearing about research studies because they demonstrated how complex the human body was and how many mysteries it held, waiting for someone to reveal them. There were so many opportunities for researchers to bring new connections and discoveries to light— which was why she wanted so much to complete her education and begin a research career of her own.

But Leo's words appealed to her in a different way. His voice had a pleasing register—not too high or too low—and his tone was conversational and surprisingly intimate, given that he was speaking to a boat full of people. His eyes made contact with everyone else's on the deck, including hers, and that made her believe that he truly wanted her to understand and connect with him. As though she mattered to him. The way he spoke to the group was intensely alluring. About as alluring as his big, dark eyes and wide, captivating smile.

"But the story is also about one divided family and the last heir to the Parissi dynasty," he continued. "As a young man of twenty-five, Patricio Parissi inherited the family's fortune, but not without consequences that changed the trajectory of many lives."

The boat was silent, except for the purr of the engine and the smack of the water against the ferry's sides. No one was speaking. Mia realized that everyone was as riveted as she was. The story Leo was telling was both universal and specific, both monumental and minuscule. It involved one family, but it also involved the whole world, generations of people. It was revelatory to think that her grandmother, who'd lived such a small, quiet life, was somehow closely connected to these consequential and devastating events of history.

After a pause, Leo went on. "You see, Patricio and his younger sister, Olivia, were the children of the patriarch, Francisco, whose wife had died years earlier," he said. "Olivia, by all accounts, was vivacious and enchanting, the apple of her father's eye, and she attracted the interest of many young and wealthy suitors. But passionate and true to her own heart, Olivia fell in love with and decided to marry a lowly Jewish tailor who was brought to the Parissi estate from a small town south of Rome from time to time to do repairs on the family's expensive clothing. Olivia's decision outraged her father, who disowned Olivia and cut off all ties with her. So when Francisco died, Patricio was his sole heir."

Mia drank in every bit of the story. Back at her lab in New York, she'd always been drawn to the narratives that cells and enzymes and chemicals told when they were combined under varying conditions. And now she saw how similar science was to history. The story of Parissi Island and the Castle of the Poet was the story of multiple factors and variables. The island might never have become what it did without all these conditions playing out exactly as they had. She felt in her heart that this was the point Leo wanted them all to understand. And she was moved by his insight and his passion, his way of creating a narrative that would touch each and every one of them.

"Now, Patricio was very different from his sister," Leo continued. "We know that as a boy, he was bookish and introverted. He dreamed of inventing devices and treatments that would cure illness—everything from the common cold to cancer and heart disease. His intellectualism and soft-spoken behavior drew the ire of his father, who wanted his son to be more assertive. We know from other sources that Patricio kept a diary, and although it was destroyed along with nearly everything in the war, a single, heartbreaking page was found in the castle with one poignant reflection written there, presumably focused on Francisco: *He hates the man Olivia married, but I fear he hates me more. And the irony is that by failing to stand up for her, by cowering upstairs as he screamed at her, I proved his point. I'll always be weak and worthless in his eyes. He'll never see me as anything else.*

"So yes, Patricio was a sensitive young man. But we know that he changed a great deal the older he got. Traumatized by his father's temper and the loss of his sister, he withdrew to the castle, speaking to almost no one except an apprentice he took on and a housekeeper who was his confidante. Though the castle was filled with artists and intellectuals, he lived and worked in isolation in the castle's tower."

Leo paused again, and the people on the boat remained quiet. The poignant and emotionally loaded words Leo had read from Patricio's diary hung in the air. He knew how to work a crowd, there was no doubt about that; but that talent didn't mask, at least not to Mia, an apparently very sincere attachment to his topic. It was almost as though Leo had personally enjoyed

Olivia's vibrant personality and sympathized with Patricio's distress. She was enthralled by his storytelling, and curious, too. Of all the places this charismatic man could have landed as a tour guide, why had he chosen this place? What was his personal interest in this island, this castle, and this flawed family?

Leo looked over his shoulder toward the castle, then faced the group again. "I'll stop now," he said. "To let you experience the scenery without distraction."

He turned his body forward, and the people on the boat remained quiet as the ferry swayed rhythmically through the water, the engine softly whirring and droplets of water splashing upward and shimmering in the sunshine. As Mia watched the island grow before her eyes, she was reminded of her schoolbook pictures of Earth as seen by astronauts in space. But this was more intense than a page in a textbook.

The colors were like nothing she had ever seen before—the rich blue of the sky, the dark greens and deep oranges of the shrubbery along the cliffs, the gradations of color of the castle walls ranging from cream and tan to gunmetal gray, the stripes of gold on the glassy blue water reflecting the castle's broad tower. Set atop a steep hillside above the jagged coast, the castle looked huge, stretching across much of the tiny island. With its two domes, imposing tower, and arched doorways and windows, it seemed straight from the Middle Ages, so Mia had the sense she was traveling not only across the water but back in time as well.

They reached the dock, and Leo hopped off the boat and once again offered his hand as people descended onto the island, handing each one a cold bottle of water for the walk ahead from a small, portable ice chest. Although the sea breeze was pleasantly warm, the sun was strong, and Mia mentally scolded herself for not bringing a hat, as everyone else had. At least she had sunglasses, she thought, as she looked almost straight upward to see how high the castle stretched toward the sky. That's when she noticed a shadow appear, and turned to see that Leo was extending his hat in her direction.

"You'll be more comfortable, Signorina," he said as he placed it on her head. "I'm more accustomed to this climate."

She started to decline the offer, but before she could tell him she didn't want to leave him hatless, or merely thank him for the gesture, he was jogging to the front of the group and onto the first step of a long stone stairway. "I'm sorry to say that the elevator planned for the back of the castle is not in operation yet," he said. "Of course, if you choose not to make the climb, please stay here and enjoy the beautiful afternoon. For those of you coming with me, let's get started."

A few people returned to the ferry, but Mia and the others continued to the stone staircase. Leo led the way, pausing at the multiple landings to let people take in the view and catch their breath. Climbing along each successive set of stairs, Mia found it hard to believe her grandmother had ever been here. The castle was grand and imposing, and her grandmother was such a tiny person—both in size and how she lived her life. Not to mention that the castle was so romantic, like something from a fairy tale, and her grandmother was the least romantic person she'd ever known. Mia had always imagined Lucy's childhood in Italy as one of scarcity, deprivation. Why else had she never spoken of it?

Because this gem of an island in the Mediterranean, this vast castle—who wouldn't want to talk about it if they'd actually been inside? Who wouldn't want to reminisce about walking the halls, looking out the windows from the top floors and seeing the gorgeous vistas? Could her grandmother have been here? And if so, what happened to make her turn her back on the place?

Finally, they reached the top landing, which opened up on to a wide courtyard. "My lord, did all the guests at the castle make this trek?" Charlie said breathlessly, wiping his face with a tissue.

"This was the only way to enter the castle," Leo said. "Other than through the kitchen in the back, which required the same long climb. Now, if you look down the hillside this way"—he pointed to his left—"you can see the boathouse, that wide wooden structure down by the water. Patricio had numerous boats to ferry guests, employees and supplies to the island. He kept a staff around the clock to ensure that nobody came onto the island without his permission. That's why the Nazi invasion caught them all completely by surprise. It wasn't so much that they weren't aware of what was going on in the rest of the continent, but they felt very safe here. They never entertained the notion of anyone unwanted showing up."

He gave them a moment to view the boathouse from their high vantage point, then motioned for them to follow him. "So let's enter," he said. "And please remember, we're still in the middle of the renovation. There is construction going on throughout the castle that could pose a danger. For safety, please stay with the group."

They walked through an arched tunnel that led to a wide wooden door with an iron ring-shaped doorknob. Leo pushed the door forward and the group filed into the entrance hall. Mia was struck by how luxurious the colors and textures were—the rich red carpet, the overstuffed Wedgwood-blue sofas and over-sized leather armchairs, the carved mahogany tables and book-shelves. She couldn't imagine how much a stay of even one night would cost when the place ultimately opened.

They continued further, and Mia reached up and took off the hat Leo had lent her. As she lowered it past her face, she noticed the scent of sandalwood combined with a slight tinge of citrus. She felt her cheeks redden as she realized this was Leo's scent. It was as though she'd been let in on a secret. Or partaken of something very private.

"Now this will be the lobby," Leo was saying as he gestured with his arm. "The alcove to your right will be a small lounge where there'll be nightly entertainment. And if you come across here with me, you'll see one of the most beautiful outdoor spaces in all of the Mediterranean, at least in my opinion. See if you don't agree."

They followed through a set of glass doors out onto a wide balcony extending along the whole length of the castle's rear wall, with a vast view of the Mediterranean, dotted with tiny islands.

"Oh my," someone murmured, and others nodded their heads.

"The architects envisioned repairing this patio so it would be just as Patricio's guests experienced it when they came down for their afternoon or evening meal, or as they went back upstairs for the night. And the staff also enjoyed this view. Many would steal away for a look whenever they could."

He gave them another moment and then motioned to them to go back inside. While the others followed, Mia lingered by the waist-high iron railing lining the space. This was a view her grandmother would have loved, especially at night. Feeling the too-familiar sense of deep loss, she pictured her grandmother back in Soundport, sometimes looking through her telescope at the stars and sometimes just staring into the darkness, listening to the water from the sound lapping along the shore. She imagined Lucy setting foot on the original patio, years and years ago, before she came to New York. What might have gone through her head while she stared out to the vastness? Mia thought about the story Leo told on the ferry, of how Patricio's childhood trauma made him withdraw. What had turned her grandmother into the quiet, secretive person she'd become? And whatever it was, could it have happened here?

"Signorina?" a voice said from behind her, and she turned to see Leo waiting at the doorway. She was the only one still on the patio, and she hurried past him. He closed the doors, giving the handles a good tug, and Mia had the feeling he was making a point, reinforcing his earlier request that the group stick together. She felt horrible for straying off. She didn't belong here to begin with, and the last thing in the world she wanted was to draw attention to herself.

"I'm sorry," she said. "*Scusi.*"

He looked at her firmly for a moment, then resumed his position at the front of the group.

They walked back to the lobby and then started up a wide, carpeted staircase. On the second floor, Leo led them down a hallway with intricate molding and small oil paintings lining the walls, each lit from above with its own tiny lamp. There were multiple doorways on each side of the hall, and when they reached the midway point, he opened a set of double doors on the right. They revealed an exquisite ballroom, empty except for four huge crystal chandeliers in a line across the ceiling. The floor was a gleaming white marble, and rows of tall, arched windows, stretching nearly from the ceiling to the floor, lined the far wall.

Leo went to the center of the room. "The nights, by all accounts, were spent here and were quite festive. Many times they would start off with a lecture or reading, but as the hours passed, the mood became almost bacchanalian. The guests would dress in their most formal attire, and musicians would play everything from stately waltzes to steamy sambas, with dancing and drinking going on sometimes until dawn. Patricio avoided these parties, although there is one account of a violin concert that he showed up for. But that was a rarity."

He made his way back to the double doors. "Now, there's one more room to see, and it's the one I'm personally most inter-ested in," he said. "It's our exhibit hall with artifacts and primary documents that reveal exactly what life was like here before the Nazis stormed the island. Our team is analyzing many of these objects, some of which have only recently been discovered within these very walls. And when they are all here, they will tell the story of this unusual place—how much was created and, perhaps more importantly, how much was lost or never came to be."

He led them to another set of doors, which opened into a square room with glass display cases positioned around the perimeter and in the center. "Most of these displays are still empty, but a few pieces are already in place. Over by the window, there are journal entries from two prominent novelists who wrote here during the 1930s. And you can also see some early models made by the Danish sculptor Hans Jerenski. Next to those are recovered sketches by Savio Peralta, an Argentinian painter who would use kitchen staff as models for his paintings. And next to those is a prototype for a microscope with focusing capabilities unknown at the time. We're still trying to identify this gifted inventor."

Missy pointed to a display case in the center of the room, the largest one on the highest pedestal. "This looks important," she said. "What's going in here?"

"Ah, that's an interesting situation," Leo said, walking toward her. "It was installed to house probably the most significant object in this room. For years, it was thought to have been destroyed in the war, but now we believe it was stolen before the Nazis overtook the castle. We believe we are close to recovering it. And, I might add, to charging those in possession of the object and making sure they are prosecuted.

"The reason it's so important is that it was invented by Patricio himself," he added. "It was intended as some kind of medical device. He called it the *schianto grandioso*."

TWELVE

2018

Monday

"Signorina?" Leo said, a little more insistently this time.

"What? Oh, oh, yes," Mia said, startled.

The others had already left the room, and Leo was standing beside her. She hadn't heard the others leave, hadn't felt Leo's presence as he approached her. She only knew that somehow she had moved to the central display case and was staring at a page taped inside with the same sketch she'd seen in Milt's office. A sketch of the very bowl she had in her suitcase.

"*Scusi*. I'm... *scusi*," she added, feeling her face redden once more.

She was embarrassed that she'd been lost in her own world and that Leo had had to come after her again. Surely the others must think her the biggest fool on the planet. No doubt they'd all been asked to stay with the group on other tours and probably were amazed that she couldn't follow such a simple instruction. And worse still, she was calling attention to herself. The last thing in the world she should be doing, under the circumstances. But she couldn't help it. Because now there was a new piece of information to process, a new threat. The resort owner wasn't simply intent on recovering the *schianto*; he was planning to file charges against the person who had it. That meant that if anyone found the bowl, she could end up in an Italian jail. And right now, she didn't even know where in the hotel her suitcase was, or who might be handling it.

"*Scusi*," she repeated. "It's just so interesting. Pretty. *Bella.* Or *bello*," she said, mumbling whatever came to mind as she backed away from the display case, hoping the tour was almost over so she could make sure the *schianto* was still safely hidden.

But as she came close to the doorway, her foot caught on the edge of another display case and she stumbled, nearly falling backward. Leo rushed to catch her, but fortunately she righted herself before he reached her. She didn't know how she could have withstood the additional humiliation of tumbling into his arms. She wanted nothing more than to cover her face with his hat, which somehow she was still grasping.

"Are you okay?" he asked, tilting his head, his impossibly dark eyes looking sympathetically into hers.

She nodded and he nodded back, his cheekbones lifting as he smiled, and then he tapped his hat as though confirming that he still wanted her to have it. If the stakes weren't so high, she'd have stayed there for a least a few seconds more, drinking in his smile and his attention, focused so intensely on her. But instead, she hurried to join the group in the hallway. He followed her, then closed the doors behind him and leaned his back against them.

"So as I was saying, *schianto* is something that crushes or causes something to shatter, and *grandioso* is grand, magnifi-cent," he said, and Mia was grateful that everyone seemed to have forgotten about her. Evidently, someone had asked about the name of the missing object, and he was now continuing with his answer. She was lucky that he was so charismatic, the kind of person who captures people's attention as soon as he opens his mouth.

"Patricio believed that by extracting certain minerals from the soil deposits along the seacoast, and then crushing them together with botanicals with a precise force, he could produce a potent mixture that would cure disease. The bowl was fashioned to his specifications with alternating sections of coarse gray granite sourced from Spain and polished pink marble sourced from Portugal, and he engaged numerous masons throughout Europe until he achieved the exact prototype he wanted. You may have noticed the tiny mallet on the sketch—he worked for years on that design, aiming for a level of force that would grind the components into fine granules without reducing their essential composition. And in the last few months of his life, he was also working on a delivery method—whether to dissolve the mineral powder into a liquid or transform it into a gas that could be inhaled."

"And he really thought all this would work?" Charlie asked.

"Well, he was a dreamer," Leo said. "That was his strength. Also his weakness, I would add. He didn't take the Nazi threat seriously. He wasn't very realistic about what could happen to the castle.

"But as far as the science goes, what he was aiming for did make sense," he continued. "Even back then, he'd have known the health benefits of vitamins and minerals. He would have known that magnesium helps muscles contract—and that was the basis for his work on heart disease. He believed that an intensive fusion of magnesium, iron, and sodium, when blended with healing plants, could improve heart function, cure heart disease, and even treat other muscular disorders."

"Fascinating," someone else said. "He believed a small bowl and lever could do all that?"

"It may sound implausible to you," Leo said, smiling. "And yet his approach could be considered a form of holistic medicine. And the mechanics—the way he thought crushing the minerals could produce a more potent effect—well, that's similar to those high-speed blenders now on the market, isn't it? How they... what's the word? Pulverize? How they pulverize ingredients to increase the value of the nutrients. So you see, he wasn't as far 'out there' as maybe he seems at first.

"Now, would Patricio's *schianto* ever have been able to cure disease?" he continued. "The sad truth is, it's impossible to know. As it's impossible to know what many of the other guests here would have achieved. They never became household names because they didn't have the time. They died here on this ground, or were marched off to concentration camps."

The group grew quiet for a moment, taking in the sobering truth.

"I hope you get the *schianto* back," Missy finally said. "It belongs here."

"Oh, we'll get it back," Leo said, his voice sounding both certain and irritated at the situation. "The island's new owner is determined. And ever since construction began several months ago, the investigation he began is starting to bear fruit. By the time the resort opens, the *schianto* will be in its proper place. And those responsible will have been brought to justice."

Mia's breath caught in her chest, and she struggled to breathe normally as she followed the group back downstairs.

Back on the ferry with Leo's hat on her head, Mia took a seat in the middle of an empty bench, hoping no one would sit next to her. She didn't feel like making small talk; it was enough of an effort to smile and nod as Leo handed out folders with projected prices for resort stays, and those around her agreed that they were high, but not out of reach. She couldn't get over the fact that her grandmother had held onto something so central to the history of the island. And considered stolen for decades. And while she still believed that her grandmother would never knowingly steal anything, she also didn't know how she could find the evidence to prove it.

Not to mention how threatening Leo's words had sounded. Apparently the efforts of the island's new owner had led his lawyers right to her grandmother's front door. Somehow they had tied Lucy to the castle and then uncovered her pathway from Italy to New York. But what were the connecting threads, and how could she get her hands on them? How could she get Leo, who clearly was in the know, to give her the information without revealing that she had the *schianto*?

The ferry picked up speed, and she pressed a hand on top of Leo's hat to keep it from blowing off. If her grandmother had intentionally taken the *schianto*, she must have thought it was hers to possess. Lucy had always prided herself on having an unquestionable character. Her reputation was something she carefully guarded, more than anyone Mia had ever known. Once when Mia was in middle school, Lucy had decided to get involved in the PTA—not because she particularly liked organizations, but because she thought it would be in Mia's best interests. And because everyone in the PTA was expected to volunteer at some school function, she'd agreed to head up the teachers' appreciation lunch. Mia didn't remember the specifics —it was all so long ago and the circumstances were fuzzy. But there was some rule prohibiting committee chairs from posting notices on the big bulletin board near the front entrance of the school, and somehow a flyer about the lunch was found tacked up on it.

Even as a kid, Mia knew it wasn't a big deal. One day the flyer was up and the next day it was gone, presumably because someone in charge removed it. But Lucy had been horrified to learn that people thought she'd flaunted the rule and posted the flyer. And she'd been determined to clear her name. In the evenings, Mia heard her making calls to all the moms in the

PTA following the flyer's appearance and disappearance, trying to identify the person who had caused her this embarrassment. Ultimately she learned the name of the guilty party, and she accompanied Mia to school the next morning to report the name to the principal.

Mia had watched the principal stare at Lucy with a look of utter confusion on her face. And at lunchtime she heard three moms, who had come to school to distribute slices of pizza, laughing and exclaiming how "bizarre" that all was and how "weird" she'd acted. Two of them she recognized as moms of her classmates. She knew they were talking about Lucy.

Sitting down at her regular lunch table, she couldn't eat a bite and barely kept back her angry tears. She hated that her grandmother was the target of their laughter, and she was embarrassed for her, too. She forced herself to put the conversation out of her mind, not wanting to contemplate for one more second the impression her grandmother had made.

But even she had found her grandmother's reaction excessive. "What's the big deal?" she'd said the morning Lucy announced she was coming to school to speak to the principal. "The stupid flyer isn't even there anymore."

"It's not about the flyer," Lucy had said. "A person spends a lifetime making it known who she is. Once you know who you are... you don't let that go."

Realizing her grandmother wouldn't back down, Mia had put on her coat so they could leave for school. Her biggest concern that morning was having to walk into the school building with her grandmother. Nobody in eighth grade walked into school with parents or grandparents. Nobody wanted their parent or grandmother to do something so strange. So she'd looked downward as they'd walked into the principal's office, and she'd put the whole matter behind her as soon as she could. She hadn't thought about it even once since that day.

But now, heading away from the castle, she remembered the

whole course of events. How important it had been to Lucy to know how honest she was, and to prevent anyone from thinking her otherwise.

And yet, she'd kept so much a secret, Mia reminded herself. How did that square with the person she claimed to be? What larger picture was there to learn, what larger story would prove her grandmother had done nothing wrong? She recalled that Leo said experts were analyzing discoveries recently found within the castle's walls. Maybe... just maybe they held some answers about Lucy's claim—*legitimate* claim, Mia believed—to the *schianto*. But with the tour of the castle now over—a tour she wasn't even supposed to be on—how could she get her hands on those items? How could she learn more?

They arrived back at Piccino Island and boarded the van for the hotel. It was almost five now, and the sky looked different than it had that morning. Lower in the sky and huge from this angle, taking up almost half of the horizon. It shone with a brilliant yellow, a color so vivid that Mia thought it should have its own name. Yellow didn't seem a big enough word to describe it.

The van was halfway up the hill when exhaustion finally hit. Having awakened before dawn to catch the train down the coast, and still recovering from the time change, she desperately wanted a shower and a good night's sleep. She knew she'd promised to touch base with Erica tonight; and she should call Ryan, too. She'd texted him yesterday to say she'd arrived in Rome, but they hadn't spoken since Saturday when he'd called as she was packing to urge her again not to take the trip.

As the van pulled to a stop in front of the hotel, Leo announced that cocktails and a selection of fruits and cut vegetables, chocolates, and cheeses awaited them in the lobby. "Dinner is on your own tonight," he said. "Feel free to enjoy the terrace restaurant, or you can order up room service if you'd like to retire early for the evening. Your rooms are ready, and the desk clerk has your key cards. Tomorrow, a shopping tour on the mainland is on the agenda.

"Now, fashion is not my expertise," he added with a charming touch of self-deprecation. "So I won't be accompanying you for that. It's been my pleasure to guide you today, and I hope it was everything you'd expected. Please feel free to find me at any point this week with any questions. *Buona sera.*"

Mia followed the others off the van, murmuring "*Grazie*" to him as all the others in line were doing, but not wanting to catch his eye. She was uncomfortable with the way he'd caught her lingering on the terrace of the castle and then near the empty display case that awaited the *schianto*. It had been a mistake for her to get lost in her own thoughts, and she regretted letting herself do that. As she entered the hotel, she hoped she wouldn't run into him again.

Inside, she walked past the cocktail area and went straight to the desk to get her key, thinking room service for dinner sounded perfect. Thanking the clerk, she started for the elevator —and then realized she was still wearing Leo's hat. *Oh, man,* she thought as she turned from the elevator. She was going to have to talk to him once more after all.

She started to search around for him, when she noticed the desk clerk pointing toward her and speaking to an older, official-looking man in a double-breasted gray suit with a light-blue pocket square. Their interest in her seemed ominous, but before she could turn away, the older man approached her with a grim expression on his face.

"Signorina?" he said and stood before her, legs parted and arms folded across his chest.

"Yes? *Si?*" she said, trying to sound nonchalant. But her voice was trembling uncontrollably.

"I'm Signor Dorria, the manager of the hotel," he told her. "There seems to be a mix-up with your reservation. We have no information about your travel agency in our system. And

Jacqueline tells me you made your reservation separately instead of going through the online form we'd set up."

"Oh," Mia said. "Oh... I..." She paused, not knowing how to continue.

It would have been so easy if he'd approached her earlier, before the castle tour. She could have explained that she wasn't a travel agent at all. Maybe he would have invited her to tour the castle anyway simply as a guest, although that seemed unlikely. But regardless, she'd let the desk clerk, Jacqueline, believe that she was part of the group. Now it would be hard to feign ignorance and say she didn't know she had joined up with a special tour.

"Do you have a travel business?" Signor Dorria said. "Because, you see, the castle tour is not open to the public. We are well aware that bloggers with large followings like to sneak into these situations to get a scoop, if you will. And if that is the case here—"

"Oh, no," she said. "I'm not a blogger. No... you see..." She paused, not sure how to get out of this mess gracefully and without causing herself any trouble. "It was a mistake when I arrived—"

"Yes, a mistake that is my fault, I'm afraid," said a voice near her shoulder, a voice that had been near her shoulder on the castle patio and again by the *schianto* display.

It was Leo.

"I was the one who took her reservation, Signor Dorria," he said. "I happened to be at the desk when she called, and I must not have entered the information properly. I apologize for not including her proper credentials in the reservation, and I'll go back and update her information as soon as I have a moment. And I apologize to you, Signorina Abrams, for creating this uncomfortable situation," he said to her. "It was my fault. Please forgive me."

He nodded to each of them and walked away, and the

manager apologized to Mia for his questions and invited her to have a cocktail and something to eat. "Or if you'd like to go right up to your room, please let me take care of your dinner. I will personally speak with the kitchen about bringing a special meal up to your room promptly," he said.

Mia thanked him, although she'd barely heard him. She was too busy watching Leo disappearing into the crowd. And wondering why he'd protected her like that. And if she'd ever see him again.

And then she knew she'd have to. Because she was still wearing his hat.

She wondered if he'd realized.

THIRTEEN

1943

August

Quietly, so as not to wake her sisters, Annalisa threw on a cotton top and a pair of wide-legged blue jeans with buttons on the sides. Although she'd decided that she and her sisters should wear skirts this morning to meet Signora Russo, she much preferred pants and was glad to dress more comfortably this evening. Closing the bedroom door behind her, she tiptoed through the tunnel to the darkened kitchen, and left the castle by the same door they'd entered through that morning. What a momentous day it had been!

Outside, she paused on the stone patio, which was lit by groups of three glass-enclosed gas lamps posed atop bronze poles. She enjoyed how the shadows flickered and swayed by her feet. The sea breeze felt delicious as it passed over her shoulders, ruffling her hair, which she'd pinned away from her face, the ends clustering around her shoulders. She spotted Aldo sitting on a waist-high stone wall that that hugged the patio's inner edge and faced shrubbery and trees, and she suddenly felt excited. She supposed it was just the knowledge that she didn't have to hide—that she belonged here now after such a dangerous journey last night. But she knew it was also because she was spending more time with Aldo.

"Hello," she said as she forced herself to approach him slowly, not wanting to seem too eager, and he swiveled to face her. He smiled, his grin wide above that cute cleft in his chin, and his eyes lit up, making her feel he was as happy to be here with her as she was with him.

"Hey," he said. "Come sit. How was your day? Did everything work out?"

She nodded as she sat, resting one knee sideways on the wall so she could face him directly. "We owe you a big thanks. We asked for Signora Russo and acted like we belonged here, and she put us to work right away. As long as the real workers don't show up to claim our spots, we should be in good shape."

"Oh, don't worry about that. Once you're in, you're in. Something to drink?"

She nodded, and he reached down and lifted a bottle of wine from the ground, then poured some into the two crystal glasses poised on the wall next to him. He handed her one. "*Salute!*" he said and clinked her glass with his.

She took a sip of the wine, which was bubbly and citrusy, full of flavor. She sipped again, then put her glass down on the wall. Letting out a luxurious breath, she tilted her head back and gazed at the sky. It was a deep blue with what looked like threads of gold, barely perceptible and mesmerizing. She shook her head, still looking up. "I will never get used to the way the sky looks here," she murmured.

"It's something, isn't it?" he said. "Island of the Brilliant Night."

She looked at him. "What's that?"

"That's the old name, the familiar name. What the island was called for centuries. It's what sailors have always called it. Why the family wanted to own this island in the first place."

"But why does it look like that? Why does it do that?"

He shrugged. "I don't know. I don't think anyone does."

"But there has to be a reason," she insisted. "The composition of the island, the rocky shoreline? The foliage, the climate? The proximity of the mainland, the moisture of the atmosphere at night..."

"All good possibilities," he said with an amused nod, and she could tell he liked her curiosity. "Which do you like best?"

"It's not about what I *like*," she told him. "It's about looking at the evidence and developing a hypothesis. And testing it and seeing if it holds up. Because there are even more solutions that could be explored. The size of the island and its angle relative to the stars... the density of oxygen in the water... the salinity—"

"Salinity?" he exclaimed as he nudged her arm with his elbow, a gesture that felt teasing and warm.

"Yes, salinity! What's wrong with salinity?" she retorted, feigning offense as she nudged him back. She was delighted with her own boldness as well as the sensation of making casual contact with his body once again.

"What's wrong with it?" he asked, his smile wide. "I'll tell you what's wrong with it. Here we are, under this gorgeous and mysterious sky, and you want to attribute this astonishing phenomenon to... salt? If you're going to stay in the castle, you need to know that people here prefer more romantic explanations. Like the ones I heard the other day—that the night sky we see is the visual reflection of the voices from antiquity that continue to echo... or the spells cast by angels and gods of mythology—"

"No, no, no," she said. "Hasn't anyone ever studied this? I mean, seriously studied it?"

"Not that I know of." He reached over and gently joggled the back of her head with his palm. "What is going on in this mind of yours anyway?"

She laughed as he took back his hand, sorry he'd let her go.

The place where his palm had been felt slightly tingly. "Because it's crazy," she told him. "This place is crawling with the smartest people on the planet. Scientists and inventors. Telescopes were designed here, and theories about life and evolution and the future. And as far as you know, nobody's studied the meaning of this sky?"

"Ah, but you're thinking about this place all wrong." He looked at her sideways, a glint in his eye. "Yes, they're scientists and inventors and creators. But more than that, they're dreamers. Castle of the Poet, surely you've heard this place called that? They're not studying this sky because they don't want to know what causes it. That would destroy it for them. They just want to bask in the magic."

"But these aren't frivolous people. I've read all about them. They don't believe in magic. They love knowledge—"

"They love the knowledge they love," he said, sounding more serious than he'd been up until now. "They want the knowledge they want. You may have read about them, but I've lived with them. Geniuses believe in magic, too—they're just more intentional about it."

"What does that mean?"

"It means, don't be fooled—all of the people Parissi invited here came not only to find something but to escape something. Like the way they danced all night last night. They see what they want to see, and they block out what they don't want to see."

She looked at her hands, sobered. "You mean the war, right? One of the other tray runners was talking about the Nazis today. You think there's danger and the people here are just refusing to face it?"

"I'm saying it's important not to fall under the spell of this island. People like us, with our heads screwed on a little tighter —we're the ones who need to keep our eyes open." He nodded knowingly as he picked up a plate of sweets from the wall and offered it to her. "Although with this kind of luxury, it's hard not to fall under its spell."

She looked at the array of bite-sized cakes and cookies, each on its own tiny doily. Choosing a rectangular morsel covered in a hard chocolate shell, she placed it in her mouth and chewed, savoring the moist sponge cake inside infused with some kind of deliciously sweet liqueur. The evening, the sky, the wine, and this delicious treat—Aldo was right, it did all add up to magic. No wonder the people who came here stayed so long and worked so hard. It was the perfect place to get lost in your own dreams. Your own vision of the world as you wanted it to be.

Aldo set the plate on his lap to survey the offerings, and she looked at his profile, which was easier to see under the light of the gas lamps than it had been late last night. Like anyone else, his face was a combination of features, but in his case, the features—the broad forehead, long nose with just the hint of a bump or two, the youthful swell of his cheek, the marshmallow-like lower lip and slight upturn of his chin—formed something very beautiful. And suddenly she wanted to understand him more, to know what was beneath this lovely facade.

He looked at her. "What?"

She let her gaze linger a moment, as he seemed more pleased than disturbed by it. "Who are you?" she finally said. "Why are you here? If you feel like all the guests here are disconnected from reality, why do you stay? What is this island to you?"

"I don't think badly of them. I don't. I'm here because of them. Well, because of one."

He popped a pastry in his mouth, then sucked some chocolate off the pad of his thumb and put the plate down. He looked out toward the woods where they'd slept last night, and Annalisa let her eyes follow his gaze. Through a small break in the trees near the path, a sliver of water shimmered silver.

"I grew up near Naples," he said. "We lived in a small

house, nice but not luxurious by any stretch. Our prized possession was a grand piano that had been handed down from my
great-grandfather. Such a huge and fascinating object. My
mother says that one day when I wasn't even yet three, I
climbed up on the piano bench and started playing. Not children's tunes, but real music, melodies I'd heard. When I was
four, I taught myself to read music. When I was seven, I started
playing in public—at the community center, at concert halls. I
was a pretty impressive sight, they tell me."

"You were a prodigy," she breathed. She would never have
guessed. He didn't look like a serious wunderkind. He didn't act
like one either.

"My parents saved up all the money they could scrounge
together and all the income from my concerts to enroll me at a
music academy," he said. "There I first set my hand on a violin.
Oh, I remember that day. I mean, piano music was beautiful,
but the sounds that came out of that petite, curved, gleaming
box! I mean... how can I put this? If anything proves that God
exists, it's the sound of a violin solo."

"So you're a poet," she said smiling. "As *well* as a
prodigy."

He chuckled. "I started at the academy when I was ten, and
I wrote my first concerto when I was thirteen. My teacher—
you've never heard of him, no one has, but he would have been
as famous a name as Vivaldi or Verdi if he had lived long
enough. He began composing symphonies, and Parissi got wind
of him and invited him here. I was fourteen, and he offered to
bring me with him as his apprentice."

He lifted his shoulders and dropped them with a sigh. "He
was working on his masterpiece when he got sick two years ago.
In the weeks before he died, he tried to convey to me everything
he wanted to put into the work, all his dreams and feelings. He
tried to tell me everything. And then he made me promise that
I'd carry on without him."

"So you're not a worker?" she said. "You're one of the *guests?*"

He shook his head. "I'm not as talented as he was. And the truth is, I'm not even sure it was worth it to him—I mean, to squirrel yourself away for years and years and to die with your life's work unfinished, with so little to show for yourself at the end. No home of your own, no family, no one to share your story except a stupid student you reached out to, not even a friend or relative... or someone who loved you, not as a teacher but for you..."

He leaned forward, clasping his hands between his knees. She'd had no idea he could have such a sad background. She wondered if he saw himself in his teacher. If he now questioned his teacher's choices because he was alone, too.

"I'm sorry, Aldo," she whispered. "I'm sorry you lost your teacher. Your friend." And without thinking, she rubbed his back lightly, her fingers feeling his heat beneath his thin shirt.

Her touch was far different than the interactions they'd had before. Those had been playful, the way they'd nudged each other and the way he'd gently jostled her head. This was tender. Intimate. She'd never touched anyone in this way before, and she didn't think she'd ever want to touch anyone else this way. She didn't think she could ever care this deeply about anyone else. And she didn't understand it. She'd only met him a day ago. What she felt was something she knew she could never explain. The forces now drawing her and Aldo together were beyond science. Beyond the scope of any conclusion she could draw by looking at evidence and formulating hypotheses.

"I don't know if I'm capable of fulfilling my promise," he said softly, his words sounding almost like a prayer, or the whispered equivalent of a beautiful sonata. "I don't know if I can even attempt to write brilliant music. Sometimes I don't know if I want to give up everything, everyone, for a single passion. Like he did, and like all the guests here do. I mean, they're all so young, some only slightly older than we are. They could be living their lives, traveling and seeing the world, making the most of every single day. Having fun, falling in love. Or at least they could have been, before the war. It's harder now. They had their chance."

"Maybe they think they are taking their chance," she said. "Maybe to them, this is exactly how they can make the most of each day."

"I guess," he said. "And I guess that's what my teacher felt. I guess it's what I should feel. But I don't, at least not yet. So I work at the boathouse. I sleep when I can. I do little jobs around the place, fixing furniture legs, oiling squeaky doors—no artist can tolerate squeaks when they're creating," he added with a grin. "Stowing notes from Signora Russo that need to go to the mainland on the supply boats. I don't know what they say but she trusts me and I do it because she asks. She believes in me, so she keeps me on.

"But I'm not sure I'm worth believing in," he added, shaking his head. "I write music when I can and I help out to earn my keep. And I think about the war. And I wonder what I will have accomplished when it all comes crashing down."

They stayed that way for a few minutes, Aldo's head down and Annalisa's hand resting on his back. She knew how he must have felt when his teacher was sick, knowing that someone he loved, someone who had given everything to him, was getting ready to leave. That's how she felt with her father. She knew her father was getting ready to die. She could see it in the way his breath grew so labored that he could no longer concentrate on the fine stitchwork he was known for. She knew it in the way he stroked her cheek, with more intention and affection than ever. He'd been telling her for months now that he couldn't last much longer. And that's why she had come here, to the one place she'd never imagined she'd ever set foot. To do the impossible and get him cured. She wasn't ready to say goodbye.

Aldo sat up straight and rubbed the tears off his cheeks. "I'm so sorry, Signorina Pippa," he said. "I don't mean to ruin this beautiful evening with my tale of woe." He waited a beat and then winked at her.

"You heard Emilia call me that last night, didn't you?" she said with a scowl. "So you must have also heard me tell her not to."

"Why? It sounds like a sweet nickname."

"It's something that my father made up when I was born. A nickname for his new little baby, and now my sisters use it mostly to tease me. My father once told me it was a way of calling me a sweet and lovely little lady. But I certainly don't want anyone here to think of me that way, silly and weak. At least, that's what I hear when my sisters say it."

"Well, nobody could ever think you silly and weak, I promise you that," Aldo said. "You, Annalisa, are a force. As strong and solid as any of those huge rocks down by the boathouse. You got yourself to this island, you tricked me into bringing you here to the castle—"

"I did not trick you. We made a deal, is all—"

"You carried two suitcases all the way up from the shore, you slept out in the woods, you got yourself and your sisters work, and now you're contemplating the sky and enjoying wine and the most delicious sweets on earth. That's quite a lot to accomplish in less than twenty-four hours."

She smiled shyly, thinking that maybe he had a point. It was nice to hear that he saw her that way. "Thank you," she said. "Although I fear the hardest part is yet to come."

His eyebrows raised, and she immediately regretted letting those words come out of her mouth. She had kept her mission secret for so long. Even her sisters didn't know the entire truth.

"So there *is* a reason you're here on the island," he said. "Something more than just a kitchen job. Now that I've told

you my story, you tell me yours. I know my way around here,
I'm a good person to confide in. Maybe I can help."

She rubbed her forehead with her fingertips. He was right,
he seemed a good person to confide in. He knew all about the
island, and Signora Russo, as tough as she was, evidently liked
him. Maybe he could help. Although she'd have to proceed
cautiously. She wouldn't tell him everything; she would only
tell him so much.

"It's not that complicated," she said. "I'm here to meet
Patricio Parissi. I've read about what he's working on, the device
he's making to treat illnesses of the heart. My father's heart is
sick, and he doesn't have much time. I want to take this device
home with me so I can cure him."

"Cure?" Aldo said. "Has your father seen a doctor? A real
doctor?"

"Of course," she said. "But he says the medicine isn't
working anymore and my father only has a few months left to
live. My mother died years ago, and we—my sisters and I—we
don't want to lose him, too. That's why I'm here. It's my only
hope."

Aldo shook his head fiercely. "Annalisa, you have to know,"
he said. "These inventions that go on in this castle... they're
theoretical. Some are pipe dreams. If any are going to work, it's
not going to be for years—"

"No, that's not true. The articles I read say that Patricio is
on the brink of something important. He's a serious scientist.
This is for real. So I *have* to meet him."

He widened his eyes, still unconvinced. "Well, even if these
articles are right—and I don't think they are—it's still going to be
a problem to talk to him," he said. "Because he talks to no one.
He communicates only in writing, only to people he has something to say to. My tutor never even met him. The times they
were in touch, it was only through handwritten notes."

"He never speaks to anyone?" Aldo nodded. "But I was

hoping to run into him. I thought if I brought his breakfast and waited, he'd eventually come out of his room and talk to me."

"I'm afraid it's not going to happen."

"But why? Why is he like that?"

"It's a long story. They say he had a younger sister he adored. But she fell in love and married the family's tailor, a Jew. Which made her father furious. He disowned her, and Patricio was too scared of his father to object. When the father died, Patricio inherited the island and the castle, but by then he'd lost all touch with his sister. The whole thing left him kind of troubled in the head. Mad at everyone who caused this mess. His father, his sister, his sister's husband, and mostly himself."

"Oh, no," Annalisa said. "I didn't know all that. I knew there'd been a falling-out with the family, but I didn't know how isolated and angry he was. That he doesn't even... talk to people..."

She tapped her fingers against her lips, hardly aware that he was next to her anymore, as she rolled over these new facts in her head.

"I'm sorry this isn't what you wanted to hear," he said. "It's all pretty complicated."

"More complicated than you know..." she murmured, mostly to herself.

But he had heard her. "Oh? Why?"

She looked at him, his dark eyes, his soft cheeks, his tender lips. There was a secret, a secret that she'd never spoken about. Not even to her own father. But she needed to talk about it now. She needed a friend. And even though she'd only known him a day, she liked Aldo a lot. The conversation they'd had this evening—it felt like one of the most meaningful conversations she'd ever had. About life and art and love. About the future and the past, and the decisions people must make.

He had trusted her with his story. And she trusted him in return.

She pursed her lips for a moment and then forged ahead, saying the words she'd never imagined saying to someone she'd just met.

"Because the sister you just mentioned? That's my mother," she said. "And the Jewish man she married? That's my father.

"The man he blames for wrecking his family is the very man I need him to save."

FOURTEEN

2018

Monday

"He told the hotel manager that you were a travel agent?" Erica said on the phone.

"Yes!" Mia answered. "I think the manager was about to kick me out of the hotel. And maybe he'd have confiscated my suitcase as well—"

"Could he do that?"

"I don't know. But it doesn't matter. The tour guide, Leo, he said that he'd entered the reservation in wrong. He was so convincing, the manager actually apologized to me!"

It was a little while later and Mia was sitting cross-legged on the white duvet cover atop the queen-size bed, rubbing her wet hair with a thick, white towel as she cradled her phone to her ear. Across the room, the catty-corner windows bordered by long, pale-gray drapes displayed an expansive view of the Mediterranean. Although dusk was settling in, she could still make out the Castello di Parissi, looking close enough to swim to from this angle.

"Jeez," Erica said. "Why do you think he did that? Was he trying to hit on you? Is he, like, creepy?"

"No, no, not at all," Mia told her. "He's very polite. And respectful. And he takes his job very seriously. And he's gorgeous, actually. Like drop-dead gorgeous."

"Oh, man! Why aren't I there with you? I could go for a gorgeous Italian trying to save me from being evicted. Why was I so stupid about the stupid passport—"

"No, it wasn't like that, saving me. He wasn't interested in me. I don't even want him to be interested in me. I have a boyfriend, remember? But I think... I think he was kind of confused by me. Or, no. More like... suspicious."

"Suspicious? What did he say?"

"Nothing bad. He's very sweet. And kind—he lent me his hat because the sun was strong and we were making this big climb to the castle. But he noticed me. For one thing, I'm alone and everyone else is in couples and groups—"

"Well, that's not suspicious. You were supposed to be there with me—"

"But then he caught me daydreaming. Twice. Once at this outdoor terrace and once at the empty display case where the *schianto* is supposed to be. And he emphasized—*emphasized*—about recovering the *schianto* and bringing the thieves to justice. He said that. Charged... and... prosecuted."

"But that doesn't mean he knows that you have it—"

"Yeah, but he knows something. The way he was looking at me and noticing where my attention was, that I was staring at the sketch of the *schianto*. No one else stayed there looking at it, just me. He didn't say anything, but I know he thinks I have something to hide. And that's why he lied for me."

"You're being paranoid. Maybe he just thinks you're cute. And maybe he thinks you got on the wrong tour for some reason and he didn't want them to make you leave. You're feeling guilty, and you have nothing to feel guilty about. You did nothing wrong."

"That's not true. I'm hiding a stolen object—"

"No, you're trying to discover where it belongs. And prevent them from falsely accusing your grandmother. Maybe even preventing them from stealing it from *you*! Maybe Lucy was the rightful owner, and you rightfully inherited it. It could be worth something, you know—"

"I don't think so. It's a bowl, that's all. A failed invention, an absurd science experiment. That's how it sounded, even though Leo was trying to be nice when he talked about it." She dropped the towel onto her lap. "I'm exhausted," she said. "I can't believe I only arrived here today. What is it, early afternoon for you? I'm keeping you here on the phone and you probably have things to do."

"No, nothing other than getting an appointment at the passport office and then stamping the date on my forehead so this doesn't happen ever, *ever* again." She paused. "So what will you do tomorrow?"

"I don't know. The travel agents are going shopping. But I'm done sticking with that group and pretending I belong."

"Think you'll run into this guy again?"

"I don't know that either. I don't know what his job is. When we got back from the castle, he told the group to have a good stay, like he didn't think he'd be seeing us again. But the way he talked to the group about their room keys and stuff, and the way he said he'd messed up my reservation—it sounds like he works here."

"Hmmm. Maybe you should try to avoid him. Just to be on the safe side."

"Yeah. I mean, he can't always be here, right?" Mia imagined looking around corners whenever she went to the lobby and ducking into hallways if she spotted him. It would be stressful but not impossible. Then her gaze landed on the wide-brimmed hat she'd tossed onto the dresser when she came in. "Oh, shoot. I still have his hat. I'm going to have to return that. Although I guess I don't have to give it to him directly. I can leave it for him at the front desk."

"Sure. Let him find some other cute American to lend it to next."

"Very funny. I told you, it wasn't like that. Anyway, that's what I'll do, I'll leave it at the desk and I'll stay away from him."

"Speaking of men, what does Ryan think of all this?" Erica asked. "How did he react when you told him I couldn't come?"

"He didn't react. Because he doesn't know."

"What? You didn't tell him about my passport?"

"I couldn't. He would have argued even harder to stop me from going. And if I tell him now... he'll be mad that I didn't tell him before. He doesn't understand any of this. He thinks I should just have Milt return the *schianto*. He says that my grandmother's gone so what does it matter?"

"Nice," Erica said sarcastically, and Mia gave a little laugh in response. Erica and Ryan generally got along, although Erica felt that Ryan was lacking in the sensitivity department.

"I'll tell him everything at some point," Mia said. "But for now, I've got to find something to eat and get some sleep. I'll call you tomorrow, okay?"

"Absolutely call me tomorrow," she said. "I want to know what's going on. All kidding aside about the gorgeous Italian. I adored Lucy, too, you know. I want to see her vindicated almost as much as you do."

"I know," Mia told her and said goodbye, then placed the phone next to the towel she'd used on her hair.

She'd always felt herself lucky to have a friend who cared about her grandmother as much as Erica did. Lucy had never come across as welcoming, especially to children, and that had made many of Mia's friends uncomfortable. She remembered how they'd hurry downstairs after an afternoon spent studying or hanging out in her bedroom, clearly hoping they wouldn't encounter her grandmother as they left the house. And if they did, they'd look down and mumble "thank you" as they hurried out the door. Mia had seen it so often, she'd tried sometimes to time their exits when she knew Lucy was outside on the deck or in the basement doing laundry. She worried that if her friends felt too weird, they wouldn't want to be with her.

But Erica was different. She and Lucy had had a relationship that had continued even after high school and college, even after Mia moved to the city, when Erica got her teaching job and settled back in Soundport. Erica recognized Lucy's big heart, and she seemed to know instinctively, as Mia did, that Lucy's reticence was not a true reflection of her character. It was more like a mask that hid who she really was. And she'd never been willing to explain what had caused her to want to hide.

Getting up from the bed, Mia tightened the belt of the hotel's cozy robe, embroidered on the breast pocket with its steel-gray logo, and went to hang up her towel. The bathroom was the most elegant one she'd ever seen, with a large all-glass shower, freestanding stone soaking tub, heated limestone floors, and a tray full of upscale lotions, creams, and other bath amenities. And the bedroom area was elegant, too, with its crisp white linens, semicircular love seat, and oval coffee table with a marble-inlay top. Mia doubted that Erica had had any idea of the luxurious place she'd found for them; back in Soundport, they'd simply been looking for a place that was close to Parissi Island and friendly to Americans. Thinking about that evening made her wish again that Erica was there. She could use a touch of her friend's carefree, animated personality. Because right now, all she could think about was what a fraud she'd been today and how she didn't deserve any of this pampering.

Coming back from the bathroom, she saw her phone on the

bed lighting up, showing that Ryan had sent a text. She opened it and read the short message:

Hey, how's it going? Tried to call you before but you didn't answer. Heading into a meeting now and you'll probably be sleeping when I get a break. This 9 hour time difference is tough! I'll try again tomorrow morning, afternoon your time. Hope you and Erica are having fun! Love you!

Reading over the text, Mia felt a fresh pang of guilt that she hadn't told him Erica wasn't with her. She felt bad, too, that she hadn't called him before going into the shower. She hadn't even noticed that he'd phoned while she was at the castle and had no service. Why hadn't she thought about him all day? And once she got back to the hotel, why had she called Erica and not him? Shouldn't a boyfriend be the first one you turn to? Shouldn't he be the one that knows you even better than you know yourself, the person that puts things in perspective when you're deep into something and feel troubled and confused?

She sighed, sinking down onto the bed, her phone in her hand. Yes, she felt guilty—but what stuck out to her most in his text, what got under her skin, was his mention of fun. *Fun?* She'd explained everything to him, all her concerns about the *schianto* and the way her grandmother had hidden it. And her total conviction that she must have come to possess it justly. She told him she knew there had to be more to the story than what the Italian lawyer had written to Milt. And she'd told him she couldn't let her grandmother's name be dragged through the mud, even among people she'd never meet. She wasn't here for fun! She'd wanted him to understand that she cared about what people believed about her grandmother, just as Erica understood. But it was as though Ryan hadn't heard her.

Or maybe he had heard it, but didn't feel it was important.

But it was important. Because it was important to her.

And that's the way he was, she thought as she sat back down on the bed. He'd always had a very clear sense of what didn't concern him. And it all came down to one rule: practical things mattered, emotional concerns could take a back seat. He'd shown that aspect of his personality when they'd met a little over a year ago at her grandmother's house. His company had bought the houses on either side of Lucy's, and he was hoping that Lucy would sell, too, so they could knock down all three at that end of the cul-de-sac and replace them with one huge, waterfront home. He'd called Lucy to make an appointment to see her, and she'd turned his contact information over to Milt. Later that week, Milt had called Mia, suggesting it was something Lucy might want to consider.

"She's over ninety now, Mia, and winter will be here soon," Milt had said. "And the house is a lot for her to take care of. Not that I wouldn't zip right over if she needed me, of course. But there are some beautiful apartments here in town, with services and neighbors right next door and a superintendent on call. Maybe she'd be more comfortable somewhere like that?"

Thinking Milt could be right, Mia had set up the meeting at the house that Sunday morning and arranged to be there when Ryan showed up. And while she'd hated the idea of selling the house and seeing it knocked down, she'd admired how sociable Ryan was and how much sense his argument made.

"My company is prepared to make it worth your while," Ryan had said. "I think you can pretty much name your own price."

But Lucy wasn't interested in the least. Not that she'd been rude. It was a nice day, and she'd had coffee and pastries waiting for him on the back porch when he'd arrived. She'd even set a pretty table with her usual centerpiece—a single white lily surrounded by silver-dollar eucalyptus. She'd listened to the proposal and asked a few questions about timing and what the new house would look like. But then she firmly told him that she liked her life the way it was, she didn't need any more money, and she wasn't selling.

Ryan accepted her answer graciously and helped clear the dishes, and after Lucy said goodbye and went inside, Mia walked him to his car.

"I'm sorry you wasted your time," she'd said. "I should have warned you. I suspected this would be the outcome. But I wanted her to hear the proposal for herself and tell you directly what she decided. I never speak for her. She doesn't tolerate that."

"It's okay," he'd said, his hands in the pockets of his pressed jeans, beneath his neatly untucked shirt. He kicked a pebble, looking unaffected, as though he didn't have a dog in the fight. "This happens all the time. It's how my business works—many ideas never see the light of day. Although I thought I had a shot when I saw the breakfast she'd made. And that fancy table, with the flower and all. I thought she was buttering me up so she'd get a nice offer."

"I hate to tell you it was nothing special," Mia said. "She always does that. A lily and silver-dollar eucalyptus. She says a breakfast table should be fragrant and aesthetically pleasing."

"Cute," he said. "Well, I gave it my best shot. I always do. Usually people have a price. But sometimes sentiment gets in the way."

"Oh, she's not sentimental," Mia said. "She's the furthest thing from that."

"Then what do you call what she just did?" he said.

"She's not sentimental," Mia repeated. "She knows what things are worth. Living here, where she can sit on her patio and watch the night sky and the stars with no city lights to intrude on the view... hearing the water from the sound splash against the shore... this has way more value to her than money. Value isn't a constant. Value is a variable."

"You sound like an economist," he said.

"I'm a scientist," she told him. "At least I plan to be. And in her own way, my grandmother is too."

They reached his car, and he asked if she'd go out to dinner with him sometime, and she surprised herself by saying yes. She wouldn't have thought he'd be her type. He was so put together, so polished. But there was something appealing in his confidence and swagger, the way he did his work without taking rejection personally. And as she got to know him over the next several weeks, she came to admire how much knowledge he had. Information about things she'd never thought about. Like safety codes and zoning laws and building materials. How to tell when a tiny crack in a section of concrete was nothing and when it was a sign of a catastrophic failure in the foundation. Or when a slightly discolored section of a wall was meaningless and when it signaled the presence of mold, in which case you had a big headache in your future. He told her stories of fires inside walls and balconies that came crashing down from eight or ten stories high, and how they could have been prevented. And when he told her all this, and he showed her how extensive his expertise was, she felt something she hadn't always felt, especially not recently.

She felt safe.

Later that night, after clearing her mind with a bowl of pasta Bolognese and a glass of Chianti brought to her room on a small wheeled table with a pink rose in the center and a selection of chocolates for dessert, Mia climbed into bed.

She thought about that safe feeling Ryan had elicited in her. How much it had meant to her over these last months, as she saw her grandmother growing frailer and taking more medicines. She'd heard the concerns in the doctor's voice when she called to follow up after an appointment. He'd explained how hard it was becoming to find the right balance of medications, because Lucy's body was becoming too weak to tolerate the high doses of potent drugs her heart needed. It was hard to bear the shakiness, the anxiousness, the... the terror she'd felt when she'd contemplated the impending loss of her grandmother. She had friends, of course—Erica in particular. She had co-workers and neighbors in her building in the city. She had Milt. She had Ryan. But her grandmother was different. From the time she was young, her grandmother was the one true constant in her life. The only member of her family she'd ever truly known.

But now as she lay in bed, thinking about how she'd navigated her way here to Italy, to this island, and over to the castle, she couldn't help but feel a small but significant sense of power. She was on a mission, she was by herself, and she was making progress. She knew more about the castle, more about Parissi, more about the *schianto* than she had back in New York. In just one day here off the coast of the Mediterranean, she had learned so much. And it was a different kind of learning. Unlike the multi-degreed researchers in the lab where she worked, who kept all the elements of their experiments tightly controlled, here the investigation was open-ended. There was so much to explore, so much she could pursue depending on the people she spoke with and the situations she encountered, the objects she saw and the objects still to be seen, whatever they were.

Getting out of bed, she went to her suitcase and dug through the clothes that hid the *schianto*. She hadn't unpacked it earlier because she'd felt it was dangerous to have it out in the open, even with no one else around. But here in the dark, with only the light from the moon and the stars coming in through the window, she thought it would be okay to bring it out and hold it in her hands. And it was beautiful and solid and glorious —its rounded shape, its molded edging, the alternating bands of grainy and smooth stone. She ran her fingertips along the mallet, feeling the silkiness of the metal, and the odd little ball at the end that was supposed to have been capable, somehow, of crushing particles into a fine, curative powder. Just contemplating the object's weight and mass and density, she felt in control. She wasn't in a position of weakness; she was in a position of strength.

Because she had what everyone was looking for. She had the *schianto*.

She rewrapped it and placed it in her suitcase, as well hidden as it could be. She pulled the zipper all the way around, then wheeled the suitcase into the closet and shut the door. Everything was neat, just as her grandmother would have wanted. Back in bed, she decided that she wasn't going to avoid Leo, as Erica had suggested. Because Leo knew all the ins and outs of the castle. All about the artifacts and documents that the renovation was uncovering. Probably way more than he'd shared with the group.

So, she decided, she wasn't going to hide, she wasn't going to cower, and she wasn't going to scurry like a scared rabbit when she saw him. He had lied for her, and she deserved to know why. What was it about her, and about her behavior in the castle, that had made him want to protect her from Signor Dorria?

She was going to speak to him directly. To learn why he wanted her to stick around. And to see what other information he could provide.

She just hoped he would help her get to the bottom of her grandmother's story.

FIFTEEN

2018

Tuesday

The next morning, invigorated by the sunshine and the gorgeous Mediterranean view from her window, Mia dressed in a pale-yellow tee shirt dress and flat tan sandals, glad that the warm weather and sunshine meant she could leave her jacket behind.

With Leo's hat in her hands, she closed the door to her room and took the elevator down to the first level. Except for a handful of hotel employees, the lobby was empty, as the travel agents had departed for their outing an hour ago. The glass doors along the sea-facing wall were open, and the breeze from the water ruffled the sheer, floor-length curtain panels and grazed her shoulders and the exposed skin just below her collarbones. She took a few steps forward and closed her eyes, thinking that she could stay in this position forever. She wondered again if her grandmother had ever felt the same breeze, seen the same water shimmering? If so, it made sense that she loved Soundport. Even now, Mia could picture the sunsets they'd seen over the sound and the full moon over the bay that they'd gone outside to see, no matter the season.

Taking a deep breath, she approached Signor Dorria at the reception desk. "Signorina Abrams," he said, as though she were a long-lost friend. *"Buongiorno*, good morning! I take it you decided not to join the tour group today?" His tone was so different from yesterday when he'd suspected she was a blogger.

"Buongiorno—and yes, I'm not so interested in shopping." She gazed around the lobby, stroking her neck absentmindedly with the fingertips of one hand, trying to give off a vacation-y vibe "So... um... is Leo here, by any chance?"

"I'm sorry, Signorina, Leo is not working at the hotel today. Is there anything I can help with?"

"Oh," she said, surprised by the response—*not working at the hotel*. She'd assumed he was a hotel employee working in guest relations or something, but Signor Dorria's comment made it sound like Leo had an additional job elsewhere. And come to think of it, Leo had seemed awfully invested in Patricio's story yesterday. More so than she might have expected from a professional tour guide.

"Is there somewhere I might find him? I borrowed his hat and wanted to return it." She lifted it to show him the evidence.

"I can take that for you and keep it behind the desk for him, if you'd like—"

"No, no thank you," she said. "I also wanted to see him. I have a question about something he brought up on the tour. He said... he would be available for questions and... such..."

"He'll be here tomorrow," the man said. "Can it wait until then? Unless you'd like me to call him—"

"Oh, no. It's not that important. I'll look for him tomorrow," she said. She preferred to run into him casually, rather than confronting him with a phone call. Especially since she didn't have a specific question in mind or know how she'd go about asking to return to the castle.

"Certainly. And what are your plans today, Signorina? Anything we can help you find?"

"I mostly wanted to look around the island, maybe explore down by the water's edge," she said. "I mean, to get a good feel for what my clients will experience when they come here." She nodded, thinking this was the way someone in the travel business would put it and hoping she sounded convincing, if he still harbored any doubts about her. "Although actually right now I would love a cup of coffee," she added, anxious to change the subject.

"Well, we can offer you coffee here, but seeing as you have the whole day ahead, I would suggest you go down to the shoreline where you boarded the ferry yesterday," he said. "If you walk past the dock, you will see some very pretty cafés. The van shuttles back and forth all day."

It sounded like a nice way to pass the time given that she wasn't going to be seeing Leo until at least tomorrow. "*Grazie*," she said and turned toward the front doors.

"Oh, and Signorina? May I suggest you take a look at this?" He gestured toward a display of glossy brochures alongside the counter. "It's a little booklet about the castle. That's the English version on the left. Maybe you'll find the information you're looking for."

She nodded as she took one and tucked it into her shoulder bag, then went outside to catch a ride down the hill. It turned out there was no one going down now except her. The driver was sweet and tried to make small talk but he didn't speak much English, so they had to make do with agreeing that the view was "*bellissima*" and the sunshine "*forte.*" She felt ashamed that she couldn't communicate with him in Italian. Why had Lucy never taught her any words? She remembered how Erica would always come back after visiting her grandparents, who were born in Brazil but moved to Phoenix, and gleefully teach the girls at the lunch table the new Portuguese phrases she'd learned: *"Eu amo sorvete de chocolate*—I love chocolate ice cream. Now you all say it. *Eu amo sorvete de chocolate!"*

But Lucy had never spoken Italian at home and had always avoided speaking about anything having to do with her childhood. Mia had even called her Nana, while Erica's grandmother preferred the Brazilian *Vovó.* Lucy had never wanted her to use the Italian version, *Nonna.*

When they reached the bottom of the hill, Mia asked "Café?" and the driver pointed toward a row of two-story buildings in bright colors like yellow, pink, and orange set back from the sandy shore. Putting Leo's hat on her head—after all, she had it still and he'd put it there to begin with—she started along the walkway. On the beach, a small cluster of people were setting up umbrellas and towels, while beyond them, scattered kayaks bounced on the gently rolling water hugging the shore.

The first café she passed had a square patio with stone-topped tables painted with lemons atop festive green leaves. At three of the tables, couples were sipping hot coffee and munching on flaky croissant-type rolls topped with butter or jam from small ceramic tubs. The fragrance made her stomach rumble, reminding her that she hadn't yet eaten today. She sat down at an empty table, and when the server arrived, she pointed to the couple next to her to indicate she'd like the same thing.

As she waited for her breakfast, she pulled from her shoulder bag the brochure Signor Dorria had invited her to take. It seemed to be mostly a marketing tool, with pictures of the castle's newly renovated courtyard, grand staircase, and expansive ballroom. But the last few pages were devoted to Patricio. There was a large black-and-white photograph of him as a teenager, standing next to a young girl identified in the caption as Olivia, the younger sister who would eventually be disowned. Mia studied Patricio's image, trying to catch a hint of the reclusive, enigmatic, bitter scientist whose story Leo had told. But none was there. Patricio had been a tall, gawky, sweet-looking teenager with wavy hair that hugged his head and a timid expression—his lips thin and straight, his eyes small and his glance downward. His sister, though, looked precisely like the fireball Leo had described: huge, dark eyes, a flirty smile, big cheekbones, and thick, dark hair that caressed her shoulders.

She turned the page and read the small text box on the inside back cover. It explained that there were very few remaining photos of the interior of the castle from before the Nazis arrived. Those that remained appeared below the text box: there was a grainy image of the ballroom, with a small orchestra playing and couples dancing, the tall windows flung open to reveal the late-night sky; another of the tunnel-like hallway which, according to the caption, led from the kitchen to the staff quarters; and the kitchen itself, where a long line of white trays—each holding a coffee cup and saucer, a selection of pastries in a basket, a small wooden board with cheeses and meats, and one or two covered dishes, along with a slim bud vase with a flower—were set out on a long table. The trays intrigued her, and Mia leaned in to read the small caption below the picture.

> Parissi's guests had their breakfasts brought to their rooms by staff members known as "tray runners" so they could work straight through the morning. The meal was hearty, with eggs, meats, cheeses, rolls and butter, fruit, pancakes, and sweets prepared to each guest's specifications. Parissi insisted that the presentation be "fragrant and aesthetically pleasing." So each tray always featured a single white lily in a vase surrounded by silver-dollar eucalyptus.

Mia gasped, her fingers starting to tremble as she grasped the edge of the glossy brochure. Now she realized why the trays had intrigued her. It was the lily and eucalyptus on each one, which had caught her eye before she even consciously noticed what they were. She'd been thinking of that very combination last night when she'd remembered the first time Ryan had come to the house, the way he'd noticed how Lucy had set such a distinctive centerpiece for the breakfast table. *A lily and silver-dollar eucalyptus*, Mia had explained. *She says a breakfast table should be fragrant and aesthetically pleasing.*

Mia had never thought much about the way her grandmother served breakfast. It seemed merely a preference. A habit. A quirk. But now Mia knew that it meant so much more. It was a habit Lucy had acquired when she was young. *Fragrant and aesthetically pleasing.* That was too particular a phrase to show up in Soundport by accident.

My grandmother lived in the castle, Mia told herself. And what was more, she'd been a regular in the kitchen. Someone who would know what centerpieces the trays featured—and why they needed to be exactly as they were.

She'd been a member of the kitchen staff. A tray runner for Parissi.

Mia set her elbow on the table and pressed her index finger against her lips. When her food came, she thanked the server but pushed it aside and looked out over the water, still absorbing this conclusion. Not too far in the distance, she saw a ferry heading toward the mainland, coming from the direction of Parissi Island. Part of the construction crew, she guessed.

Then she looked more closely at the people on the deck, and suddenly spotted one that looked like Leo. The more she watched as the boat glided by, the more she was certain it was him. He had the same straight back, broad shoulders and longish, dark hair. And the same style of clothes as he'd worn yesterday—a white shirt with rolled-up sleeves, khaki pants, and boat shoes. Plus he seemed to be the only one without a hat, which also made sense, as she was wearing his. She kept her eyes on his figure as the ferry picked up steam, drawn by his handsome stature and the memory of his enchanting smile. At one point he lifted an arm, and waved to someone he recognized on shore as the ferry sped along. Watching it pass, she wondered why he had been on Parissi Island today. He hadn't seemed to be part of the construction crew, didn't dress like a builder or say anything that would suggest he was.

But whatever his job was, she knew she'd been right. He had access.

And access was what she needed. So she needed him.

After returning to the hotel that afternoon and eating dinner in her room again, Mia went back down to the lobby. It was just after nine, and the space was dimly lit and quiet. The only other person in sight was a young clerk at the reception desk who was reading a magazine. Mia had decided to have her food brought up to her room, choosing not to participate in the pasta-making class and five-course dinner she'd read about in the tour group folder. She'd received an email that afternoon from Signor Dorria telling her that the charges to her credit card had been reversed, as the travel agents were invited guests of the hotel, and he was sorry for the inconvenience. She didn't want to continue taking advantage of meals and activities she wasn't entitled to. She'd decided to keep a running tally of her charges and to pay for everything once she returned home.

But she'd also felt she wanted to be alone, after reading the brochure at the café this morning. She'd spent the rest of the day walking by the beach, watching the kayaks nearby and the open water in the distance, and taking in the castle as she moved along the shore. At one point Ryan had called, and she'd told him about the lily-and-eucalyptus photo and how it made her believe that Lucy had worked in the castle's kitchen. He said he didn't remember anything special about how Lucy had set the table and asked her again if she and Erica were having a good time and if she'd thought any more about selling the house back in Soundport.

But she'd barely heard his questions. All she could think about were the lily-and-eucalyptus centerpieces that had been so much a part of her life. So beautiful, so fragrant, and apparently so meaningful as well. And Ryan hadn't even remembered them. Worse still, he'd been dismissive on the phone. He'd changed the topic when she brought it up. He hadn't been interested in hearing what feelings the discovery had stirred in her.

Passing by the sofa in the lobby, Mia smiled shyly at the clerk. She was aware of what an outsider she must seem like. Roaming around, while the rest of the group—the group she was believed to be part of—had turned in so they could be refreshed for tomorrow's activity, whatever that was. But as the night unfolded, her room had started to feel small and the open windows, though large, hadn't seemed to let in enough air. As a kid, she'd always gone outside to sit with Lucy at night because she thought Lucy was lonely. But now she realized that she, too, liked being out in the night air, under the wide night sky.

She stepped onto the terrace adjacent to the lobby. The restaurant was closed now, and she walked along the waist-high stone wall that lined the perimeter. At the far end, she sat on one of the backless carved stone benches, so she could face Parissi Castle, which the stars and partial moon made vaguely visible.

Why had she never asked Lucy about the lily-and-eucalyptus centerpieces? It had never occurred to her to do so; it would have been like asking her grandmother why she chose blue toothbrushes over any other color, or why she wore shorts in the summer over skirts or dresses. Some things just *were*. But now she found herself wondering what had been wrong with her. What kind of granddaughter had she been? Lucy had been utterly devoted to raising her, being there every day when she came home from school, always having meals ready, clothes washed, rooms nice and clean so Mia could concentrate on her homework. And taking in work as a proofreader, too, to pay the bills while ensuring that Mia rarely had to be by herself.

But Mia had never taken the same level of interest in Lucy. Okay, kids and teenagers are notoriously self-centered, she understood that. But it was fourteen years now since she'd left for college—plenty of years as an adult while Lucy was still around. How had Lucy felt knowing that her granddaughter had never cared to learn all her truths? Was Mia right—had Lucy been glad that Mia took her cue and never asked questions? Or had she been waiting, even hoping, for an invitation to open up, especially in the last few years when she was starting to face her own mortality? Had she wanted a sign that Mia would be there for her as she pored over memories she'd worked so hard to suppress? Might she have even opened up about the *schianto* and the wedding dress if Mia had shown a morsel of interest?

"So pretty, right?" said a voice from a few yards away, and she looked up to see Leo walking toward her. "You know, there was a story about Parissi Island, that the sky above it would stay light and sparkling even when there was no moon, no stars," he said. "That's how it got its nickname, *Isola della Notte Brillante*. I don't know if it's true or someone just made that up. But I like to come out here and close my eyes and imagine what that would look like."

He reached the bench. "May I?" He gestured toward the spot next to her.

"Of course," she said, embarrassed that he'd caught her so deep in thought.

He sat down and leaned forward, clasping his hands between his knees and tilting his head toward her. "I heard you were looking for me."

"Yes... I..." She remembered how emboldened she'd felt last

night, how she was going to challenge him, asking why he'd lied for her. But she didn't feel so bold right now. The revelations about her grandmother had unsettled her. "I still have your hat," she said softly.

"Is that all?" he said, and she couldn't tell if he was saying it was no big deal, or if he was disappointed that she didn't have a more important reason to want to see him. His eyes gleamed in the moonlight, and the dimmed lamps from inside the hotel produced a golden aura behind him. "You can keep it while you're here," he added with a smile. "I have others. Somewhere."

"Thank you," she said. She didn't need his hat. She could get one of her own. And yet she wanted to know that she'd see him again. After tonight. In case there was something she might still have to ask.

"So, did you enjoy your coffee this morning?" he said. "And did you try one of their *cornetti*? You probably would call it a croissant, but it's a little more special than that. I hope someone told you not to miss it."

She looked at him, speechless.

"You didn't see me?" he said. "I was on the ferry coming from the castle and we passed when you were seated. I waved. I thought you saw me."

"No, I... I saw the ferry and the people. I... wasn't sure it was you," she stammered, not wanting to reveal that she'd spotted him, too. But then she wondered again why he'd been in the castle today. How was he able to return there?

"You were at the castle?" she said. "Leading more tours?"

"No, I was working with the renovation crew today. They opened up a wall in the kitchen and I thought there might be something interesting in there."

"So you're working on the renovation? I thought you were a tour guide."

He shook his head. "I'm neither, actually. I'm a professor of

Italian history. I was teaching at the University of Chicago until last year. Then this opportunity came up to curate the exhibit for the island's new owner, and I couldn't resist. I've wanted to come and see the castle since I was a kid. I also agreed to work with the hotel here to help out with the marketing program. Which leading tours falls into."

"Oh?" she said. That was the last thing she'd expected to hear. She hadn't pegged him as an academic. He'd seemed too casual for that. And she hadn't pegged him as a Midwesterner either. "So that's why you don't sound like everyone else. You sound almost like an American."

"I am American," he said. "I was born in Philadelphia, but we moved near Rome when I was young. My mother is Italian. My father is Argentinian, but his people were originally from northern Italy. We have a long history with this country."

"And how did you become interested in Parissi?" she asked. It didn't seem like too forward a question to her. She felt that he'd opened the door to talk more, having offered up the information about his background.

But surprisingly, he seemed to feel that her question did cross a line. "Let's just say I have a special interest in the place," he said.

She pressed her lips shut, feeling bad for evidently seeming to pry. "Well, I can see why anyone would be interested," she said after a beat. "It's quite a story you told on the boat. Who wouldn't want to know more?"

He looked out toward the water, and she could tell he wasn't going to say anything else about himself just then. "And you?" he said. "What do you do back in the States?"

"I work at a hospital in New York. In medical research."

"So you're a researcher, like me. What are you researching?"

"Immunology. That's what my lab is focused on. But actually, I'm the lab coordinator. I supervise the techs and help the scientists conduct their experiments. Although I hope to do my own research someday."

"I see." He turned his eyes away from her. "So, Signorina Mia. I'm told the tour group has a boat trip scheduled tomorrow. Will you be going on that?"

She looked at his profile. His face was calm, but she knew he was playing with her. Daring her to open up. Why would he ask that question if not to see how far she was willing to go to avoid admitting the truth? "You know that I'm not part of that group," she said quietly.

"That's true. I just didn't want to put you in a difficult position, if you intended to continue to pretend that you were."

She watched him as he looked out at the water, frustrated because she couldn't yet figure him out. "I don't understand," she said. "Why did you lie for me? You don't know me. Why would you care if I was kicked out of the hotel?"

"Because..." he said slowly. "Because I think you have information I need."

She froze. *He* was the one with information! He was the one who had access to the castle, who had spent today there in anticipation of possible new artifacts. Why would he think that she knew anything? "What... makes you think that?" she asked, haltingly, picturing the *schianto* in her suitcase.

"As a historian I deal with lots of different people," he said. "And I've learned to spot when people have information. It's how you looked during the tour. You weren't like the others."

"I was just... looking..."

"No, there was something more." His tone was even. Certain. "I was watching you after you lingered on the balcony. And then I saw the way you looked at the empty *schianto* case. Almost like you'd seen a ghost. I think you did see a spirit in there, didn't you?"

She held her breath. It was shocking, how much he had deduced about her. But still, there was a lot he didn't know. He didn't know she had the *schianto*, of course. And he also didn't seem to know that she was the granddaughter of the woman suspected of stealing it. Maybe he didn't even know about the letter in Milt's office. Maybe he was out of that loop. And in that case, she wanted to get his help while he was still in the dark. She needed to convince him that she did know something —but not show her cards. She had to give him a reason, a need, to bring her back to the castle with him.

"Let's just say that like you, I have a special connection to the castle." She decided to go one step further. "A special connection to the *schianto*."

"You know where the *schianto* is?" he asked, looking at her, his eyebrows raised and his voice steady.

"Someone I loved lived in the castle when Patricio was there," she said, ignoring his question. She wasn't going to give away any more just yet. "And I need to know why sh... this person went there and then left. I need to get onto the island to discover that story."

"Who is this person?" he asked.

"I'm not ready to tell you that."

"I see," he said. "Well, I would gladly bring you back to the castle if it were possible. But I can't. It's prohibited. We could both get in trouble."

"It's a risk I need to take. I can't go home knowing no more than I did when I left."

"I don't think I can help you." He started to stand. "I'm sorry, but—"

"No. Wait," she said. "Okay, I do know about the *schianto*. A lot. And if you help me learn about my... *person*, I can help you locate it."

He looked at his hands on his lap. Then he looked back at her.

"I believe you, Mia. And I want to know what you know."

"And I want to know what *you* know," she said with a sly smile.

He laughed. "You have something I need, and you need something I have," he said. "So I guess we're in this together." He breathed in. "Meet me at the dock tomorrow at nine in the morning. Don't tell anyone where you're going or that you're meeting me. And don't be late."

With that, he got up and went back into the hotel. By the light of the stars and moon, and the golden glow emanating from the hotel, she watched his figure fade away.

SIXTEEN

1943

August

"Wait—your mother is Olivia Parissi?" Aldo said. "Patricio's sister?"

Looking down at her lap, Annalisa sensed Aldo shift his weight on the wall, turning his body toward her, and she felt his hard stare.

"Yes, she *was* his sister," Annalisa said. "She died many years ago."

"So Signor Parissi is... your *uncle?*"

She nodded.

"But don't you see what this means? You're a Parissi! You don't need to be sneaking into the castle and working in the kitchen. You own all this." He spread his arms wide, indicating the castle, the island, and more. The air, the sky, the water below, maybe. Too much to even quantify.

"No, that's not true," she told him. "My mother was disinherited. I own nothing. And the way he feels about my father, he wouldn't even want me in the kitchen. He may not even know that my mother died. He'd probably hate us all even more if he knew that."

"But he didn't hate your father. His father did."

"So why didn't he ever try to find us?"

"Because he didn't know how. That's what my mentor said. He didn't know where your mother was."

"Are you sure he doesn't hate my father just as much? For breaking up his family?"

Aldo sat back. "Well, when you put it that way…"

"I know," she said. "It's very complicated. And my father doesn't have much time."

"So what are you going to do? How are you going to get him to share his invention with you?"

Annalisa folded her arms across her chest. Although the day had been warm, it was now starting to feel a little cold. "I don't know. I guess I didn't anticipate how big this place is. And I definitely didn't realize that nobody ever sees him. Or that we'd be working all day in the kitchen and there'd be so much to do. I guess there's a lot I didn't know.

"But that's okay. I can do this," she said, tapping her fingers together by her chin. "I just need to make a plan."

She turned to him. "Emilia said that he likes when the workers are curious and want to learn. So… so I can show him how interested I am in his invention. I *am* interested in it—that's why I'm here. Maybe I don't have to tell him who I am at first. Maybe I can just be an interested student and win him over that way."

"You think he'll share his invention with you just because you're… interested?" Aldo said, his raised eyebrows emphasizing his skepticism.

"Why not? Maybe it's best to keep the family out of this for now. I can tell the truth later, after he likes me." She looked at him. "No? What do you think?"

He lifted his palms in a playful show of surrender. "I don't even know what to think. I've been here for months, and I'm still trying to figure out what to do with myself. But you... you get here and, in one day, you already know what you came to do, how you're going to do it, and what you're going to do when it's done."

"Because I don't have much time. My father needs help."

"I only mean I'm impressed," he said. Then he hopped off the wall. "I'd better get down to the boathouse. Hopefully it'll be a less eventful night than last night."

"Wait!" she said, hopping off after him. "Will I see you again?" She knew it was a mistake, to grow attached to someone here. It could be distracting and throw her off her game. But she couldn't help it. She liked being with him. And she suspected he felt the same way.

"Sure," he said. "I'm always around in the evening, although not always at the same time. It depends on what they have me doing."

"Then how will I know when to find you?"

"Hmmm." He ran his tongue along the inside of his upper teeth as he thought. "What kind of an arrangement can we make? I don't want to keep coming to your room and waking up your sisters. And probably you don't want all the people here seeing me knocking on your door. People like to gossip here. A lot.

"Hey, I've got it," he said and kneeled by the edge of the wall. "Look, this stone here"—he jiggled it—"it's loose. Signora Russo sometimes puts lists of supplies here for me to give to the boats going back to the mainland."

"Why does she hide lists of supplies?" Annalisa said.

"What? I don't know. That's not even the point," he said, shaking his head. "The point is, there's a pad of paper and a pencil deep inside. When I know what time I can get here at night, I'll write it down and leave it for you. You can come out and check when you're having dinner or something."

"Okay," she said. "That'll work."

"Yeah, for sure. Now you should get some sleep. You were up all last night. And you have busy days ahead."

He waved and started for the front of the castle, and she watched him until he was out of sight. Then she looked at the stone that would hide his notes to her, feeling exhilarated. Maybe it was because the night really did seem to shine, thanks to all the brilliance and possibility concentrated right here in this place. The promise that existed within the walls of this castle was infinite. She now believed for sure that she could go home a different person than the one she was when she arrived. She could be someone who could reverse her father's all but certain fate. Repair the schism in her family. Maybe even redirect the course of human history. She could be someone who knew how to make sick people well.

Because the truth was, she already was changing, she thought. She was becoming someone she hardly recognized.

Someone who knew how it felt to be falling in love.

Three days later, she got her first sighting of Patricio.

She'd been carrying his tray ever since that first day, leaving the bedroom before dawn, trying not to wake her sisters, although Emilia was a light sleeper and would inevitably groan and cover her head with her pillow. In the kitchen, she would wait for Signora Russo to finish preparing Patricio's tray and grab it off the metal table before any of the other tray runners had arrived to start their shift. Then she'd make her way to the fourth floor and walk through the hallway toward the tower. To her left was an astonishing balcony built so far out from the castle that it seemed to be floating on air. She'd stop and gaze out over the water before continuing to the tower. Then she'd rest the tray on her left arm and push the heavy wooden door with her right, letting it ease closed slowly so as not to make any sound. This part of the castle was dark, with streaks of light coming in from narrow windows high above in the circular spire. Across the landing, there was a wide doorway that she suspected was Patricio's suite. She'd place the tray on the table right outside and hurry back through the tower door, keeping it open a crack so she could see him. She didn't want to meet him right away; instead she wanted to get a good look at him first.

Two days passed. In the mornings, she'd hide behind the tower door, peering through the slim crack for as long as she could, leaving before she would be missed downstairs. In the late afternoons, she'd check for Aldo's note to see what time he could meet up with her. Over dinner in the small room where the workers ate, she'd pretend to listen to Emilia's complaints about having to rewash the soup pots three times until they met Signora Russo's approval, and to Giulia's pining over Vincenzo, as she anticipated seeing Aldo again. When they met each night, they'd analyze her tray deliveries and try to determine how she could position herself in the tower at the exact moment Patricio retrieved his breakfast.

Then, on the third day, she felt skilled enough to balance two trays on his, delivering them first so she wouldn't arrive with his breakfast so early. The strategy worked; from her hidden perch, she saw his door open—and there he was.

Her first thought was that he was far gentler looking than she'd expected. Despite having seen his pictures in the publications she'd read, she'd still imagined him, from what Aldo had said, as a kind of ogre—stout, hunched over, walking stiffly, maybe with a gray matted beard. Instead, he was very tall and very thin, with short copper hair neatly parted on the side and no facial hair at all. He had a few wrinkles around his eyes and on his forehead, which was in keeping with a man who was in his mid-forties, according to her calculations. His clothes were loose, his shirtsleeves draping down below his wrists and the tail of his white shirt hanging down past his hips.

"He's not scary at all," she murmured to herself as she went back downstairs for more trays. "Not scary at all," she repeated to Aldo later that night.

The next morning she followed the same routine, bringing his tray to him as her third delivery, and sure enough, he came out to retrieve it as she hid in the hallway. So on the next morning, she slowed her pace, and waited in the hallway with his tray as she heard his footsteps approaching.

He opened the door and stared at her, looking more surprised than angry. "You're late," he said. A simple statement of fact. His voice was higher than she'd expected of someone so tall. She looked at his face, and felt tears form in her eyes, as she took in his thin lips, rounded chin, red cheeks, and fine, delicate eyelashes. In those ways, he was the spitting image of her mother.

He took a slice of hair between his third and fourth fingers and combed it away from his face. For a moment, she wondered if he'd simply snatch the tray from her and close the door in her face. But then she realized he wouldn't. There was something in his amber eyes, the same shade as hers, that reminded her of her mother. It wasn't the color—her mother had had dark eyes—but it was a softness in their expression that seemed so familiar. He was bitter, she knew, and hurt, but he wasn't mean. She could tell that immediately. His eyes looked lonely. Like her mother's had sometimes looked when she gazed out the window. Maybe thinking about the family she'd lost.

"I'm sorry, sir," she said. "I wanted to see you."

His eyebrows raised. "Wanted to see *me*?"

"I read about you," she said. "You're working on a medical device. You're why I came here to the island with my sisters. To work in the kitchen, but I was hoping to learn from you, too. I want so much to know about your device—how it works and what it can do. Do you... do you need an apprentice?"

She saw his shoulders relax and his eyes grow warm. He was moved by what she'd said. "You read about my invention?"

"Oh yes, tons," she said. "All the articles and book chapters I could find." It was true. She had found him through her reading when she was trying to look for cures for her father. And when she'd seen a photo of him in one of the books, she'd recognized it as identical to the one her mother had kept in her dresser drawer. Her mother had sometimes talked fondly of her big brother, Patricio, whom she'd loved, and her awful father, who didn't believe in love. Annalisa had always assumed that Patricio had died—but when she saw his photo in that book, she'd put two and two together.

"What's your name?" he asked.

"Annalisa," she murmured. She wondered if she should have made up a name, but that could have created additional problems with Signora Russo and the other tray runners. She could only hope that he had no way of knowing he even had nieces.

"Do you know I speak to no one?" he said. "Didn't Signora Russo say not to talk to me?"

"We were told not to bother any of the guests," she said. "But I want to learn. I wanted so much to meet you and to learn from you. I'm sorry."

"You know, I never talk to anyone," he repeated, a note of surprise coupled with a tinge of outrage in his voice, as though he couldn't believe anyone in the castle could fail to have grasped this simple, unchanging fact.

"I know," she said. "But I also know you believe in education. I know you encourage others here to teach the workers. I don't want to learn from anyone else but you. I want to help you. I want to make sick people better."

He studied her and she licked her lips and waited, keeping her eyes locked on his. She didn't want him to think she was the kind to back down.

Finally, he spoke. "Can you do exactly as you're instructed? And not ask too many questions? Can you do your work quietly? Can you stay out of my way?"

She nodded. "Yes. I'll work exactly as you want me to."

He considered this. "You are right. I did say that about education. I do mean that. It's important to hand down knowledge. Not to cut off the next generation. Okay. If you want to learn. Come in."

She followed him into his suite. The main bedroom was huge and darkly furnished, the window covered with heavy red drapes. As he led her through an internal doorway, she noticed a tiny bald spot on the back of his head. It made him seem vulnerable, and she smiled with affection. Her mother's big brother.

The back room appeared to be his lab, and she looked around. It was sparser than she would have expected. There was a long, heavy table, iron maybe, and a stool. On top of the table were two piles, one of wet sand and soil, and one of leaves and petals.

He picked up a handful of soil. "There is so much power, so much potential, here by the sea," he said. "There's a reason people gravitate to these shores. It triggers something very deep inside. It's primal. You see, there are minerals within the sand and water here. Curative minerals. Magnesium. Sulfur. Iron. They've been sustaining life forever. I just need to harness them. Extract them and use them."

"How do you do that?" she asked, then gasped and covered her mouth, remembering he didn't want her to ask questions. But he didn't seem to mind. Maybe he was okay with questions at this stage, when he was introducing her to his work.

"With this," he said as he walked to a polished mahogany cabinet, like a wardrobe, on the opposite side of the room and pulled on the brass doorknobs. Inside were heavy wooden shelves. The entire cabinet was empty except for the center shelf, which was lit by a small fixture on the bottom of the shelf above, and which cast a golden glow.

"The *schianto grandioso*," he whispered.

It was a wide-mouthed bowl on a gleaming black base, with alternating bands of rough stone and smooth pink marble running through it. The bowl was almost in the shape of a wide V, but the top pink marble rim was slightly curved inward. There was a metal rod attached with a hinge to the edge. It jutted straight out into the center of the bowl and looked like a dense, solid mallet, with a round pink ball at the end.

He brought it out and put it on the table. She was dying to touch it, to examine it with her own hands. From the way he held it, it looked heavy and breakable at the same time. She yearned to touch the mallet, to understand how it moved and how it would function. She ached to touch the surfaces, to confirm in her mind the differences, the smoothness of the rod and some of the bands forming the bowl, the roughness of the others.

He ran his fingers around the perimeter of the bowl, as gently as her father had stroked her cheek when he told her that her mother had died. "It will knead the sand and release the minerals," he said. "Once I perfect it. And that's the job of this mallet. This little ball here." He touched the rounded part of the rod.

She was excited and thrilled, wanting nothing more than to study with him. To learn from him. To help him make this device work.

"This is... amazing," she whispered, too awed to do anything but stare.

Then she lifted her gaze to study her uncle's eyes. She saw her mother in them—the same thirst for knowledge, the same reverence for the potential of the human mind. And she knew she would find a way into his heart. Because there was something wrong about a broken family like theirs. The magic of the *schianto* was not just the cure it would provide, but also the reunion. She was her father's daughter, but she was also her mother's daughter and Patricio's niece. She was the sum of so many parts.

And if she could bring them together, who knew what else she would accomplish?

That evening, as usual, she and her sisters had dinner with the other workers. While everyone was exclaiming over a gift that one of the tray runners had received from Patricio via Signora Russo—a slim wood-bound notebook and a fountain pen—Annalisa discreetly left the table and went onto the terrace to fetch Aldo's note, which said he would meet her at nine thirty.

Later in the bedroom, she braided Emilia's wet hair and listened as her sisters chatted about their favorite meals so far and tried to figure out if Signora Russo was older than she looked and whether she was on her own or might have a husband or children living elsewhere. Not ready to admit, not even to them, her growing feelings for Aldo, she waited for the specified time and then slipped out the door.

"I'm going to the kitchen for some water," she whispered, coming up with an excuse as she did every night if she left before they'd fallen asleep.

"Bring some back for us?" Emilia said.

"Fine. But I have to check something, too, so it may take time... so don't wait up," Annalisa said impatiently and left the room.

In the kitchen, she maneuvered into a dark corner and changed into her favorite green cotton dress from home, which she'd tucked beneath her arm as she'd left the bedroom. Smoothing her hair behind her ears—never one for fancy hairdos, she suddenly felt she wouldn't have minded a pretty clip or flower to affix to the side—she went out onto the terrace. He was sitting on the stone wall, waiting for her.

"Word is that you penetrated the impenetrable force," he teased as she approached him. "It's all over the castle. Patricio has an apprentice."

"How did you find out?" She sat down next to him, and he handed her a glass of wine.

"The kitchen doesn't miss a thing," he said. "And this wasn't a hard one. Apparently, Patricio sent a message down that he wants only you to deliver his breakfast from now on. And you are relieved of some kitchen duties because he wants you to work with him every morning. You did the unthinkable, my very clever friend. You broke through a stone. Just wait. He'll be moving you up to a fancy bedroom. You'll start having your breakfast delivered to you."

"No, no..."

"It's going to happen. This is what you came for. You're on your way up—"

"But you can be, too. You have your music. None of us has to stay in the kitchen. Isn't music why you came here?"

He shrugged. "I told you, I don't know why I'm here. I followed my teacher, and now he's gone. But you... you got Patricio to talk to you. You're changing everything." He squeezed her elbow. "I'm glad for you. I knew you were something special. Ever since you tricked me into bringing you up here—"

"I did not trick you—"

"I know, I know. But you are headed somewhere great. I'm glad I got to know you."

She looked at him, more serious. "What are you saying? This isn't goodbye. He still has a lot of work to do. I'll be here for a while. I'll still meet you here every night."

"And I'll be here, watching the sky and waiting for you."

They sat in silence for a few minutes, and then it was time

for him to go to the boathouse. Unexpectedly, he reached one arm around her shoulders, and she slipped her arm beneath his and encircled his slender waist. It was kind of a hug, she thought, and although it lasted only a moment, she felt as though her whole life had changed. He felt so warm and his arm felt so strong, and he smelled lovely, like the earth after a rainstorm. Then he released her and gave her hand a squeeze, and she watched him disappear around the side of the castle. At that moment she realized that as much as she wanted Patricio's cure, she also wanted Aldo. She wanted the cure, she wanted to tell Patricio who she was, and she wanted Aldo, too. Her mother had chosen love over her family and Patricio presumably had chosen his obligation to his family over his love for his sister. And had devoted himself to a lonely life.

But were those choices necessary? Couldn't she have both Aldo and the cure for her father? Love and family? Friendship and knowledge? Couldn't her heart and her head be reconciled? It was just like a different type of science experiment, she thought. A problem-solving challenge. And she could figure it out. She figured out how to get here and how to meet Patricio. She could figure out how to keep Aldo in her life, too.

Because she had to. She wouldn't have it any other way.

She continued to believe that over the next few days, as she began spending way more time with Patricio than in the kitchen. He'd hypothesized that adding plant matter to the mineral compound would increase its potency or absorption in the bloodstream, so he put her to work researching the properties and effects of botanicals that he could source. Day after day she'd read through books and, as he'd requested, record her findings in the simplest of terms into a hard-backed journal:

Chamomile: Relaxes muscles; reduces inflammation; calms nervous energy

Sage: Fights infection and pain

Hyssop: Aids digestion and respiration

Fennel: Reduces inflammation

It was arduous work, as the books he'd given her, even the ones he'd recently ordered, were full of scientific jargon and Latin abbreviations that she didn't understand, so she had to find their definitions in other books before she could return to the initial book. Sometimes she'd jump from book to book to book with new questions, until she couldn't even remember where she'd begun or what she'd been reading when she'd started hours earlier.

Other times he'd give her some plant samples and have her analyze and record their properties so he could predict how they'd behave when combined with minerals. She loved when he did that, since this was the type of research she preferred— using all her senses to understand the nature of what was presented before her. She'd always believed that this was the only way to truly know something—to confront it head-on. She'd look at each sample, gently turning it over and around with her fingertips to analyze the shape, the shade and uniformity of the color, the presence of markings. She'd smell it to ascertain the fragrance and even touch it lightly with her tongue to determine the taste. She'd knead it with her fingers and rub it against her cheek, and then write down all her findings: translucent, vivid or veiny; acrid, earthy, or grassy; sweet, bitter, or metallic; rubbery, powdery, sticky, or prickly.

She'd return to her bedroom each night after meeting Aldo on the terrace to update him on her work and her increasingly fond relationship with Patricio. Usually when she came back to her bedroom, her sisters were asleep. But one night, she returned to find Giulia waiting up for her. She motioned to Annalisa to follow her to the hall, so their conversation wouldn't wake Emilia.

"I've been sneaking down to the dock to meet Vincenzo when he brings supplies," she whispered. "I didn't tell you because I thought you wouldn't approve, and I know you didn't believe how much I care for him. But today he told me some-thing you have to know. He heard from the cousin who lives in our town." She paused. "He says things aren't so good with Papa."

Annalisa felt her breath catch. "What do you mean? His heart?"

"Yes, but not just his heart. It's getting worse for Jews. A lot of people won't even go to his shop anymore. Vincenzo says Papa should get out of Italy soon."

"Out of Italy? Where will he go?"

"He won't go anywhere without us." She started to cry. "I'm scared for him, Pippa. I think we need to get back to him fast. Vincenzo was told he's getting very thin. He needs help."

Annalisa didn't bother to tell Giulia not to use that silly nickname. This was terrible news, and she had to do something. She'd thought she had at least three or four more weeks with Patricio before she'd have to tell him about her sick father. Three or four weeks to earn his complete trust and affection. Then, she'd thought, she could tell Patricio who she was; and after he had accepted her, she'd tell her sisters that he was their uncle.

But now it seemed she didn't have much time at all. She needed Patricio to finish up with the *schianto* and let her take it home with her.

She had no choice. She would have to reveal her identity to Patricio tomorrow.

SEVENTEEN

2018

Tuesday

After Leo left, Mia stayed on the terrace for a few moments to absorb what he'd told her. Then she went up to her room to call Erica. She wanted more than anything to fill her friend in on what had happened, and she would have reached out even if it had been the middle of the night back in New York. Thankfully, though, it was four in the afternoon.

"And he doesn't know the *schianto* is right there in your suitcase?" Erica asked when Mia had finished her story.

"No, I didn't want to tell him," Mia said, sitting on the bed, the night table lamp glowing gold and the stars outside large and hot white. "I told him I know something about it. But I wanted to hold the truth back, so he'd want to help me out more. Plus, it scared me the way he talked yesterday on the tour about how they intend to prosecute whoever has the *schianto*. I can't tell him it's here until I can prove that my grandmother didn't steal it."

"And he agreed to take you to the castle?"

"Yes! Tomorrow. I feel bad not telling him the truth, but I don't have a choice."

"Wow, no choice but to spend the day with a dreamy Italian. Poor you..."

Mia rolled her eyes. "It's not like that, Erica. And he's not Italian, by the way. He's American. He's from Philadelphia, although his family moved here when he was a kid. But that's not what this is about. I mean, I have a boyfriend. That's not why I'm here."

"And yet, he's made quite an impression on you..."

She paused as she realized Erica was right. "He has," she said slowly, choosing her words thoughtfully. "Because there's something else to him, something more. He's got this... earnest quality to him. And a kind of sadness. Oh, maybe it was just because we were sitting out there alone and it was so dark and empty. But it sounded like he was searching for something. I mean, yes, he's searching for the *schianto*, but he also said he has a special connection to the castle. It sounded very personal. More than it should be, if this was just some run-of-the-mill exhibit and he simply wants the thing returned. And I'm so curious about what his stake is in all this."

"He's probably asking himself the same thing about you," Erica said.

Mia nodded, then paused, again struck by what Erica had said. Did he see the same intensity in her as she saw in him—and was that why he was willing to bring her back to the castle tomorrow? Could he be searching for information about someone, as she was? Was it possible that they both saw in each other a need that mirrored their own?

"I hate to say it, but you don't have that much time," Erica said softly. "Tomorrow is Wednesday already. You're heading back to Rome Sunday morning to catch your flight home."

"I know." Mia sighed, leaning back on the padded headboard. "That's why I need to get back to the castle first thing tomorrow. And Thursday and Friday and Saturday if need be. I can't bring the *schianto* home and be back where I started. And I can't leave it here without knowing why I have it in the first place." She clenched a fist. "I need answers. And he does, too. At least I think he does. And you know what? He's not getting his answers until I get mine. That's just the way it has to be."

"Absolutely. You went there for a reason," Erica reminded her.

"Right. And I can play hardball as well as anyone," Mia said. "I've seen Ryan do it. Just dangle what they want and keep sweetening the deal until they fold. Okay, it didn't work with my grandmother when he wanted to buy her house, but she was an unusual case. Everyone has a price, that's what Ryan always tells me. And the *schianto* is the sweetest deal there could be for this guy—right?"

"I suppose," Erica said, sounding unconvinced. "Although maybe he just doesn't have the answer you're looking for. Maybe it's not that he won't help you, maybe he can't. No matter what you can give him in return."

Mia sighed. She'd been thinking the same thing. "And you know what else?" she said. "I don't want to play hardball with him. He's a nice guy, and he doesn't deserve to be messed with. Especially since his goal is... noble, you know? Returning the *schianto* to what he believes is its rightful home." She looked down at her lap. The truth was, Ryan never let himself get caught up in questions of principle. When someone like her grandmother resisted his argument, he shrugged and walked away.

"Ryan doesn't come off particularly well in this comparison, does he?" she added, hating to verbalize the thought. And yet she wanted to say it. Her view of Ryan seemed to have changed since she'd gone back to her grandmother's house on Thursday. And more to the point, she knew she'd always been aware of the way he was; she'd just never been so directly impacted by his apparent lack of empathy before.

"No, he doesn't." Erica sounded certain but also regretful admitting this to her friend. "But hey—you're both under stress and you're far apart right now. Texts and phone calls are not always the best way to communicate."

"That's true," Mia said, although she realized she wasn't having any misunderstandings with Erica—and they were far away from one another as well. Erica hadn't sounded at all harsh or unfeeling this week. She'd been as wonderful a friend as always.

"Well, don't let yourself get upset," Erica said. "Just think—you're doing something very exciting tomorrow, and who knows what will come of it? We thought we'd be lucky to get to the castle once—and look, you're going back a second time. Be hopeful, okay? They're doing renovation. They're breaking walls and tearing up floors. And apparently Leo is intimately involved with the construction crew. He's right there in the thick of it. Who knows what you two might find?"

Mia promised she'd stay hopeful—it was what drove her to come here in the first place—and hung up the phone. Erica was right, there were things going on in the castle this week that could be very revealing. She just couldn't get her mind off Leo. It felt bad to move forward without being more honest. He'd lied *for* her, and she was lying *to* him. By not saying the *schianto* was right here. Two flights up from the terrace where they'd been speaking.

She felt her phone buzz and looked down to see that Ryan had texted. He didn't ask how she was doing or whether she had learned anything more about her grandmother. He didn't seem to understand how much she felt was riding on this trip. No, his message was all about his own goings-on, as evidently he was convinced that his top priorities were hers as well. He said he was sorry he'd been too busy to call, but the deal he'd put together looked like it was going to work out, as everyone who'd had objections was now coming on board. *So cool, right?* he'd written.

We'll celebrate big time when we're both home!

She put her phone down on the bed next to her, wondering what he had done to win all those decision makers over. Had he bluffed, stonewalled, or sweetened whatever he was offering? How shrewd had he been to get exactly what he wanted? She wondered, too, if anyone in that meeting had looked at him the way Leo had looked at her, with a need and an intensity that had nothing to do with money.

Tapping her lips with her fingers, she thought of her grandmother's steadfast piece of advice, the piece of advice Mia had internalized above all others: *Face facts head-on, using all your senses, when there is a decision to make.* There wasn't much she could rely on right now as far as her senses went, since she was alone in a hotel room in Italy. And yet she knew that in this case, her grandmother would want her to confront the evidence nonetheless. Mia had been watching Ryan and learning about him for a long time now. He'd proved himself to be, at his core, a responsible person and devoted boyfriend. Even so, there was a piece of him she couldn't relate to. A side to him that didn't sit well with her.

She had told Erica she could be just like him in dealing with Leo. That she could play hardball. But then she'd corrected herself. In a fundamental way, she could never be like Ryan. She wouldn't want to be.

So with those facts in mind, she had no choice but to ask herself the next logical question: what was she doing with him?

The next morning Mia dressed in leggings, a tee shirt, and sneakers, assuming she'd be walking through rubble and dust.

She was about to grab Leo's hat from the closet doorknob when her phone rang, and when she lifted it from the night table, she saw it was Ryan. She paused before answering, not wanting to hear him say anything that might cause her to doubt herself and her purpose again; but he hadn't called her at this hour ever since she'd arrived in Italy, and it made her worry that something could be wrong.

"Ryan," she said. "Everything okay? What is it, like, the middle of the night there?"

"Yes," he said, sounding angry. "And I guess you could say something is wrong. I texted you last night about my deal getting green-lighted. And you didn't even text me back to say congratulations?"

"Oh... I..." She stopped, having no words. He was right—he had texted her with good news, news any normal girlfriend would have been thrilled to hear. But she hadn't thought for a moment about calling him back. No, his text had made her think about the differences between Ryan and Leo. And the way Ryan had come up short.

"I'm sorry," she finally said. "I should have texted you back. It's just I'm so far away, and a lot is going on here—"

"It's okay," he said, sounding like he didn't really forgive her. "It's just kind of hurtful, you know? This means a lot to me, that things are going well out here. I thought it would mean a lot to you, too. There I was, in this conference room with two lawyers, an accountant, and the senior managers..."

She nodded as he went on, thinking that a week ago she'd have responded exactly as he'd wanted. If he'd called or texted her at work and left that same message, she'd have called back to hear the whole story: who in the meeting had been skeptical, who'd called him out on insignificant points, how he'd been able to think on his feet and turn everyone's resistance on its head so it seemed they were all in support of his proposal and the reasons behind it. She knew how much he wanted to leave his firm and go out on his own. Making money—commission and bonuses—was the way he could finance his dreams. And he believed his dreams were hers, too. That they were building something together.

And she was partly to blame. She had let him believe all these months that she was behind him. She had never asked him to support her dreams, never expected him to acknowledge in any meaningful way her desire to return to school for her PhD. Maybe it was because she'd never felt her dreams were as important as his were. She'd never felt entitled to his support.

Why had she allowed their relationship to progress that way? Why had she never before demanded his respect? And why was she only now recognizing this was a problem?

As Ryan spoke, Mia tapped her phone to see what time it was. She didn't want to be late for Leo, and she didn't know how long she'd have to wait to board the van down to the shore.

"That sounds great, Ryan," she said. "I want to hear more. But I have to get going—"

"What's up—Erica's getting antsy for breakfast?" he joked. She could hear the swagger returning to his voice, as speaking to her had evidently assuaged his ego. "Tell her it's my fault. Tell her I needed to talk to you and it's no problem to get out on the beach ten minutes later. You tell her I said that. Okay?"

Mia inhaled deeply, her lips pressed together, regretting she'd been apologetic. A moment ago, he was criticizing her for overlooking his feelings, and now he was doing the same thing to her. No—what he was doing was worse. He was negating her feelings and reframing her trip into the simple beach vacation he wanted it to be. He was rewriting her story, the story about her past that was unfolding this week. He was even scripting her, telling her what she should say to her friend.

"Fine," she said coldly. "I'll be sure to tell Erica exactly that."

She hung up, took Leo's hat from the doorknob, and she left the room.

In the elevator, she took a few deep breaths to slow down her heartbeat. Today was all about discovery and connection with the past. It would be suspenseful and exciting, as Erica had said. And she wasn't going to let the phone call with Ryan ruin it. In the lobby she saw Signor Dorria behind the desk, and when he asked where she was going, she kept her promise to Leo and said she wanted to return to the café from yesterday for another *cornetto*, which she had found irresistible. He wished her a lovely morning and said the van was at her disposal, as the tour group was not scheduled to leave for its next outing—a boat trip among all the other small islands in the area—for another hour.

The van left soon after she boarded, and when it arrived at the dock, she thanked the driver. Having had no time for breakfast, what with Ryan's phone call, she now found herself longing for a good, strong cappuccino. So she was delighted when she spotted Leo coming out of yesterday's café, holding a bakery bag and a cardboard tray with two coffee cups.

He was wearing jeans and a deep-green tee shirt, the breeze stirring the bottom hem and tousling his hair. Walking toward her, he jerked his head to shake his hair away from his face as he set the food on a railing alongside the dock. Then he waved to her to join him. Drawing closer, she saw once again how impossibly handsome he was. With his wavy hair and his tantalizing beard trimmed to the perfect length, not too tame and not too scruffy. With his broad shoulders and slim waist, his strong, straight stance. But perhaps what she found most lovely of all was his wide, welcoming grin—his mouth slightly open, his chin raised, his cheekbones high and his eyes crinkling. He was so appealing when he smiled. She knew she'd probably spend the whole day trying to make him smile again and again.

"*Buongiorno*," he said when she reached him. "I asked

inside about the American woman who was here yesterday morning with the big hat"—he smiled and gestured toward her head with his chin—"and they remembered you. They said you'd enjoyed the *cornetto*. So I bought us some more. And coffee."

She felt guilty that she'd strong-armed him into bringing her back to the castle, and instead of being mad, he'd shown up with coffee and croissants. She shook her head. "You didn't have to do that—"

"Did you have breakfast yet?" he asked.

"No, but—"

"Then I had to do it. We may be on the island for a long time today, and there's no snack bar. I can't have you fainting in the middle of the construction site. You may not get another bite until dinner."

She followed him onto the ferry, where he spoke in Italian to a few hefty men dressed in jeans and work boots. Then he waved to the captain and led her to a bench.

"I said you were my assistant," he told her as they sat and the boat's motor revved. "Nobody seemed to care—they're tearing down the old kitchen now, so everyone's pretty excited. Do me a favor and don't get hurt. And try to act like you go to these kinds of sites all the time. Okay?"

She nodded, glad that she'd been smart enough to dress in leggings and sneakers instead of a dress and sandals.

He put the coffees and the bag in between them, then handed her a cup. Lifting the lid, she let the fragrant steam waft up and then took a sip. It was sweet and delicious, just like yesterday's. Leo unfurled the bag and held the opening her way, and she reached in and brought out a *cornetto*. It was steamy with condensation and looked delicious, and she bit into it, feeling both delighted at the taste and embarrassed at the cascade of flaky crumbs that rained onto her leggings and the front of her tee shirt.

"So you said everyone's excited," she said, both because she was interested and because she wanted to distract him from the mess on her clothes. "What do they hope to find?"

"Nobody knows," he said as they both continued eating and brushing away crumbs. "But if something big is going to be found, the kitchen is likely where they'll find it. Like I said on the tour, Patricio's sole confidante was Signora Russo. She was the head of the kitchen—not really a cook, more like a manager for the whole place. She kept all the records about the guests— what they liked for breakfast, what books they read, what they liked for entertainment, even how they liked their clothes folded and what kinds of sheets and towels they liked. She also kept track of the staff. And she wrote up all the lists for the supply boats coming back and forth from the mainland.

"We've identified her handwritten notes in many places in the castle," he added. "But we feel that much of what she wrote, she would have hidden in the kitchen, which is where she spent most of her time."

"Why would she hide it?" Mia asked.

Leo swallowed some coffee and put the cup back down on the bench. "She's a bit of a mystery," he said. "While most of the guests were pretty naïve about what was going on with the Nazis, or maybe they just didn't want to know, Signora Russo seemed to have a sense of what was happening. And her writings—nothing all that special, just lists of names of the kitchen workers and guests, breakfast orders, and so on—she seemed to deliberately hide them inside closets and cabinets, and in compartments cut into walls. We think that she suspected the island would be destroyed and wanted to safeguard all she could."

"But if she did suspect something, why didn't she speak up? Why didn't she leave and get the others to leave as well?"

"That's an excellent question," he said. "I don't think she quite expected the devastation that was to come. The evil of the

Nazis, the unbridled cruelty. And what's more puzzling is that her remains were never found, and there's no record of her being sent to a concentration camp. Some believe she was working with the Americans, receiving information and sending out messages on the supply boats. There's speculation that Russo wasn't even her real name. I think she may have been taken from the island and tortured for information before she was killed."

"Oh my God," Mia said. She wasn't expecting such an awful story. Leo hadn't suggested anything like this during the tour the other day. He'd focused on the inventions and creations, on Patricio's contribution to art and science. The tone had been nostalgic, not horrifying.

"That's my theory, and others', too," Leo said. "I'm sorry if I've upset you, but history isn't nearly as sanitized as what you'll hear on a tour of a prospective luxury resort. I think Signora Russo left a treasure trove of documents to make sure history was never repeated. I'm hoping that's what is going to be uncovered as they move through the demolition of the kitchen. If Signora Russo was a hero, she should be acknowledged."

Mia looked at him. This was not the charmer she and the travel agents had met on the tour. This was a far more complex person, and she was drawn to him.

"This means so much to you, doesn't it? To uncover this," she said.

"It should mean something to everyone," he said. "Doesn't it mean something to you? Didn't you say you have someone connected with this island?" She heard the passion in his voice.

"Yes, of course. It does. And I do." She paused, not wanting to inflame his mood more. She'd clearly offended him by sounding so removed, as if this was his project and not something that mattered to the world. And would continue to, for generations to come. And yes, she did have someone connected with the island, as she'd said. But her grandmother had apparently left before the Nazi invasion. Her grandmother had lived a long, good life. This was the first she'd heard of the horror that happened there.

"I have someone I believe lived in the castle at some point," she said. "But she didn't die here. She ended up in New York." She paused, then decided to offer one more piece of information she hadn't given last night. "She was my grandmother," she said.

"Your grandmother?" He looked at her, surprised. Evidently he hadn't realized her connection would be so personal.

"Yes. I think she was one of the people who brought the breakfast trays to the guests. It's a long shot, but that's what I believe right now. It has to do with a picture I saw of the breakfast trays, the centerpieces. And what Patricio Parissi used to say about them, which I read in the brochure from the hotel. My grandmother used the same centerpieces all through her life. And said the same thing Patricio did about them."

"I see," Leo said. "So you knew your grandmother well?"

Mia tilted her head from side to side. "In some ways. She raised me, you see. But in other ways not so much."

"You are lucky to have known her at all," he said. "I never knew my grandfather. He died here. With Patricio and the rest. At the hands of the Nazis."

She instinctively drew her hand to her chest. "Oh, I'm so sorry," she said.

"He was a painter," he said. "Savio Peralta. And he was invited by Patricio to work on his masterpiece. A mural of a series of dresses. A wedding gown, a ball gown, a nightdress, a mourning outfit. He was a student of fabrics, actually. He wanted to portray with precision the way fabrics sway and drape and crease. He had young people from the kitchen staff who would come to sew and model the dresses so he could study their movement, and there was one apprentice who handled the most complicated sewing. I never met my grandfather. I only heard his stories from my grandmother. He left her and their home in Argentina to come to the castle and devote himself to his art. My grandmother never recovered from his murder."

"Oh, Leo. I'm so sorry," Mia repeated. She knew it was a flimsy response, but she didn't know what else to say.

"He wrote her letters telling her how happy he was to be here. He was so honored when Patricio wrote to invite him. We have none of the work he did here. All destroyed, or so we believe. The only thing we have are sketches he sent my grandmother. I will show you back at the hotel. My grandmother heard so much about that mural in his letters. After he died, she wanted only to recover that mural. It was her deepest regret that she never found it.

"He had so much talent," he said, sighing. "And never got to let the world see. I grieve for him, and I grieve for the world." He shook his head and she could hear his voice catch. "We are here for a moment, Mia. Just a moment in the vastness of time. And all we want is to make our presence known. And when we're gone, all we deserve is for the story of who we are and how we lived to be preserved."

She paused for a moment, struck by his beautiful sentiment. "Do you think you might find that mural in the castle?" she finally asked.

"I hope so. But now it's a bigger mission to me. People should know what happened here, all of it. Every story should be told and everything that belongs here should be returned. I feel so strongly about that, Mia. It makes me angry, and it will continue to make me angry until everything is uncovered and found."

She looked out toward the sea, as the castle grew closer. "You're talking about the *schianto*?" she asked in a whisper.

"Yes, everything, but surely the *schianto*," he said. "It was the object that was supposed to cure disease, change the world. Patricio was so damaged, but he had a vision for how the world could be. He meant the world to my grandfather. And it's outrageous that someone would take this thing and keep it as their own.

"I mean, why would they steal it?" he said, his voice growing stronger. "What's the value? What's it worth? Of course, it doesn't cure anything. It never worked. But it's the dream—the hope. That's its value."

"Maybe it wasn't stolen," Mia offered. "Maybe there's a reason why whoever has it—"

"It still belongs here. It's part of the story of who we all are and how we came to be at this moment. It's a story of loss and war that must never be repeated. The *schianto* is my story, your story, everyone's story. The invasion is our story. The story of the Jewish people is our story. How else do you live in a world if you divide stories into mine and not mine? That's the root of all war, isn't it?"

Of course, Mia knew he was right. And his words touched her. She was moved by this man, who was so passionate and full of emotion. She had never spent time with someone like him before. She'd always been taught that staying calm was the best way to be, that it brought you where you needed to go. Her grandmother had never been one to show emotion. But maybe it wasn't because she didn't want to; maybe she didn't know how. Or maybe it was frightening to do so, because of whatever she'd gone through that caused her to leave Italy. She felt sad for her grandmother. And protective. It couldn't have been easy to hide everything. It must have been exhausting.

"What is it, Mia?" Leo said. "I'm sorry. I didn't mean to upset you..."

"No, no, I'm okay," she said. "It's okay. I'm just confused. There's so much I don't know. And I'm trying to make sense of it. I'm just..."

She shook her head. "I'm thinking about my family now, too. I found things at my grandmother's home. She hid things from me. I don't know why."

"And that's the reason you've come to Italy?"

She nodded.

"I'm glad you're here," he said.

They both grew silent as the boat reached the shore. When it docked, Leo pulled two bottles of water out of the cooler on the deck, and she thanked him, then took a deep breath as they approached the steps and began the climb.

They reached the courtyard and Leo smiled as she leaned against one of the benches. It was such a hard climb, and she couldn't believe that he wasn't falling apart, too. He gave her his bottle, which was about half-full, and she took his hat off and poured the water over her head. It may not have been dignified, but it felt so good, and she was glad she'd done it.

"You're laughing at me!" she said, pretending to take offense at his smile.

He shrugged. "Tourists," he teased.

She paused and then shook her head fiercely, sending the water from her hair spraying in all directions. It was spontaneous and fun, and they both laughed out loud as she put the hat back on her head. It was a relief, a happy change, from the seriousness of the boat ride.

Just then a man appeared from around the side of the castle. "Leo!" he called. "*Sbrigati!*" And he turned back and disappeared.

Instantaneously Leo stopped laughing. "They found something," he said, his voice filled with controlled tension, like a balloon withstanding pressure before it pops. "He said to come quickly."

And with that, they took off for the kitchen.

EIGHTEEN

2018

Wednesday

Mia followed him across the courtyard and around the side of the castle. Beyond the walkway was a huge, sloping, woodsy area that seemed to stretch out to the horizon and up to the sky. She'd never seen such an expansive view of greenery—tall trees and thick shrubbery cascading down the hillside, making her feel as though she were poised on a cloud. But Leo was stopping for nothing and almost seemed to have forgotten she was with him. He turned the corner and made his way along the terrace backing the castle. She caught up with him, their footsteps resounding against the thin plywood boards covering the broken-up stones beneath their feet.

Halfway across the terrace, a makeshift wooden door appeared, and Leo threw it open and charged in, Mia at his heels. She assumed they were in the kitchen now, but only because of the old farmhouse sink and some fittings where a large gas oven might go. Other than that, the space was empty, with exposed beams and columns, plywood boards on the floor, and exposed pipes overhead. There was one folding table in the center of the space with floor plans and diagrams rolled out flat and held down by rocks at the corners. Six or seven people were surrounding the table, all wearing hard hats, and they looked up when Leo approached. Most of them were wearing boots and toolbelts, so appeared to be construction workers. One man and one woman were dressed in khakis and button-down shirts, and Mia thought they might be engineers or architects.

Leo grabbed two hard hats from a stool next to the sink. With a scowl, he took his hat off Mia's head and replaced it with a hard hat. She could tell that the time for playfulness was over. His mood was serious and anticipatory, like a doctor heading into a difficult surgery. He put the other hard hat on his own head and tossed his sun hat impatiently onto the stool.

"*Cosa succede?*" he said as he strode to the table.

Feeling lost in the interchange of quick-paced Italian, Mia stayed a few steps away from the table. Looking past Leo's shoulder, she saw that the group wasn't examining floor plans at all. Instead, they were leaning down to study a sheet of lined notepaper. It looked as though until recently it had been folded up, and one man was trying to smooth it flat with the palm of his hand. It was some kind of handwritten list.

Leo looked over his shoulder and motioned to her with his head to come alongside him. She moved toward him, and he turned the paper so it was right side up from her perspective. She appreciated that he was including her. She didn't know why she'd changed for him from suspicious to someone trustworthy, but he had changed in the same way for her too. Maybe it had to do with their conversation on the ferry, the symmetry between the loss of his grandfather and Mia's loss of her grandmother. Yes, his grandfather had died decades ago under the most evil of circumstances, and her grandmother had died peacefully after a good, long life; but they both wanted answers.

Leo picked up the thin, yellowed page, holding it firmly and intently with both of his hands, as though it would crumble like a butterfly wing if he didn't treat it carefully. "Oh, *Dio mio*," he mumbled, shaking his head. Some of the others nodded.

"What is it?" Mia asked.

"Come, sit," he said as he led her to a rickety wooden bench pressed against the wall near the sink. "This is very big."

She sat down beside him, feeling that in drawing her over, he was saying that he wanted her input, and that she had a right, or even a responsibility, to ask questions and help analyze whatever this list revealed.

Still holding the paper, Leo leaned his lower back against the wall, his shoulders slightly drooping. He shook his head, as though he couldn't believe what he was seeing.

"They found it under some rubble when they were opening up the walls where the pantry once was," he said. "Signora Russo made lists of all the workers when they arrived at the castle, what job they held, what their interests were. But they ended with the May 1943 arrivals, and we knew that couldn't be the end, because we know others came that summer. And here they are. The names of the people who came to work here in July and August of that year. The ones who were living here right before the invasion happened."

She looked over his shoulder at the list. There were eight names on it, and Leo explained that alongside the name was their job assignment.

"And see the triangle next to some of the names?" he added. "Patricio was a big believer in offering gifts to the staff that would help them make something of themselves. Books, tools for sculpting or fine paintbrushes, sometimes a piece of sheet music. As you know, he lived his life mostly as a recluse, so he would send notes to Signora Russo on what to give, and she would list it and put the triangle to show when she'd given it. Last month we found a book where she wrote up all the guidelines. She inscribed it to her niece, who was getting ready to take over here at the castle, as Signora Russo planned to leave the following year to take care of her elderly mother. But she never made it."

He looked down again at the paper. "Now this is interesting," he said, taking a pair of rectangular, black-framed glasses from his shirt pocket and putting them on, then looking at the page more closely. "See these little brackets next to the names? When Signora Russo drew those little brackets, we believe that meant they were siblings. Lots of siblings came to work here. And it looks like the last three kids to come work here were siblings, see? They seemed to have shown up in August of that year."

He leaned in, cupping one hand around the faded print to try to reduce the glare from the sun coming through the windows. "The ink is so faded, it's hard to read the names... the middle one, does this say Giulia?"

She moved in closer to see the handwriting. "I think so..."

"And look there—it says she worked as a *sarta*, a dressmaker. And she apprenticed at the painter's studio." He shook his head. "She would have known my grandfather. My grandmother always said my grandfather had one apprentice, a young girl he thought the world of. He said she had such talent in working with fabrics, silks and linen and fine wool. He thought she'd be a fashion designer one day. This could be her, Giulia."

He took off his glasses and rubbed an eye with his pinky finger. Mia gave him a minute to absorb what he'd read. She knew she'd be affected, too, if she came upon the name of a young person who had known her grandmother.

He sat up again, seeming to shrug off his personal reaction, and studied the page closely again. "Okay... now this name seems to be Emilia, right? And the top one, the oldest sister... does that say Annalisa?"

She nodded. "That's what it looks like."

He chuckled. "What do you know? We finally found

Annalisa. The tray runner who became Patricio's apprentice. Now we know exactly when she came."

Mia's ears perked up at the words "tray runner." As she'd told Leo, her grandmother had been a tray runner. She was certain of it. And her grandmother had had some connection to Patricio—hadn't she always described her lily-and-eucalyptus centerpieces as "fragrant and aesthetically pleasing"—the very description in Patricio's quote in the hotel brochure? If her grandmother had been an apprentice to anyone, surely it would have been to a scientist. She'd never have apprenticed with an artist or musician. Not if her interests were taken into account.

Still, her grandmother's name was Lucy, not Annalisa. Close but not the same. Plus, her grandmother didn't have sisters. Lucy had never explicitly told her that, but Mia had grown up knowing it. She'd never met anyone related to her—no cousins, no aunts, no uncles. And no one had reached out after Lucy died, claiming to be a relative, even though the obituary had been on the funeral home's website and had shown up in some online postings.

Suddenly Mia froze, as she thought of a strange coincidence. Her mother's name had been Julia, the English version of the Italian Giulia. And although she was called Mia, her legal name was Emilia. Just like the third sister on the list. Her grandmother had told her long ago that she'd suggested that name to her daughter when Mia was born.

Plus, that name—Annalisa. Wasn't that one of the names the Italian lawyer had mentioned in the letter Milt had shown her? He'd accused Lucy of going by other names. And Annalisa, she remembered, was definitely one of them.

Could it all just be a coincidence?

She noticed that Leo was no longer sitting next to her and, looking around, spotted him speaking to the people by the doorway. After a few moments, he came back to the bench.

"They're closing the site to start some major excavation," he said. "No one else can be in the castle when they do that kind of work. The rest of the team is packing up for the day. We should head down to the dock—the ferry will be leaving soon. I'm sorry, but that's how it goes sometimes. The construction comes first."

"But—" Mia started to protest. She hadn't seen anything she came to see. She hadn't explored more of the castle, as she'd hoped to do; and although the similarities between this Annalisa person and her grandmother seemed like more than a coincidence, she didn't know for sure what they meant. But it made no sense to argue. This wasn't Leo's decision.

And she still had tomorrow, Friday and Saturday, she thought. Leo was going to have to bring her back as many times as she needed. Because that was the only way she was going to reveal where the *schianto* was.

She was not giving up.

Back at the hotel, Leo said he was scheduled to lead the tour group on an evening cruise around the islands and then to the mainland for a festive banquet and an overnight stay. But he had a few hours before then, and asked if she'd join him for lunch on the terrace. She agreed, glad for the chance to spend more time with him, as she was growing more and more fond of him. She only wished she'd had time to change her clothes. She hated feeling so dusty. This was the kind of setting that called for a flowy skirt and silky top, maybe in a pale blue or buttercup yellow, with espadrilles. She didn't usually worry about her clothes. At the lab, she was often covered up by a lab coat, goggles, and gloves. Everyone dressed that way for safety; despite best intentions, chemicals could drip or splash, so it was critical to be as covered as possible. But today felt so different. She felt different.

They were seated at a table on the terrace, and when a server brought over a pitcher of iced tea, she and Leo both nodded. He poured, and then he and Leo chatted in Italian for a few minutes. Everyone she'd seen today seemed to know Leo well and like him a lot. He was a fixture here, even though he'd said he'd been on the island less than a year. He had such an easy way about him, and everyone responded so positively.

And now, as she studied him, she realized he wasn't merely "dreamy," the word the woman on the ferry had used. No, he was unique. Complex and smart. Kind and warm and soft-spoken, but firm and passionate, too. She thought about how she'd classified him when she first met him as simply handsome. How often did she do that—jump to conclusions about people with very little information? What did that say about her?

Maybe it was due to the kind of work she did. Classification was essential in research. And it was a process that could help someone feel safe. Because if you could label something, if you could name it, you could own it. Her grandmother had classified people all the time. Milt was attentive and generous, Ryan was clever and dependable, Erica was a good friend. This was Lucy's shorthand, her way of assessing stimuli so she knew how to proceed. It wasn't meant to be mean; it was self-protective.

She sipped some iced tea, taking in the flavor of the lemon slices floating in the glass. The lemons here were nothing like the ones she bought at the grocery store back home, she thought. They weren't simply sour; they were tangy and so full of flavor that they made your mouth pucker wildly, but not in an unpleasant way. It was sort of like squinting in the sunshine—the way it was possible to appreciate a strong sun so much that the squinting was part of the experience. It was an intense flavor and she realized that was exactly why she liked it. Intense experiences and sensations were good. The intensity of being alone, of coming here to Italy by herself. She realized now she'd had a whole life of avoiding intensity. And intensity, while sometimes overwhelming, made you know you were alive.

Leo turned back to her and said the server recommended

the selection of *tramezzini*, which he explained were small triangular sandwiches with tuna, olives, prosciutto, or other fillings. She nodded, as she was enjoying trying new Italian fare.

"So, tell me what was so special about that last name you read on the list. Annalisa," Mia said when the server stepped away. She wanted to hear more about the island, and she loved the way Leo spoke about the people, as though he actually had known them. But more than that, she wanted to find out about Annalisa. Despite having grown up believing that Lucy was an only child, she couldn't help but wonder if Annalisa and her grandmother were possibly one and the same.

"She was Patricio's apprentice," he explained. "And we knew she'd only been there a short time. But now we know exactly when she arrived. And what's so important is that Patricio never took on an apprentice, never wanted anyone around his research, until she showed up. So he was taken with her for some reason. And another thing. We know that sometime in the weeks before the invasion, he attended a concert in the ballroom—a debut, actually, by the Italian composer Aldo Verga. Again, something else he never did before Annalisa arrived."

"So you think it was because of her? That she changed him somehow?"

"Maybe, but maybe not. Do you know Verga?"

She shook her head no, as the server returned with their lunch. He'd divided the sandwiches for them, and they each dug in. The food was delicious—the bread warm and crusty, the fillings fresh and flavorful. But Mia couldn't concentrate on the taste for long. She was riveted by the idea of a young female apprentice, a scientist by nature, who might have changed the lives of the Parissi heir and a budding composer. She wanted to hear more.

"Verga was a world-class composer and violinist," Leo said.

"And he started out as an apprentice on the island. Not too long ago he penned an extraordinary memoir that included a brief section about his time at the castle. There's actually an English copy of it in the hotel's conservatory—I can show it to you if you'd like. Verga completed and performed his most famous work all over Europe a few years ago. And in his memoir, he wrote that he'd begun composing it decades earlier, when he was at the castle, and had been inspired by someone he met there. He dedicated the book to her. He called the piece 'For Pippa.'"

Mia gasped. Pippa! She remembered it immediately. That was the other name the Italian lawyer had mentioned in his letter. Annalisa and Pippa.

"Pippa," Mia said, trying to keep her tone even. "What does that mean?"

"Evidently it was the nickname of the person who inspired him. Some kind of pet name, maybe something her family called her. But you see, the important point here is that Annalisa was in the audience the same night as Patricio was. The night that Verga performed this piece of music for the very first time."

"What do you make of that?" she asked. "Do you think Annalisa and Pippa are the same person? But why would Annalisa being there make Patricio want to attend?"

"Again, I don't know," Leo answered, finishing the last bite of one of the sandwiches on his plate and wiping his hands on his napkin. "But that's what I do—I look for patterns, things that happen concurrently. And Annalisa becoming Patricio's apprentice, going to the concert the same night Patricio did... it makes me wonder."

"Did anyone ever ask Verga who Pippa was?"

"Of course. And he toyed with his interviewers. Sometimes he said Pippa wasn't a person at all. That he'd simply been referring to the moon."

"But you don't believe it," Mia said, predicting from his tone that the answer would be no.

Leo raised his palms in response. "It's crystal clear," he said. "His music is full of passion. Love and heartbreak and yearning. It wasn't about the moon. Here, I can get it on my phone. Listen."

He opened his phone, tapped a few buttons, and then held it up. "The Viennese Orchestra," he said. "This was the last time it was played."

She listened. The sound quality wasn't great, but Leo was right—it was a warm, emotional piece, full of long notes and haunting minor-key chords. It built to a crescendo and then tapered off to a quiet longing. It was poignant and beautiful. She didn't know if she'd ever be able to get the melody out of her head.

"I believe that Pippa was a woman," Leo said firmly. "Someone he loved. Someone he met at the castle and feared would break his heart. The music—it doesn't end with happiness, does it? It ends with a question. See?" He pushed the line back on his phone to play the last several notes again. "See? It's hopeful, but it's not certain."

He was right. The ending didn't sound like an ending. It sounded like there should be more. The melody was left slightly hanging so the listener didn't know what would come next.

"But why wouldn't he admit he wrote it for someone he loved?" she asked.

"Who knows? People have many reasons to lie. Surely you have learned that yourself."

She looked down at the napkin on her lap, hoping he didn't notice her face turning red. Or that he'd think it was caused by the sun.

"We do know that Verga went on to have a happy marriage that lasted more than fifty years," Leo said. "He was lucky enough to be away from Parissi Island when the Nazis arrived.

He settled in Switzerland, married, and had six children and fourteen grandchildren. And two great-grandchildren. Maybe that's why he never admitted to loving Pippa. Can you imagine telling your spouse, after fifty years of marriage, that you loved someone else? And that it was this other person who inspired the most beautiful, breathtaking work of your life?"

Mia considered the question, knowing that she couldn't possibly imagine what Verga felt about his inspiration and his music. She'd never been creative like that. She didn't know what it was to be truly inspired by love.

"But still, can't someone talk to him again?" she asked. "Now that you have this list with Annalisa's name? Can't someone ask him if Pippa was Annalisa?"

He shook his head. "He died last year, shortly after his wife. There was lots of speculation about why he went back to perform something he'd composed so long ago. Maybe he knew he was dying. And he wanted this piece of music remembered. Or... I know this sounds morbid, but maybe with his wife gone, he felt free to return to his memories of the woman he had loved before. And the truth is, from what I've learned during these last few months, I have a sense, a strong feeling that Annalisa was Pippa—that Pippa was Annalisa's nickname. It adds up.

"So you see, this list with Annalisa's name means a lot," he continued. "We know she was here, she was real, and the year she arrived. And we can maybe start to imagine where she came from, and if she was able to escape as Verga did. Because there's one thing we haven't even mentioned yet. As Patricio's apprentice, she would have had access to the *schianto*.

"And on a personal note, this is the first time I've found the name of someone who would have known my grandfather," he added, his eyes wide and hopeful. "If even one of these sisters escaped—Giulia or Annalisa, or the third one whose name I don't remember—if one of them is still alive or there are descendants, who knows what more I can learn?" He smiled. "Would you like to see my grandfather's work?"

"Very much," she said, and he waved to the server, indicating he'd settle the check later, and then led her to the lobby. There was an art book on the table, and he flipped through the catalog until he came to a photo. "This is my favorite, a sketch," he said. "He sent the original to my grandmother. It was based on her wedding gown, sewn by hand here on the island..."

He turned the page in her direction and she recoiled as she drew in a sharp breath. There was no mistaking it.

It was the wedding dress she'd found in the garment bag in her grandmother's closet.

NINETEEN

1943

August

The morning after she'd learned that her father was getting sicker, Annalisa went up to the tower as usual. Patricio got her to work with the botanicals in his collection, cleaning leaves and snapping stems as he continued to polish the mallet and the deep bowl. After a few minutes, he walked over to survey her work.

"Nicely done," he said. "Do a bit more, and then you can return to your books."

She looked up at him from her chair, hoping to catch his attention before he returned to his work. "Professor Parissi?" she said.

"Mmm?" He went back to his table and picked up the mallet, looking at her over his glasses.

"Are we getting closer?" she asked, walking over to him.

"You can't rush science, child," he said, directing his eyes downward at his work. "Didn't I tell you not to ask silly questions?"

"But what if there was someone who really needed this cure?" she said. "Someone you cared about deeply?"

He raised his eyes. "Is there someone you have in mind?"

"Well... yes..."

She saw him soften, looking so much like her mother. "Someone you're close to?"

"Very close."

"Someone who's ill?"

She nodded.

"I'm sorry," he said. "I thought you understood. Science isn't for the individual. Science is for the whole."

"I know but—"

"Science isn't personal. You should know that."

"I do, but—"

"I'm sorry," he repeated. "I can't help your family."

"It's not just my family," she said.

"What was that?" he asked, his focus on his work.

"I said it's not just *my* family," she repeated, louder. "It's your family. *Our* family."

He let go of the mallet. "*Our* family?" he asked, sounding riled. "What are you getting at? What does this have to do with me?"

"It has to do with my mother."

"What about your mother—and no! Enough! Enough of these riddles—"

"Please listen!" she cried out. "It's not riddles! My mother was your sister. And the person who's dying is my father. Your sister's husband." She took a deep breath, not sure what to expect next. "I'm your niece. Olivia's daughter."

The silence that followed seemed endless, and she clasped her hands together, ran her tongue along the inside of her cheek, moved her toes around in her shoes, not knowing what to do with herself. Patricio stared at her, and his expression was uninterpretable. He took off his glasses and stood, and she noticed most how his eyes sagged, the pouches underneath them forming long, baggy loops, as he leaned onto the desk. She saw him open his mouth and then close it again.

"You're *what?*" he asked, his voice almost a growl. She didn't know what to do because she didn't know what he would do next. He could do anything—scream, go to hit her, or storm out of the room. That's how little she knew him. And what would she do if he left? Would she stay there and wait? Should she continue the research? She froze, her eyes glued to his.

Then, after a few terrifying moments, his shoulders softened and his gaze lowered, and she knew it was going to be okay.

"You're... Olivia's daughter?" he asked, his voice hoarse.

She nodded, even though he was looking down so she wouldn't see. "There are three of us. I'm the oldest. My sisters are here too."

"Olivia has three daughters... three grown daughters?"

"Yes. Well, not quite grown. I'm eighteen. Giulia is seventeen. Emilia just turned fifteen."

"And your mother... did she send you here?"

She tilted her head, hoping the truth wouldn't be too painful. "My mother died. Years ago. I'm sorry."

"Olivia... is dead," he repeated. He walked to the window, put his hands in his trouser pockets, facing the Mediterranean. Then he looked at her over his shoulder. "How did it happen?"

"She died giving birth. To a fourth sister. There was a complication. Neither one of them made it."

"Didn't she have a doctor?" he shouted. "Couldn't they do anything?"

"I don't know," she said. "I was only six." She remembered going to the neighbor's home for the night and coming home the next morning to find out that her mother and the baby were gone. Her father had sat by the window, barely moving. A distant aunt from his side of the family stayed for a few months to help out, and then when she had to leave, another relative took over.

Annalisa had almost no recollection of those early months. She only remembered her father's intense grief, how he grieved for weeks. How she tried not to cry because she worried it would somehow cause him to leave, too. Eventually he pulled himself together and began working again. Still, there was always a sadness about him, a frailty that showed even before his heart started weakening. Annalisa remembered deciding at some point that she didn't trust marriage. Not if this could be the outcome. Not if it killed one person and left the other reduced to a shell.

"Olivia... is dead," Patricio repeated and looked back out the window, his back to her. "And now you're here for your father? You want me to save the man who destroyed everything?"

"It's not his fault," Annalisa said. "He loved her."

"Did she love him? As much as she told us she did?"

"Of course. She gave up everything for him."

"She told you this?"

"I saw it. I was young, but I remember. She loved working in the shop with my father. They held hands all the time. She loved my father's hands, because of the work they did. Even with all the needle pricks and calluses. She would tell me that was a sign of love. When you were happy just holding some-one's hand.

"Professor Parissi... Uncle," she continued, the memory of her parents emboldening her. "I loved my mother, and I love my father, and don't want him to die. I want him to get well so I can take him away, somewhere safe. People might say it was foolish, the way we snuck over here so I could meet you and make you like me. And maybe it was foolish, too, when my mother left her family. But she did. And now I'm here."

He lowered his chin and shook his head. "I heard her fighting with my father in the study," he said. "He called your father awful names. He told her he'd cut her off completely if she went ahead with her insanity. But I knew it wasn't insanity. I knew your father, I'd met him. He was a good man."

He paused. "I didn't even try to help her. I was so scared. My father called me weak all the time. I could have done something, but I didn't. I wanted to prove to my father that I wasn't what he thought."

"She didn't blame you."

He looked at her skeptically. "You know this for a fact?"

She nodded. "She told me she had a brother she cared about deeply."

"She screamed at me that night. She called me a coward. She didn't even say goodbye."

"She forgave you. She had good memories of you. She remembered walking on the shore here and picking up shells and rocks. She remembered how you examined the rocks and you wondered what was deep inside. She said she would ask you about the sun and the rain and the clouds. She said you were the most brilliant person she knew.

"She didn't think you were a coward," she added. "The coward was her father. Your father."

He went back to the window. "I tried to find her after my father died," he said. "But I didn't know where they ended up."

"They settled in a small village not too far from Rome," she told him. "We had a very happy life. I remember friends and parties and lots of wonderful times. She was happy, I promise you. Her only regret was losing her big brother."

He walked back to his table and eased himself into his chair. "And your father... he's sick now?" he asked.

"He's very weak. He can barely walk."

"And he wants my help?"

"No," she said. "He doesn't know we're here, my sisters and me. He would be mad if he knew. He blames you and your family for my mother's death. Same as you blamed him."

"But you came anyway."

"Because... because you were her brother. And *we* need you. Isn't it possible that we can get along now?"

He chuckled softly. "You remind me of her. So open, so inquisitive. You don't take no for an answer."

She smiled. "You remind me of her, too. I noticed it the first time I saw you. Sometimes it made it hard to concentrate...

"She would want you to help my father," she said. "She would see this as a way for everything to be okay again."

He put his elbow on the table and rubbed his forehead. She watched him staring down at the table for a few moments. When he looked back up, his eyes were red and his cheeks ruddy. Then his thin lips spread in a gentle smile, and she thought she could see the person her mother had seen when she was a little girl.

"I'm glad you came, Annalisa," he said. "I'm glad you're here. And I know she'd want me to do what you ask. So, let's get the *schianto* finished. And then let's see what else we can accomplish together. I will make it up to her. I will make you a scientist, the scientist she could have been if she had stayed. And that will be my gift to her. That will be her legacy."

He held out his arms, and without any hesitation at all she ran into them and hugged him. And it felt for a moment as if she had her mother back. She knew her mother would be proud that she'd engineered a reunion of their broken family, uniting the head and the heart—the head of her uncle, the heart of her mother.

And soon her father would be cured.

From that point on, Patricio was newly energized, as though he were a teenager again. Annalisa couldn't believe the change in him. She realized he'd been beating himself up for years over the division in his family, the loss of his sister, the terror he'd felt of her father; and now, with her in his life, he saw the chance to make things right.

That evening, she brought her sisters into the kitchen, which was always empty at this time of day, to explain that Patricio—the head of the whole castle, the scientist she'd come to see to find their father a cure—was none other than their uncle. At first they couldn't quite grasp the news, and had a million questions: How did she find out about him? How did he respond when she told him who she was? What was Papa going to think? And what would happen now? She started to explain, but it was Signora Russo who provided the answer to the last question. She showed up while Annalisa was talking to tell them that their things had been moved out of the servants' quarters and into a guest suite with adjoining bedrooms of their own.

None of them had ever seen such luxury before. The feather beds and feather pillows and large closets and beautiful mahogany furniture. They even had their own glorious bathroom, with a big marble tub and plenty of thick, soft towels.

By the time they had moved in and set up their rooms, it was after eleven and the three of them were exhausted. Annalisa realized she had forgotten to check behind the stone on the patio to see when Aldo would be waiting for her. She felt bad that she'd missed their meeting. He'd warned her that their friendship would end as soon as Patricio learned her identity, but she hadn't believed him, and she didn't believe him still. She would apologize to him as soon as she could for failing to show up. And he would understand. And he would be happy for all that had happened.

In the days that followed, Patricio met Giulia and Emilia, and instructed the three girls to call him "Uncle." He invited them to have their meals in the main dining room, and even made an appearance in there himself, so he could introduce them to all the guests. When he heard that Emilia liked preparing food, he put her in charge of proposing menus and helping to manage the cooking staff; and when he heard that Giulia loved to sew, he introduced her to the painter Savio Peralta, who made her his apprentice and put her to work helping to create all the dresses he'd designed, including an exquisite and elaborate wedding dress.

His enthusiasm for change became boundless, as did his energy. He instructed Signora Russo to begin a complete revamping of the tower, taking down the heavy drapes and replacing them with sheer curtains that let in the sun. He requested that all worn carpets be removed and replaced with area rugs in colors that mirrored the aqua of the sea and the blue of the sky. He began hand-delivering gifts—books and trinkets— to staff members he wanted to reward. He even began adding the orange triangles to Signora Russo's notebook himself.

And in the tower, Annalisa and Patricio applied themselves even harder to completing the *schianto*. It wasn't just theoretical or scientific anymore; now there were real consequences, a real person who could benefit from their work. And with the knowledge that this person was the father of his nieces, Patricio appeared even more devoted to his work than before. He and Annalisa worked so long into the night that sometimes Annalisa fell asleep on top of her botanicals books, waking up with a page stuck to her cheek. She'd shake herself alert and get back to her research, recording the plant names and their properties:

Psyllium: Helps with digestion, may strengthen the heart muscle

Rosemary: Reduces inflammation, may treat infections

Meanwhile, in his lab, Patricio worked on the mallet's hinge, aiming for the optimum tension to crush the mix of minerals and botanicals into a powder that would dissolve in water to make for a drinkable, effective brew.

The one thing that was absent from Annalisa's life was Aldo. The days sped by, and then a week had passed, then two. She never seemed to have a moment to go downstairs and through the kitchen to check behind the loose stone for a note. She wished she had more time for him, and she hoped he knew how much she thought of him, how she wished he could run upstairs to see her in her guest room, the way he'd come to her in the staff quarters on her first night in the castle. She hoped he'd learned from Signora Russo how hard she and Patricio were working to perfect the cure for her father, and she hoped, too, that he understood why things had changed. And most of all, she hoped he still wanted to be her friend. She missed him— his smile and his laugh, and how interesting he was to her. She missed the way he listened to her and made her feel important, and she missed hearing his thoughts about music, the castle's guests, and the future.

One day when she couldn't bear not knowing how he was, she went to the kitchen to talk to Signora Russo.

"Have you seen Aldo?" she asked, trying to sound like her interest was official.

Signora Russo smiled, clearly aware of the true nature of Annalisa's interest. "Not today. Not recently. He's been busy. But the last time I spoke with him, he had news. Didn't you hear?"

Annalisa shook her head.

"He's working on his music again," she said. "Even though he'd stopped for so long. He has a whole new determination. He even asked to present his work at a concert next Thursday night. One week from today. We hear him rehearsing every evening." She raised her eyebrows. "I think he's doing it for you, Annalisa. I think he wants you to admire him, just as everyone around here admires you."

Annalisa broke into a smile, feeling her chest tingle as the tension gave way. What a relief, what fabulous news, that he was okay and still thinking of her! "I'm so thrilled to hear this," she said. "I never see him anymore, so I had no way of knowing. Can you tell him something the next time you talk to him?"

"Of course."

"Can you tell him that I will be at the concert to hear his music? And that I can't wait, and that I am so happy for him?"

"I will. I know he will love to hear that."

Annalisa ran back upstairs to work, feeling so much better than she'd felt on her way down. It was already coming on three weeks since she'd arrived at the castle, and she'd given herself a month to return to her father. She'd soon be heading home with his cure.

And she was happy, too, that she'd be here for Aldo's performance. She wouldn't have wanted to miss it for the world.

TWENTY

2018

Wednesday

"I'm tired and so confused," Mia sighed into the phone. "I mean, she had sisters, that's what it looks like now. And she came to this island with them, and she apprenticed with this very important man. But she never wanted me to know any of it until she was gone. Why would she do that?"

"I don't know," Ryan said. "But she was always a little weird, Mia. You never wanted to see it because she was all you had growing up. But everyone else saw it, and you need to face it, too. She wasn't that great a person."

"Wait... she wasn't *what?*" Mia said.

She could hardly believe what she was hearing. She had come straight to her room after seeing the wedding gown sketch downstairs, mumbling something to Leo about a headache, because she needed to think about what she'd learned and what it all meant. Sitting on the carpet in her hotel room, her legs outstretched and her back against the mattress, she'd been glad that Ryan had woken up early to call her. She thought he could help her process what she'd seen, and what she'd learned. She hoped he would make her feel safe, as he usually did. That he would help her believe that no matter what happened next, it would all be okay. The last thing she'd expected was for him to start criticizing Lucy. And more harshly than he ever had before.

"What are you talking about?" she went on, her back stiffening. "What does that have to do with anything? She just died, and I'm still dealing with that, as well as all the things that don't make sense now. Why are you trying to make me feel worse?"

"I'm not trying to make you feel worse!" Ryan's voice grew louder and his tone became more aggressive, as it always did when he felt defensive. "She didn't just die, Mia, she died a month ago. And it's time you faced who she was. It's time you called a spade a spade."

Mia stood and walked across the room, too outraged to sit. "You couldn't be more wrong!" she exclaimed. "She wasn't a bad person, Ryan. She wasn't, no matter what you think—"

"I didn't say she was a bad person. But she wasn't the saint you always made her out to be. She wasn't very likeable. She wasn't even normal."

"Normal? What's that supposed to mean?"

"It's supposed to mean that she never could be what you wanted her to be, what you pretended she was. It doesn't strike me as so unbelievable, frankly, that she would steal the stupid thing. Look, I get it. You grew up wanting to be like your friends, and wanting her to be like your friends' mothers. Every kid wants that. So you convinced yourself she was just a tiny bit quirky and unemotional, but in an endearing way because she was a scientist at her core. But she was never that person. You invented that person. She doesn't exist. You needed her to be—"

"Stop! Just stop!" Mia shouted, pressing her palm against the air. "You think you have me all figured out? Well, you don't, okay? Don't tell me who I was and what I wanted as a kid. How do you know what I needed?"

"I'm trying to tell you what you're not seeing yourself—"

"I never asked you to interpret my childhood for me," Mia cried, her voice trembling with anger. "I asked you—no, I *expected* you to comfort me and embrace what I'm doing here and tell me that you understand it's important. If for no other reason than because I'm telling you it is. Can't we agree that everything that came before we arrived in the world deserves to be explored and remembered—and maybe even honored, if it's deserving of that? Don't talk about my grandmother the way you did just now! She went through things—she and the people she lived with here—they went through horrors you can't even imagine. Your life is easy compared to theirs. Your deals and your green lights and your meetings and dinners are *nothing* compared to my so-called abnormal grandmother's life!"

"What has gotten into you, Mia?" Ryan said. "You're like a whole different person. Ever since that night you spent last week in your grandmother's house—"

"And let me tell you something else about my grandmother," Mia interrupted. "I never said she was a saint. I never called her personality endearing. But she loved me, and she gave me everything she could. She stood by me and all my dreams. She was so proud of every step I took to move forward, my job and my plans—"

"So why aren't you one?" he said smugly.

"Why aren't I one what?"

"Why aren't you a scientist yet?" he said. "Why are you still only an assistant? You've been talking forever about running your own lab someday, and it's getting old. Mia, face it. You took this career path because you were desperate for a crumb of approval from her—"

"That is not true," she shouted, furious at this unfounded, unfair depiction of Lucy.

"Then why haven't you gone back to school to get your PhD already?"

"Because it takes money to quit your job so you can go back to school full-time!" she said. "Not everyone grew up with a family that could bankroll their education like they were buying a cup of coffee. My grandmother worked as a proofreader after my grandfather died so she could make some money and still be home to raise me. Do you know how hard it was for her?"

"It was hard because she didn't want to do it," he said. "That was so clear. She wasn't meant to raise a kid, let alone a grandkid, and you spent your whole life trying to please her because you were scared that if you crossed her, she'd abandon you and you'd have no one. Mia, it's time to end this craziness. She's gone, okay? Give Milt the bowl thing, give the wedding gown in the closet to whoever showed you this sketch, sell the damn house, and let's move on with what's best for our future."

"You mean what's best for *your* future, right?"

"I mean, what's best for both of us. Look, the meetings out here weren't just good, they were great. They showed me I can leave the firm and go out on my own. Six, eight months from now, tops. And I need you by my side to start things up. She's gone, so don't let her haunt you with all she demanded of you. It's over now. You owe her nothing!"

Mia stood by the bed, resisting the urge to slam the phone onto the nightstand, as that wouldn't do her any good. She needed the phone because there was something she had to say. And she wanted Ryan to hear her loud and clear.

"Now you listen to me," she said, her voice low but seething with fury. She couldn't tell for sure because she wasn't near a mirror, but she could feel her lips tense and her eyes narrow. It was the very expression Erica had described that night when they'd gone to Caryn's for dinner, the expression she said she'd seen in Lucy's face as well. There was no doubt about it. She was her grandmother's granddaughter through and through.

"You have *no idea* what you're talking about," she told him. "You are so far off base—what you said, and the ridiculous idea that I would somehow appreciate hearing it. You don't know anything about my grandmother, no matter how smart you think you are. And what's even worse is that after all this time together, you don't know me either. I didn't change, Ryan, from the person I was before I slept at my grandmother's house last week. I'm finally finding my own voice. This is me, Ryan, whether you like it or not. This is who I am!"

She hung up the phone, then flung it on the bed as she let out a loud "*Ahhh!*" She wanted to let go of all the tension that was making her feel as though her chest were in a vise. She walked onto the balcony and looked out at the castle. How had things come to this? Hadn't she and Ryan spent so much time together, shared the same experiences, viewed the same situations, taken in the same data, so to speak? How could he possibly say that her dream of earning her PhD was nothing more than some wild attempt to win Lucy's affection?

Coming back into the room, she sat on the love seat and drew her knees up to her chin. She remembered the night she'd found her grandmother outside crying about her father. She'd gone upstairs afterward to put herself to bed, shivering under the covers even though the evening was warm, staying awake for as long as she could. She'd hoped to hear Lucy's footsteps on the stairs, to see the glow from Lucy's bedroom lamp appear under her doorway, to sense activity in the bathroom as Lucy washed her face and brushed her teeth. But she fell asleep before any of that happened. The next morning, she'd run downstairs, where she'd spied Lucy at the stove cooking oatmeal.

"What's wrong? Why is your face all red?" Lucy had asked. "Are you sick?"

"I'm... fi-fine," Mia had stammered.

"Was your room too warm last night?"

"I don't think so."

"Then splash some cold water on your face and get dressed for school. Breakfast is almost on the table."

Mia had nodded and climbed back upstairs, then paused outside the bathroom. She'd leaned against the wall and closed her eyes, breathing deeply as she pressed her fingertips to her chest to feel the gradual slowing of her heartbeat. She'd been so worried the night before that Lucy would never come upstairs. That the memory of her father's birthday had been the last straw. That she'd finally decided she couldn't live here anymore.

Thinking about that night, Mia supposed it would be easy for someone like Ryan to conclude that she was terrified of being abandoned and willing to do anything to convince Lucy to stay. But Ryan's theory was too simple. Mia hadn't decided to become a scientist because she was scared about Lucy; no, it was because she *loved* her. She'd felt from that night on that she'd do anything to mend what was broken in her grandmother. To heal all the sadness Lucy had suffered, sadness that seemed to have started with her father's diseased heart. Even so young, Mia had understood that pain like the kind Lucy felt, pain that spanned generations, could turn a person into someone they were never meant to be. And Mia knew that she needed to attack that pain—to uncover its mysterious source and render it powerless. That was why she wanted to be a scientist. To get to the bottom of the suffering she'd seen right there in her own home, day after day. Pain that even love—the love she had for Lucy—couldn't fix.

Of course, Ryan didn't see any of this. He wasn't built to read between the lines. She remembered a time last spring when one of his colleagues had secretly negotiated a great price on a parcel of residential properties in Manhattan. Ryan had been apoplectic. And not because he was jealous of the guy or wished he'd been part of the deal; no, he'd just wanted to be in the know. She thought now of the instructions he'd given her about the house before she left for Italy: get timers for the lamps; install cameras and motion detectors; make sure the gardener clears the leaves. They weren't bad suggestions, of course. But his instincts were always to throw light on everything. Unlike Lucy, he didn't trust the darkness. He didn't know that sometimes the most important answers were hidden away, in crevices or corners, in old art books, in attics or storage closets or castles left to rot long ago.

Or in the deepest recesses of a person's heart.

Mia stayed sitting on the chair for a long time. She didn't know how long until she went to retrieve her phone and saw that it was five o'clock, more than an hour since she'd answered Ryan's call.

Feeling her skin itch from all the dust in the castle, she went to take a shower. Peeling off her leggings and tee shirt in the bathroom, she was astonished at the layer of dirt clinging to the garments. It had come from the walls and floors and ceilings of the castle when she'd been there with Leo that morning. And from the shoreline, the stairway, the rocks. Structures that had been there for decades, if not centuries, and elements of nature that had been there for even longer. She couldn't help but wonder which of the dust and dirt particles on her now had maybe touched her grandmother's shoes or grazed her grandmother's skin. And which had touched Giulia's skin or Emilia's skin. Or Patricio's, Aldo's or Leo's grandfather's skin. Who were those people—those poor, innocent people, who should have had so many creative, productive, loving years ahead of them? She ran her fingertips along her arm before getting into the shower. How she wished she could have known them, and could have absorbed and embraced their heat and light.

In the shower, she lifted her chin, letting the cool water stream down her face. A part of her wished she hadn't answered Ryan's call when she got back to her room. Because she didn't know how they could possibly move past this point. And it was hard to face that when she was all alone, so far from home. She'd come to rely on him because, up until now, he'd seemed always to know how to make her feel grounded. Especially in the last few months with her grandmother getting worse and worse news from the doctor. It had been a relief to be with someone who took everything in stride.

Ryan had grown up in a big house in Michigan, and his parents were lovely—she'd met them once when they came to visit. They had three boys, Ryan the middle one, and a huge family on both sides. That evening over dinner, they'd talked with Ryan endlessly about aunts and uncles taking bucket-list trips, cousins having babies, grandparents already making plans to host Christmas. And they were smart, too, talking about the most esoteric accounting matters. "So what did you decide to do with that IRA?" his mother had asked Ryan. "You didn't keep it to give away, did you?" And they'd all laughed. She'd had no idea why.

But she had liked them a lot. Especially his mother. She'd looked so stylish, in a pair of tan, wide-legged pants and a sleeveless black top. And so self-assured. And so present. That's what she'd been struck by most—a mom who was *there*. Unlike her own mom. She remembered feeling almost paralyzed when she was growing up, not knowing how to respond when friends asked about why she lived with her grandmother and then expressed sympathy when she said her parents had been killed in a car crash. She felt foolish, having no details to share, but her grandmother had no interest in discussing the matter. Sometimes she'd try a roundabout way to approach the subject, hoping that would get her grandmother to talk.

"I wish I had a mom like Erica's mom," she'd said one Saturday, after coming home from a sleepover party at Erica's house for her twelfth birthday. "Who's pretty and hugs and tickles her."

She'd worried for a moment that her grandmother might be

insulted by what she'd said, but Lucy didn't react with any emotion. "Wishes are not the best use of your time," she responded as she put Mia's lunch on the kitchen table.

"But it's still how I feel," Mia said, settling into her chair. "I can't help how I feel."

"No, you can't, that's true. But feelings cause us to make bad choices. Feelings need to be controlled and managed."

"Is love a bad choice? Is my loving you a bad choice? Or you loving me?"

"Love is not a choice," Lucy had said. "It's sad, it ends. If I could, I would choose not to love. But I love you despite anything else, Mia. It's the one thing I can't explain. Humans are flawed. Humans love."

That night in her bed, Mia took comfort in her grandmother's words. *I love you despite anything else.* But later, as a teenager, she would feel the anger simmering inside when that conversation came to mind. *If I could, I would choose not to love.* What kind of a messed-up message was that to give a kid? What would prompt a grandmother to say something like that?

Coming out of the shower, she put on a pair of jeans and a tee shirt, and as she towel-dried her hair, her eyes landed on Leo's sun hat, now hanging from a knob on the dresser. Was her grandmother really the Annalisa on the faded list Leo had held in his hands? But then why had she never mentioned having any sisters? Maybe the list was wrong, the brackets intended to surround another set of siblings. Then how could Lucy have ended up with the wedding gown that the girl named Giulia had sewn? Could Giulia actually have been her grandmother's sister, her own great-aunt?

And what of the concert, Aldo's concert, that both Patricio and Annalisa attended? Could her grandmother have been called by the nickname Pippa? Could she have inspired the musician's masterpiece? Mia sat on the bed, the wet towel around her shoulders. Her grandmother had never been a romantic person. And yet there had been a hint of that spark, that magic, just once, Mia suddenly remembered. It was August, two months ago, and she and her grandmother had taken the ferry across the sound for their yearly trip to Shelter Island. They'd sat on beach chairs, Lucy with a scarf around her neck, staring at the rising moon as it came into view. At one point, Lucy mumbled something in a slow, rhythmic tone. It sounded like Italian, and Mia was surprised. She'd never heard her grandmother speak Italian before.

"What did you say?" she'd said.

Her grandmother spoke, this time in English, such a beautiful sentence that Mia asked her to repeat it twice, so she could memorize it word for word. "You are too far to hold, too close to resist, too strong, but not too strong to have to turn away," she said. "I long for you, I bow to you, I embrace you from a distance, my star, my muse, my words, my music."

"What is that? A poem?"

Lucy shook her head. "Just the words of a friend."

"What friend?" She'd never heard her grandmother speak about friends either.

"It doesn't matter," Lucy said. "It was all so far away. It was never going to be. He was talking about the moon. Not me."

"What does that mean?" Mia had said.

"What does what mean, dear?" Lucy suddenly seemed to have no idea what Mia was talking about. Even though she'd just uttered the words.

Later, Lucy had insisted they go into town for dessert. They used the flashlight on Mia's phone to carefully make their way from the sand to their car in the parking lot, and then found a small Italian place that was still open. They'd sat at a small table on the patio, admiring the boats moored at the dock. Lucy had ordered limoncello for both of them, and she'd laughed and flirted with the handsome young server who brought their drinks. It was as if something had changed for her grandmother that evening at the beach, Mia had thought. Something that had eased her mind and given her a kind of freedom Mia had never seen before.

It was the last evening she'd ever spent with her grandmother.

Thinking of that conversation now, Mia went back to the question she'd asked Ryan at the beginning of their disastrous phone call. Why had Lucy hidden so much? It wasn't because she was unfeeling, as Ryan had argued. No, she loved enormously. But everything she did, everything she said, was borne of great hurt and pain and loss. Lucy had kept secrets, Mia suspected, because she couldn't bear to expose the truth. Maybe she was scared to face her demons.

Still, whatever the reason, Mia thought as she looked out the window toward the castle, she had learned her grandmother's lessons very well. Because she kept secrets, too. It came naturally to her when it seemed necessary.

She had kept the truth about Erica's passport from Ryan; she hadn't wanted to hear his increased urgings to cancel the trip, which no doubt would have resulted. She had kept the truth about the storage unit from Milt; she had rationalized that she wanted to protect him, but she knew she also didn't want him to believe for one moment that her grandmother was guilty of the accusations against her; she had kept the truth about the *schianto* and the wedding gown from Leo; she had worried that he wouldn't help her with her own search if she gave up too much too soon.

And there was more, a fact she now confronted. She had even lied for years to her best friend, Erica, who believed that Mia's parents had been killed in a car crash. Mia had made that up when the two girls met in school in third grade. Because she was scared Erica wouldn't like her if she had said her parents had abandoned her, first her father and then her mother, when she was just a baby. A car crash had sounded "normal." It wasn't hard to sound convincing. It wasn't a hard story to stick to. She even all but convinced herself of the explanation. After all, it could have been a car crash; that was as likely as any other explanation, right?

But in the end, she thought, Lucy had decided to open up. She must have regretted keeping secrets. She must have decided it was better to own her own story, even if she couldn't face doing it while she was still alive.

Mia wanted to own her own story, too. But the difference was, she wanted to do it now.

Because she couldn't let Ryan control her story any longer. The illusion of safety he offered was not worth the price. She'd shown a drop of initiative, of individuality, when she'd stayed at the Soundport house by herself, and a bigger drop—a dollop— when she'd decided to go to Italy all to protect her grandmother's good name.

How much more individuality would she show as the rest of her week here in Italy unfolded? A cup? A vat? An amount too big to measure?

She didn't know. But what she knew for sure was that the answer was up to her, and her alone.

TWENTY-ONE

2018

Wednesday

Too wound up after her call with Ryan to stay in her room, Mia went back downstairs to the lobby.

It was six o'clock, and she hoped Leo was still in the building, maybe working behind the reception desk or chatting with guests. She thought he might now know when the excavation would be done on the castle and they could get back over there —maybe even today, while the sky was still light and the ferry still running. But when she reached the first floor, he was nowhere around. Outside she could hear the van starting up, and thought about going down to the shore to get a coffee. Maybe that's where Leo was. She went to the front steps, and saw the van full of passengers, with Leo standing inside near the driver, his back to the windshield. That's when she remembered that he'd told her he was going to be busy this evening, leading the tour group on a boat trip around the scattered islands and then to the mainland for a banquet.

She started to wave, as being with the group and Leo sounded like a better way to spend the evening than staying here all alone. But the van was on its way down the hill by then, and nobody saw her. She dropped her arm. She didn't know what Leo's schedule was, or when he'd be returning to the castle. The only thing she knew was that he would be gone overnight. The soonest she could speak to him and tell him the truth about who Annalisa and Giulia were, and the soonest she could hope to get back to Parissi Island, was tomorrow.

She went back into the hotel and sat down in the lobby, watching the breeze from the open doors make the sheer white curtains on the nearby windows flutter and dance. At least now, without any distractions, she could think about all she'd discovered today. Like the fact that her grandmother, assuming she really was Annalisa, had arrived at the castle in August of 1943, part of the last group of workers to leave the mainland for Parissi Island. That would have made her only eighteen years old. What would have driven her to travel to the castle—and with two sisters in tow? Where did she come from and what could have made her want to leave? Mia didn't know where in Italy her grandmother was originally from. How long was the journey? What had her home life been like, her family? Mia didn't even know if Lucy's parents—her great-grandparents—were alive in 1943. She didn't know anything about them. The only thing she knew was the snippet Lucy had revealed that night on the patio: that she'd adored her father, and that he had died of heart disease.

So maybe it made sense that she'd want to meet Patricio. But had she come here *after* her father had died, or had she come here while he was still alive? Had she known about Patricio's medical device, or had she learned about it once she got here? Did she believe in the logic underlying his far-fetched invention? And even if she knew about Patricio and his project, how did such an important man come to know about her, a young kitchen worker? Why did he pick her as an apprentice when there were apparently dozens of workers, maybe more, at the castle? Why had he even taken an apprentice, when he kept to himself so much that people called him a recluse? Was there a connection between her arrival and his decision to hear Aldo Verga's performance?

What was the thread, the connective tissue, between Patricio Parissi and her grandmother? And how had that led to her possessing his *schianto* and choosing to hide it away?

Mia rose and walked across the lobby to look out at the sea. What was almost more mystifying was the revelation about the two sisters. Even if Mia could concede that maybe Lucy had a good reason for hiding the *schianto*, what on earth was the reason she'd denied the existence of Giulia and Emilia—the very sisters her daughter and granddaughter were named for? Mia and her grandmother had always been so alone—a tiny, closed circle—with caring people like Milt and Erica on the outskirts. Yes, Lucy had shut herself off from so many other people with whom she'd had some familial ties, such as Mia's grandfather's family and Mia's father's family. But those weren't blood relations—not to Lucy. Her sisters were in a whole other category. Where were those sisters now? It was awful to think about, but had they been murdered in the castle? Or had they escaped, as Lucy had? Was it possible that Mia had cousins somewhere? How had her grandmother never even wanted to discuss, and possibly investigate, that possibility?

Her phone rang just then, and a part of her wished it would be Leo. She wanted to keep talking with him about his relatives and hers, about what else he could reveal of the workings of the castle. She'd never given him her cell phone number, but she assumed he could easily find it in her hotel reservation. She took out her phone from her bag and saw that it was Erica. They'd planned to talk later, but she knew that Erica must be curious about her trip back to the castle. A chat with her friend was something Mia now realized she could desperately use.

"Hey, how was your morning?" Erica said. "Did you make it back to the island with the tour guy? How was it?"

"Yeah... and I don't know what to think. I had the biggest fight with Ryan on the phone a little while ago. He said horrible things about my grandmother, but I think it was more about me and why I had to come here and what it says about us... and honestly, I don't think I can be with him anymore."

"You're breaking up with him? Mia, what on earth happened? Start from the beginning."

Mia sat on the lobby sofa and described what she'd learned about Parissi, the list, the sisters, the name Annalisa and nickname Pippa, and the wedding dress. "She kept so much from me," she said. "And all it's done is leave me with questions and no answers. She should have told me about all this, instead of leaving me with a whole puzzle and so many missing pieces. So then Ryan calls, and I tell him about everything, and rather than helping me try to understand what she did, he says this was exactly the person she was—cold and strange and not very likeable. And more, things that he must have been thinking about her all along."

"But that's ridiculous. He's wrong... He's done this before, Mia. He says things to help get his own way."

"I know. I know he does. And I knew he never liked my grandmother. But it was hard to hear him say all that. Because she wasn't cold. I think she was just so hurt and so damaged. And someone who claims to love me and to want to spend his life with me—well, he should be able to see all that."

"Of course he should."

"And what I found out today, it's all so much bigger than we expected. You and I read online about the Nazis and the castle, and it was awful, but nothing like what I've learned here. They stormed the island and brutalized people and then killed all of them, or sent them to the camps, people who should have lived on and loved and made things and had families and memories.

And my grandmother was here when it happened. I don't know how or why, but somehow she escaped, and I'm not sure what she saw, but I'm sure that whatever she went through—it destroyed her inside. I think she'd have been a very different person, if not for this."

"Oh, no," Erica said. "Mia, I'm so sorry you're alone and learning all this. I'm so sorry I'm not there."

"I know you are, and it's okay. I can handle it. But what I hate is that I don't see a way to protect her from the accusations. After everything she went through, to still have her remembered as a thief—I can't let that happen. But I'm right back where I started. Leo is convinced that the *schianto* was stolen. And even if I tried to explain her character to him, I don't know why he'd believe me..."

"Is there any good explanation for why she took the *schianto* to New York? This rich guy she apprenticed with. The owner—"

"Patricio—"

"Yeah—is it possible he would have given it to her?"

Mia thought about that possibility, then shook her head. "It doesn't look like it. There was this housekeeper who kept all the records. Detailed records of everything. Including gifts, because he gave out a lot of gifts. And the housekeeper recorded all of them with little triangles in her notebook next to the recipient's name. And there was no triangle next to my grandmother's name. And it wouldn't make sense that he'd give the *schianto* to her or to anyone," she added. "It was his life's work."

Erica paused. "So what are you going to do?" she asked gently.

"The right thing to do is to tell Leo the truth about who I am and what I have in my suitcase," Mia told her. "He deserves to know, and I don't want to keep lying to him. It didn't feel wrong yesterday, but it feels wrong now, when I'm getting to know him and understand why he needs all these pieces to come together.

And how... I don't know, how noble his motives are. He's thinking about Patricio's legacy and the legacy of all the people who once lived here. But how can I expect him to believe that my grandmother didn't steal the thing?"

Mia sighed. "I don't know who to trust or what to do anymore. I can't keep trying to exonerate my grandmother when there's not a shred of evidence in her favor."

Neither one of them said anything for a moment. Then Erica spoke up. "Look, first things first. Get everything Ryan said out of your head, okay? Your grandmother was a loving person, and you have to remember that. She had a good heart, and she felt things so deeply, even if she didn't always show it. I remember—I don't know if I ever told you this, but that time last month I took her to the doctor—when you had to work and couldn't get back here to take her yourself? She was quiet that day. But as we left the doctor's office, she spoke this verse, from a poem. So beautiful. Something about a star... a muse..."

"You are too far to hold, too close to resist, too strong but not too strong to have to turn away," Mia recited. "I long for you, I bow to you, I embrace you from a distance, my star, my muse, my words, my music."

"Oh my God! That's it!" Erica said. "So you know it, too?"

"She recited it on our last trip to Shelter Island," Mia said. "I asked her to repeat it and I memorized it. I'd never heard her say it before."

"So what does it mean?" Erica said.

"I'm not sure. But there's something else. Leo told me about this concert just nights before the Nazis stormed the island. My grandmother was there, and Patricio was there, too. And there was this Italian composer, he became very famous and he died a year ago, and Leo thought it was significant, that my grandmother and Patricio were both there..." She thought again of the lunchtime conversation when Leo had spoken about the musician, Aldo Verga. And the composition he returned to just before he died, the one he played in his only castle concert... and...

"Oh my gosh, I have to go," Mia said hurriedly. "I just thought of something. I'll call you later, Erica. I really have to go—"

She hung up and ran down the hall until she came to the conservatory Leo had mentioned. There was a tall set of bookcases, and she hurried over and scanned the spines. And there it was, a hardcover black book with gold letters: *Pippa: A Memoir by Aldo Verga*.

She pulled it out and opened it and looked at the cover, a photograph of a young man, maybe in his early thirties, wearing a black tuxedo and conducting an orchestra on a large concert stage, the audience appearing out of focus in the background. He was beautiful—dark curls that wrapped around his collar; a baby face, sweet and gently angled; a wide forehead; big, wide eyes. She opened the book to find a smaller picture of him as an old man, weathered and wrinkled but still lovely, with white hair that still curled around his collar.

She leafed through the book, not sure what she was looking for. There was a photo of him taking a bow, another of him as a young, handsome boy and a third of him surrounded by what she assumed was his family—adults, children, babies, and an older, stout woman, no doubt his wife, sitting alongside him.

She flipped a few more pages. The type was dense, and she didn't have the patience to read it. So she turned to the index, where there was a list of podcasts he'd made when he started his world tour for the debut of "For Pippa." Many of them were in foreign languages, but then she spotted one hosted by a local public radio station in Pittsburgh, where his tour had begun. She didn't know what she expected to hear, but that didn't stop her from pulling out her phone and copying the link into her browser. She hoped the interview was in English.

It was.

The interviewer introduced himself and Aldo, and then began his questions. "Tell me, Mr. Verga," he said. "What was the inspiration behind 'For Pippa'?"

"So many influences," Aldo said with a chuckle. His voice was thin but friendly, his accent thick and melodic. "But mostly it was begun back when I was an apprentice on the *Isola della Notte Brillante*, the wonderful artists' residence, as a young boy of eighteen. You see, the sky was so light then and you barely saw the moon, and any stars were so faint. And so the idea of holding onto something that couldn't last was profound. The war was coming. It was so clear. But nobody wanted to face that."

"Oh, yes. The castle. The Parissi dynasty," the interviewer said. "I heard you spent time there."

"I came with my mentor, who died soon after we arrived. I stayed and tried to use his lessons to compose my own work. And I also worked in the boathouse and around the kitchen. It was a wonderful place while it lasted. So much art, so much beauty. So much love."

"And it's about love, your piece, isn't it? Is that why you went back to it so many years later?"

"There were many, many people I cared about on that island," he said. "I went back to it for them. For all of them."

"But for anyone in particular? Was there a woman named Pippa?"

"Mmm," Aldo said, as if hesitating to answer. "As I said, it was for all of them. Signor Parissi. Signora Russo—"

"Yes, Signora Russo. There were rumors that she was a spy for the Allied forces. Did you know that?"

"I learned of that many years later," he said. "I think I suspected it at the time. She would hide lists of supplies she needed in this little space behind a loose rock on the terrace, and I would take them down to the supply boats to ferry to the mainland. I think there were messages hidden in them. She was so brave. Sadly, it was probably because of her that the Nazis were so brutal when they arrived. The truth was, we all thought we were invincible back then. We weren't."

"And how did you escape?"

"A group of us were sent to a nearby island," he said, his voice cracking. "Ostensibly, we were excavating for a new castle, but I think Signora Russo thought those of us who were helping her with the messages would be safer there. So we were gone when the Nazis arrived. At first, we didn't know what was going on. But no boat came back to get us, as we'd expected, so we knew something was wrong. Fortunately we'd brought plenty of food and water, and we had enough tools to build a raft. We floated on the water for three days, until some fishermen rescued us. We wanted to help save the people in the castle, but it was too late."

"And you eventually made your way home?"

"Yes. I married, I had children, they grew up and had children. The ultimate act of defiance, of courage. Of faith. I lived a good life. I was a good husband and a good father. What else can one do, in the end?"

"And what of your muse, Pippa?" the interviewer asked. "Surely she was real? Will you say so for sure?"

"Ah, I do not know how to answer," Verga said. "You see, the Pippa I remember is just an ideal in my eyes. I look and I believe I see her sometimes in the night sky."

"May I ask you one more question?" the interviewer asked. "Would you recite the inscription you wrote for the piece? The one that's in the program for tonight's performance?"

"Of course," Verga said. "You are too far to hold, too close to resist, too strong but not too strong to have to turn away. I long for you, I bow to you, I embrace you from a distance, my star, my muse, my words, my music."

Mia didn't hear the rest of the interview. The words he'd recited echoed in her ears. Feeling numb, she went to replay the end of the interview, but then her phone signaled a text. She didn't recognize the number, but it came from somewhere in Italy. She opened it up.

Mia, it's Leo. The excavation is finished. I'm leaving here after breakfast tomorrow to go back to the castle. I can have the ferry stop for you at eleven. If you'd like to come, meet me at the dock.

She responded in a fraction of a second.

Of course. I'll be there.

TWENTY-TWO

1943

August

That week, Annalisa worked harder than she ever had before.

The news about Annalisa's identity and her father's decline continued to energize Patricio, who became as determined as his niece was to perfect a cure for her father. The two pored over her botanicals notes and agreed that the anti-inflammatories were likely the best complement to the curative minerals Patricio was aiming to use in his mixture. He put her to work with the anti-inflammatory plants he'd had supplied from the mainland and those he'd found on the island, directing her to pull off the stems and shred the leaves and petals, then rub them with a variety of rough and smooth stones from his collection and report how they responded: Did they tear, shred, or flake? Display scratch marks or pigment changes? All changes could prove significant, Patricio stressed, in determining the effect of his medicine and the dosage that would be required.

As Annalisa worked on the plants, her mind sometimes wandered and she pictured Aldo composing and rehearsing his music. She was happy for him and proud of him, so glad he had finally found his way forward after the loss of his mentor and all his questioning about the island and his purpose there. It made her feel good that the two of them were creating works that had never existed before, and it inspired her to focus more intently and complete her tasks more quickly, knowing he was proceeding with intensity, too. She couldn't wait to hear him play.

When Thursday came, she returned from the tower after her day's work to get ready for the big performance. As she walked through the castle, she saw the elaborate preparations underway. It seemed all the guests and workers who had known Aldo's mentor were fond of Aldo as well, and everyone was going all out to make it a spectacular evening.

Peeking into the ballroom, she could tell that it had been cleaned from end to end, as the chandeliers were sparkling, and the marble floor was gleaming. A wide platform stage had been set up by the wall of windows, with a set of red velvet curtains hanging from a rod and a row of spotlights aimed upward. Wooden ballroom chairs with thickly padded floral cushions were arranged in rows opposite the stage, and porcelain vases with lilies and fragrant eucalyptus leaves were positioned along its front edge. Against the far wall, a long table was covered in a red damask cloth, where desserts—Signora Russo's wonderful cakes and custards, tarts and chocolates—would no doubt be placed for the celebration after the concert.

The evening was set to be the most glorious one the castle had ever seen. Not only did it mark Aldo's debut, but it was also the first time ever that Patricio himself would attend an evening event. Word had spread for the last several days that Patricio planned to be there, and although Annalisa hadn't asked him directly—she hadn't wanted to distract him when he was working so hard to save her father—she could tell from the extraordinary steps taken to set up the ballroom that he must have confirmed he was coming. The dress code for the evening was formal, so she was delighted when Giulia showed up at their room to say that Savio, her mentor, had invited the sisters to wear any of the gowns that had been crafted for his paintings.

Annalisa, Giulia and Emilia had a quick supper and spent the early evening in the expansive closet in Savio's studio trying on the various possibilities. Emilia chose a bright-pink gown with sparkles, while Giulia selected a blue dress with a V neck and a low back. Annalisa chose a more modest gown, deep amethyst in color with a high neck, fitted bodice, and full skirt. She didn't care much about fashion but she found the texture of the dress fascinating, the way the skirt draped in rounded, symmetrical folds as it flowed from her waist down to the floor.

She knew it was frivolous to care about a dress. After all, the only thing that mattered now was her father's health. But at the same time, she couldn't wait for Aldo to see her in something so pretty. She hadn't seen him since the night before she'd told her uncle who he was. And oh, how she remembered that night so well! The hug they'd shared, the way he'd smelled so good, and his arm had felt so strong. She'd never felt a young man's arms around her before. She wondered now if her mother had experienced the same thing the first time she'd hugged her father. If so, it didn't surprise her that her mother wanted to be with him more. The way she'd felt with Aldo's arm around her that night, she could imagine wanting nothing else but to experience that again. It seemed reasonable, understandable, that someone would give up everything to be able to have that feeling, that level of delight, over and over for the rest of their life.

She desperately hoped he felt the same about her. Because the only way they would see each other after tonight was if he felt as unable to deny their connection as she did. The odds were against them—Aldo had acknowledged that the last time she saw him. They came from different worlds, he'd said, and the minute she told her uncle who she was, their friendship would change. She wondered if it wasn't that their paths simply hadn't crossed lately, but if he'd been avoiding her ever since she'd revealed her identity to her uncle. Or if she'd been avoiding him without consciously intending to. She understood now how much her mother had to weigh, leaving one life for another, because her mother had been caught between two worlds, too. Even after the *schianto* was finished, there would be other experiments to do and cures to find. She was her uncle's partner now, his fellow researcher. He wanted to make her what his own sister had never become: a real scientist.

And yet this yearning she felt for Aldo—for his friendship and his beautiful smile and the feel of his arms. How did a person choose? It was like choosing between the sun and the moon. All that Patricio represented and all that Aldo could offer —she wanted both. She needed both. But was that possible?

Nine o'clock arrived, and the castle was electric with energy. Annalisa felt it as she and her sisters walked into the ballroom and sat down on the seats reserved for them near the front. The open windows reminded her of the first night she'd arrived, the way they'd seen snippets of dancing through the open windows as Aldo led them up the steps to the castle. Oh, how she'd wanted to be part of this world, a world of glamour and learning and passion. Aldo had said that none of the guests paid attention to the outside world, so caught up were they in the affairs of their minds and the giddiness of discovery and art.

And now she felt a tinge of insecurity, which she suspected must have been lurking there in the ballroom that night as well. She had a sick father and the war was getting fiercer and Jews were increasingly unsafe, and perhaps soon nobody would be safe anymore. Maybe Aldo had been right. Maybe the guests danced and drank because they needed to aggressively push the world out of their thoughts.

She heard the crowd gasp and then go quiet, and she looked toward the rear of the ballroom. There was her uncle, Patricio, standing at the doorway, a combination of boldness and shyness, clothed in a tuxedo that was slightly too big for him. He looked at the stage, and she wasn't sure if the glassiness in his eyes was caused by tears or just the reflection of the spotlights. She felt for him. He was not made for this kind of extravagance: no, he was a quiet, awkward man who would have been happy not to have been born a Parissi; who wanted only to devote himself to his books, his experiments, and his love of what the human mind could produce. Then she saw him notice her and her sisters, and she was sure he was crying. He'd chosen to be alone all these years, but now it seemed clear that he hadn't wanted to be alone at all. He'd been a victim of his upbringing and his family's name.

The silence suddenly broke as the guests stood and applauded. She saw her uncle looking around as if he couldn't believe their affection for him. He'd had a hard life—having no mother when he was growing up, fearing his father so much, and then losing the one person who lit up his life, his little sister. Shutting himself off from the world, maybe feeling unworthy of anyone's affection because he'd disappointed his father and his sister both. She was glad that he could appreciate all this love and gratitude. He had created this amazing space for all these people. He was a good person.

A moment later, Savio, an elegant, long-limbed man with a mane of slicked-back brown hair, came up to the stage. As the most long-standing guest on the island, Giulia had told her, he served as master of ceremonies at events, and he'd been working on his speech all week.

"Signor Parissi, we are so honored to have you join us tonight," he said. "And it's an honor to have here your young nieces, whose youth and energy are inspiring to us all. We are so grateful to you for giving us the space to do our best work and hopefully bring art and beauty to the world. The contributions we make to this frail, broken world, we owe to you."

The group broke out in applause again as her uncle walked down the aisle until he reached her. Giulia and Emilia slid down a seat and he crossed in front of Annalisa to sit between her and Giulia. She took his hand and she felt it shaking. He seemed so fragile and needy in this moment. He reached up and patted her cheek, and she was glad she had taken the risk and come to the island.

"Tonight, we have a special surprise," Savio continued. "Because we know how much you appreciate young talent and helping the next generation learn, we are pleased to present the debut composition of one of the most talented newcomers we have seen in a while. He came to the castle as an apprentice to Flavio Rusetti, whom we sadly lost. But Flavio's talent and legacy live on in the beautiful composition you will hear tonight. Ladies and gentlemen, I give you Aldo Verga playing his debut piece. It's called 'For Pippa.'"

Annalisa inhaled sharply, instinctively raising her hand to her lips. He'd titled the piece after her, after the nickname he'd heard Emilia call her. It was like a private little joke that only she and her sisters understood, and she slowly lowered her hand, feeling the closeness inherent in his decision.

The curtains parted to reveal a single wooden chair on the stage, and the audience applauded again. Aldo came onto the stage, a violin tucked under his arm. He looked beautiful in his tuxedo, his hair parted on the side and neatly combed. She felt Giulia touch her elbow. Aldo stood for a moment by the chair and looked out at her and when their eyes met, she didn't think she could ever look away. She'd only known him a few weeks, only spent a few evenings with him, but suddenly she knew she loved him. And she could feel he loved her too. He pulled out a sheet of paper from his breast pocket, and read the words: "You are too far to hold, too close to resist, too strong but not too strong to have to turn away. I long for you, I bow to you, I embrace you from a distance, my star, my muse, my words, my music."

He sat down on the chair and raised the violin to his chin as the lights dimmed so there was just one spotlight on him. There was no music stand, as evidently he knew the piece by heart. He lowered his chin slightly and began to play.

Annalisa was certain it was the most beautiful music ever composed. Nothing had sounded so lovely to her ears before, and she believed that for the rest of her life, nothing would. It started off slow, with smooth movements, a haunting melody that repeated two notes up and two notes down. It moved into a quicker melody, playful, a lovely beat that quickened her heart rate, and then it moved into a sadder section. She felt it mimicked their relationship, the slow beginning, the joyful middle, the tense final section with the hint of an ending possibly coming soon. It was a whole love story, a whole life story, in one piece. There he was, on stage all by himself, and it was as though he was telling the most intimate story of a love—a love so beautiful, so strong, so personal and so eternal. His arm seemed to be dancing as he moved the bow; the bow was an extension of his arm as his arm was an extension of the music. She couldn't take her eyes off of him, even as she felt tears streaming down her cheeks, even as she felt her uncle's eyes on her. She was transfixed.

He ended on a long, chilling, almost questioning note and then dropped the bow to his side. It took a moment for the audience to realize, to hear, that it was over. But then they erupted in applause, everyone standing and shouting *"Bravo!"* as the spotlights came back on. She stood, too, and they continued to look at each other as though they were the only two people on earth that mattered. And she knew she had found the one thing that made life worth living. Yes, science and art were important, but it was the connection between two people, the magical coming together, that made it all make sense. No wonder her mother had left her family and her future behind. No wonder.

Aldo bowed his head and the spotlights went out as the curtains closed. She turned and rushed past her uncle to make her way out of the room, because she had to see him. But there were so many people coming to introduce themselves to her and her sisters. She finally made it out of the ballroom, trying to figure out where she would find him. There were so many turns and corners, and she kept running and turning until she came to a small hallway lit only by the night sky coming in at the windows.

That's where she saw him. And she ran into his arms and felt him kiss her, and she kissed him back, hard and deep. She didn't think she'd known how to kiss, but it came as easy as anything could. She was kissing him for all the love stories written in the past and yet to be written, all the love stories destroyed by hate and fear and war. She was kissing him to try to find something lasting, something that couldn't be destroyed. She was biting his lip and feeling his tears wetting her cheeks. She wanted to tell him that he was beautiful, his creation was beautiful, they were beautiful together. That she could never love anyone else, not after feeling the way she felt now. This was it, the meaning of life, the reason people were put on this earth. How could her mother's father, how could the world not understand that—

"Stop!" came a loud, angry voice. And a wall sconce was switched on. It was Patricio.

"Uncle," she said. "It's okay. This is—"

"It's *not* okay!" he barked, as he pulled Aldo away by the arm. "Don't you bewitch her with your music and your words. She is made for greatness! Don't you get in her way!"

"But I'm not—" Aldo started.

"You're nothing. You're nowhere near what Flavio was. You're not worthy of—"

"Uncle, stop!" she said. "Don't do this! You're wrong! He's talented and brilliant, and he's not taking me away from anything—"

"Annalisa," Aldo whispered in her ear. "It's okay—"

"No," she told him, pulling back so she could look directly into his eyes. "He's not going to destroy how I feel! He's not going to destroy you! Uncle, stop, you don't understand. You're wrong—just like you were wrong about my mother!"

"You're not your mother," Patricio growled. "You're different. You're better. You have a future—"

"I'm no better than her," Annalisa said. "She was right to leave to be with my father. You're so wrong—"

"Annalisa, no," Aldo said, pressing her hand. "Your uncle is upset. Don't yell at him. He deserves your respect." He leaned in for a second so his cheek brushed hers. Then he walked past her and into the darkness of the hallway.

She turned back to Patricio. "Look what you did! You hurt him on the night he's been waiting for! Why are you doing this? I love him."

"You don't know what love is."

"I do. I love him."

"You have more important things ahead of you. You can be a scientist!" he exclaimed. "You are on the brink of greatness. You can change the world. Don't throw away your life like your mother did—"

"She didn't throw it away. She loved my father—"

"She accomplished nothing. And she died—"

"She accomplished plenty. She loved my father. She had us —my sisters and me."

"She could have had that and more—"

"No, she couldn't. She had to choose. Don't make me choose!"

"If you want to devote yourself to science then you have to be completely invested. Your father is waiting—"

"I am invested! I want both!"

"You can't be throwing your attention around on a little boy who plays a pretty song. Put this foolishness out of your mind!"

"No! Uncle, no, don't make me choose! I can't choose between my father's health and my love. I can have both."

She ran down the hallway and toward the grand staircase, past the guests and the food and the wine and the dancing in the ballroom. It all seemed so unimportant now. Yes, she could eat and drink and dance and learn and put the rest of the world out of her mind. But she didn't want to. She didn't want to trade one life for another, as her mother had done. She didn't want to settle and she didn't want to run away. She was a human being with a mind and a heart, and she deserved the chance to try to have the life she wanted. The whole life. She deserved that freedom. As everyone did.

Reaching the first floor, she went through the kitchen, hoping that Aldo would be on the terrace, as he'd been on those nights when she and her sisters were still workers. But the terrace was empty. Thinking that maybe he'd gone to the boathouse, she was starting for the steep steps when she noticed something sticking out from behind the loose stone on the terrace wall. She ran over and pushed the rock aside. Inside was a sheet of paper with the short poem Aldo had read at the start of his concert, the poem in which he'd called her his muse. Below that was an additional note, the handwriting, though rushed and shaky, still clearly Aldo's:

> *Your uncle is right. You don't belong with me. I was wrong to play for you and name the piece after you. Live the life you were meant to live, Annalisa. Be happy. Aldo*

She couldn't believe he'd give up so easily. How could he let her go? She sank against the wall. Maybe her uncle was right. Maybe he wasn't the person she thought.

She crumpled the note, then pulled out the pad of paper and pen and wrote back to him.

Fine. You be happy too.

TWENTY-THREE

2018

Thursday

The next morning, Mia dressed in jeans and sneakers again and went downstairs. The lobby was empty, with the tour group still on the mainland. Breakfast was being served on the terrace, and she sat at a table and ordered a cappuccino, which arrived along with a delicious-looking assortment of *biscotti*. She sipped the warm drink, bracing for the characteristic she'd come to expect of Italian coffee—the strong, almost bitter, taste beneath the light, frothy swirl of milk and cocoa powder on top.

Looking out over Parissi Island, she thought back on the interview with Aldo she'd listened to, the way he spoke so cryptically yet poignantly about Pippa, the woman she now believed was her grandmother. To have written the words he'd recited at the end of the interview, he must have loved her very much. And judging from how Lucy had remembered those words through the decades and recited them at the end of her life, she must have loved him too. They'd been apart, on two different islands, when the Nazis came—but still, why hadn't they reunited? What had drawn Lucy to go to New York without him? And why didn't he try to find her?

And why had she ended up with Mia's grandfather, a man she never really loved? It was so evident even in the wedding picture back home, on what should have been the happiest day of her life. Lucy couldn't even bring herself to smile for that photo. What had happened to the girl who had inspired Aldo to make music?

She didn't know, and yet she needed to make Leo understand who her grandmother had been when she finally told him the truth. How could she convince him that Lucy was a good person? How could she convince him that Lucy wouldn't have stolen the *schianto*, even if all evidence was to the contrary? She had to be honest with him. Because the truth was, in an unintentional but very real way, she and her family were responsible for his failed searches and some of his grandmother's heartache as well. His family had been left with only a sketch of the wedding gown, while she had the actual dress; and he had only an old, faded drawing of the *schianto* when the real thing was in her suitcase.

She didn't know if her grandmother ever could have been aware that people would be looking for these objects. But still, it was disturbing to think that she and Lucy had been secure in their Long Island bubble while Leo and his family were searching for any scraps that would make them feel more connected to Leo's murdered grandfather. Would Leo understand that she'd been ignorant? Or would he point out that Lucy was never ignorant—she knew what she possessed? Could she make him understand that Lucy was damaged by all that had happened at the castle? Because in the end, she would need his help. After she revealed that she had the *schianto*, would he be willing to help her prove that Lucy didn't steal it? Or was the evidence against Lucy too overwhelming? Mia didn't want to ruin their time together by revealing the extent of her secret—and yet the longer she waited, the angrier he was sure to be.

The bottom line was that he had a right to his grandfather's story, just as she had a right to her grandmother's. But it was her grandmother's unwillingness to open up that had caused him pain. And now she was causing him pain, too. By being as secretive as Lucy had been.

After breakfast she came back upstairs to get her bag and Leo's hat, and when she entered her room, she noticed a button on her bedside telephone flashing red. She couldn't imagine who would be trying to reach her by contacting the hotel, since anyone she knew—even Leo—would call her cell phone. Tossing her key on the bed, she pushed the button, and after a recorded announcement in Italian that she didn't understand, there was a beep and then the voicemail message.

"Mia, hello, this is Missy! We haven't seen you at any of the events this week, and just wanted to be sure you're okay! Charlie thought he saw you getting onto the ferry for Parissi Island yesterday morning, and we're wondering how you managed that. I mean, we have so many questions! The castle is exquisite, but we are very concerned about how that elevator up the hillside is going to work. And how about a more luxurious way to travel across the water? If people are going to spend a fortune for this trip, they're going to want a more elegant transfer. Anyway, if you have any more information, please call us back and shed some light!"

Mia returned the phone to its cradle. It was nice that Missy had called to make sure she was okay—although also sneaky that they'd seen her with Leo and were curious if she'd made some special arrangement to get back into the castle or had been privy to more information than they had. She supposed she understood; if she were in their position, with so much at stake for their business, she might be looking for additional access to Leo or the castle. Funny, she thought, how in a strange way she and Missy were alike. They were both searching for answers. As was everyone, she guessed. Maybe what made people human, she mused, was not opposable thumbs, but the need to always know a little bit more.

Back downstairs, she boarded the van. With the tour group still on the mainland, the driver—whose name she'd learned was Giuseppe—looked bored, but quite happy to see her. Thinking how she only had a few days left here, she realized as the van shifted into gear that one of the things she'd miss most about her trip was this drive to the shore. No longer apprehensive about the van's ability to navigate the turns, she opened her window and settled into the gentle swaying and rocking that eased her left and right. She loved the smell of the sea that grew more noticeable as they approached, and the swelling sound of water hitting the rocks. At the shore, she stepped off the van and walked to the dock. The morning was hot, the sun almost exactly overhead, and she thought how glad she was to have Leo's hat. The water was light blue and seemed to go on forever. From this angle, the Isola di Parissi looked longer and more slender, the castle almost two-dimensional. More like a drawing, a figment, than an actual structure.

"Mia!" came a voice from the deck of the ferry, and she turned to see Leo waving his arms to catch her attention. She waved back and hurried to the boat.

He was dressed a little more nicely than yesterday, in a white button-down shirt and jeans, and she supposed it was because he was coming from the event on the mainland. She was glad to see him, and not only because he was her ticket to the island. She enjoyed his company and how much he cared about all that had come before. She took his hand to climb onto the boat, wondering if he was happy to see her too. But then she silently scolded herself for the thought. Whatever was going on with Ryan, whether they were going to make it as a couple or not, she was still in a relationship with him. It felt wrong to be having feelings for another guy, and she felt guilty, even though she couldn't help it.

The motor purred softly as they sat on a bench on the deck. The captain gave Leo a wave, and they were on their way, steaming toward the blinding yellow sun. Like yesterday, the castle seemed to grow in stature and density, drinking in the sunshine like a child taking in nutrients to grow. She was reminded of one of those time-lapse documentaries on TV, where you see a flower blossom at warp speed, or a busy city street grow empty as the sun goes down in a matter of moments. It struck her that nothing, really, was constant. Everything was relative. The castle never looked the same; it changed depending on where you were, when you were, as you approached.

Leo's voice interrupted her thoughts. "What are you thinking?" he asked.

"Nothing important," she said. "Just about how the castle looks. And maybe if others from the past would have seen it and felt it the same way I do. How it seems to get bigger and more solid as you approach it. The whole experience of being about to set foot on the island and climb up those steep stairs."

"I suspect they did," he said. "Although it's impossible to know. I can never experience what my grandfather did. I can imagine, but I can never know his world as he lived it."

"I guess," she said. "But I want to know for sure. I want to know what people felt when they came here, how it changed them and or made them do the things they did. Isn't that what you're trying to do, after all? You've put your career on pause to be here in this isolated place. You're trying to recreate what was. What's the point if we can't know the truth?"

"Well, we can come close to the truth, I believe," he said. "You're right, I did give up a lot. And I can tell you for sure, it's not just to put together an exhibit that rich tourists can linger over between seven-course meals and exclusive shopping sprees. What is it for? Yes, it's about my grandfather and the others. But what would change for me if I found more of my grandfather's creations? I don't know. Still, it's important." He shrugged and dropped his shoulders. "Important enough to give up a relationship, actually."

"Oh?" she said, curious to hear that he'd had someone in his life.

"Not everyone understands what it means to want to know the past before finding a future," he said. "We broke up when I came here. She thought I was chasing ghosts and she wanted no part of it. And I couldn't see changing who I was for her. It didn't sound like a recipe for happiness.

"So enough about me," he said as the boat picked up speed and a spray from the sides lightly showered them. "Tell me about being a scientist."

"Well, like I told you the other night, I wouldn't call myself a scientist yet," she admitted. "I work for scientists. Brilliant people, actually. I like my job a lot. But what I really want is to be a PI—principal investigator. That means running my own research lab."

"Oh? And when will you get to do that?"

"Not very soon," she said with an embarrassed laugh. "I need to save up so I can afford to go back to school. Then I need to apply and get accepted."

"And where would you go to?"

"I'm not sure yet. Boston University was always my first choice. There's a professor who's working on the most fascinating research into the molecular mechanisms that lead to heart disease. But I never wanted to move so far away from my grandmother." She looked at her hands. "Although that's not an issue anymore," she added.

"Why?" he said softly. "I'm sorry. I don't mean to pry—"

"No, it's okay. It's hard for me to say. But the reason I don't need to stay in New York anymore is because... well, my grandmother died recently."

"Your grandmother? Who raised you? I'm so sorry," he said. "And she's the person you believe was a tray runner?"

Mia nodded.

"I'm so sorry," he repeated. "I had no idea." She felt his hand on hers. "And this is why you've come here?" he asked. "Because of her? To discover her life?"

"Yes. In a way. She left some questions. Like your grandfather did."

"So we both put our lives on pause to answer them."

They reached the dock, and Mia followed Leo to the steps leading off the boat. He leaned down to grab two water bottles and then had a quick exchange in Italian with the captain. "He says he'll wait for us," he told her as he handed her the water. "Ready for a climb again?"

They left the boat and started up the staircase. "I am glad you came today, Mia, especially after what you told me," he said. "I think you're going to love where we're going."

"Why? Did they find something in the excavation today?"

"No, I don't think they did," he said. "The plan was to break up the stone terrace by the kitchen to replace it with one that will meet building codes. But I did want to show you some more lists of people who got here earlier. Because you said you believe the person you're connected to—your grandmother—may have worked in the kitchen? Those lists are here, and we can go through them if you'd like."

"That's very nice of you, to do this for me," she said, feeling guilty. Because she'd already found the list with her grandmother's name—Annalisa. She just hadn't told him yet.

He paused on the first landing, and they both leaned against the wall and drank some water. "Well, the truth is there's another reason I wanted to bring you back," he said. "You looked so troubled when we found that list of the new arrivals yesterday, and then again when I showed you my grandfather's sketch of the wedding dress. It's hard to take in, these discoveries, these stories about people long gone under the worst of circumstances. And you weren't prepared for that. I want to make it up to you."

"Oh, no, I was okay," she said, realizing that he thought she was sad by how much loss he'd shown her. When she was actually stunned at the revelations about who her grandmother was and how she was connected to his grandfather. And how she was responsible for so much of what was missing. "You didn't have to make anything up to me," she added.

"I'm glad you wanted to come," he insisted. "Because what you also need to know is what Patricio created. For so many years, this was a place of brilliance and beauty and light. Everyone who came here knew it and felt it. And I wanted to share with you something I stumbled upon one day. I think you can count on one hand the number of people who've ever set foot where you're about to."

He stood and began to climb again and she followed. Despite her guilt, she was curious to see where he was going to bring her. They reached the courtyard and he led her through the front entrance and up the stairs, the same route they'd taken when he'd led the tour two days ago. But this time they went beyond the doorway to the exhibit. Soon they passed through an archway and the space changed drastically. They were out of the restored part of the castle. He led her further down the hall and through a set of double wooden doors. Ahead was another set of doors—these ones made of small panes of glass, the wood of the frame cracked and rotting—which led to one of the most astonishing structures Mia had ever seen.

It was a balcony, vast and semicircular in shape, jutting out past the hillside below.

"Come," Leo said and gestured for her to follow him onto it. Mia hesitated. "Is it safe?"

"Completely," he said. "This was one of the first things the engineers worked on. Because it's so magnificent. And built so well, our crew was shocked at how sound it was. Patricio called this the *terrazzo galleggiante*."

"Which means?" she asked.

"The floating terrace. He had one of the most esteemed architectural firms in Rome design it. He said he wanted to be so far out from the edge of the island that he wouldn't feel limited by time or space at all. That he would feel as though he were floating on a magic carpet. He wanted to be both close to the sky and overwhelmed by its vastness. Can you imagine all the great thinkers who stepped out here while they worked on their masterpieces? Can you imagine how they felt—both part of the universe and yet distinct from it, too? To some extent infinitesimal, to some extent all-powerful. Patricio loved contradictions, and this was the ultimate one."

They stayed in silence, as Mia contemplated that glorious and puzzling desire. How can a person feel both small and all-powerful at once? But it was strange; in a way she felt exactly like that. A part of the universe and whole in and of herself. What brilliance, to have envisioned this. And to give it to his guests. And built it so well that it would last indefinitely. And to hear all this come from a person who had given up his relationship to be here.

She admired that he'd done that. She was starting to think that she'd done the very same thing.

He led her back to the hallway, then closed the double doors behind them.

"Well, we should get on with finding those lists of workers for you," he said. "I don't have all that much time. I need to get back to the hotel to do some paperwork and then change and help with preparations. Tonight there's a banquet and a dance at the hotel for the travel agents."

"That sounds nice," Mia said.

"I'd rather stay here and explore more. But it's part of my job. And it turns out I have some big news to share tonight. I received an update today from the lawyer in Rome who is handling the investigation. They've gone through travel documents and accounts and records and even photographs of the ports in the days before the Nazis invaded the island. And they think they've found someone who would have concrete information about the *schianto*'s whereabouts. A woman named Lucy, who's been living in the United States for decades. They're sending a team out next week to her home. Some town called Soundport.

"Now, you have information about the *schianto,* too," he said. "Does this square with what you know? Or are you still not ready to tell me? You don't have to decide now. We still have time to go back downstairs and look through those lists—"

"Leo," she said, touching his arm. She couldn't hide it anymore. She was separate from him yet a part of his story. Both at the same time, the kind of contradiction that Patricio loved. And more important, she cared for him. Unlike Ryan, he'd been so good to her. So understanding of her need to be here. Even without knowing all the facts.

"Hmmm?" he asked.

"Those people who are going to look for the woman in Soundport? They're not going to find her. Because she died. And they're not going to find the *schianto* either."

"What?" he said. "Why?"

"Because the woman is Annalisa, although she changed it to Lucy when she got to New York. She's the Annalisa you found on the list two days ago. And the reason I know is because I'm her granddaughter.

"The two things you've spent so long hoping to find?" she said. "My grandmother's had both of them all along."

TWENTY-FOUR

1943

September

The next morning Annalisa stayed in bed long after Giulia and Emilia had left to start their day. They didn't know what had happened with Patricio, and when they all reunited in their suite well after midnight, she hadn't wanted to tell them. She'd pretended to be asleep this morning when they'd awakened, and she heard Giulia telling Emilia not to disturb her.

"Let her be," Giulia had said. "Something bad happened last night. I have a feeling."

"What?" Emilia whispered back.

"I don't know. But don't bother her. She'll tell us when she's ready."

Lying in bed after they'd left, she knew she had to get up and get back to the lab. There was still work to be done to finish the *schianto* and create a potion that would cure her father. But she didn't want to see her uncle. She wondered if she could work in the lab on the botanicals without running into him. Maybe he'd plan to try to avoid her, too, which would be perfect, as far as she was concerned. She no longer cared for him or trusted him. Such a change from last night when he'd stood at the threshold to the ballroom, taking in all the applause, and her affection for him had been boundless! But last night he'd shown his true colors. The colors that had made her mother call him a coward.

Because he'd destroyed something that was so important, so valuable to her: what she had with Aldo. She'd been so happy last night to see Aldo perform his beautiful composition. And not just happy; she'd been proud of him. Proud that he'd made something beautiful and extraordinary. The piece had been so heavenly that it had made people cry. Art *could* transform people, just as she and Aldo had agreed. And he had named the piece "For Pippa." He hadn't forgotten about her these last couple of weeks. She'd been an inspiration to him the whole time he was composing and practicing his music. And she'd been thinking about him and missing him as well.

She sat up and opened her nightstand drawer, where she'd stuffed the crumpled note he'd left behind the stone last night. Unfolding it, she smoothed the paper with her palm and read the poem. "*You are too far to hold, too close to resist, too strong but not too strong to have to turn away. I long for you, I bow to you, I embrace you from a distance, my star, my muse, my words, my music.*" She'd been his muse—that's what he'd said.

But if that was how he felt, why had he walked away? She understood that he feared he would be harming her by turning her away from her family: her uncle, whom she'd just reunited with, and her father, who needed her back. She understood, too, that he knew about her mother's estrangement from her family and wouldn't want her to suffer the same fate. But why hadn't he stayed to tell her all this? And to show her how hard it would be for him to lose her, if it came to that? She'd told him her deepest secrets about her parents and her fears, her father's health. And he'd opened up about his past, too. With everything going on in their lives, all that was going on in the world, how could that not matter?

The only answer was that he never felt for her as strongly as she'd felt for him. That it was an illusion, the narrative she had built in her mind about the two of them. No matter how he looked at her as he finished the piece, no matter the poem he'd written for her, no matter that their eyes had locked until the lights on the stage went down—whatever he'd been feeling, it couldn't have been anything like what her parents had shared. Because her mother hadn't been able to walk away.

She slowly got dressed, took a few bites of the breakfast her sisters had left for her outside the room, and went up to the tower. Her uncle's breakfast tray was on the table, untouched. She wondered if he was suffering as much as she was from their argument last night. She'd been so proud at the start of the evening that she and her sisters were the reason he'd decided to reunite with the outside world. But now he'd retreated again. What had she done so wrong? Perhaps if she'd spoken to him before the concert, she could have given him a better picture of who she was and what she wanted from life. She could have told him that she was like her mother—more than she'd ever before realized. But she hadn't known how strong her feelings for Aldo were, not until that indescribable embrace after the concert. How could she have explained her feelings when she didn't know them?

Looking at Patricio's closed door, she wished she could go back to the way she was when she first arrived on the island. Devoted to science and determined to meet Patricio and bring his experiment back home. She'd had such a singular focus. How had she let that get away from her?

Because I'm human, she thought. It was human to love, it was human to care, it was human to want to connect. And she was glad she was human. She'd never want to erase all she had felt for Aldo. She was glad she'd kissed and held him. She would do it all over again if she had the choice. Even knowing what would come of it, she would do it again. She wouldn't have been able to listen to his concert and then leave the ballroom.

Annalisa stayed where she was for a few moments more, then went into a small side room where she'd stored some plant matter to continue sorting, observing and manipulating the leaves and petals and then recording her findings. After a few hours—and still with no sighting of her uncle—she grew worried and decided to go downstairs to see if anyone had spotted him yet today. She arrived at the main dining room as lunch was being served to the guests, and since she didn't feel like eating, she stood at the doorway. The mood around the table was subdued, so different from the boisterous, raucous lunches she was used to. She could hear the clink of silverware against china, the sound of liquid rushing as the servers filled glasses with lemonade and water. She'd never heard those sounds before, as the conversation and laughter usually drowned them out. Were they all just tired? Had there been dancing that continued to dawn, as it had on the night she and her sisters arrived? Or had they heard her fight with her uncle? Did they think Patricio had retreated to his room again—and if that's what they thought, did they blame her? She turned away because she didn't want to have to defend herself, if she was indeed the person who had made them all so sad. If she had ruined everything.

She went to the kitchen to see if Signora Russo had seen her uncle at all today. But the woman seemed as distracted as the guests in the dining room. She was sitting at the worktable, gazing forward, her chin on her hand, her fingers extending over her lips. She seemed deep in thought and jumped in her chair when Annalisa walked in.

"Oh, Signorina Parissi!" she said. "I'm sorry, I was lost in my own world. Lunch is underway—would you like some? And what of your uncle? Is he coming down?"

"No, thank you," she said. "And about my uncle—I haven't seen him all day. I was wondering if maybe you had?"

Signora Russo shook her head. "Strange. He hasn't hidden like this since before he came to know who you were. Perhaps he's hard at work. Or perhaps he's still asleep. I understand it went on very late again last night after Aldo's performance."

"Is that why everyone is quiet today?" she said. "The mood in the dining room is somber."

"I suppose," she said. "There also were some news reports that made it back from the mainland this morning. The good news is that the Allies have overtaken Sicily, but now there's worry about how the Germans will respond. Things may get worse before they get better. Although... what am I saying? The guests wouldn't pay much mind to that. They don't keep on top of the news or think about the outer world, especially after a big night of celebration."

"Which reminds me... I haven't seen Aldo today either. I wanted to say goodbye before he left," she said.

"Left?" Annalisa demanded, sounding more upset than she'd intended to. "Left where? The castle?"

"They're doing some exploratory work on the small island to the west that your uncle is considering buying. Blazing trails and such. A group of the boathouse crew went."

"Do you know how long they'll be gone?" Mia asked.

"A few days. Maybe more. Depends on how quickly they get the work done."

"Oh." Annalisa gazed downward as she took this in.

She wondered if Aldo had left because he saw her note: *Fine. You be happy too.* Had she driven him away? She'd been angry and hurt when she wrote it, but she didn't expect never to see him again. Trying not to seem too anxious, she went outside and over to the loose rock on the stone wall, hoping there was another note for her. Telling her he was wrong, they were wrong. That what they felt when they kissed last night—that it mattered, and they couldn't let it go. That they'd convince her uncle they needed to be together.

She pushed aside the rock and peeked in. Nothing was there. Her note was gone. He'd seen it and left.

She sat down on the stone surface, her knees folded and her hands in her lap. She had to talk to him now. About everything—his performance and her uncle and her father; the mood in the castle and the news Signora Russo had just shared; her warning that things could get worse before they got better. What did that mean? Aldo had said the war was coming, that the guests at the castle were like ostriches with their heads in the sand. Signora Russo's concern was apparent, the way she'd been staring into space when Annalisa interrupted her just now. Was Aldo right, that the Shangri-La her uncle had built had a conclusion date stamped across it? What did that mean for the two of them? What did that mean for all of them?

She put the stone back in place and walked inside, wondering if she should ask Signora Russo for more information. But before she could, Signora Russo approached her with an envelope.

"Signorina Parissi, I meant to give this to you," she said. "It was with the supplies that came up from the boathouse this morning. From the sweet one who brings the flour and such, Vincenzo. The boys said to get it to you right away. They said he's waiting at the boathouse for a reply."

She took the envelope and pulled out the note.

Annalisa,

I'm told that your father has taken a turn for the worse. He has chest pain every night now and is having trouble breathing and is very weak. He can barely stand. He seems to have given up hope of ever seeing you and your sisters again. Please let me know what message I can give him. Something to help him

bear up a little bit longer until you are ready to return. I will
wait for your reply.
 V

Oh no, Annalisa thought. What have I done?

Tucking the note into her pocket, she went upstairs to
Savio's studio. She was glad to see Giulia alone there, as Savio
hadn't yet returned from lunch to start his afternoon's work.

Giulia looked up from her seat, a white gown in her lap and
a threaded needle in her hand above the beaded bodice. "What
is it? What's wrong?" she asked.

Annalisa handed her the note.

"Oh Pippa," Giulia said after she'd read it. "What should
we do? He needs us. Should we go back?"

Annalisa shook her head. "We can't. The *schianto* isn't
finished yet. I don't have medicine."

"But waiting for it is killing him. Do you think the cure is
really going to work? Or is our uncle a dreamer like the rest of
them?"

Annalisa looked at her. She hadn't realized Giulia could be
that perceptive. But it was the very same question she was
starting to ask herself.

"I don't know," she said. "But I'm not ready to give up yet.
It's a good idea he has. I trust that he knows what he's doing."
She thought for a moment. "Okay, Papa can't be alone anymore,
so we'll send Emilia back to take care of him. She'll cheer him
up and she'll let him know I'm working on something and we're
coming back soon."

Giulia nodded.

"Go down to the boathouse and tell Vincenzo what our
plan is," Annalisa said. "He's waiting there. I'll get Emilia and
help her pack her things. Tell him we'll be there as soon as we
can."

. . .

A little over an hour later, Annalisa and Emilia reached the shore, Emilia in her traveling clothes from the night they came to the island. Emilia was quiet, and Annalisa knew she had mixed feelings about going home. She was scared to see how sick their father was and didn't feel confident that she could build him back up on her own. Annalisa understood how she felt. She'd never expected to send Emilia back like this. She'd never imagined how complicated everything would become, back when they were making that heady trip over that first night. And now she realized how naïve she'd been back then. Thinking she could cure her father, win over her uncle, and fix her whole world. She hadn't even thought about how the war would impact everything or how sick her father could become without them.

Vincenzo was by the boat, holding Giulia's hand. He took Emilia's suitcase, then helped her into the boat. The sky was darkening. A storm was approaching.

"We'd better get moving," Vincenzo said. "And you both had better get back up to the castle. It's not a quick walk."

"Take good care of Papa," Annalisa told Emilia. "Tell him we are coming back soon with a cure. Make sure he eats well and takes the medicine he has."

"I will," she said. "And hurry! Come back as soon as you can."

"Don't worry, I'll keep in touch with you about them," Vincenzo said to Annalisa. He turned to Giulia and she touched his cheek. Annalisa watched her sister, realizing that both Giulia and Emilia had aged in these last few weeks. Emilia was no longer a baby and Giulia was no longer a flirty schoolgirl.

Vincenzo climbed into the boat and soon they were on their way.

"Do you think Papa will be okay?" Giulia asked.

"I think he can hang on for a bit more. He'll be glad to have Emilia back. That will cheer him up."

"And you'll have a cure to bring him soon?"

"I believe so," she said.

Giulia looked hard at her. "What's going on? What happened to you last night? We looked around for you after the concert. And Aldo was gone and Uncle, too. And then you didn't want to get up this morning."

Annalisa shook her head. "It's nothing. I'm fine."

"Someone said they heard Uncle shouting. Did it have something to do with you?"

Annalisa stayed silent.

"And I saw the way Aldo looked at you when he played his piece," Giulia continued. "Everyone saw it. He named it after you, didn't he?"

"It was just a name. Not for me."

"Of course it was for you. Don't try to make me feel like a fool, Annalisa. I know what I saw."

Annalisa raised her palms in surrender. "It doesn't matter, whatever the name of the piece was. It was silly, the way we looked at each other. I shouldn't have allowed it to happen."

"But he's a good person. He's a very good person." She paused. "Do you think Mama was thinking about big things when she left? About legacy and the future and her rich family? Because I don't think so. I think she just knew that she'd met a good man. I think that's all that matters—to have a very good person love you. I mean, the war and the fighting and all the danger and illness. Don't you think that maybe it all comes down to having one person who loves you for a minute? Even just for a moment?"

Annalisa looked toward the water, where she could see Vincenzo's boat receding. She didn't know how to answer Giulia. Not now, not after losing the love of both her uncle and Aldo. She stood still, contemplating the vast sea and the islands and mountains in the distance, the sky that always stayed light even after dark. Wasn't there anything a person could do that was eternal? Wasn't that the goal of science, to build something to last? Or did it really all come down to what Giulia said—to having a love that lasts only a moment? If Patricio's medicine worked, it would only keep Papa alive for what, a few years, a decade maybe? In the history of the universe, wasn't that just a moment as well?

She turned and started back up to the castle, watching Giulia give a final glance toward the boat. She wondered what her mother would have advised her.

But there was no way to know.

TWENTY-FIVE

2018

Thursday

Mia watched Leo take in what she'd just told him.

Though she'd only met him this week, she'd spent a lot of time with him, and she'd never seen the expression on his face that she was seeing now. It wasn't angry and it wasn't startled. It was almost blank, his chin lifted, his lips slightly pursed. But it was his eyes that said far more than she thought he was ready to say. He looked like he'd taken a slap across the face. And he was trying to figure out why. Not so much so he could retaliate. More so that he could see where he'd gone wrong. What mistake he had made. Why his trust had been so misplaced.

But she hadn't betrayed him. She'd followed the rules like any good scientist would have. The problem was, this wasn't science. They were two people trying to understand where they came from. Searching for confirmation that it meant something, what those who had come before them had endured. Searching for a route forward, a way to have peace for themselves, because it was a kind of peace for those who were no longer here. And she had hidden her secret for too long. Just like her grandmother.

They made their way to the entrance hall and out the castle doors in silence. When they reached the courtyard, she moved ahead of him and turned so they were face to face.

"Leo, I'm sorry," she said. "I'm sorry I didn't tell you sooner. I'm sorry I let you think I was sad about the island when I was really just stunned by what I'd learned about my grandmother."

He put his hands in his pockets and shook his head, looking down. "It's okay," he said, his tone even and dispassionate. "You were coming for information. You said you weren't going to tell me anything until you got what you wanted."

"I know. I did," she said. "But when you brought me here today to show me the floating terrace and how beautiful it was, and explain what it said about creation and imagination and vision... I realized I'd been wrong. That what we're doing is so much more than just exchanging information."

He turned his head toward the stone staircase at the far end of the courtyard, seemingly to avoid her eyes. "Come," he said. "The boat will be waiting."

They were silent again as they went down the hill. She knew that technically he had nothing to be angry about, but still she felt terrible. She cared about Leo, and she hoped she hadn't destroyed the friendship that was forming between them.

The ferry was there as expected, and they sat down on a bench, her on the end and him about a foot away. He reached into a cooler beneath the bench for some sandwiches he'd brought from the hotel, and went to hand one to her, but neither one of them felt like eating. Mia faced forward, not wanting to watch the castle recede from sight. She suspected that Leo would feel no obligation or desire to bring her back, that she'd never be there again, and the thought was almost unbearable. She wanted to be where her grandmother had been, to learn more about her life and her sisters. To learn about Patricio, why he chose her grandmother of all people to mentor. She wanted to learn about Aldo—and how he and her grandmother had escaped from the Nazis. She wanted to go back and learn more. And maybe she would have been able to if she'd been honest sooner.

The boat picked up speed, and she turned to Leo. "I need you to know how things were for me when I came here," she said. "You and I are so different. You're from a close family that came together, that rallied, after your grandfather died. I know your grandmother grieved after she lost her husband, but she had her children and grandchildren. She shared what she knew so you would all know, too. Isn't it ironic? Your grandfather died and your family stayed strong. My grandmother lived, and yet she was so damaged. She loved me, but it wasn't with the love that most grandparents have. Love wasn't a source of comfort to her. It was a sign of imperfection. I don't think she was always like that. But she changed."

She dropped her chin. "And now I know why," she said, with resignation. "I wasn't the granddaughter she wanted. The family she wanted was the one she would have had with Aldo. Because she was Annalisa, his muse. And when she lost him, she lost herself."

A moment passed, and then Leo slid closer and put his arm around her shoulders. "Oh, Mia," he murmured and drew her toward him.

She let herself lean against him and felt the welcoming warmth of his body through his shirt. A piece of her felt guilty, craving the closeness when, at least technically, she still had a boyfriend. But she couldn't move away. Although she'd known Ryan for a year and Leo for less than a week, she was certain that Leo would understand what she was going through far more than Ryan ever could.

"I never knew my grandmother had sisters," she said, her head near his shoulder. "I never knew she had a love so much more meaningful to her than the one she shared with my grandfather. I never knew she aspired to be a scientist, the kind Patricio would make his apprentice. I never knew she was his apprentice, or that she even lived here. I never knew any of it until I saw the letter the lawyer in Rome sent, which led to everything else.

"And the only reason I saw that was because she died," she said. "That's the only reason I found the *schianto* and the wedding dress. Because when you die... things come out."

She felt his chin gently make contact with the top of her head. "I'm sorry, too, Mia," he said. "I'm sorry that you're learning all this now, so far from your home, with your grandmother so recently lost. You're right. In a strange way, even though my grandfather died, I'm lucky. And in a strange way, even though your grandmother survived... it's not always the survivors who triumph, is it?"

He pulled away and she lifted her head so their eyes could meet. "Tell me about the wedding dress. Have you seen it?"

"Yes, and it's lovely," she said. "An incredible combination of structure with a beauty that seems to float on air. With these shiny stone beads, and the fabric that drapes in curves and dips... I can't even describe it. You have to see it. You will. I promise. I will get it to you."

"And the *schianto*?" he said. "You've seen that too?"

She smiled. "I have. And that I can show you. Right now."

As the boat reached the shore, Leo radioed to Giuseppe to come meet them with the van. Soon after, they were in the hotel. She led him to her room, then kneeled by the suitcase and unzipped it. She removed the sweaters and held it out to him.

He squatted, and she could feel his warmth right beside her, as he took it from her hands. His fingers cradled the sides below the rim. "Unbelievable," he breathed. "Oh my. Oh, Mia, do you realize how this feels? I have been looking for this for so long."

"It's astonishing, isn't it?" she said. "I knew it was. Even before I understood the full meaning behind it."

"It's even more amazing than I imagined," he said, almost in a whisper. He stood and carried it to the window, holding it up as the rays from the lowering sun filtered through the glass to graze it. "Look at this. It's exquisite. Look at how the facets in the granite sparkle. Look at the veins in the marble. Patricio was a scientist but he was an artist, too. He corresponded with my grandfather about this, letters delivered from the tower to the art studio, because he had to talk to someone. He had the stone-cutters work on it for months. He sent it back time after time—that's what my grandfather wrote to my grandmother. He speci-fied how the marble should look, where the veins should be. This was what he hoped would mend the world. He wanted to heal people. Because he was so badly hurt."

"It's so sad," Mia said. "He wanted this to work so much."

"Sad that he had no family to honor this. At least my grand-father had me. But Patricio had no one. No one who could feel the magic that I feel when I touch my grandfather's sketches. That I'll feel when I see the wedding dress."

He shook his head and came back from the window. Handing her the *schianto*, he sat on the foot of the bed. "Your grandmother had it this whole time? And she never told you? How did you happen to find it?"

Mia rewrapped the *schianto* and placed it in her suitcase. Then she sat next to him. "She wanted me to find it after she was gone. She left me clues that sent me straight upstairs to the attic to find the gown and then to a storage unit where the *schi-anto* was.

"So what happens to the *schianto* now?" she asked. "Does the lawyer expect that I'll hand it right over?"

"Do you have another idea?" he asked. "It's Patricio's. It

belongs to the castle. It belongs to the island. The developer bought it all, that's why they're going after it so aggressively. Do you think otherwise?"

"No... but it seems that she's being accused of taking it when it didn't belong to her. And I don't think she would have done that. She wasn't perfect, she had a lot of faults that left me very confused. But she had integrity, and she was honest." She told him about the PTA flyer and her fierce defense of her reputation.

"That's why I came here," she said. "To prove, somehow, that she wasn't a thief."

"Well, I believe you, Mia," he said. "But that's not going to hold water. These guys want it back for the exhibit. They're not going to accept that she legitimately owned it unless there's proof."

"Couldn't Patricio have given it to her?"

"You think it was a gift?"

"I don't know. But you said he gave gifts..."

"He gave pencils, trinkets. And besides, I told you about the record-keeping. If he gave something, it was on the list with a triangle. Otherwise, no way."

He studied her. "Mia," he said. "Do you want to keep the *schianto*? Is that what you're trying to do? Keep it hidden in that storage place? Is that where you think it belongs?"

"No. No, I don't want to keep it locked up. And if it rightfully belongs to this place, then I'm happy to hand it over. But I can't live with people thinking she stole it."

"No one will think that. No one will know it. They just want it back at the castle."

"But *I'll* know it. And she'll know it, wherever she is. It's just wrong. She'll go down in history as a thief. And I can't do that to her."

He stood. "What's the alternative? We could search for years and still never find anything that proves she took it for a legitimate purpose. I think you're asking for the impossible. Either keep it and fight for it or hand it over. But what you're asking for... they're not going to entertain the possibility that she took it legitimately unless you have proof.

"You have to choose, Mia," he said. "If you want me to deny I saw it, I won't say a word. But they'll find you. These investigators don't miss a beat. And they'll go after you. They'll drag your grandmother's name through the mud to get the *schianto* back. And then what will you have?"

"You think I should just give it up and walk away?" she said, her tone demonstrating that that was the last thing in the world she'd agree to do.

"I don't know what to tell you. I just don't know."

She went to the table and collapsed onto a chair.

He stood and started for the door. "I need to get ready and change, and go help set up for the banquet tonight," he said. "Why don't you plan to meet me down there? Put this aside for now."

"No, I don't think I could stand a party," she said.

"You need to eat something," he said and gestured toward the cooler with the sandwiches that he'd brought back from the boat.

"I will," she told him.

He sighed. "I hate to leave you like this," he said. "But I have to get down there. It's part of my job."

She smiled, thinking it was sweet that he felt the need to explain why he had to leave. As though he would have preferred to stay. But he didn't owe her anything. This was her problem. He'd gotten what he wanted from her, and he'd intended to give her what she wanted. But he couldn't. He had nothing in his possession to confirm that her grandmother wasn't a thief. And no way of finding such a thing.

"Of course, you should go," she said. "It's fine. I'm fine." But she wasn't fine, no matter how she tried to sound convincing. And she knew he knew it, too.

"You're certain you won't come?"

"I'm sure. But be prepared," she added, trying to lighten the mood. "Missy has some questions for you. She wants to ask about a nicer way for her clients to get onto the island than the plain old ferry."

He shrugged. "I guess she has a point. Thanks for the warning."

She got up to walk him out, and he turned to her when he reached the door. "If you change your mind, just come down-stairs anytime this evening. And if not, I'll see you tomorrow, okay? We'll spend some more time together before you go back home."

"That would be nice," she said.

He left, and she walked away from the door. Sitting down on the carpet, her legs outstretched and her back against the bed, she sent quick texts to Erica and Ryan letting them know she was okay but busy and would call them tomorrow. She didn't feel like talking to anyone. This was not how she expected her trip to wind up. This was not what she had been thinking as she watched the sun lower over the airfield at JFK. She'd been determined to exonerate her grandmother. To free her from horrible allegations.

And suddenly it felt like one more failure, one more time she had let her grandmother down. She had failed all her life to make her grandmother truly happy. She had failed to show her that love, even the love between a grandmother and grand-daughter, is far from imperfect; it's the most wonderful thing in the world. She'd felt so guilty all her life that her parents had taken off, first her father and then her mother, as though she'd caused it simply by being born. And she'd tried so hard to make it up to her grandmother—to prove to her grandmother that life and love were still valuable, despite the pain her grandmother felt.

And she had tried so hard to make do with less, because her grandmother had had to. The truth about why she'd never gone to graduate school—the truth she could admit to herself only now, when she was at her lowest point—only partially had to do with saving money and not wanting to move too far from her grandmother. The other part was that she couldn't bring herself to apply to schools and continue her education and her career. It had always seemed too selfish. She couldn't stand the thought of achieving more when her grandmother, who'd been smart and had so much potential, had had to make do with less.

And now the one thing she'd wanted above all else to do for her grandmother—to save her grandmother's reputation—was not going to happen. Her grandmother would be remembered as a thief if she were remembered at all. Mia had come here and was about to surrender the one thing Lucy had wanted to keep hidden. She'd resigned Lucy to a sad and unfair legacy.

There was a knock at the door and she pulled herself up and went to answer it, thinking that possibly it was Missy inviting her to come down and have a drink with her, Charlie and Pete before the party. She was thinking of the best, most polite way to turn her down when she opened the door and saw Leo there.

She looked at him and shook her head. "I... can't..." she said, not sure what she was saying. That she couldn't go to the party, that she couldn't see him again, that she couldn't go home, that she couldn't stay alone in this room one more night looking at the island and knowing she'd failed. But nothing came out except "I can't" a second time.

She started to close the door, because she didn't want him to try to convince her that she was a good granddaughter or that she'd done her best or any of the other lovely things she knew were probably on the tip of his tongue. But he placed his palm against the door and held it open.

"No, wait," he said. "I thought of something. It may not work, but it's worth a try. But you have to follow my instructions. You have to do exactly what I tell you. Can you do that?"

He didn't have to ask twice.

TWENTY-SIX

1943

September

The next few days were almost impossible for Annalisa to bear. She tried to continue her work, but it was so hard to concentrate. The mood in the castle stayed tense, and Signora Russo appeared increasingly distracted, making it seem that she'd been wrong, that the guests were aware now that the war was intensifying, and danger was imminent both for themselves and the families they'd left behind. Annalisa worried about her father and Emilia, feeling anxious when she awoke every morning and despairing every night when another day had passed without word from Vincenzo. She couldn't bring herself to go out on the terrace near the kitchen because that made her think how much she missed Aldo; and she hated being in the workroom because through the window she would see her uncle way down by the shore, scooping up soil from the water's edge and letting it pour through his fingers.

Even from this height, he looked like a shell of himself, weak and crestfallen. She wondered what he was thinking as he studied the soil. Did he regret letting her and her sisters into his life? Did he wish she'd never shown up? But what had she done that was so terrible? She'd fallen in love. Was he too bitter from his past to accept that? To understand that there was more to life than what the mind could imagine and the hands could build?

And when she thought about his unyielding attachment to his invention, she couldn't help but remember what Aldo had called the guests who came to the castle: dreamers with no grasp of reality. She couldn't help but think about Giulia's question as they walked back from the shore after watching Vincenzo's boat take off: Was it really true that they'd soon be going home with a cure for Papa? Or was Patricio chasing a pipe dream?

It seemed so much had gone wrong already. But then, six days after Emilia and Vincenzo left, the unthinkable happened.

Annalisa was awakened early by the sound of people rushing and shouting. Leaving Giulia to sleep, she peeked out her door to see the castle in a hubbub. The guests, who should have been awaiting breakfast, were rushing from their rooms, many carrying suitcases or dragging big trunks, mingling with staff in a way they never did. Doors to the guest rooms were flung open, and from where she stood, many looked like they were no longer occupied, all the books and framed photographs gone. Tray runners were carrying not breakfast trays, but large cardboard moving cartons.

After dressing quickly and silently so as not to disturb Giulia before she knew what was happening, Annalisa ran downstairs to the kitchen. There she found Signora Russo slicing bread and layering on cheese and meat for sandwiches, while one of her assistants wrapped each one in a cloth napkin.

"What's going on?" she asked.

Not stopping her work, Signora Russo answered soberly. "We got word early this morning from the men on one of the supply boats. Italy has surrendered to the Allied forces, and now the country is under attack from the Germans. The Nazis have invaded from the north. Rome is under Nazi control."

Annalisa crumpled into a chair. Although she'd heard Aldo and she'd known about the war, it seemed she'd been almost as oblivious as the others on the island. It was a great relief that war with the Allies was over. But a Nazi onslaught was catastrophic. She'd sent Emilia back home to Caccipulia to take care of their father. Their village was not far from Rome. How could she save them now?

"It's not safe to stay here," Signora Russo continued. "If the Nazis are approaching, they'll no doubt make their way to the islands in this area. You and your sister had better start packing up, too. I've never seen anything like this before. We don't have much time."

"Does my uncle know?" Annalisa asked.

"Nobody has seen him," Signora Russo said. "I sent some tray runners up to the tower, but he refuses to open his door. I wish he'd come down. We need someone to take charge." She pointed to the hallway, where people were rushing and shouting to one another to get out of their way. "It's chaos," she said.

"How long do you think we have?" Annalisa asked.

"A few days before the Nazis get here. That's what the men on the supply boat said."

"And what of the people working on the other island?"

"You mean where Aldo is? I'm worried about them, too. We're trying to get word out there. Hopefully we'll get them back here later today so they can leave for the mainland with everyone else.

"Oh, and I almost forgot," she said. "One of the boatmen brought a message for you. Here." She reached into her pocket and pulled out the envelope.

Annalisa ripped it open and read:

Dear Annalisa,

I am so sorry to tell you that everything has changed for the worse. I'm told that your poor father went to sleep two nights ago and never woke up. I hope he is in a better place now. I pray for his soul. But the news is more troubling for Emilia. Her life is in danger because of the change in the war, and because she is Jewish. I'm told she's gone into hiding, so my plan is to find her and try to help her escape to Switzerland. Please take care of Giulia and let her know I am thinking of her and hope we will all be reunited before too long.

Yours,

V

Annalisa stepped away from Signora Russo and looked outside onto the terrace, too sad for tears. Her father was dead. She hadn't saved him, and she hadn't even been there to comfort him or say goodbye. She'd left that awful job for Emilia, who now was in terrible danger herself. Why had she been so selfish and headstrong, so intent on delivering a cure that never materialized? She was no better than all the guests these last few months. Dancing and eating with their heads in the sand. Refusing to see what was happening.

Only Aldo had been clearheaded. He had seen the danger that the guests were in, deluding themselves. He'd said they were foolish and naïve, like children. She'd heard him say so. And yet, she hadn't changed her plans. She shouldn't have stayed here, no matter how wonderful it was, no matter how much Patricio's research intrigued her, no matter how much she adored Aldo. She should have gone home with her sisters weeks ago and taken her father out of Italy. Yes, he'd been frail, but they could have helped him travel. And maybe if they had, he'd still be alive now.

She stuffed Vincenzo's note in her pocket. There'd be time later to lambast herself. For now, she had to take responsibility for her sisters. Giulia was in danger here, and Emilia was in danger back home. She'd brought them here and now she needed to find a way to make them safe. But how?

Immediately after she asked herself the question, she knew the answer. She had to get her uncle to help her. They needed to get through this together. She thought about how happy he'd ultimately been to learn that she was his niece. Now everyone on the island was leaving, going to their families, going home. Patricio was her family. She had to reconcile with him.

She ran up the stairs to the tower and looked in his room, with no luck. Then she realized where he was. She left the tower and found him on his floating terrace. He was in his usual outfit, a too-big white shirt and baggy trousers, looking out to the Mediterranean. She saw the back of his head, the small thinning bald spot she'd noticed before. His back was rounded, his shoulders sunk. He was seeing everything he ever cared about, the one thing he'd done right in his life, crumbling to pieces.

"Patricio," she said, then paused. "Uncle," she whispered.

He turned around. "Is everyone making plans to leave?" he said.

She nodded.

"Is there panic?'

"No. No panic. Just... determination. To leave quickly."

He shook his head and looked back out on the sea. "Why doesn't anything ever last, Annalisa? When you think you've made something wonderful, and it can only get better and better—why doesn't it last?"

She stayed silent for a moment, not knowing how to answer. She didn't like seeing him like this. It was frightening, finding out that the people in your life who are supposed to have the answers no longer do. "I don't know," she finally said. "But isn't that what science teaches us? Nothing stays? The seasons, the tides. The setting of the sun, the rising of the moon. You know that. It was what you based your invention on. That natural elements can become curative if you manipulate them the right way. You taught me that."

"Yes," he said. "Yes. But I... I thought the perfect things stay. The music. The art. The genius. Everything here. It's permanent precisely because it comes from the human imagination. It's not changeable, it's evolutionary. Things are supposed to get better and better. When they come from here." He tapped his head. "From thought, from the brilliance of the human mind. It's not changeable, like matters of the heart. It's not the sea and the tides and the moon. It's knowledge. It's the mind.

"I must have done something wrong," he said, shaking his head fiercely. "I must have thought wrong. Otherwise, this couldn't be ending."

"You did nothing wrong," she told him. "It's war. It's evil. You don't control that."

"But I thought I could escape it. Escape the evil and the ugliness. Embrace the beauty that has always been a part of humanity."

"You did, for a time."

"I thought it could be forever. And that was my folly. My foolishness. I never thought I was a foolish man, Annalisa. But I'm a fool."

"That's not true—"

"Then how is any of this explained?" he said, facing toward the window as he raised his arms overhead. "All my decisions. A failure. Like my father said."

"No, they weren't," she said. She didn't want him to think this way. Despite what had happened between them, despite his rejection of Aldo, she cared for him. More than she would have imagined at this point. They were all people, everyone in the castle, doing their best, living under the illusion that they had way more power than they really did. Thinking they had control over their destinies. She was no better than he was, or than the guests in the castle were. She had thought she had control, too. Because... why not? Was there any other way to live? Her mother had thought she could control her own destiny, too, never imagining she'd leave a grieving husband with three motherless daughters. If Patricio was a fool, then they all were. But they weren't fools. They were human.

And he hadn't been a failure. He'd created something wonderful, even if it lasted barely a moment in the long history of the universe. That's what mattered. And he had done it from the heart, she knew that now. It had taken faith and hope and belief. Those were matters of the heart.

Even while denying it, he had acted with his heart. It was what being human meant.

He turned to her. "But I didn't come to you just now. You came to me. What is it you came for?"

"To ask for help," she whispered.

"Help to get back to your father?"

She shook her head. "We got word this morning. My... my father's dead."

"Oh, my child," he said, and moved toward her. "I'm so sorry. I'm so very sorry. I thought we could save him. I wouldn't have kept you here if I didn't."

"I know," she said. "I thought so, too. I wouldn't have stayed otherwise. But there's something else," she added. "Emilia left a few days ago to take care of him. And now she's in hiding. Vincenzo, our friend who runs one of the supply boats, he's gone back to try to get her to safety. I have to go there to help him."

"But you can't," he told her. "You can't go back. You are your father's daughter. You are Jewish, too."

"I can't abandon my sister. And I can't put all that responsibility on Vincenzo—"

"No. I have a better idea." He went to his desk. "I can get you on a boat to New York. I'd arranged that before, for you and me when our invention was done and your father was healthy again. I'd planned for us to stay temporarily with a former student of mine who now teaches there. You go ahead without me. Take Giulia. The two of you." And here—" He went to his desk and gave her a packet of what looked like travel documents. And then he took out a wad of bills from the drawer.

"Take this, you'll need it," he said, pushing it all into her hands. "My student's address is there with the tickets. Pay whatever you have to, whomever you have to—"

"But what about you?"

"I will find Emilia and Vincenzo. It's safer for me than for you. And I have money, which your friend Vincenzo doesn't, I'm sure. I'll find them both, and we will all meet in New York."

He went to the cabinet and took out the *schianto*. "And here. Take this, too."

"What?" she said. "Your experiment? No, no—this is yours."

"It won't be safe here. And I can't take it with me. Please take it, Annalisa. It means nothing to me now."

She thought for a moment, then took it from his hands. "Okay, I'll take it, but only temporarily," she said. "I will take it because your journey is more uncertain than mine. But I will keep it so we can continue to work on it in New York. Together. In my father's honor. In my parents' memory."

He reached out and held her face with his hands, then kissed her cheek. She moved the *schianto* to one hand and hugged him with her free arm. Because he was family. They were a family again.

Holding back tears, she started for the door. "Annalisa?" she heard him say.

She turned back. "Yes?"

"What of Aldo?"

With the mention of his name, she felt tears well in her eyes. Regret was a useless sentiment, and yet all she could think of was how foolish she'd been to write that note to Aldo. She pictured him, his cheeks drawn and his beautiful eyes downcast, as he kneeled by the stone to read it. How she wished she could take back everything that had happened since they'd kissed after he played the piece he'd dedicated to her.

"I don't know," she said, her voice breaking. "I don't know what will happen to him."

"Where is he?"

"He left after the concert. He went with the crew to the other island. They're trying to get a message to them, to make sure they know all that's happening, but..."

"Oh, no," Patricio said with a deep sigh. He reached his hand out to touch her shoulder, then withdrew it, as though he didn't feel entitled to embrace or comfort his niece. "I am so sorry for what I did," he said.

She met his eyes with hers, knowing how hard that must have been for him to say. "It wasn't your fault," she told him.

"But the things I said..."

"It wasn't," she told him. "Believe me." He wasn't the one who'd sent Aldo away. She had done that, by lashing out with her cold-hearted note. She closed her eyes, knowing she had to compose herself. She couldn't fall apart now. She still had to save her sisters.

"I need to find Giulia," she said as she wiped her eyes with her fingers. "We need to move ahead with all our plans."

"We do," he said. "Go—go get Giulia. We're the ones who can make this work, Annalisa. We're the ones who can save our family."

She nodded and, with the *schianto* in her hands, she ran downstairs to Savio's studio. It was empty, all the paints tucked away. So she turned and ran back up to their suite. Giulia was there packing their things.

"Oh, Annalisa! I didn't know where you were," she said, running to embrace her sister. "We need to go to Papa and Emilia. We can't wait for Patricio's cure."

Annalisa put the *schianto* on the dresser and led Giulia to sit down. "You don't know all the news. It's worse than you think," she said as she reached in her pocket for Vincenzo's note.

Giulia read it, then looked up, big tears forming in her eyes. "What have we done?"

"We did what we thought was best," Annalisa said, swallowing hard. "We tried to save Papa. He was so sick."

Giulia nodded. "So what do we do now?"

Annalisa told her about Patricio's plans to find Emilia and Vincenzo, and about the passage he'd booked to New York.

"And what about Aldo?" Giulia asked.

"He's away on the other island."

"But he's coming back, isn't he?"

Annalisa shrugged, tears filling her eyes again. "I don't know. He went with the crew to the other island days ago, and they're trying to reach them and get them back right away. Oh, Giulia, I can't... I can't think about him now. If I start now, I won't be able to think about anything else except how... how I love him..."

She looked down, and a moment later she felt Giulia gently enveloping her in her arms. "That was a silly question for me to ask," she said. "Of course he's coming back. They'll get word to them, and he'll come back as soon as he hears what's happening. He loves you. He should be the one going with you to New York. He should use the second passage Uncle gave you."

"No, you need to come with me. You're my sister."

"I'll be okay," Giulia said. "Savio is going home to Buenos Aires and he offered to take me and two others who helped with the dresses. I can travel to New York from there. Then you can travel with Aldo." She got up and went to the closet to pull out the wedding dress she'd helped sew for Savio's painting. "And here. You take this."

"The wedding dress you made? But why?"

"Savio wants me to have it. And I think it belongs in New York with you and Aldo. You'll wear it when you marry him and we'll dance all night, the way we saw the people do when we first got to this crazy island. We'll celebrate your wedding and we'll always remember how you and Aldo met. I always knew you'd wear it. I had you in mind when I sewed it.

"And you know what else?" she added. "Maybe I'll wear it too, one day. When we are reunited with Vincenzo. We have a whole future to look forward to."

They hugged one last time, and then Giulia took her suitcase and started back to the studio to find Savio. Annalisa watched her, willing herself to believe that one day soon they'd all be together in New York. Then she started toward the stairs to see if there was any word yet from Aldo and the others on the smaller island. All around her people were scurrying, rushing, carrying suitcases—musicians, artists, writers and staff members too, young and old. She wondered for a moment about all the beautiful works begun here that would never be finished. Aldo had said these guests were full of potential, and many had yet to make their mark on the world. They had years of creativity ahead of them. What would come of everything they'd started to create, all that was still simmering in their imaginations? Who would have thought even yesterday that this would be the outcome of their talent?

She started down the steps when she heard her uncle calling from behind.

"Annalisa! Wait!" he said. "There's one more thing I have to do."

TWENTY-SEVEN

2018

Friday

The next evening, as she'd been instructed, Mia came down to the lobby at six o'clock. Leo had told her not to wear jeans and sneakers, as he didn't want anyone who saw her to suspect she was going back to the construction zone on Parissi Island. Instead, he advised her to dress as though she were joining with the tour group, which had one final cocktail party and buffet dinner on the terrace. Then they were leaving for a cruise that would wind up at the mainland, where they'd spend their last night and catch a train back to Rome early tomorrow morning.

Hardly able to sit still and thinking she was too nervous to risk meeting anyone in the lobby and having to carry on a conversation, Mia stayed in her room most of the day, making her way downstairs for a little while when she started to go stir-crazy, and staying on the quiet side of the terrace. Following Leo's directions, she put on a flared skirt with a sleeveless top and her jacket, as it was sure to be chilly on the water at night. She'd worn her nicer sandals, since they'd look more appropriate at a cocktail party than flats. She hoped she'd be able to climb the stone stairs in them—and quickly. Leo had said they wouldn't have much time.

The lobby was busy, as the travel agents were all checking out. The perimeter was lined with suitcases of varying sizes and colors, all with distinguishing ribbons or other decorations that would make them recognizable on the baggage carousel when their owners finally reached their home airport. As Leo had instructed, Mia stayed near the elevator bank until she caught sight of him by the entranceway. He locked eyes with her and nodded, and she hurried over. He didn't even wait for her to reach him before leaving the hotel. Outside, Giuseppe was waiting by the van, and he hopped on when he saw them approaching. Mia followed Leo on board and Giuseppe immediately took off down the hill. Inside the van, nobody said a word. The only sound was Leo's fingers lightly tapping the metal pole that separated the benches from the driver's seat. She could tell he was tense, that he was doing something he wasn't supposed to be, and although she didn't know what was wrong, she felt anxious just watching him.

When they reached the shore, she followed Leo and paused to drink in the view. The dusky sky was lavender, with touches of orange and hints of gold threaded just above the horizon. She wondered if this was what the sky had looked like when it was given the name *Isola della Notte Brillante*. And had it looked like this, too, on the first night her grandmother had spent here? Had Lucy been as wowed as Mia was right now?

"Unbelievable," she murmured.

Leo exchanged a few words with Giuseppe in Italian, and then Giuseppe drove the van back toward the hotel while they headed for the dock. "Come, Mia," Leo said. "We have just over two hours if we want Giuseppe to drive us up to the hotel. Otherwise, he'll be busy with the tour group, and we'll be on our own. So, let's go. Not a moment to lose."

She followed him toward the ferry and stepped aboard,

sensing the now-familiar feel of moving water underneath her feet. She started for her usual bench and sat down. But something was different—and she soon realized what it was. There was no captain in the wheelhouse. And then she saw why. Leo was climbing up the stairs to where the captain should have been.

"Leo!" she called, standing up. "What are you doing?"

He looked down at her from the top step. "I'm taking us to the castle."

"You're steering the ferry? Do you know how?"

"Well enough, I hope."

"But why no captain?"

"Because we're going someplace nobody is allowed to be. Now you'd better take a seat. It may not be as smooth a ride as you're used to."

She sat down on the bench. She didn't know what to say, and he didn't sound like he wanted to entertain any more questions. She supposed she could leave the boat if she truly felt unsafe. But she trusted him, and if this was the only way she could get back to the island to check out his idea, then she was willing to stay.

She looked out over the side of the boat as it began to pick up pace. The night sky darkened slightly, and with no moon visible, the surface of the water turned a bluish black, with what looked like a carpet of tiny gold pebbles reflecting the light from the hotel. The castle looked like it was made of onyx, its silhouette dense in the near distance.

"Quite a view, right? Even better, in a way, than in the daytime, isn't it?" she heard Leo call from above.

"It is," she said and stood to walk a little closer to the stairway leading up to his perch, starting to relax as she realized he could handle the ferry after all. "Breathtaking. And you know, the sky actually does have a strange lightness, don't you think?"

He paused. "Maybe."

"I think it's glowing." She studied it some more. "I'm sure of it."

Leo docked the boat smoothly at the pier and climbed down the steps from the wheelhouse. Though the sky was lighter than she'd have expected, the trees and shrubbery on the island made the ground almost impossibly dark. Leo pulled out his phone, so Mia did, too, and they both used their flashlights to illuminate the way as best they could. They reached the steep stone staircase, and Leo kneeled by a makeshift electrical box she hadn't noticed before, mounted to a wooden board attached to a pole. Opening the box, he flipped a switch and suddenly the staircase was illuminated by two lines of tiny white bulbs running up on either side.

Mia drew in a breath. "That's so pretty," she said.

Leo closed the box and stood back up. "Not authentic by any means. It was put in for the resort, with the idea that there could be midnight nature walks and ghost tours and such. In Parissi's time, nobody would be going up or down these stairs at night. Way too dangerous to navigate these steps at night with only a lantern or two to guide you."

"But we're not supposed to be here, right? Aren't you scared they'll see us from the hotel?"

"I don't think it'll be visible there. There's a lot of other light interfering, and these bulbs are pretty small. I'll turn this off when we get to the top. But it's the only way. We'd never be able to make it all the way up without any light but our phones."

They proceeded up the stairs. At the top, Leo walked to another electrical box to switch the staircase lights off, and they went back to using their phones' flashlights. They stepped through the front doorway and proceeded upstairs, Leo switching on only enough light to guide them. They passed the places they'd passed before—the ballroom, the exhibit hall, and the floating terrace, and then continued further down the hallway, to another set of stairs. At the top, he reached a wire hanging down with a small switch in the middle, and he pushed the dial forward with his thumb. A series of bare lightbulbs suspended from the ceiling lit up.

Then he led her through a narrow hallway and to a closed door. She wondered what he could possibly want to show her in this unfinished portion of the castle. But as soon as he opened the door, everything changed. It was as though they had stepped back in time eighty years. This was not a renovated replica of what the castle had once been, as the rooms downstairs were. This was the actual space. There was a faded, dusty red carpet on the floor and a long hallway with intricate molding above and blue toile wallpaper ripped and stained in places.

"Where are we?" she whispered.

"This is an area that will never open to the public," Leo said. "It's Parissi's suite. His private space where he spent all his time, alone. He never left here until a week before the Nazis arrived. When he went downstairs to hear Aldo play."

"And you've never been here before?"

He shook his head. "I think if you add you and me, you'd still have only a handful of people who've ever set foot here."

He led her through another doorway, the door split nearly in half and partially off its hinges. They were now in a big room. The floor-to-ceiling windows were cracked and covered in tape, and the floorboards were loose and warped. There was a row of battery-operated lanterns on the floor and he switched a couple of them on. Looking around, Mia saw a large bed, two night-stands on either side, and a wooden desk with six drawers. Across the room was a tall wooden cabinet with a curved top, and a metal table.

"Was this his bedroom?" Mia asked.

"His bedroom and his study," Leo said. "I imagine the Nazis used this room as an office. Which was why it wasn't ransacked as so many of the other rooms were."

"It's like we've stepped back in time," Mia murmured.

Leo nodded. "This was where he did all his work. I guess there are worse places to be holed up. And... oh, wait. Look here." He walked over to the cabinet and opened the double doors. Inside was a series of shelves. The center one was the tallest and seemed to have had a light fixture attached to the bottom of the upper shelf at one point to light whatever was on display.

"I've only seen this shelf in books," he said. "This was where he kept the *schianto*..."

Mia felt chills run down her arms. "I can't believe it sat right there when he was doing his work."

"He brought it out to work on it every day. And tucked it away safely every night."

"So what do we do?" Mia asked.

"We search," he told her. "This is the only place I can think of that hasn't been explored yet. I haven't seen anything yet to show that your grandmother was entitled to take the *schianto*, but maybe if there is some proof, it's hidden in this room. The furniture here has been untouched since the Nazis left. Let's just see how much we can open and what's inside."

She nodded and the two of them got to work. Mia opened the drawers of the desk while Leo concentrated on the night-stands. They both examined the spaces underneath the bed and beneath the yellowed mattress. Mia spotted a clothes closet and looked inside there, too. But it didn't take them much time to cover the whole room. There was nothing but dust and empty spaces, other than some blank sheets of paper and old pencils in the desk, and a random beaker and weighted scale on the table.

Mia looked at Leo, who was across the room by the cabinet. "There's nothing. How can there be nothing?"

"I didn't expect this," Leo murmured. "Either he destroyed everything, or the Nazis did. Or someone the new owner sent over to scout out the place." He shook his head and started to sit down on the bed, then evidently changed his mind when he realized how old, dusty and unstable it no doubt was. Then he raised his hands, like a show of surrender. "I'm sorry," he said. "It came to me last night. I thought if we'd find some proof anywhere, it would be in Patricio's private quarters. That if he wrote something about the *schianto* and where he wanted it to spend the future, it would be here. But I guess I was wrong."

She sighed. "It's not your fault. Thank you for trying. I know you risked a lot doing this."

He shrugged. "I did my best. Come. I need to get the ferry back before anyone misses it."

Mia followed him all the way back downstairs and out of the castle. All she could think about was how she'd let her grandmother down. She'd come here certain that as long as she arrived on Parissi Island, she'd discover the proof she needed. But here she was, coming up empty. Her flight back to New York from Rome was less than two days away, and she didn't want to accept she was destined to remain in the dark. There was a gap, a crater, between what had happened and what she could gather. And yet she still believed the truth was knowable. Somewhere on this island, she believed, there was proof that her grandmother had been entitled, even asked, to take the *schianto* to America.

And if the proof didn't exist in Patricio's room, that didn't mean it didn't exist at all, she told herself. Who else could have known that Lucy came by the *schianto* legitimately? Who else could have known the truth and written it down, then placed it where it wouldn't have yet been disturbed...

She pressed her lips together and narrowed her eyes, cataloging in her mind all the evidence she'd encountered since she'd made her first trip to the castle: the balcony, Signora Russo's lists, the brochure she'd read at the café, the recording of Aldo's interview... *I embrace you from a distance, my star, my muse, my words, my music...*

"Oh my God!" she said. "Leo, wait!"

"What?" he said, turning around.

"What if we're looking at the wrong man? The wrong hiding spot, the wrong person who would have known? What if whatever was said about the *schianto*, whatever was communicated… what if it wasn't between Patricio and my grandmother —but between my grandmother and Aldo?"

"You mean Aldo gave her the *schianto*? That doesn't make sense—"

"No, it's what Aldo said in an interview he gave in Pittsburgh when 'For Pippa' debuted. He said Signora Russo would leave messages for the Allies behind a loose stone in the terrace, and he'd take those messages to the boathouse. Maybe he left other writings there, too. He knew my grandmother so well, and they loved each other, and they must have shared everything. What if the proof we're looking for wasn't written by Patricio— but by *Aldo*?"

"I don't know," Leo said. "But it can't hurt to look."

They went back into the castle, through to the kitchen, and out to the terrace, the ground still covered in plywood. Using the flashlights on their phones, they kneeled on the plywood and crawled along the stone wall, feeling for the loose stone. A few stones were loose but turned out to be false alarms, as they couldn't be removed from the wall. But then Mia found a stone near the edge of the wall that pulled right out when she tugged it.

"Oh my gosh," she whispered, feeling her breath catch in her throat. "This is the loose rock Aldo described in the interview." It was where he'd pulled out messages to transfer to the Allied forces. She felt like she was touching history.

Feeling the edges cut into her fingertips, she pushed aside the rock and brushed away the dirt behind it with her fingers. Then she reached inside. "Leo!" she said. "There's something here!"

She stuck her hand all the way inside the small opening, and pulled out a yellowed sheet of paper, covered in mud stains and torn where it had been folded. Straightening it out, she shone her phone light on it. The handwriting was faded, but she recognized it anyway. It wasn't Aldo's after all. It was her grand-mother's.

She gave the note to Leo and he translated it from Italian as he read it aloud.

My dearest Aldo,

I came here in pursuit of science, a cure for my father, and I leave with feelings and dreams I never imagined I'd have. Feelings of love for you and dreams of being together forever. I am leaving for America tonight and I want you to come with me. My uncle has secured passage for us. All the details are on the sheet folded into this letter. Giulia is going with Savio to Argentina and then to America, and my uncle is going to find Emilia and meet us there too. And if all goes well, we will all be reunited in New York. Giulia gave me the wedding dress to take, and I have the schianto, too, so we will always remember what we had here. I love you, Aldo. I want to spend my life with you. Please come with me to America. I long for you, I bow to you, I embrace you from a distance.

With all my heart,

Annalisa

Mia took the page from him and studied the foreign words. If she were the crying type, she was sure she'd be sobbing by now.

"Oh, Leo," she said. "My grandmother wrote this. It's her handwriting."

"And he never received it," Leo said. "He didn't know she was waiting for him. He never came back to the island. He never got this note."

"No wonder she was always so sad," she said. "She was in love. She thought they'd all be reunited. And she probably never knew if he got this note or not. If he never saw it, or if he saw it and decided he didn't love her back."

She sighed. "But this doesn't prove anything about the *schianto*, does it? It proves she had it, but it doesn't prove she was the legitimate owner, does it?"

Leo shook his head. "I'm afraid not."

Mia stood and walked to the end of the terrace, looking past the trees toward the water. "I don't know what to think anymore," she said. "Maybe I've been deluding myself all this time. Maybe I misread her. Maybe she did steal it. Maybe she thought she was saving it, with the Nazis coming. Maybe her intentions were good. But it says it right there, what you read: *I have the schianto*."

"You can't blame her," Leo said, coming up next to her.

"She was so honest. She never wanted to steal anything."

"Maybe that's why she hid it. Because she felt so bad about it all these years."

Mia shook her head. "I didn't want to believe it," she said. "But I have no choice now. I need to admit the truth and give it back. I guess it always should have been here."

Leo stroked her hair. "She may have been right. She may have saved it by taking it away."

"But hiding it for decades after the war? Why would she do that?"

"Maybe she was scared of being accused of stealing it. Or maybe she didn't know how to go about giving it back."

"But she should have," Mia insisted, facing him. "It was wrong to keep it if it didn't belong to her. No matter the reason. She should have found a way to get it wherever it truly belonged." She pressed the back of her hand to her forehead, her fingers still clutching the note. She was exactly where she'd started.

"Oh, my—I don't believe—oh, Mia!" Leo exclaimed.

"What? What?"

"Look! Look at the back of that note!"

She turned it over and saw more Italian handwriting. But then she saw something that didn't need to be translated.

It was a triangle. The sign of a gift from Patricio.

Then she sounded out the words, even though she didn't know what they meant: *Per Annalisa, mia nipote. Lo schianto di terra. Da tuo zio, Patricio.*

"What does it mean?" she asked Leo. "Is it Patricio's handwriting?"

"Absolutely," he said. "I've seen it in books a million times."

"It's a gift, right? With the triangle? Isn't that what it means?"

"It means more than that," he told her. "*Mia nipote* means my niece. *Tuo zio* means your uncle. Your grandmother wasn't just an apprentice. She was his niece. He gave the *schianto* to his niece.

"She was a Parissi," he said, smiling. "And Mia. That means you are, too."

TWENTY-EIGHT

2018

Saturday

The terrace was quiet with the tour group gone and the hotel empty. Mia was wearing the one fancy outfit she'd brought, a deep-blue tiered dress with spaghetti straps and a cinched bodice. Erica had urged her to bring something nice in case they went out on the town during their one evening in Rome. Mia had thought the chances of that were slim, since they had to get up so early the next morning for the train ride down the coast. But she was glad she'd brought it. She'd have to remember to thank Erica for insisting that she prepare for a possible special night.

Leo was leaning against the stone wall, but he stood up straight when he saw her. He, too, was dressed differently from the way she'd seen him all week, and she thought he looked stunning, in a blue-striped button-down shirt and tan pants, his hair combed smooth, and just a skimming of hair against his jaw.

Over his shoulder, she could see the dim outline of the Castello del Poeta. Even though the moon was just a sliver, the sky looked radiant tonight. Just as it had last night, as Leo had commandeered the ferry to take her to Parissi Island. What was causing the light, the *notte brillante*? She wondered if there actually was a geological explanation. Or maybe it was the specter of the many, many souls, long gone now, who had made this place so magical. Too magical to last. Maybe their spirits were lingering. Because energy didn't disappear, it just changed form. She knew that. She was a scientist at heart. Like her grandmother.

"*Buona sera*," he said as he took her hand and kissed her cheek. "You look lovely."

She closed her eyes and savored the kiss, then opened them to see him gesturing toward a small, round table in the center of the terrace. It was beautifully set for two, with pink linens, crystal wine goblets and sparkling silverware. A lily surrounded by eucalyptus was the centerpiece. At the far end of the terrace, two servers in tuxedos were arranging food from platters onto two dinner plates.

"What an evening," she said. "I can't believe you did this..."

He chuckled. "I didn't. Signor Dorria did. The news has only been out for twenty-four hours, and yet you're already a celebrity. Nobody expected to ever meet a real Parissi."

"I still don't believe it," she said. "It doesn't make sense."

"I know," he said. "I never thought this was how things would end up this week either."

"You thought I was some annoying tourist trying to get secret information."

"And you thought I was someone obsessed with power and holding all the cards."

She laughed. "I'm so glad you decided to lie for me that night."

"I am too, Signorina Mia," he said.

He touched her back lightly and led her to their table. She was surprised she was even awake. They'd rushed away from the castle last night in order to get the ferry back to the shore and board the van within the timeframe Giuseppe had been able to allot them. They'd watched the tour group leave, then sat down in the lobby staring blankly at one another, both absorbing what they had discovered. Then Leo had gone to the office behind the reception desk to craft an email informing his employers about the discovery of a Parissi descendant and the recovery of the *schianto*.

Meanwhile, Mia had gone straight to her room. She needed to be alone with her thoughts. Sitting on the freshly made bed, her grandmother's note to Aldo in her hands, she suddenly—and so unexpectedly—found herself crying. Crying like she never had before. With big gasps and heartfelt bursts of breath. She hadn't cried when Milt had called to tell her that Lucy had died, and she hadn't cried at the funeral either. How do you cry for someone you barely know? And that was the truth—she'd barely known her grandmother until the discovery of the note hidden in the stone wall.

Of course, she'd thought all her life that she knew Lucy. She had no reason to think otherwise. Her grandmother was the strict, quiet, and strange but always loving woman she'd spent her whole life with. Distant from strangers but utterly devoted to people she knew and cared about. And somehow incredibly appealing to people like Milt and Erica, who admired her straightforward, take-no-prisoners approach to life. The woman who loved the night sky, who loved the nighttime and the water more than she could ever express. The woman who persevered on her own to raise her granddaughter.

But now Mia saw the real person deep inside. The girl who came to an island in pursuit of science, in pursuit of a cure for her father, and ended up falling in love. The girl who once had big hopes and was left with nothing but loss and grief. The loss of her sisters, her father, her uncle, and the man she wanted to spend her life with. She'd tried to reach out to Aldo and ultimately lost him. Had she thought he'd rejected her? Or had she thought he'd been killed along with the others? Either way, he never read her note. He never knew she wanted him to escape to New York with her, and she never knew he didn't get her message. No wonder she married someone she didn't love and spent her life so closed off. No wonder she never danced or sang or traveled. No wonder she'd always been so quiet. How do you go on after that loss? How do you process the grief and the guilt of surviving? She went through the motions of life, but she never could be the person she once was.

They'd been so young, she'd thought. Lucy and Giulia and Emilia and Aldo. Even Patricio, who'd only been in his forties. And the guests, as Leo had told her—the artists and writers and inventors. Young and so full of promise and industriousness. But it didn't last, and for Lucy, it didn't even transform into a more mature but equally hopeful way of living. No, there'd been no hope in their house, Mia remembered. There had been facts and chores and day-to-day obligations and commitments. Things to take care of. Is that why Mia's own mother had left— because she couldn't handle the overwhelming grief that suffused the household? Mia cried now for her grandmother and all the people who were on that island. For everyone on earth who faced such unspeakable evil. For everyone who had their lives ripped away, and everyone who survived but lost their innocence, their dreams, their openness, and everything else that made them human. Their capacity to love. To give it and receive it openly and with joy.

She saw now that her grandmother's love of the darkness, her love of the night, was maybe just a way to feel safe, to live undercover. She wondered how it must have felt to her grand-mother, to find fear in the rising sun or a trip anywhere more than an hour from home? To cling to people like Milt and Janet, whom she somehow found the power inside to trust? She thought back now on how brave it must have been to say goodbye, as Mia moved out of the house for college. How hard to say goodbye when your life was filled with losing people you cared about. Mia had had no idea what her grandmother was hiding inside. No idea of all the pain. No idea why she'd never even considered opening up. Maybe she'd wanted to protect her granddaughter. Or maybe she thought it would hurt too much to reveal it.

But one thing Mia had always known was that her grand-mother loved her. She'd loved her ferociously and with every inch of her soul. She'd loved her and protected her and watched over her so closely. She'd stayed involved in school events even though she'd hated getting involved. She'd attended raffles and picnics and ballet recitals even though she couldn't bear to be around people. And most important, she'd kissed Mia goodbye when the time came. With all she'd lost, with all those who she'd never see again, with all the goodbyes that were so tragic, she'd still been able to say goodbye to Mia when Mia's life began and she was ready to leave.

That was love. And it was remarkable that despite everything, Lucy had still been able to love.

Now sitting opposite Leo at the beautifully set table, Mia decided it was time to put all the sadness behind her and enjoy her last night in Italy. She was glad to be here, on this beautiful terrace in this still, dark night. Because sometimes darkness wasn't avoidance, she thought. Sometimes it was the gateway to a place you'd never been before. And sometimes that place was exactly where you wanted to be. Sometimes life really was an *Isola della Notte Brillante*—even if just in your imagination.

Soon after she and Leo sat down, a small quartet of musicians appeared and picked up their instruments. They started playing a slow jazzy tune.

"What is all this?" she asked.

"Dorria arranged it," Leo answered. "He thinks all Americans love jazz, so he wanted you to hear some on your last night here."

"But why?"

He laughed. "I could be generous and say he wants you to have a wonderful last night here. Or I could be cynical and say he wants you on his side if it turns out you have an ownership stake in the castle."

"What does that mean? He thinks I could cut off his access to the castle?"

"I guess he's worried about it and wants to cover his bases. This was all so unexpected. Anything could happen. That's why the press is all over this." She supposed he was right. Leo had sent the email to the island's owner late last night, and by this afternoon, reporters were calling up the hotel and even arriving here from the mainland to ask if the rumors they'd heard were true.

"But why? Why is this such big news?" she asked.

"The Parissis are practically mythic here in Italy, and Patricio's death at the hands of the Nazis was never forgotten. The ownership of the island and castle was in dispute for many years. I don't even know how it came to be purchased last year. But if there's a legitimate heir..."

"I don't think that's what I am—"

"Well, you must get used to people looking at you as though you are," he said. "Although not for tonight. For tonight, you are Mia. And we are having dinner. Let's just say that Dorria wants us to share a beautiful night. A *notte brillante*."

Mia nodded. That's all she wanted right now, too. The music was lovely, and since dinner hadn't yet been served, she decided she wanted to dance. So she took Leo's hand and led him to the dance floor, then wrapped her arms around his neck as they swayed in time with the music. As they became one with the breeze and the darkness and the beauty that was the Mediterranean.

"Nana," she whispered to herself as she held Leo even closer. "This dance is for you."

"Okay, so I'll get that all set for you, Mia, if you're sure this is what you want to do," Milt said.

She nodded. "It's time."

A month since she'd returned from Italy, to be specific. She had just completed tying up all the loose ends in her life. And now she was ready to move on.

Milt stood up and came around from behind his desk. "I don't know how I'll ever drive past that house again, knowing other people are in there," he said. "How many times did I plan to come see her with papers to sign or something, and she told me to come over after the sun went down? Sometimes even when it was twenty degrees! She told me she always thought better out on the patio. I'd suggested pretty often she enclose it and put in some heating. But no, she liked to do things her way."

"She liked the night," Mia said smiling. "She always did."

"I'll get the house listed right away. I'm sure it'll sell pretty quickly."

She nodded. It was hard to give up the house. But she didn't belong there. There were so many other aspects to her life now, so many other parts of the world where her story had started. She felt as though she was discovering herself for the first time, because she knew so much more than she ever had before. She was a blend of multiple traditions, the great-granddaughter of a Jewish tailor and a disowned Italian heiress who'd descended from one of the wealthiest yet hugely anti-Semitic families in Italy. It was puzzling and confusing... and stimulating, too. She was both a Jew and the great-great-grandchild of someone who hated Jews enough to disown his own daughter and cut all ties with her. How did she move forward now? Would this knowledge change her? Should it?

"So, my dear, when do you head back to Rome?" Milt said.

"I leave tonight."

"Don't worry, I'll take care of everything."

"I know you will."

He sat on the corner of the desk. "I only wish you'd told me..." he began.

"I didn't want to get you in trouble or make you have to compromise for me," she said, an explanation she'd already given but evidently he needed to hear again.

"I know, but thinking of you running all over Italy by yourself with this presumed stolen object in your bag—honestly, Mia, this could have all gone south really fast."

"But it didn't. And I'm glad I handled it on my own."

"Your grandmother had made me promise I'd watch out for you. It was one of the last things she ever asked me."

"But if she had wanted you to be involved with this, she would have left you the key to the storage unit and not me. I think she wanted me to go looking on my own. I think she knew that finding her story was something I needed to do myself. At least it seems that way. From everything she set up."

He shrugged, as if he still regretted what she'd done but accepted her reasons. "And what will you do there?" he asked.

"It's still up in the air, but there's so much more to learn," she said. Which included finding out for sure what had happened to her great-aunts Giulia and Emilia. It seemed there was evidence that Giulia had died in the Nazi siege, but no proof. And the fate of the youngest sister, Emilia—the sister Mia was named after—was unclear, too. Could both of them have escaped—and could Mia have relatives somewhere?

And, too, as Leo kept insisting, there was the issue of whether, as a Parissi descendant, she had any rights to the island or the castle, notwithstanding Olivia's estrangement. It was startling to think her grandmother had known all along that she was a Parissi but had never done anything about it. Mia assumed it was because Lucy hadn't felt she deserved anything. She'd hidden the *schianto* and the gown presumably because she hadn't even felt entitled to those, despite the fact that they'd both been given to her. Or because they made her so sad. Either way, Mia ached for the guilt and despair her grandmother must have felt. She wished she had insisted on knowing more sooner. She had let her grandmother down, by not finding a way for her to bare her soul and relieve her burden.

She would always feel bad about that. But not so bad that she would withdraw, as her grandmother had done. Lucy hadn't wanted Mia to shut herself off from the world. She'd made that clear when she'd planted the clues that led her to *Isola della Notte Brillante*.

"And what of your job?" Milt said.

"I'm taking a leave of absence," she said. Although she wasn't sure she'd ever come back. She was a different person now. And it was time for her to do bigger things. Like go back to school and get her PhD, finally, so she could pursue the research she wanted. She could use the money from the sale of the house. She was sure her grandmother could have thought of no better way to finance the next step of her education. Of her whole life.

She rose and hugged Milt. It was sad to say goodbye, but she was looking forward to returning to Rome. For many reasons, the most important of which was that Leo would be at the airport when she arrived. Leo was part of a new chapter in her life that she could now envision. The old chapter, the one in which she was heading toward a future with Ryan, now belonged in the past.

She had texted Ryan from Da Vinci Airport on the day she'd left Italy, a month ago, to say she was on her way home. He'd responded that he was soon heading back to New York as well.

"I know you have a lot to catch up with, and I do, too," he'd added at the end of his text. "Maybe we should wait a week before we see each other."

Seated by her gate, she'd stared at that last sentence for several seconds. Knowing him, she could tell it meant that he thought their relationship could be ending. She wasn't surprised, and she wasn't upset. Actually, it was a relief that he evidently understood something profound had changed between them. He wasn't going to feel blindsided when she told him she wanted to end things—which was good because she knew how much he hated being blindsided. But sitting there waiting to board her flight, she took a moment to reflect. Ryan wasn't a bad guy, but he was no longer *her* guy. Her grandmother's death had tested their relationship, and rather than reinforcing its strength, it exposed its weaknesses. Sometimes even when things are at their darkest, light prevails.

She'd met Ryan for dinner the Saturday night after she'd returned, at a Mexican place near his apartment building. He was wearing a blue-striped shirt under a gray half-zip pullover, a pair of pressed jeans and brown loafers. His honey-colored hair was gelled away from his forehead. He was chic and polished as always, and while she appreciated the efforts he'd made to look his best, she couldn't help but picture Leo as he waited to take her back to the castle on Thursday morning, his hair ruffling around his neck as the warm breeze picked up on the water.

They were seated, and their food came quickly after they'd ordered. Over tacos and chips, she told him about the note that exonerated her grandmother, and he'd told her about the colleague he'd spoken to in Los Angeles who wanted to explore starting up a new firm with him.

"I'm going back there in two weeks to talk more," he'd said. "It might make sense for us to base our start-up there. I like L.A. I think I could be happy there. And you?" he said. "What's next for you?"

She told him that she was going back to Italy at the end of

the month. She'd be supervising the installation of the *schianto*, which she'd left with Leo, in the exhibit hall of the castle. And she also intended to do some research into her family's past. "I may have aunts, uncles or cousins that I never knew about. In one way, I found the answer I was looking for, but I also have a lot of new questions."

"So... there's no reason to ask you to consider coming with me to Los Angeles?" he asked. "No way we can patch things up?"

She tilted her head, touched by the question. Then she shook her head no. "I think you know that wouldn't work, not for either of us."

He looked to the side, then turned back to her and shrugged in agreement. "Tell me something," he said. "Is there someone else?"

She nodded, because even though she had no desire to hurt him, she wanted to be truthful. "But even if there weren't, it still wouldn't be right to stay together," she told him. "We were okay for each other for a time. But not anymore. What about you?" she asked. "Anyone else?"

He shook his head. "Maybe some possibilities for the future. But up until now... it was only you, Mia."

She narrowed her eyes, trying to find the words for what she wanted to tell him. "I didn't see this coming either," she said. "And maybe if my grandmother hadn't died, or if she hadn't left all those things for me to find, maybe we wouldn't be doing this tonight. But at some point, we would have. I don't think I ever would have stayed the way I used to be. So, it's better that we do this now, right? Before things got any more serious. Before it became even harder."

He took a sip of his beer, then tilted his head from side to side, as though reluctantly admitting she had a point.

"I'll miss you, Mia," he said. "It was great while it lasted."

She knew he was right. The relationship had worked for a

while. But now her world was opening up. In a way her grand-mother's never had.

When she'd finished her goodbyes to Milt and Janet, she left the office building and went back to her grandmother's house to get her suitcase. Milt had said to keep the house as it was—it wasn't overly furnished and the realtor had said it showed very well. But the one thing she did take with her was the wedding gown, which she'd planned to give to Leo. Her grandmother had hoped to marry Aldo in it. And she wondered now whether someday, if things worked out, she'd have it restored so that she could wear it. Maybe even as she married the grandson of the man who'd designed it.

But that was a story still to be written.

Finished packing, she went downstairs to wait for Erica to pick her up, as she'd done the night she decided to go to Italy. Erica would be taking her to the airport after they had an early dinner at Caryn's. They'd have burgers and fries and beers, as they always did when she came back to town. And no doubt they'd reminisce and talk about the future and how much they'd miss one another. But how glad they were that they both had their lives on track.

Because they were friends. And they'd always be. Having dinner with Erica was the best send-off Mia could imagine. A way to put a button on her past. The past that she knew. So she could start her exploration of the past she didn't know.

As she heard Erica's car reach the driveway, she opened the door of the hallway closet and pulled Leo's hat off a hook, where it had been hanging since she'd arrived back home. She'd been holding it when Leo had walked her from the van to the ferry to begin her journey back to Soundport. She'd handed it to him as she promised to text him flight information once she'd booked her return.

He'd taken it and placed it on her head, just as he had the day he met her. Then he'd held her face in his hands and kissed her, a sweet, meaningful kiss that made her forget the rest of the world, if only for a moment. He adjusted the rim and then kissed her again.

"You take it," he said. "I'll be at the airport when you return, and you can give it back then."

She'd pressed the hat to her head and then took the initiative to kiss him one last time, happy to have his hat as she made her way to New York.

Stepping out of her grandmother's house for the last time, she smiled, thinking of what a chore it had seemed after her first visit to Parissi Castle to have to find him to return the hat. She hadn't been sure that she wanted to see him again. She wasn't sure if he was friend or foe.

But this time, it wouldn't take any work at all to give it back to him. He'd be at the airport waiting for it. Waiting for her. So they could tie up the last threads of their pasts.

And begin their next adventure together: the future.

A LETTER FROM BARBARA

I want to say a huge thank you for choosing to read *Secrets of the Italian Island*. If you did enjoy it and want to keep up to date with all my latest releases, just sign up at the following link. Your email address will never be shared, and you can unsubscribe at any time.

www.bookouture.com/barbara-josselsohn

Last summer, as I was deep into writing this book, I had the great fortune to spend two months in Greenport, a lovely small town on the North Fork of Long Island. Greenport is set right in between the sound to the south and the bay to the north; and the sunsets and moonrises, the rocky coasts and the lapping water, the ferry leading to and from Shelter Island, and the steady string of warm days and quiet nights helped put me in the shoes of Mia and Annalisa as they made crucial decisions during the transformational moments of their lives.

But Long Island had additional significance to me last summer, as I grew up there. And even though I left long ago, being there felt like coming back to my real home—something I hadn't expected when I made my travel plans. If you've read my earlier books, you know that one of the themes I like to explore is *home*—where we find home, how a place becomes home, and what happens when home feels elusive or, worse, non-existent. My time back on Long Island was so inspiring, as *Secrets of the Italian Island* is also about home—and the courage to prevail when you find out that your home and your family are not at all what you thought they were.

Too, *Secrets of the Italian Island* is about a granddaughter and a grandmother. And in writing it, I found a meaningful new closeness to my own grandparents. Although they all were gone by the time I was a teenager, I'm now keenly aware of the lesson Mia learns—that I am who I am because they were who they were.

I hope you loved *Secrets of the Italian Island*, and if you did, I would be very grateful if you could write a review. I'd love to hear what you think, and it makes such a difference helping new readers to discover one of my books for the first time.

I love hearing from my readers—you can get in touch on my Facebook page, through Twitter, Goodreads or my website.

www.BarbaraJosselsohn.com

f facebook.com/BarbaraSolomonJosselsohnAuthor

twitter.com/BarbaraJoss

instagram.com/Barbara_Josselsohn_Author

tiktok.com/BarbaraJosselsohnBooks

ACKNOWLEDGMENTS

I knew that writing this book, my first historical novel, would be challenging—but to say I had no idea just how challenging is quite the understatement! Even more than ever, I am so grateful to all the people whose support, expertise, encouragement, and friendship proved indispensable during my very intense writing year. I am glad for the opportunity to offer my thanks as I send this book, which I couldn't be more proud of, out into the world.

As always, I am beyond grateful to my agent, Cynthia Manson—a superb reader, sage professional, unwavering cheer-leader, and treasured friend all rolled into one. Her involvement at every stage of this book, as always, was invaluable. If I didn't know she had many authors to represent, I'd be convinced I was her only one! She's steered my career with such care and wisdom, and I couldn't be more thankful.

As an author, it's wonderful enough to work with one great editor—so I consider myself extra lucky to have found myself with two this go-round! The amazing Jennifer Hunt—my editor for my last four novels—worked tirelessly with me in late 2021 as I conceptualized and started to write this book, offering her great-as-always perspective and guidance. And when she left on maternity leave, the incredible Jess Whitlum-Cooper took me on. While I'd never known Jess before, I instantly recognized her expertise, trusted her insights, learned from her strong sense of story and character, and warmed to her as a person. The transition from Jen to Jess was remarkably smooth and stress-free, and I couldn't be happier with how the year unfolded!

Thanks, too, to the publishing, marketing, and editorial professionals at Bookouture—I am so proud and thankful to be part of the team! And a special thanks to Kim Nash, Digital Publicity Director, and the talented PR crew! A shout-out, too, to my fellow Bookouture authors, whose talents never fail to wow me with each new book release.

I am privileged to have a wonderful community of author friends who inspire and teach me every day. Thanks from the bottom of my heart to Jimin Han, Patricia Dunn, Jennifer Manocherian, Marcia Bradley, Veera Hiranandani, Diane Cohen Schneider, Patricia Friedrich, Maggie Smith, and Susan Schild.

A second thanks to Patty Friedrich, as well as to Ines Rodrigues, Paolo Aversa, Kathy Curto, and Laura Tommaso, for help with the Italian and Portuguese terms in this book. Your expertise and quick turnaround are much appreciated! Special thanks, too, to Kerry Schafer, a fabulous social media whiz who's also a wonderful novelist and a simply great person!

My deep appreciation also goes to the Women's Fiction Writers Association, the Writing Institute at Sarah Lawrence College, the Scarsdale Library Writers Center, and Westport Writers Workshop. And a big virtual hug to the amazing book bloggers and reviewers who have become such a big part of my writing life! Although our interactions have been online, I feel so connected to you all, and I'm glad to call you my friends.

Much of this book was written during an intense two months last summer in the beautiful community of Greenport on Long Island's North Fork. I loved my time there—so much that the book's fictional town of Soundport is based there, and nearby Shelter Island also appears, in chapters that are most dear to my heart. While out on Long Island, I met some remarkable people as dedicated to books as anyone I've ever known. Thanks to Scott Raulsome, owner of Burton's Bookstore in Greenport, and to Janet Olinkiewicz at Floyd Memorial

Library, Jessica Montgomery at Shelter Island Public Library, and Dennis Fabiszak at East Hampton Library for making my stay so memorable. Thanks, too, to Rosemary Nickerson, for opening her lovely home to my family.

Thanks to Ben Pall for great insights into visiting Italy, and to Brittany Glassberg for reviewing the sections on medical research. And huge thanks to Jessica Kaplan and Mark Fowler, owners of Bronx River Books, my hometown bookstore, for supporting me and so many other authors!

Finally, as always, my deepest and most heartfelt thanks to my husband, Bennett, and our kids—David, Rachel, and Alyssa. You are all always willing to make editorial suggestions on everything from fashion choices to academic terms to career and life goals, and my characters are indebted to you for setting me straight! But most important, thanks for being my family. You guys are everything to me, and I couldn't love you more!